THE SOUND
OF BLUE

ALSO BY HOLLY PAYNE

The Virgin's Knot

THE SOUND
OF BLUE

HOLLY PAYNE

DUTTON

DUTTON
Published by Penguin Group (USA) Inc.
375 Hudson Street, New York, New York 10014, U.S.A.
Penguin Group (Canada), 10 Alcorn Avenue, Toronto, Ontario, Canada M4V 3B2 (a division of
Pearson Penguin Canada Inc.); Penguin Books Ltd, 80 Strand, London WC2R 0RL, England;
Penguin Ireland, 25 St Stephen's Green, Dublin 2, Ireland (a division of Penguin Books Ltd);
Penguin Group (Australia), 250 Camberwell Road, Camberwell, Victoria 3124, Australia (a division
of Pearson Australia Group Pty Ltd); Penguin Books India Pvt Ltd, 11 Community Centre,
Panchsheel Park, New Deli - 110 017, India; Penguin Group (NZ), Cnr Airborne and Rosedale
Roads, Albany, Auckland, New Zealand (a division of Pearson New Zealand Ltd); Penguin Books
(South Africa) (Pty) Ltd, 24 Sturdee Avenue, Rosebank, Johannesburg 2196, South Africa

Penguin Books Ltd, Registered Offices: 80 Strand, London WC2R 0RL, England

Published by Dutton, a member of Penguin Group (USA) Inc.

First printing, January, 2005
1 3 5 7 9 10 8 6 4 2

 REGISTERED TRADEMARK—MARCA REGISTRADA

LIBRARY OF CONGRESS CATALOGING-IN-PUBLICATION DATA

Payne, Holly.
The sound of blue / by Holly Payne.
p. cm.
ISBN 0-525-94792-2 (alk. paper)
1. Teacher-student relationships—Fiction. 2. Americans—Hungary—Fiction.
3. Americans—Croatia—Fiction. 4. Dubrovnik (Croatia)—Fiction. 5. Brothers—Death—
Fiction. 6. English teachers—Fiction. 7. Women teachers—Fiction. 8. Refugee camps—Fiction.
9. Composers—Fiction. 10. Hungary—Fiction. I. Title.
PS3616.A97S68 2005
813'.6—dc22   2004006710

Printed in the United States of America
Set in Simoncini Garamond
Designed by Leonard Telesca

FOR
SANDOR AND JEN

Where the rivers meet
you tell me of your black dreams.
Your memories make me uneasy.
But I listen because I know
my listening, like all listening,
allows you to heal.

HLP

THE BALKANS
1992

1

On the forty-eighth hour, everything had changed. Sara Foster stared, sick and uncertain, at the snow falling on Csokhid erasing any evidence of her arrival. It was as if she had always been there, that there had been no arrival. The tire marks were gone from the van; nothing but poles from the Red Cross tent, the pens frozen and strewn on the sidewalk. She was surprised to see the girl in the navy pea coat sprawled alone in the driveway making snow angels. As soon as the girl finished with one, she jumped up and dropped onto her back, starting another beside it, forming a chain of snow angels as if she believed they protected the refugee camp. She lay with her mouth open, catching snowflakes on her tongue, unaware Sara was watching her.

Sara leaned against the window, staring at a moonless milky sky, glimpsing through the clouds the three stars in Orion's belt. It struck her that the hunter was inverted in this part of the world, as if he were not saluting heaven, but stood on his head slashing through hell. The hunter was like the girl making snow angels, she thought, determined to defy the desolation here. Csokhid, the town of many bridges, was a crossroads, a place where the hills of the west spilled into the uncertainty of the great plain to the east. It was a land of folktale and illusion. A magician's playground, the confluence of past and future. Deception was its nature. She had been warned.

She held the passport in her hand, fingering the edge of the pink visa, already distrusting its sanction. She resented the director's thumbprint smudged on the page, committing her to him and the refugees. Until now, she had not considered why he had chosen only her for the camp in Csokhid, and she wondered where the other teachers were, what conditions they had inherited, if they were better or worse, if snow angels were guarding them, too. She wondered if they had decided to stay, and if they had, why. She had no reason. Anyone in her right mind would have turned around, found a bus, caught the next train to Budapest, returning home in time before the differences defined themselves, before they mattered. Sara feared that more than anything because she did not want a reason to care. Her gut said stay.

She watched the snowflakes stick to the glass as if each were the opportunity she was supposed to recognize, but could not because it was too small to see. She could read French and German, but not the language in snowflakes. If she could, she would convince herself to stay, realizing she was the only one in the refugee camp faced with this predicament. The refugees from Croatia had risked their lives getting here, but she was willing to risk hers to get out. She stared down at the driveway. The girl with the navy pea coat leaned against a telephone pole now, casting her shadow over the wings of a snow angel. She positioned herself carefully until the wings appeared to be her own, as if she possessed the power to fly home.

⌇

Teaching was not Sara Foster's wish. Or her dream for that matter. She was an American girl raised on promises, and her dreams were the dreams of many: Marriage. Family. Career. A reputation.

Hers was the confidence and pride of graduating summa cum laude from a notable school whose notable future depended on alumni with big dreams. Sara dreamed of becoming a partner in a big law firm in a big city in a big building with big doors that opened, not to streets, but to avenues and boulevards that had no end. She spent the last semester of her junior year cooped up in the library, studying for the law-school exam. She intended to graduate early, missing formals and parties and weekend trips to the beach. The taste of study foods, stale saltine crackers and burned coffee, vanished from her mouth while she waited to hear from Harvard.

She had withdrawn slowly, unknowingly, using the law-school application as an excuse to be alone. Sara was not one to believe in premonitions, and instead she believed this need to be alone was her way of preparing for the punishing first semester of law school. Then the letter came. She had done well, but not well enough. She did not believe the test score, demanding the company check it by hand, mistrusting the computer that counted the black dots and the number-two pencil that had made them. Two weeks later, Sara learned that the computer had missed two questions she had answered incorrectly. She burned the test score and the rejection letter from Harvard. Nobody would find the truth in ashes. She expected an acceptance. Everybody did. There had been no other options.

Sara had already found a brownstone in Cambridge with a view of the Charles River. She would apply again, next year, when she knew more, but for now, she could not bear to answer the inevitable question of what a valedictorian would do with her time. She decided to go abroad.

⌒

Sara received the call on a steely November afternoon, the campus deserted for Thanksgiving. She had prolonged her stay, delaying her drive home because she did not want her parents to see her like this, eyes bruised from lack of sleep, hair dull and lifeless. Her father would worry that she wasn't eating. Her mother would worry that she had eaten too much. If she timed the drive right, she would arrive at the end of the Thanksgiving meal for the leftover turkey, hoping the tryptophan would help her sleep. Sara needed rest, but she could barely sleep a minute past sunrise, arriving at the dining hall before the morning shift could unlock the doors.

A job posting blew off a kiosk while she waited and caught around her ankle. She tracked it inside, annoyed, regarding it as if it were a damp leaf stuck to the bottom of her boot. She thought it was a joke. Teaching English in Hungary. Nobody fantasized about the Eastern Bloc. Even the Eurail pass omitted those countries, probably, she thought, to spare travelers from their monochrome skylines and industrial disgraces. Still, the idea of crossing borders seduced Sara with the possibility of anonymity. Nobody would know her in Hungary. She would be a stranger. Nobody would expect anything from her. She could rest and read and recover. Hungary, the perfect escape. Hungary, the place where she could bide her time before Harvard realized the grievous mistake they had made by rejecting her.

The more Sara considered the possibility of working in Hungary, the more it appealed to her. The Ministry of Education needed teachers. The positions could not be filled fast enough since the Berlin Wall had fallen. The Eastern Bloc had shifted from communism to capitalism and was scrambling to catch up with its Western neighbors. By teaching English, Sara would play a role in Hungary's history, helping it to master the world's business tongue. And this, she believed, was noble.

Sara understood the importance of language, that language was its own currency, that the number of languages a person could speak influenced, if not determined, their rank and value. She herself knew French, Spanish, and German and could recite Italian from operas she had never attended but had listened to on CDs from the public library. How hard could Hungarian be? She would get paid to travel. She could taste the opportunity, its possibilities fresh.

～

The caller had promised Budapest. Good students, sons and daughters of businessmen and ambassadors. Children in starched uniforms. Sara imagined a school near the Buda castle with a view of Fisherman's Bastion and enough cake and tea to get her through the winter. She had researched it well. She had discovered the glamour of Hungary. She expected a summer along Lake Balaton, a fall in Eger, stomping grapes in the Valley of the Beautiful Woman. She had dreamed of red pepper markets, the bike she'd ride through the streets, negotiating her way over cobblestones. She would take lunches along the Danube, spend the evenings in cafés where poets and politicians gobbled cakes and cobbled history, mixing ink with icing, calling it sweet.

The Hungary she discovered was different from her dream. She had never been to Europe. She had never left the country. Her family did not fly. They did not ski, or sail, or take summers on Padre Island. Her travel experience, besides going to her grandfather's fishing cabin, included Disney World via train when she turned thirteen. Even then Hungary was not included in the Epcot tour. Her family had confused the name several times, even recently.

"For Christ's sake, Sara. It's Thanksgiving," her father said, muting the football game on the TV. "We've got plenty to eat."

He was frustrated. Dallas was losing. He swore at the Steelers. Sara stuck a candied yam with her fork.

"I'm *going* to Hungary," she said from the kitchen.

"Honey, get her another potato."

Her mother looked up from the table, holding pinking shears, the blade open. Her plate had been cleared, covered with coupons she had cut from the Sunday paper. Her forehead was shiny from the lamp above the table, and she dabbed the oils with a coupon for Healthy Choice.

"East of Austria," she said, running her fingers along the zigzagged edge. Sara's mother, like her, had never left the United

States, but she *had* traveled. Her two-day Greyhound ride from Alabama to Texas to marry Sara's father had been the biggest trip of her life, which is why, Sara believed, her mother taught seventh-grade geography, to learn of the places the bus had gone without her.

"Can't hear you," her father said, slouched on the floor against the edge of the couch. He opened another beer, tossing the empty can into the veritable recycling center that had taken over the living room during football season. Only they didn't recycle. She imagined her town was the last to get an ATM machine. Change came slowly and not without suspicion in central Texas.

Sara raised her voice, competing with Ed McMahon's exhortation to check the Publishers Clearing House Sweepstakes.

"The country," Sara said, rubbing her eyes.

"Honey? Get her some leftovers."

Her father called helplessly to her mother, who clipped another coupon for two frozen dinners.

"South of Slovakia. West of Romania," her mother said.

"Honey?"

The clip of pinking shears punctuated the silence. Sara spoke to the blades.

"*Hungary,* Dad. I'm going to Hungary."

Her father turned to her, eyes hidden by the shadow of commercials flickering from the TV. His face was drawn, confused. He looked somewhat assaulted, as if the mention of Hungary contained some sort of elusive profanity.

"What about Harvard?"

"I've deferred."

"What?"

"I want to take some time off."

Her father pressed MUTE again, waiting for his only child to continue. Sara lowered her voice. She developed this habit, realizing her father had selective hearing. She wanted his attention.

"I need a break."

Her father's eyes darted from the TV to her mother, then after checking the score, settled on Sara's face the way they did after he checked her report card in grade school or roved the high-school transcript when it hadn't met his approval. He sat up.

"What about the apartment in Cambridge?"

"I cancelled."

"You're giving up the view? Like that?"

He cocked his head, disappointed. Her cousin Mark had chosen it.

Sara nodded. "I'll find another view."

"Hungary over Harvard."

Her father pumped the pronouncement with judgment and the kind of criticism he used when Sara had mentioned, years ago, that she admired Ansel Adams and wanted to be a photographer. Her father believed a photographer's work did not rely on a brain, that her brain was worthy of more than lenses and light.

He proposed the question. "You're choosing Hungary over Harvard?"

Sara shrugged, pressing her lips together as if she had the power to squeeze out the lie. "Yes."

"How long has your mother known?"

Sara pushed the coupons together, squaring the edges. Her father peered up over the denim-covered La-Z-Boy, searching for an answer from her mother, who, without lifting her eyes, pulled the comics from the pile of newspaper pages and opened to the Family Circus.

"She's doing the right thing," her mother said, reaching for the pinking shears.

"There's a *war* going on," her father said.

"I'm not going to Iraq."

"But what about those other places? Croatia."

"I'm going to Budapest, Dad."

Sara caught her father stealing a glimpse of the television. The game was back on. He fiddled with the remote, his thumb grazing the orange MUTE button.

"Why would you want to leave America?"

"You did."

"That was different."

Sara stared at him. Vietnam veteran. Three years in Saigon. His choice, actually. He could have stayed and sold clothing at the Army PX, but her father liked to build things. He built parade floats with the hands that would have built houses had he not been hit by a grenade. He called the accident the Palm Frond Discount. The Jungle Thief who stole his dreams. He ran a shuttle service now, crossing the Trinity River twice a day, driving passengers to the Dallas–Fort Worth International Airport, reminding himself of the possibilities of travel but never once traveling. He said there was nothing to see outside Texas, that they had everything they needed. Sara never believed him, because he always wanted more.

"They need teachers," she said.

"For what?"

"Golf."

"What?" he asked, surprised Sara raised her voice.

"They need to learn English."

"Why? They have a language of their own. Let the Hungarians speak Hungarian."

"Magyar," her mother said, correcting him.

"Huh?"

"Nothing," Sara said.

"Hold on, honey."

Her father turned up the volume on the TV, surfing channels to the news, getting the latest on the war in Iraq. Her cousin Mark, a captain and West Point graduate, had been sent with the Chemical Corps in late January. Mark, the local hero and future leader appointed by Senator Ratliff. Mark, their hope for a better world. The pastor of their church mentioned Mark's name in the weekly prayer along with a flotsam of words, names, and places half the congregation could not pronounce let alone identify on a map. But the churchgoers listened whenever they heard the mention of Iraq. It was a new word that had burst onto their tongues, exploding their vernacular, a mystery they wanted to solve because it involved one of them. They didn't have family in Hungary or Yugoslavia. They knew nobody there. They didn't have to care.

"They need help," Sara said, not realizing she blurted the words in the middle of a touchdown. She was surprised by the honesty in her tone, uncertain if it were her or the students who needed the most help.

"Help? They're a goddamn miracle, Sara."

Her father reached out and slapped the TV, elated with the touchdown, certain Dallas would beat the Steelers. He cracked open another beer and brought it to her mother, careful not to set the can on the pile of coupons. He thought glasses were pretentious, so he didn't offer one. He kissed the mole on his wife's forehead.

"We might win the Christmas ham," he said. "How's that for choosing sides?"

Her mother looked up and smiled. Her fingers, laced through the handles of the pinking shears, wiggled, dancing for his joy. "One less thing to worry about," she said.

She winked at Sara, teasing. Her father hopped and slid in his white tube socks back across the kitchen floor for more football and scores that excited him.

"Mark might be home by Christmas," he said, kicking a few of the beer cans out of his way.

"Mark can eat my share."

Sara's mother lay down the pinking shears. Sara didn't wait, catching her father sliding down the couch, his knees cracking when she made the announcement.

"I leave for Hungary on Christmas."

⤺

The plane circled the Danube at dusk. The river was frozen, and ice skaters slid across pearls of light that glowed from the Chain Bridge connecting Buda and Pest. Sara pressed her cheek against the window, trying to see beyond the snowflakes, a lace veil draping the grandeur like an antique she was not supposed to touch. Her eyes darted from the spires of castles and cathedrals to clay roof tiles and cobbled squares, leaping through styles she had read about in school. Romanesque, Gothic, Baroque. It was certainly an endeavor in architecture. Budapest. A city that had risen from the ashes of its assailants and offered refuge.

Sara expected the plane to land at any moment, but it banked sharply to the left, sloping toward the Parliament building, flying south over the treetops of Princess Margaret Island, the lights of the city scattered like the beads of an unstrung necklace. Her plane had been in the air for forty minutes, flying in circles. Nothing below but fields now, the river snaking its way, feeding a great plain that lay fallow and indifferent to her arrival.

Sara turned, looking around at her peers. Faces she had never seen but understood, scrunched in worry like her own. She had met them in the Frankfurt airport, where a group of UN civilians greeted the party with welcome bags filled with gummy bears and beer, escorting them to the terminal for Malev, the Hungarian national airline. The teachers appreciated the gesture and drank the beer, hoping to forget their circumstances. Most of them were plugged in, drowning out the holiday with songs from headsets, the bass thumping with techno music.

Sara had never missed Christmas, and she wasn't sure if she missed her family or the holiday more. She missed the worn leather chair that overlooked the hill outside the university library. She missed being a student and wasn't quite comfortable telling people she was a teacher already. Two weeks ago she was finishing final exams, signing the honor code in the last blue book of her college life. She could live without the rituals of school, but Sara truly missed the holiday, sitting on the dock of the fishing cabin, wrapped in worn wool blankets, singing, her grandfather's voice rubbed by the legs of Irish whiskey. She wondered if her family had sat down to eat the ham yet, if the U.S. Army served Mark his share, if they ate ham in the desert. She thought about the pearled onions her mother made to remind them of their roots. Sara never liked pearled onions. They were canned and soggy, but she would have rolled the onions around her tongue to keep them from getting lost had they been offered on the flight.

It was a small flight and oddly private for a commercial airliner. Each of the teachers had been given their own row, and most of them had sprawled out, trying to stretch their legs across the seats. It was strange not to see any other civilian passengers, and Sara wondered if it was the Hungarian custom to be so thorough and welcoming.

Her ears popped. The plane had begun to descend. She pressed her face against the glass, straining her eyes, watching the sliver of moon on the wings. The plane dipped right, heading straight for the peaks of a mountain that rose unexpectedly from the plain, the smoke of farmhouse chimneys curled into the blackness. Her throat tightened. The plane was not turning. It dropped faster, directly over the mountains. The magazine she had been reading slipped off her lap and slapped the floor.

A flight attendant walked by her row, offering cherry juice from a carton. She was young, with large dark eyes and hair that had been split and stained with chemical dyes. She stared at the handprints on Sara's pants.

"You okay?" she asked, handing Sara the juice. Sara wiped her hands on the seat cushion and opened the tray.

"They usually fly this close to the mountains?"

The flight attendant shook the carton, staring. "No mountains in the *puszta,*" she said.

"The what?"

"The great plain," she said, following Sara's eyes to the window. "Nothing but wheat and sunflowers down there."

"I swear I saw a mountain."

Sara jabbed the window, pointing to the shapes in the sky, then turned, shocked to see they had vanished with her breath on the glass.

The flight attendant laughed, speaking louder over the rattle of the engine, the screech of brakes popping open. "A mirage," she said.

"What?"

"You saw a mirage."

The plane bounced through a band of clouds that had suddenly gathered in the darkness. The cup of juice flipped over, splashing the seat.

The flight attendant handed Sara a stack of napkins and grabbed the cart. "You can't believe everything you see here."

⌒

They landed on a broken runway in the middle of a field where the earth breathed blue fog and red lights blinked beneath snowdrifts. The door opened to darkness, and a blast of cold air rushed into the cabin.

A garbled voice came over the intercom. "Happy Christmas."

A round man who called himself Gabor met them on the tarmac. He negotiated his way through luggage, checking off things from a clipboard, intermittently scratching the small goatee on his double chin. He was short and thick and wore nylon sweatpants, his chest inflated by a flak jacket zipped over his coat. He reminded Sara of a body builder. A gold chain dangled from his neck, the cross catching the moonlight. He talked into a mobile phone, brandishing it like a wand or a weapon, pawing the broken runway with the toe of his boot, chipping away at a puddle that had frozen. He spoke a spare English.

"Teachers here," he said. "Translators there."

They stood still, unaware of the division. Sara turned to the man beside her, a tall, blond Canadian whose coat with the red maple leaf patch she had followed through the Frankfurt airport because it made her feel safer, closer to home. She touched his shoulder.

"I thought we were all teachers."

He shook his head, lowering his voice.

"It's not teachers they need."

Sara straightened and stared at him, curious. She had seen the same expression on his face when the flight attendant mistook him for an American. He shook the maple leaf on his coat when she passed his row.

"Most of us are translators," he said.

Sara shifted on the ground, feeling her toes go numb. The lace on her boot had come undone, and she bent down to tie it, her fingers stinging from the cold. She looked up.

"What do you translate?"

"Stories."

"Stories?"

The Canadian tilted his head back, searching the sky with his mouth open as if he could catch a star. He spit out the words, too pointy for his tongue.

"Refugee stories," he said.

"Refugee stories?"

He smiled, reading her wide eyes. "First time teaching?"

"Yes."

"English as a Second Language?"

Sara nodded.

The translator continued, trying his best to help her understand. "My job is to translate their past. You teach them the present tense and help them to forget it."

The weight of his words lifted Sara's face, the muscles strained in her back. She held her position, kneeling, fingering the loop on the shoelace. The Canadian studied her face. She was younger than the other passengers and obviously unprepared or uninformed, too naïve to know exactly why she was there.

"Good luck," he said.

"Where are you going?"

"Zagreb. Belgrade. Dubrovnik," he said, and shrugged. "Wherever there's a story to be told. Why do you think we landed here?"

The Canadian stepped away and joined the translators, who were boarding a bus; the door closed behind them. Sara stood, following him with her eye to the back of the bus. The tailpipe spat smoke into the blackness. She dug her fists into her pockets, picking at her fingers, no longer cold. She was numb, making sense of the Canadian's job. Of her own. She wanted to run after the bus and ask him more. She wanted to know where he was going. Where all of them were going on Christmas. Where they would be tomorrow. Or the next day. Next year. She thought of the lace curtains blowing in a classroom in Budapest and felt her stomach sink, regretful. She had chosen to be here.

"Sara Foster?"

She turned, feeling the weight of Gabor's hand on her shoulder through the bulk of her coat. His fingers wrapped around the joint as if he could pluck the bone from the socket and toss it. He snapped his fingers.

"Your passport."

Sara looked at the other teachers. There were six of them, each wide-eyed and spooked, the only passengers from the flight left on the tarmac.

"Passports, please."

Gabor held out his hand, impatient. The teachers struggled with their money belts, peeling back layers of wool and thermal underwear. Wind blew across the runway, retarding their movement, thickening their blood in the cold. There was nothing hospitable about the *puszta,* the great plain chewed raw by nature and man, corroded by its own corruption.

Gabor stepped forward, collecting the passports. He took out six work visas, pink squares that looked like postage stamps,

licked them, and pasted them into the pages. He smeared the
saliva with the pad of his thumb, initiating the English teachers
into the crude formalities of southeastern Europe, entitling them
to its health care. Gabor handed back the passports and shook
the teachers' hands.

"Csikos Gabor," he said, introducing himself, saying his last
name first as was the custom in Hungary.

Gabor had not taken his eyes off Sara since they had met. She
shifted uncomfortably in his presence, the cold air sweeping
around her ankles, making its way to her bones. The engine had
been shut off, and the runway was quiet and dark. Gabor stood
as a silhouette between her and the plane. His face was bearded
and waxy, fixed in eternal perplexity, it seemed. The whites of his
eyes flickered in the cigarette lighter cupped between his hands
and suggested that Gabor was a haunted man.

"I'm the director of the refugee camp," he said. "You report
to me in Csokhid."

"Choke-heed?" She thought she heard him incorrectly.

"Yes. Town of many bridges."

"What about Budapest?"

Gabor closed the lid over the lighter, stepping closer to Sara in
the dark. His breath smelled of licorice and cigarettes. "Budapest," he said, "is filled."

"But we signed papers with the Ministry of Education."

"They couldn't place you."

Sara stared at him, confused. "They could hardly fill the positions."

"Things change quickly here, Sara."

He pronounced her name, stressing the accent on the first syl-
lable, Hungarian style, as if he had rehearsed it a thousand times.
He perfected the pronunciation not to impress her, but to feel the
way it forced his tongue against the tip of his front teeth as if he
could touch her by merely saying her name.

"Sara? You are Sara?"

"Yes," she said. "I don't understand."

Sara looked at the other teachers. They said nothing, sucking on their cigarettes, the cherry embers flickering.

"The refugees aren't in Budapest. They're here in Croatia, crossing the border."

"Croatia?"

Gabor massaged the bare patches of his temples, then took out his cigarette, and smiled. "Don't worry," he said. "You're going to Hungary."

"You're serious."

"What?"

"We've landed in Croatia?"

Gabor nodded. He was accustomed to the startled reactions and had derived an odd enjoyment from seeing the discomfort the word caused, using it like a magic trick, the rabbit on his tongue, testing the media's accuracy or lack thereof. He could tell Sara and the others were just as uninformed. They had not taken the time to understand the conflict and, worse, dismissed it as too complicated. Croatia was not Ireland. The civil war in Yugoslavia was orchestrated by the minds and hands of human beings. The war was not as inevitable as it had been portrayed until now, and the worst of it was around the corner. The poison fruits of independence for Croatia would be earned with great human loss and suffering and an economic disaster that would plague the country for generations. The problem was not exclusively rooted in Croatia or Serbia, Bosnia, Slovenia, Albania, or Macedonia, but in the rise of nationalism perpetrated by the power-hungry men who represented each state. All it took was one man to love power more than he loved his own country to bleed it, leaving neighbors like Gabor to mop up the blood.

Hungary had inherited forty-eight thousand refugees, and Gabor needed help running the four camps. The teachers *were* teaching in Hungary, but they weren't teaching Hungarians. Their jobs were not so much to teach English as a Second Language, but to foster the hope that learning English inspired, the hope of starting a new life in the West and eliminating their burden on the country they had fled. Gabor hadn't lied. He'd omitted the details.

"Maybe you made a mistake," Sara said.

"No mistakes. Only lessons."

Gabor smiled, flashing bits of metal in the darkness. Sara's jaw tightened. She glanced at her watch. Midnight. The twilight zone in southeastern Europe. Four o'clock at home, leftovers on the kitchen counter. The Christmas cactus blinking from the living room. Her faced burned. She was not supposed to be here. She did not care if the other teachers stood silent. It was wrong. She would be back on the plane and in Budapest by morning. Her heart raced. She grabbed the money belt, accidentally dropping the contract with a photocopy of her passport and credit cards, a thousand dollars in one-hundred-dollar bills. All soaked with slush. She swept up the papers, shaking out the contract, pointing to the signatures.

"What about the contract?"

Gabor ripped the page away and studied it. "Pen means nothing here," he said, crushing it into a ball. "We sign our contracts with blood in the Balkans."

He tossed the ball at Sara's feet.

"I don't understand."

"*Nem erted?*" Gabor asked in Magyar. He mocked her, his voice suddenly higher, that of an impatient schoolteacher or music instructor who had grown weary of his students' questions.

Sara stepped away, lowering her voice. She had studied the basic phrases from a book on tape but was self-conscious of her pronunciation. "*Nem. Nem ertem,*" she said.

Gabor dug his fists in his sweatsuit pockets, rubbing the material until it whistled beneath his fingers.

"*Besel magyar?*"

"*Nem jol beselek,*" she said, hoping he would stop there. Her words were limited. She had memorized only a few phrases, practicing in the bathroom of the plane over the din of a flushing toilet. Hungarian was notoriously difficult, an agglutinative language with a complex system of suffixes having little in common with the Indo-European languages with which she was familiar. There was nothing at its base to make it easier, no Latin or Slavic roots. The closest language was Finnish. She had read that Hungarians and Finns descended from a tribe in Russia.

"It's a hard language," Sara said.

"Yes. But not the hardest."

Gabor carried her words with him to a white van marked with a red cross parked on the tarmac. He gestured for the teachers to climb in, grabbing a fistful of snow when Sara passed him at the door.

He lowered his voice. His words were softer, infused with apology and regret. "Survival."

Sara looked back.

"Survival is the hardest language," he said.

Gabor held her gaze as if he meant to say more, his finger drumming the lock before he shut the door.

⌒

Sara sat with the English teachers between boxes of syringes and sterile pads, frozen bags of blood. The famous Welsh soccer player Ryan Giggs smiled from a Manchester United sticker peeling off the back door. His boyish grin was the only welcoming face they would remember. The radio had been tuned to a local station. Gabor sang along to Balkan folk ballads, lost in the words of a dark carnival, his tone one of merriment and reckless abandon. He tossed the teachers around in the back of the van when the road turned, and it turned a lot. They had no idea which direction he had taken them. None could see outside. The window, a glassy web spun from bullets, had been taped and covered with butcher paper that flapped and tore in the wind.

Sara hugged her knees, thoughts drifting, chasing borders and time zones, trying to make sense of everything that was happening to her. She did not want to teach refugees in Hungary. She wanted to teach the children in the starched-white uniforms. She wanted to meet their parents and dance with ambassadors above Baroque balconies overlooking the Danube. But now, sitting there, bracing herself against the cold steel walls of the van, Sara Foster had the sobering feeling that her expectations were nothing more than a big joke, a prank at the expense of good-natured people who thought they played a role in making the world a better place. But this world, with its broken runway and cracked earth, was another world with different rules and sometimes no rules at all.

Sara's head hurt, not from hunger or cold, but from worry. She could not remember the last time she had eaten. She had lost yesterday. The events were blurry, and even if she had been thinking straight, she did not want to know the source of Gabor's dark joy. The van turned abruptly, the ripple of rubber on railroad tracks. A tower of blood slid away, crashing on the floor. Sara reached out, taking a frozen packet between her hands, wondering whose blood it was, whose life was saving the refugees.

꩜

They traveled north along the Danube, passing whitewashed farmhouses and thatched-roof cottages, hills draped by vineyards and almond trees, arriving in Csokhid at dawn. Gabor opened the door of the van, permitting the teachers to get out. They stood outside a former hospital with bars on the windows overlooking the river, crossed by an elaborate network of wooden bridges too narrow for cars. The old boards creaked, sagging beneath the burden of refugees crossing into the camp. It was cold and foggy, the air acrid with coal smoke and a stench as foul as death itself.

Gabor gave each of the teachers a handkerchief, pressed and folded, smelling of mothballs and cedar. He did not explain, certain they would soon make sense of the gesture, directing them to the Red Cross tent, comprised of three wobbly card tables set up under a tattered tarp. The frayed plastic whipped in the wind, carrying with it the smell of decayed and rotting grass. But there was no evidence of grass anywhere; the ground denuded with snow. The English teachers pressed the handkerchiefs against their faces, grateful for the camphor relief. The refugees carried the past and present in their smell, and Sara wondered if they would ever be capable of washing it off completely, if the scent of a refugee was universal, if in a crowded room or bus they could identify each other, even blind, by recognizing the stench they shared.

From the bridges, above the rush of the water, the refugees shouted out the names of countries in English. Canada. America. Australia. The only countries they had heard would accept Yugoslavian passports. Their papers were worth nothing elsewhere, and knowing this, the Red Cross workers, bleary-eyed and caffeinated, fidgeted with pens, clicking them on and off between entreaties. The refugees scribbled on the tables, not trusting paper, the numbers and names of people they knew could help them. Children roamed lost and hungry in the snow, sliding down a bust of Stalin that remained stalwart in its defense of the camp, a former Communist hospital. The steps glowed blue with salt and the bright white socks of priests who administered last rites to those who did not believe they would live another day, and if they did, asked God to make it their last.

The sidewalks were blocked by ambulances and police cars, vans, public buses, and hand trucks from local hotels loaded with boxes of soap and shampoo. The university radio station received word of the migration at midnight, and locals scampered over in pajamas to serve coffee and tea from hand-painted cups taken from their kitchens. Children donated blankets from their own beds, adding them to the piles of wool still warm with body heat and the smells of their homes. Special cakes and pastries circulated through huddles of the beleaguered, but failed to comfort them. The refugees were too embittered and outraged over their fallen city, too traumatized to be gracious.

Vukovar had officially fallen to the Serbs in November. The locals believed Croatian President Tudjman had sacrificed it in order to garner international sympathies. Mortar had decimated the charming city along the Danube. Thirty-five thousand people had fled by the end of August. The other fifteen thousand stayed, believing President Tudjman would protect them. But he never declared war, even by September, when columns of tanks six miles long arrived from Belgrade along the Highway of Brotherhood and Unity to claim the city as its own, destroying what they claimed to liberate. Two thousand men from Vukovar had disappeared. Now their wives and children stood before the refugee camp workers apologizing for spilled tea.

"I'm sorry. I'll clean your coat," one of the women said to Sara. She wore white industrial shoes with thick soles, the shoes of a nurse. She spoke English like most of the younger Croatian women. She was bright with intelligent eyes, her forehead creased with worry. She carried a small child's suitcase covered with stickers of dancing bears.

"It's okay," Sara said. "It's only tea."

The nurse looked at her with glazed eyes, shaking her head. Nothing was okay. Not today. She gasped when a soccer ball, kicked by one of the children, flew into the tent, grazing her cheek. Sara caught it.

"That was close."

"It's always close," the nurse said, staring at the ball as if she were seeing a ghost. She lowered the ball from her eyesight.

"I'll keep catching them."

The nurse looked up, dabbing her eyes.

"Elana," she said, and smiled, extending her hand.

"Sara."

The nurse glanced down at the ball and lowered her voice as if she were speaking to herself, not to Sara.

"Be careful what you choose to hold dear."

She excused herself, carrying the suitcase with her. Sara expected to see a child, but Elana entered the refugee camp alone, pausing at the door, eyes fixed on the boys with the soccer ball. The woman reached out, grabbing hold of the walnut tree growing beside the building as if to brace herself against the onset of rootlessness.

A Swedish woman leaned toward Sara and whispered. "Don't get their hopes up."

"What did I say?"

"You said it's okay."

The Swede turned back to guide the hand of another woman who had misplaced her reading glasses and could not see to fill out the registration form. Cradled in her left arm was an infant wrapped inside a sport jacket, the sleeves dangling at the woman's waist. The child's face was the size of the coat's pockets, its eyes closed. Sara could not tell if the baby was asleep or dead. She felt a tap on her shoulder and turned to find a group of children waiting for her to return the soccer ball. She tossed it gently, realizing that no one was supervising the kids, who wore their jackets unzipped, their noses drippy and raw with cold.

"Shouldn't they be with their parents?"

"They can't."

"Why?"

"They don't have any."

The Swedish woman read Sara's face, watching trauma *absorb,* flush her cheeks. The Swedish woman had seen this look before in other Red Cross workers. She bet Sara would not last more than a week. Sara was too soft. Too trusting. Too naïve. Too easily affected by the hardships of others. The refugees would weaken her, sending her packing before she had a chance to unload her bags. The Swede had seen several teachers, all women, come and go through the camp, none of whom had the courage to live among the refugees without becoming one of them. It took the kind of people whose compassion did not compromise their sense of survival. To work in a refugee camp was to survive it, but Sara Foster did not appear to be a survivor of any kind. She was a tourist, this girl, with the long red curls.

"What happened to them?" Sara asked.

"You don't want to know."

"Don't *you* want to know?"

"It's not our job to ask questions. Not the kind you want answers for," the Swedish woman said, blowing on the tip of her pen. "Details can be deadly. Stick to the basics. Shoe size. Inseams. Allergies. Medications."

Sara stiffened, watching the advancing queue, aware of the many women, the widows who waited for her. They clung to each other, bracing themselves against the cold, hands stuffed inside the other's pockets, terrified of being separated again. Hanging at their sides were nylon bags bulging with clothes and photos, a child's doll, a plastic alarm clock, a wall calendar, baby spoons, small souvenirs they had managed to salvage before their homes had burned. They smelled of wood smoke, faces smudged with ash. They carried the stench of urine and sweat, cigarettes and alcohol, transferring their trauma to those they met on the other side of it.

Sara had never seen such collective exhaustion. She wondered if the refugees' weariness was not so much from the lack of sleep, but from the fear of sleeping, as if closing their eyes would flood them with the horrors they wished never to see again. They stared at her, faces vexed by humiliation and defeat. Their minds were not pressed by the deaths they had seen in the last few days, weeks, months, but by the decimation of their lives and city. There was nothing they could do to reverse the events, their fate, the fate of Vukovar. It was the mundane, not history, that deceived them now. The simple tasks of daily life haunted them, and their eyes held lists of things left undone. The lights left on in the kitchen. The bread burning in the ovens. The clean laundry, still damp, probably frozen by now in the windswept plains of northern Croatia. There were videos stuck in VCRs. Homework left incomplete. Grades unrecorded. Gifts unwrapped. Concerts unattended, appointments missed, holidays anticipated but not celebrated this year. They stared at the English teacher as if she could assure them there was another life at the end of the line that took them from Croatia to here.

A small girl stepped forward, letting go of her mother's hand, the fringe of her polka-dot dress peeking out from beneath a navy pea coat. She dug in the pocket and lay a gold locket in front of Sara, her tiny fingers too cold and stiff to open it.

"Let me help you."

Sara wedged her nail between the metal, feeling the girl's warmth, opening it to a photo not of a parent or sibling, but of a Dalmatian puppy wearing a red bow around its neck. The girl pointed to herself, curling the blond wisps of hair that stopped at her chin.

"Our dog," she said. "School dog."

Sara smiled, understanding the girl meant mascot.

"He's very pretty."

"My friend."

"Good friend," Sara said.

The little girl nodded and took a deep breath, fighting for the right word. "His name Miki," she said.

"Mickey?"

"Gone," she said.

The girl reached for the dangling sleeve of the ski jacket. Her mother turned, offering Sara an apologetic look, then moved into the building to start her life again.

Sara wanted the woman to stop, for everyone and everything to freeze. She wanted to reach out and feel the safety and static of a TV screen, knowing she would never touch the people it projected or the lives that entered her living room but never truly affected her own. She wanted to reach for the remote or any device to control the images, to mute them or fast forward to make them disappear, because none of this felt real. Refugees were not really people. She did not have to know them. She did not have to care what they did or who they were or how her life might affect them. She watched them on the news while she drained pasta over the sink and heated jarred marinara in the microwave.

Sara's jaw stiffened. She shifted her eyes, watching the other teachers. One was doubled over behind the bust of Stalin, wiping her face with snow. The others were talking excitedly to Gabor, voices raised, panicked, arms flailing with their trilingual arguments. It was only Sara who remained fixed under the tent, unable to move.

"Sara."

She looked up to find Gabor standing in front of her with a steaming mug hand-painted with the American flag, missing too many stars and stripes to make it authentic.

"Hot chocolate," he said, offering it to her, but her mouth hung open, and she could not reach out to take it, too self-conscious to accept it in front of the other refugees.

"Don't burn yourself."

Gabor set the mug in front of her. Sara did not respond and instead covered her mouth with the back of her hand. Her lips were too numb to move for words.

"Are you okay?"

Sara shook her head.

"Drink," he said, noticing her hands. "Your fingers are blue."

She felt a surge of heat through her body, and turning, vomited into the snow, splattering Gabor's shoe. He flicked it defiantly against the back of the chair. The Swede reached out and touched Sara's shoulder.

"Shit happens to everyone. Not just the refugees."

Sara shifted her eyes and forced a smile, feeling the burning in her body move into her cheeks.

"Go inside," the Swede said. "I'll get the others."

Sara turned and stared at the refugees, helpless. One of the older women in line walked up to the table and pressed a linen handkerchief into her hand. It smelled of lavender and leather. Sara took it and wiped the corner of her mouth. "Thank you," she said.

The old woman smiled. She was blond with huge blue eyes and a face that reminded Sara of an apple doll, her lips outlined in pink from a lipstick that had feathered and caked in her transport. But she had bothered to apply it in the first place.

"Get up, Sara. You're freezing."

She had been sitting for four hours; the sun was already sinking behind the camp. Gabor quickly lifted Sara from the table, swiping the locket and depositing it into his pocket like a coin he had found on the street. He guided Sara into the building, past the other teachers who were stuffing suitcases into the trunk of a blue Mercedes en route to the camps in Bekescaba and Debrecen. Sara glanced over to the van, seeing the red duffle bag soaked with slush by the rear wheel.

"They forgot my bag."

Gabor held the door open with his toe and nudged her inside, the glass fogged from the heat of his breath.

"I'll get it for you. You're staying here," he said, closing the door behind her.

Sara was too tired to ask why and stood in the hallway on squares of maroon linoleum streaked and stamped from shoes and crutches. Her mouth tasted sour, and she scanned the dim hallway, searching for the bathroom, seeing little beyond the flicker of a fluorescent tube. The only other lights blinked from a fake pine tree strung with paper angels and tinsel, flashing red and blue like a police light on the face of a clay baby Jesus.

⮎

It was hot inside and smelled of stale, recycled air, the odor of fur-lined boots soaked with tears and slush drying under the heat vents. Sara followed the stink of urine to the bathroom, where an old man was passed out at the urinal, snoring, content in his stupor, his bony fingers wrapped around the neck of a beer bottle.

She crossed to the sinks and ran the water, the pipes spitting chunks of rust. She turned them off immediately, catching in the corner of her eye a paper she had not seen in the old man's lap. It was a picture of herself, the edges curled, soiled with fingerprints as if it had been touched too many times for the wrong reasons. She doubted if the old man needed the English lessons advertised in Serbo-Croatian beneath the picture.

Sara flicked water from her fingers, rubbing her eyes to get a better look. The photo lay upside down, and she reached out and lifted it slowly from the old man's lap. He hiccuped, startling her, then resumed his stupor, suckling the empty bottle. His breaths were labored, and she wondered if he were dying or having a bad dream. She wanted to wake him, ask how long he had had the photo, where he got it, but he fell asleep again, slobbering on a silver locket that dangled from his neck like a moon.

She had not submitted the photo. She had few photos of herself and did not like to pose for pictures. She believed they were false. She had no idea how Gabor received it. Who had sent it, if her mother or father had dug up the past to fish for an image that best reflected their only daughter, capturing her intelligence and charm. She remembered the photo being taken by her cousin Mark at the fishing cabin in July. His engagement party. The cabin, a watering hole for family affairs. She was sitting on the dock, barefoot, reel in one hand, bass in the other, her face shaded by dappled light. She had forced a smile, offering congratulations to Mark and his fiancée, who stood behind him while he took the picture and studied with a barely perceptible longing the intimacy they shared.

The photo had been changed now. It was a black-and-white photocopy. A sticker had been placed across Sara's chest making it appear as if she were wearing a T-shirt silk-screened with an American flag. Gone were the details of the moment. The searing heat. The rotted wood of the deck, soggy beneath her legs. The barbecue pit belching smoke. The smell of sparklers burning prematurely, before dark, before they could shine most brightly. It was as if the copy had been drained of its color on purpose. All that remained was Sara's toothy smile, a promise that the life inside the photograph was easy and safe. The photo pricked her memory. The image deceived whoever stared back at it, like a painting whose story extended far beyond its frame.

Sara peeled off the flag and let go of the photo, hearing Gabor's voice.

"My wife thinks you look like Meryl Streep."

She turned, seeing Gabor in the doorway. "Meryl Streep doesn't have red hair."

"True. But her eyes take you places."

Sara's cheeks burned. She was not good at taking compliments, not because she did not believe they were true, but because she did not trust the intention behind the praise. She would have rather Gabor said nothing at all. She knew nothing about the director, finding it odd he had taken to her so quickly, even on the tarmac, as if he had prepared for her, anticipating her questions and fire.

Gabor shifted his gaze to the old man. "He's been drunk for a month."

He marched over to the old man and wrestled the beer bottle from his fingers. The man woke up, startled. Gabor swore at him, then tossed the bottle against the wall, shattering it above the old man's head. He reached out and yanked the man to his feet and pointed to the door. The man, still shaky from his stupor, walked his hands along the wall, feeling his way to the hallway, his pants stained. He paused, looking out through his milky eyes, seeing Sara, then yanking the locket, stepped forward and kissed her on both cheeks, calling her Maja.

"Maja's dead!" Gabor shouted, pulling him off Sara.

The old man, stupefied, lowered his face in shame. Gabor

shoved him through the door. Sara wiped the old man's slobber
from her cheek, smelling him on her fingers, her disgust and em-
pathy competing. Gabor smiled, bending over to pick up the
photo.

"You've got one of those faces," Gabor said. "You remind
people of things."

Gabor reached out to the wall and rubbed off the man's fingerprints from the tiles. He scanned the bits of glass on the floor,
disgusted by the mess.

"It's not always like this. There is hope for some."

The old man coughed from the hallway.

"Will he go back?" Sara asked.

"To what?"

"Home."

Gabor lifted his finger and pressed it over his bottom lip as if
she had uttered a curse.

He whispered, "A refugee has no home. That's why they're
here. They can go anywhere in this world and still be a stranger
because they have no country."

The lightbulb above them buzzed in the silence. It hissed then
popped, leaving them in darkness.

⌒

Gabor led Sara down the hall, past frantic women and children who were sorting through belongings, dividing themselves
into groups of ten to fifteen people before they moved into the
rooms. They paused, staring both covetous and curious at Sara's
shoes and watch, recognizing her instantly. They crowded her,
pressing small gifts into her hands and pockets, plastic flowers, a
button, a half-eaten chocolate bar, lace doilies, and empty cigarette cases. Others retrieved hard candies from their pockets,
picking off lint. Someone found a crocheted tissue case in the bottom of her bag. Another a stone from the banks of his beloved
Danube. They dug for tokens, ingratiating themselves to Sara,
hoping she would remember them when everyone else had for-

gotten. Even the children had managed to give her drawings rendered in crayon and colored pencil, featuring rainbows and rivers, houses and trees, and in some pictures, the tanks that had destroyed them all.

Most of the children and younger mothers sat on the floor, staring up at Sara, but the elderly managed to stand, fighting exhaustion, struggling to reach out and touch her, jabbering in their native tongue greetings of good cheer and welcome. She shifted, unable to return their touch, withdrawing her hand from the introduction. She was grateful the teenagers had kept their distance. But it was the teenagers that challenged her most, bracing themselves, cross-armed.

"Don't let them bother you," Gabor said, reading her face. "They don't like anybody."

The teenagers refused to get up from the bunk beds in which they lay listening to headsets, drumming the air with their thumbs. Behind them, the walls had already been covered with posters, strips of empty Marlboro cartons, a lone crucifix and advertisements torn from magazines in their own language. Someone had traced a hand, leaving the middle finger extended, writing above it in English TEACHER LEAVE ME ALONE. They stared, judging, taking sides, refusing to let her in. She wished for only a subtle nod, something to assure they would be her allies, that together, they would help each other in the camp. But they had already built walls, stacking the pain behind anger, sandbagging their hearts. They breathed slowly, however not without recourse, as if they were fighting themselves, wanting to trust her, the teacher that could help them to understand their calamity, the teacher that could help them to recover.

Sara wanted to shake them, to wake them and confess. Couldn't they see? Didn't they know? She had no intentions of rescuing them. She had come to rescue herself.

～

She would leave in the morning. She had already made up her mind, absently following Gabor's tour through the refugee camp. She caught bits of its history, how Gabor had been the director since God knew when, how he loved the idea of America, an entire country created on the basis of refuge. Gabor reveled in the idea of escape. "Give me your weak, your weary," he said, having committed to memory the engraving on the Statue of Liberty from a postcard he kept folded in his wallet along with a sticker from Graceland. He named his first daughter Elise after the island, he said, scowling when Sara corrected his pronunciation.

"Ellis Island."

"No. Elvis is my *dog*."

Gabor would not be bothered with trifles. He gave Sara a tour of his office, dusting off snifters of brandy as if they were trophies on his bookshelf. He was proud of his job, all the baubles he received from the various countries supporting the camps: boxes of Swiss chocolate and Danish butter cookies in blue tins that had not been opened.

"You get a lot of gifts?" Sara asked

"Not really. Most of it's for the refugees."

"You have willpower."

"How's that?"

"You keep them for yourself," she said.

Sara was appalled not only by Gabor's gross sense of entitlement, but also mostly at the facilities of which he was so proud. She had no idea how all those people would take a shower, how they would be fed in the cafeteria, what they would do all day, not believing for a moment they had any interest in learning English. There was nothing she could teach them that they didn't already know. They knew too much. Saw too much. Cried too much. Everything about the refugees was too much. She had heard of people waiting for years to serve in the Peace Corps digging wells in mosquito-infested swamps of Third World countries, building schools and bridges where there were none, but there seemed to be no opportunity to build much of anything for the refugees. No trench could be dug deep enough to hold their losses.

Tomorrow Sara would take the train to Budapest, find the school for which she was best suited, the school that she deserved. It would take a few phone calls. A fax or two. Perhaps she could leave Hungary altogether and take her chances in Prague. She knew the Czech people wanted to learn English. According to *Let's Go Eastern Europe,* there was a basement Kmart in the center of the city that sold Kraft macaroni and cheese. She would feel at home and maybe even learn to like pilsner.

Sara was not prepared to feel at home in the refugee camp. Nothing about it had suggested anything remotely comforting. Not even the steam of hot goulash that wafted through the halls and fogged the windows. She was surprised, then, even dumbstruck, when Gabor led her through a series of narrow hallways on the seventh floor, the top floor of the refugee camp, to a room reminiscent of a five-star hotel. There was a king-size bed, a large desk, bookcases filled with English textbooks whose seals had not yet been broken, an overstuffed leather reading chair with ottoman, and an entertainment center stacked not only with stereo equipment, but also a huge television and VCR. The screen spanned the mirror on the opposite wall from which stared the noble eyes of Hungary's former King Matthias painted in oil. The bed was covered with expensive pillows, silk and velvet shams, the goose-down comforter gathered in a dimple beneath the weight of Sara's red duffle bag.

"We want you to feel at home."

Sara nodded numbly, standing at the threshold. Gabor looked up from the bed and gestured, excited to welcome her, his mood suddenly joyful, even playful, dignified by the choices he had made to please her. He fingered the gold cross dangling from his neck and inspected the room.

"Good taste, huh?"

Sara braced herself between the doorframe. "You get a lot of guests at the camp?" she asked.

"No guests," he said.

Gabor unwrapped one of the chocolates from the pillow and slid it into his mouth, chewing while he spoke.

"The room is yours."

Gabor expected Sara to smile, to oblige his joke, but she said nothing, her face crestfallen. She crossed to the desk and sat, still nauseated, fingering the plastic ruler from a ceramic vase stuffed with pencils and pens. The squeak of beds in the room below broke the silence.

"We want you to feel special."

"I feel sick," she said.

Sara massaged her forehead. She was overwhelmed by the hospitality, even suspicious. How could she ever feel at home here? She would never sleep knowing three families had stuffed themselves into the rooms below this one. She did not need even one night in a king-size bed to reconsider.

"I can't stay here," she said.

"Why?"

"It's unacceptable."

"But I don't understand," Gabor said.

"Neither will the refugees."

Gabor pressed one of the pillows against his chest, jowls flushed. He had expected her to be overwhelmed, as if he had remembered her birthday or her name day, the latter of which was even more important in Hungary, but he could not understand the forlorn expression, as if he had delivered news of tragedy. He wanted to make her comfortable, give her a place to recover from the trials she would endure teaching at the camp. He couldn't afford for her to leave. Not now. He had done everything in his power to buy the right things, finding the television on the black market and a satellite dish from a Russian priest. He had installed it in a snowstorm, anticipating Sara's arrival. She would like the television and soon, he was certain, she would thank him.

Gabor crossed to the entertainment center, lifting the remote control from the television, pressing the power button. He clicked forward to the BBC and European MTV, stopping at a rerun of *Dallas* dubbed in Hungarian.

"You know J. R.?" he asked in all seriousness, pointing to the screen. Larry Hagman, dressed in a white suit, kissed the inside of Victoria Principal's wrist. The scene excited Gabor, and he pressed the remote against his thigh, grazing the seam of his sweatpants.

"I don't watch TV," Sara said.

"Everybody watches TV."

"I don't want it."

"You don't want a television?"

"Give it to the refugees."

She stood. She was slightly taller than Gabor, but smaller, too. She snapped the ruler against the desk. She was angry now, feeling her head throb from fatigue and hunger.

"Don't look so sad," Gabor said, trying to distract her wet eyes. "There are worse things here than the refugee camp. Look at the view."

He walked to the window and pulled open the curtains, pointing to the twin-towered eyesore across the river, a Gothic spire that had once been the site of Csokhid's oldest structure, dating back to the twelfth century. The sun had already dropped behind the castle, the city draped in darkness.

"The organ is the only thing worth seeing. Eleven thousand pipes. Very good concerts."

Sara walked over to the window, seeing for the first time the small island in the middle of the river. A boathouse sat abandoned, burdened by snow. It looked so out of place, so alone, as if the festivity of the place had frozen, too. She felt a tightness in her throat as she stared at it, an odd pinch in her chest. She

pressed her fingers against the glass, tracing the long colon-
naded portico of the boathouse, stopping on a man in a long
white raincoat who stood with a bulging suitcase at the end of
the line of refugees. A streetlight threw halos of light on his face,
but before Sara could see him fully, he stepped into the shadow
of a tree.

"They keep coming," she said.

"Yes. As long as there is war."

Gabor stepped aside as the door swung open. A homely
middle-aged woman with nylons rolled around her ankles entered
with a tray of cheese and local sausage pricked with Hungarian-
flag-bearing toothpicks. A green glass bottle had been opened,
and the smell of liquor laced the air.

"Just in time," Gabor said. "To make you feel better."

He waved the woman away, pressing a cigarette into her hand.
She smiled, but did not speak.

"We'll see you downstairs."

"Sara?" The woman studied her with expectant eyes.

Gabor sighed, the introduction perfunctory and pained.
"Sara, Vera. Vera, Sara."

Sara smiled and offered her hand. "Nice to meet you," she
said, already aware of the dumbing down of language, stripping
out the idioms to make the simplest connection with a stranger.

"You are America?" Vera asked, her delivery mechanical like
a language tape that had been overstretched and expired.

"Yes. I'm from America."

"You teacher English?"

"Yes. Will I teach you?"

Vera shook her head, face flushed, the inadequacies of her
tongue shaming her. She waved her hand over her mouth.

"No. I am clean woman."

Sara nodded. "Yes. You are."

"I like job as clean woman."

"*Cleaning* woman, Vera," Gabor said. "Cleaning."

The woman turned to Gabor. He was annoyed and cracked his knuckles as if he'd corrected her a thousand times. She nodded, repeating him. "Cleaning woman."

"You do very good work," Sara said.

Vera nodded, hands behind her back like a schoolgirl, staring. Sara was uncertain of what else to say. She wasn't sure what Vera wanted, but she continued to stare, waiting for a response. Gabor plucked one of the flags from the cheese and popped a chunk into his mouth.

"Okay, Vera. See you later."

"I like speak with you."

"Thank you. I like speaking with you."

Vera turned to Sara, bowing her head, then disappeared into the darkened hallway. Gabor walked over to the bed and picked at a pillow. Every time he spoke, he reminded Sara of a count from Transylvania, the way his vowels tumbled at the back of his throat, softened, oddly with what sounded like a Texas drawl.

"Never thank a refugee," he said.

"Why not?"

"They should thank you."

"Thank me?"

"Yes."

"I haven't done anything for them."

"You will," Gabor said, slapping the sheets. "You have not tried the mattress. You will sleep like a queen."

Sara stared at him, incredulous, shaken by his contempt and careless confidence. He smothered the bedspread with the back of his wrist, catching in the threads the links of a watch that had greened his skin.

"Why should I sleep at all?"

"You have come to help. You need your rest."

Sara scratched her neck. The wool wet and itchy. Gabor rushed toward her, carrying two snifters of *palinka,* plum brandy, the national drink of Hungary. He offered her the glass cautiously,

but she turned from him and faced the window, pressing her fingers against a spider web stuck to the glass.

"How can I possibly help anybody here? They all seem to speak English anyway."

"It's not about English."

"That's why I'm here."

"Wrong," Gabor said.

"You hired me to teach English."

"I hired you to give them hope."

Gabor clicked off the television and tossed the remote to Sara, static crackling from the screen, then silence.

~

Sara wanted her own bed. She could not sleep the sleep of a queen in the king-size bed whose feathers floated on the dreams of refugees. Instead of entangling herself in the sheets, she negotiated the darkened hallways, trying to find the telephone. It seemed impossible that a thousand people would share one phone, that only one phone worked, but she was thinking of herself, not of the refugees, most of whom had no one to call.

She walked quietly, pressing the back of her wrist against her nose, not yet used to the smells. If she were blind, she would have believed anybody who told her that she walked not through a locker, but a barn. The camp was filled to capacity, and she was surprised order prevailed. Tidy stacks of shoes already lined the doorways as if the refugees needed a routine, not a roof for their survival. She crept past their rooms, hoping not to disturb them.

She found a pay phone in the stairwell, the light on a timer ticking as she picked up the receiver. Even as she dialed the international operator, she realized the call was ridiculous. Nobody would believe her, because she was not sure she believed herself. She had not rehearsed the conversation and shifted uncomfortably as the phone rang.

The operator answered. "How can I help you?" The voice was southern, like her mother's, but sounded light-years away.

"Miss, how can I help you?"

The operator sipped something—tea perhaps, or burned coffee—and Sara imagined a half-eaten muffin on the edge of the woman's desk crammed with photos of family and friends, her front row smiling back at her, giving her reasons to work and come home. For a moment, Sara found herself envious of the operator. It amused her, really, shaming her as much, to think of herself answering telephones with a college degree. But this voice on the other end of the line was in the business of connecting people—lovers, friends, families, strangers—and there was nobility in that.

Sara's father picked up on the fifth ring, provoked from his place on the couch. He answered the last ring before the answering machine went off. It was dinnertime. Five o'clock in Texas.

"Hello?"

"Dad?"

"Sara?"

A commercial singing praises for toilet cleaner played from the television. Then the laugh track for a sitcom when the channel changed.

"You sound good."

"I'm tired. It's late."

"It's dark there, right?"

"You could say that. Very dark."

She heard the folding of a newspaper, her father finally interested in talking.

"So how is it?"

"Cold. Snowing."

"Honey?"

"What?"

"You sound strange."

"I feel pretty strange. I flew through Christmas," she said, wanting desperately to add, for drama and laughs (what the hell, why not), *I landed in Croatia only to drive three hours in the back of some shit-for-tin van, vomited at the sight of a thousand refugees from a place we've never heard of and won't because it's been blown to bits.*

"How was the flight?"

"Surprising."

"Surprising?"

"Turbulence. You know."

"Thank God you got there. I had a dream you landed in a cornfield. By helicopter. Imagine that? Too much beer before bed. Hold on, honey. Your mother's coming."

Sara felt her cheeks burn. Her throat was tight, and she rubbed it with her sleeve, preparing herself, hoping to sound cheerful and mask her panic. She forced a smile, pressing the phone tight against her ear. A chair slid out from the kitchen table. The scratch of the receiver against her father's pajamas as he passed the phone to his wife.

"Turn it off," she said.

"The game's not over."

"Turn it down, I can't hear her."

"Mom?"

"How is it, sweetheart?"

"It's crackling. I can't hear you, Mom."

"She can't hear, honey."

Her parents shared the phone, their lips pressed against the receiver as they scuttled around the kitchen, trying to get reception for a new cordless, her father's Christmas gift to himself so that he could watch football and compare scores with his brother in Ohio.

"Can you hear us?"

"It's still crackling."

"Can you hear us now?"

"That's better."

"Sounds like you're calling from Mars."

Sara nodded, biting her lip. Her mother was right. It *was* another planet. The light in the stairwell went off, and she walked as far as the cord permitted, lifting her leg, pressing the button with her foot to reset the timer.

"Are they nice?"

"Who?"

"Your students."

"I haven't met them yet. Not officially."

"Did they have a party for you?"

"A party?"

"A welcome party. After all, you volunteered."

Sara drew in a breath, tonguing the sore on the roof of her mouth from eating too many gummy bears. "No party. Not yet. They're working on it."

"How about your flat?"

"I have a room."

"Honey, I expected that. There's at least one room in a flat, isn't there?" Her mother used the word *flat* as if she had spent her summers in Paris.

"It's not a flat. Not really. Just a room."

"Can you cook in your room?"

Sara hadn't even thought about cooking or about any food since she landed. The phone buzzed. The door to the stairwell opened, and one of the refugees, a tall middle-aged man, walked past Sara, greeting her in English. She waved, but the refugee sat on the stairs, wearing a hat made from a newspaper. He gestured for her to hang up.

"What did he say?"

"Good morning."

"They speak English," her mother said, impressed.

Her father said, "They're up early."

"I don't think they actually went to bed, Dad."

"Christ. You *live* with them?"

"Yes."

"Christ."

Every time her father cursed, she felt her heart sink because she believed in a way he was cursing her, the way he mishandled language. She told him once that language was fragile, but he never listened.

"What kind of school is it?"

Sara paused. "A boarding school," she said finally, realizing no answer would suffice. Instead of telling her parents the truth, she decided to tell them what they wanted to hear, what she herself wished were true, driving deeper the wedge of her lie. The phone call was over. She could not tell her parents that she was in a refugee camp. Not now. Not yet. She would have to get used to the idea first, wean herself from wanting to leave, realizing in the blackened hallway that stank of refugees that she had no choice but to stay. She would rather face the uncertainty of life in a refugee camp than the humiliation of having a college degree without a life.

"One of my students needs the phone," she said, watching the refugee gesticulate, pleading with her.

"Honey? We're losing you."

The phone went dead. The tall refugee stood behind her, his arm arched over her shoulder, pressing the cradle with his thumb. He lifted the phone from her hand and hung up. The light went off in the stairwell, and all she could see were the whites of the refugee's eyes. Her heart raced.

"Why'd you do that?"

"Candles burning," he said.

"What? Where?"

"Come. Come."

"Is there a fire?"

The tall refugee took Sara by the elbow, ushering her through the darkened stairwell to a room at the end of the hall. The lights were off, and the walls flickered with shadows from firelight. She was surprised he paused at the doorway to kick off his shoes, and she followed suit, seeing not a flame but a single taper candle drilled into a large square of chocolate on a plate in the middle of the floor. The tall refugee nudged her inside. She stood, barefoot, surrounded by other refugees. She recognized some of them from the Red Cross tent, the little girl with the locket and Elana, who stared listlessly at the candle flame. The beds had been pushed against the walls to make room for a party, the windows draped with paper chains made from old newspapers, headlines from Vukovar tucked and twisted into flowers. The Red Cross worker from Sweden stepped out from behind the door with a bottle of red wine.

"I didn't think you'd be sleeping."

"People sleep here?"

"The living dead," she said, and winked, "can party."

Sara smiled, feeling the irony twist her lips. "So this is the party."

"Yes. First day of the rest of their lives."

The Swedish woman pulled the cork on the bottle, the loud pop punctuating the announcement. Filling a glass, she lifted her eyes to meet Sara's. "Yours too," she said.

Sara waved her away.

"I don't drink."

"Neither did I," the Swedish woman said, pressing the glass into Sara's palm, forcing her to take it anyway.

The Swede walked around the room and filled the cups, any cups the refugees had managed to salvage or find, finishing one bottle then another, encouraging them to drink more, three bottles, four, opening a fifth for the tall refugee, a gravedigger, who paced the room, eyes drifting south toward the window, haunted not by the bodies he had collected but for those left putrefying in the streets. An old woman sat alone in the corner, folding newspapers written in her native tongue, a magician of sorts turning the ugly words of despair and de-

struction into art, flowers, hats, crucifixes, props for the theater of war.

Sara's eyes wandered the room, searching for somebody she
might recognize, smiling at the nurse Elana, who seemed lost, too,
trying to control the tremor in her hands. A middle-aged man
with a wounded leg, his head wrapped in bandages, pressed a
crutch to his heart, teeth sunken into the foam, gnawing absent-
mindedly like a horse chewing wood. The little girl who had lost
the locket drummed the ghost of it at her neck, her pea coat
dusted with snow.

The old woman in the corner pushed herself off the floor and
crossed the room to Sara, dragging a chain of paper flowers. She
wound them into a circle and crowned the girl's head, lifting the
curls off her back, delighted by the beauty as if it had been a long
time since she had seen anything beautiful.

Sara noticed the feathered pink lipstick, recognizing the
woman who had given her the handkerchief that afternoon. The
woman was drunk on whatever spirit had been distilled into the
bottle, passing it to the only other man beside the tall refugee, both
too old to be a threat to any Serb conscript. They were all drinking now, and they rocked listlessly, staggering to the windows to
watch the snow.

The Swedish woman, dizzy from circling the group, sat on the
floor beside Sara.

"Where are all the men?"

The Swedish woman ran her finger around the rim of the
wineglass as if the high-pitched ring were enough of an answer.
But she knew the girl wanted to know more.

"Buried. Mass graves."

"What?"

She pointed to the tall man standing at the window. "The
gravediggers lived. The Serbian army needed them. But that
man's actually too young to be alive."

"Too young?"

"You won't see men between the ages of eighteen and forty here. If you do, you wonder what they did to survive."

Sara roved the faces, her cheeks flushed with wine. The refugees talked quietly among themselves in Croatian.

"Are they all from Vukovar?"

"Most of them, yes. But there will be more Serbs. And it will get ugly." The Swedish woman tapped a metal flask. Sara had not noticed, but the bottom rim had rusted.

"You've been here a long time," she said.

"Three years. First wave Romanians. Then the East Germans."

"That's a long time not to know what happened to any of them."

The Swedish woman raised a finger in the air, not to make a point, but to admonish the girl. "I don't need answers to do my job."

"And you've managed not to get involved?"

"Never."

"Not once?"

The Swedish woman took a sip, passing the flask, as if it were the answer she refused to give to Sara. She threw her gaze into the glass, surprised to see it was full. "You don't drink."

"No. I told you. I get headaches."

"Too many details will do that," the Swedish woman said, swiping the glass. She drank the wine in one gulp, tipping the glass over, shaking the excess on her wrist. "It's contagious, you know."

"Headaches?"

"Trauma."

Sara stared at her, listening.

"Their trauma is your trauma if you ask them to share it. Keep a forest between you," the Swedish woman said, lowering her voice. "The minute you open your heart to a refugee, you will suffer everything they have survived. They will earn your sympathy but you will not earn theirs. And you will hurt as much, sometimes more, because you suffer the horror not of one story, but of all the stories you learn when you ask what happened."

"Which is why you don't ask."

The Swedish woman shrugged, reading Sara's face. "You don't like it, do you?"

"It's not very compassionate," Sara said.

"The camp. Not my morality."

"No. It wasn't my first choice."

The Swedish woman laughed. She undid her braids, the dark hair falling in thick waves down her back, draping the straps of her overalls. She appeared to be almost too comfortable in the camp, indifferent, as if she could be anywhere in the world and call it home. However, it was not so much a posture of apathy as it was avoidance that Sara detected most, as if in the Swedish woman's effort to appear unfazed and carefree, she had used up all her energy trying to protect herself from caring at all. She was not coldhearted. She lied, yes. She drank and had obviously drunk a lot, especially tonight. The smell of plum brandy, not wine, lingered on her breath. She took out the flask again and drank as if she needed a spirit as strong as her own to keep her wits about her. Her eyes were bloodshot. If it weren't for the dim light of the candle, Sara could have sworn the Swedish woman had just finished a long hard cry before the party started.

"You think there was a mistake?"

"I didn't choose to be here," Sara said.

"Neither did I," the Swedish woman said, wiping the brandy from her lower lip. "Neither did they. Nobody chooses to be a refugee."

Sara turned to her. "You're not a refugee."

"That depends. We're all here because we've escaped something, right?" The Swedish woman screwed the lid on the flask, speaking to Sara's reflection in the metal. "It's not a choice," she

said. "It's a last resort. The worst choice of all is the one that's decided for you."

Sara's jaw tightened. She crossed her arms over her chest,
feeling a chill. One of the refugees had opened the window to
smoke, and a cold wind swept around her ankles. She could hear
music playing from a distance outside, a solo violin straining to
tune itself against the wailing of a child who had awakened upstairs, most likely, from one nightmare before descending into
the next. The music ambled at first, off-key, grasping for a new
key as if hidden inside the notes was a promise for everyone who
listened.

Sara, too, turned toward the sound. It was not so much the
beauty of the music that moved her to listen with such attention,
but the map she detected in the arrangement as if it had invited
her, expressly, to listen. The coupling of notes was unlike any she
had ever heard. It was not beautiful. Not in the traditional sense
of a harmony. It was a bruised sound, pained, choking on imper-
fections, yet it offered a certain release she had never experienced
from music. She did not consider herself a musical person. One
year at flute. Two at piano. All miserable lessons. She had no patience and no sense of pitch, yet she felt the force of the music
now. The sounds pierced and jabbed her heart, the bow fighting
all the friction between her and the world. The notes gathered in
circles, releasing halos of sound that floated up for each of them
to hold.

The tall refugee, feeling the energy, began to clap, performing
a folk dance to dissipate the angst. The girl without the locket
took his hand, skipping, trying to keep up with his long legs. Soon
the others joined, lacing sticky fingers, swirling in their stupor,
drunk on Bull's Blood and bitter hops, minds restless and agitated. They danced a dance both mournful and merciless, silent,
as if movement itself could displace their loss.

Sara sat watching, her knees pulled to her chest, wondering
what had given them the courage to go on, not willing to believe

it was simply the music. She was doubtful the dance would last much longer, but when the refugees reached out and lifted her off the floor, sweeping her into their own reverie, she experienced a deep and immediate stillness. She remained powerless over their will to dance, as if the music itself gave them a reason to move beyond the pain and uncertainties of refugee life. Squeezing their hands, she wondered if they had anything in common besides the need to hold on to each other.

2

~

The boy's name was Luka, and he wanted his drum. It was not an unreasonable request for a nine-year-old cooped up in a bomb shelter for six weeks. He accidentally dropped the drum on the street the day he went underground with seven hundred people who, fleeing their homes and the Serbian soldiers burning them, decided to stay in Vukovar. It was mid-November. Nobody walked the streets now. Nobody sane, anyway. Bridges were mined. Windows sandbagged. The street, his mother had admonished, was where the drum would stay.

The lid of a toilet seat would have to do for now. Luka could handle the stink if it meant he could hear the rhythms. He didn't mind using the women's bathroom. Not that they were any cleaner than the men's—they were worse—but they had stalls with doors whose locks worked, and the privacy they offered was a small luxury for a boy who wanted to be alone. He left the lights off, using a small flashlight instead, and crossed the bathroom, his stride stiff. He carried two unsharpened pencils to use as drumsticks and slipped into the last stall, sliding the latch into place on the door.

The walls had been tagged with fingernail polish, the names and dates of people who had recently died. Luka recognized some of them: a dentist, two neighbors, the plumber who recovered his mother's wedding band from the pipes below the kitchen sink. They were all men. And they had all disappeared. They had never made it to the shelter. Luka reached out with the pencil and tapped BRONCO, the plumber, then leaned in and kissed his name. Luka's mother had spent more than half the money she received for hawking the recovered wedding ring to buy Luka a set of drumsticks in September. Luka had used them only once before the Yugoslav army set his neighborhood on fire, burning every building except the church. His mother advised him to forgive the wrongdoings, that the Serb troops were mostly conscripts, at least at this stage in the war, bewildered boys twice his age who were only doing what they were told. Luka could forgive them, he promised, if they had only burned his house. But the Yugoslav army had destroyed the drumsticks, and for that he could never and would never forgive them.

Drumming on toilet seats was beyond reproach. Luka knew that drummers had always held a privileged position on the battlefield since the beginning of time, and it was considered dishonorable to strike or wound them. He was not a fighter of any kind, and he had never been in a battle until now. He understood the victory in seizing a drum, but knew there was no glory in destroying one. Only despair. When a drum fell silent on either side, there was barely a will to fight. And without a will, there would be no winner. Even a conscript knew that.

He turned off the flashlight, preferring to drum in the dark. He faced the toilets, kneeling, holding the pencils lightly in his hand, tapping out the rhythms to "The March of Paris." He drummed softly at first, slowly adjusting his hearing to the echoes in the bathroom. The acoustics were worse here than anywhere else in the shelter, but it was the only place he could drum without disturbing the other refugees. The Croatian National Guardsmen had confiscated the empty coffee can that Luka's mother had given him to drum. Luka argued that the rhythms would calm them, but to no avail. Only the toilet seat had been faithful to his drumming, guaranteeing the briefest connection to a place beyond the shelter, beyond Vukovar, beyond the battlefield and its blood, to the only place the boy could find peace.

Luka had always found safety in the edges of rhythm. He played in it, too, climbing rhythms as if they were the trees in a secret forest only he could enter at will. He respected the fluidity of rhythm, how it understood and obeyed gravity. Just as water made its way to the lowest levels in the earth, the vibrations of a drum traveled to the places that needed it most: to the body, mind, spirit, and soul. Drumming established order, organizing the chaos in the boy's heart. There was a predictability about drumming that established a sense of security in him, and he learned to depend on it when everything else had failed to alleviate his fear and rage. The drumming permitted Luka to wrestle the trauma of war until his arms burned and his head ached and his hands fell limp from silencing guns. The boy believed a drum could freeze a bullet.

Occasionally Luka would sit for hours alone without the drumsticks, mining for other sounds. The silence of the shelter was unbearable, and the boy was starved for real sound, missing the rhythms of the Danube, the dance of rain. He lingered in the bathroom instead, listening to the tinny drip of water from a leaky faucet or the slow rush of toilets flushing. Sometimes he spent hours with his ear pressed to the walls in his dorm, listening to the buzz of electricity in the wires, the scurry-tap of termites inside the wood. He had developed a highly sensitive way of listening and was aware of the inner voices that crept through the most inanimate of things—leather, stone, paper, bone. The boy believed everything had a sound, even faith, because his patience rewarded him by hearing it.

The march of boots on the tile stopped his drumming. He could hear the click of the National Guardsmen walking through the corridor. There were more than two of them, the uniformed staccato steps interrupted by the patter of bare feet slapping the ground, defiant, resistant. The guardsmen stood outside the women's bathroom, whispering, the smell of cigar smoke and smoked ham drifting in with the voices.

Luka quickly tucked the pencils behind his ear. He climbed on top of the toilet, straddling the seat, hands outstretched and braced against the walls for balance. The lights were turned on, and he could see through the cracks in the stall two uniformed National Guardsmen with a bony woman between them. He recognized her. The old woman and her husband sold baklava from the bakery on his street. They worked long, hard hours. The old woman was strong, but the boy had never seen her like this, frail and wobbling. She fell to her knees and pressed her face to the floor to pray, as a Muslim would, but the guardsmen lifted her by the elbows, wrestling the prayer beads in her tiny hands. Her eyes were swollen, ringed from lack of sleep. She dabbed her cheeks with the ends of a head scarf, trying to compose herself, but she could not control her sobbing, and they slapped her. Not once. Twice. Drawing blood.

Luka stiffened, accidentally dropping one of the pencils. It bounced off the tile and rolled under the door, stopping in the drain by the sinks. One of the guardsmen's hands swooped down to pick it up. Without hesitating, the man marched to the last stall and jiggled the door, frustrated to find it was locked.

"Who's in there?"

The guardsman pressed his round face against the slat, peering in at Luka. He turned back at the other guardsman, coughing up a laugh.

"It's the drummer boy again," he said, then turned back to Luka, eyes narrowed to slits. "How many times do we have to tell you to stay out of here? You're not a girl. This is the women's bathroom, for Christ's sake."

The guardsman wedged his thick fingers through the slat, trying to open the latch, but Luka jumped off the toilet and bit him. The guardsman howled, and Luka dropped to his stomach, dragging himself beneath the stalls. He met the boots of the second guardsman, who reached down and pulled Luka out by the shoulders. The man was old enough to be his father and scowled the way his teachers did when they caught him drumming on his desk during class. The man held out his hand, gesturing for Luka to show him his papers, but the boy stared up at him with wide eyes and shrugged.

"My mother has them."

"Where's your mother?"

"At the hospital. Working the night shift."

"Saving Serbs."

"What?"

The boy looked at him confused.

"She's always been fond of the Serbs."

Luka shifted on his feet, uncomfortable, feeling the cold tiles beneath his toes. He shook his head. The guardsman leaned in to the boy and whispered, poking Luka's sternum with his index finger.

"You're father was a handsome man. Lucky you got his dark curls and blue eyes."

Luka nodded, slowly, hating the man's questions, the insidious way the words slithered over his tongue.

"Too bad she didn't save him."

"She tried," Luka said.

His mother told him the story every year on his birthday because it was also the anniversary of his father's death. His body was found in the Danube a week before he could bring a case to trial. The case involved World War II war crimes suffered by Luka's grandparents, two of ten thousand Bosnian Serbs exterminated by the Croat *Ustashas*. Luka received a drum the day his father died. A gift from his uncle to keep his father alive. The drum was a Tibetan prayer drum and had the power to wake the dead.

The older guardsman took the pencil from the other guards-

man, who was still sucking on his finger. Luka had bitten through
the man's nail. The older man pulled the pencil from Luka's
pocket and, holding both of them in his right hand, snapped
them in half, dropping the pieces on the floor, where they rolled
back into the stalls. Luka pressed his lips together, blinking back
tears. Even pencils were hard to come by in the shelter. It had
taken three weeks to get them since the last time he had been
caught drumming in the bathroom. Luka crouched, reaching for
the broken pencil, wondering if they could be saved with medical
tape, but they had already splintered. He struggled to lift his eyes
to the guardsman.

"My mom says you're trying to save Croatia."

"We are," the guardsman said, alarmed. "We will. As long as
your mom doesn't save Serbia first."

The man laughed, and Luka stood, flinging the broken drumsticks at the man's waist, silencing him. The old woman cupped
her hands, catching the blood dripping from her nose. Luka
stepped toward her and reached for her hand.

"Should I get my mom?"

"No, Luka. I'm fine. Go back to your dorm."

"You're bleeding," he said, spooked by the stains on her
cheek. She forced a smile, staring at the boy. Her lips moved
slowly, trying to tell him something, but the guardsmen ushered
her toward an old man with a cane who stood waiting in the doorway. She stepped away from the guards and buried her face into
her husband's shoulder, but the guardsmen prodded them with
his rifle.

"*Hadje.* Get going."

The old woman shook her arms free from the guards and bent
over, rolling nylons down around her ankle bones. She proceeded
to peel bills wrapped around her swollen legs and offered them,
limp and soggy, to one of the guardsmen.

"We don't want your money."

"Don't be a fool. They're deutsche marks. Look."

The old woman dangled them in front of his hands, but he leaned in and spat on the already soggy bills.

"Your money's no good."

"I don't understand."

The guardsman flicked the bills with his fingers. He spoke slowly as if he were talking to a child. "Understand this. You are a Muslim," he said, then looked over at Luka. "And you. You are half a Serb."

The old woman reached out and slapped him. "We're Yugoslavs," she said. "I've lived my entire life in Vukovar and gave birth to three sons here. You have no right to tell me what I am."

The man with the cane nudged her gently, yanking the ends of the pink cardigan draped over her shoulders.

She turned to Luka. "We have as much right to be here as anyone."

Luka's face burned. He was a Yugoslav, too, and he didn't understand why that should shame him or the old woman. Who cared if he were as much Croat as he were Serb? What difference did it make if the woman was a Muslim? She made the best baklava in town. And she was kind. And she let him ride the bikes her husband repaired in the shop behind the bakery. How different was she from the other women he knew? They married, gave birth, lived, and died. Some of them crossed themselves with two fingers, others with two fingers and thumb, and still others, like the old women, didn't cross themselves at all but kissed the floor instead. He didn't see the big deal in the way they contacted God. The only difference is that Luka had never seen a woman slap a man before, and he was awed by the old woman's behavior. He giggled. It delighted him. The guardsman deserved it, and if it hadn't been for the old woman, Luka would have slapped him, too.

The guardsman, humiliated, chased Luka from the bathroom. "Get out of here, Chetnik."

Luka ran down the corridor finding his way in the dark to the dorm, the old woman calling after him.

Her words echoed in his head. "Never let them tell you who you are."

⌐◡

Luka searched the sleeping mats in the dorm for toothbrushes, hoping to find extra to use as drumsticks. He could not understand how anyone slept in the dorms and was startled by the snores that arched over each other. There were no clocks on the walls, and it was always dark, a kind of permanent night, but the hall light had been turned on, and he smelled coffee from carts being wheeled through the shelter, waking the refugees to a new day, a different day, he hoped.

Luka would have risked anything for a change, even a new sound. He wished it had been him, not the old couple who were leaving, although he did not trust it was a good place where they were being taken. He imagined any place was better than the shelter, even the wrong place. He was restless there, tired of walking in circles, sleeping on the floor, tired of the old men and women whose breath smelled of crackers and cured meat, sausages that had been saved from root cellars and spared from looting. He was tired of the nagging, the tears, the commotion, none of which was making any sense. Thirty-five thousand people had left by the end of August, but he didn't know why, since the Serbian army had only recently taken over Vukovar.

Luka overheard the guardsmen outside his dorm room discussing the news, and he got up to listen. Five hundred twenty bodies had been registered and taken to the only available burial ground in Vukovar, but they weren't sure where that was, a field perhaps, a mass grave in the meadows where the same bodies had shared picnics and fallen asleep, drunk and exhausted in the grass. Hundreds of bodies remained uncollected, they whispered, spitting out bits of fingernails. They had chewed their fingers raw, leaving nothing but the quick of the nail beds.

Luka had tried to understand the problem by watching the news on television. President Tudjman said Croatia did not want

war. At least that's what Tudjman said on TV. Croatia wanted independence. Slovenia wanted independence. Serbia, on the other
hand, did not want independence from Yugoslavia and insisted
on preventing the other two from gaining it. His mother had
called the dispute a pissing contest before the first bomb fell on
Vukovar.

Luka didn't know which side he was on or if it even mattered.
His mother was a Croat. His late father, a Serb. His paternal
grandfather was a Bosnian watchmaker who married a sculptor
from Belgrade and moved with her to the mountains of Kozara,
where they were just two of a million people, mostly Serbs, exterminated at the camp in Jasenovac in June of 1942. Luka's
mother's father, an Italian cobbler from Trieste, married a milliner
from Split. Luka was as much Croat as he was Serb, as much Italian as Bosnian. He was no different from most of the people who
lived in Vukovar. Holidays had always been interesting, plum
brandy favored over pilsner, everyone drunk on spirit and song,
fluttering tongues bleating, *"The world's heart beats loudest in the
Balkans."*

Luka's family was characteristic of most mixed marriages from
eastern Slavonia, the fertile plains stretching toward the Danube
valley whose rich cornfields fed generations of families in Central
Europe. The people of Vukovar and its environs comprised a
unique tapestry of Serbs, Croats, Slovaks, Czechs, Hungarians,
Italians, and until the end of World War II, Germans, all living
harmoniously in the southernmost sphere of the Austro-
Hungarian Empire. They lived a life of peaceful coexistence,
sharing apple strudel and polka dances until 1918, when waves of
southern refugees, after living under the Ottoman Turks for five
hundred years, moved into the homes of older families killed in
the First World War. The divide between old and new, *starose-
dioci* and *dosljaci,* the sophisticated settlers and the barbaric im-
migrants catalyzed a new conflict. The difference between a Croat
and a Serb had never been part of the problem, and Luka was not

sure why it was now. He was a child, and his concerns were those of a boy.

And like any child, Luka longed for what he had lost. He missed climbing the plum tree outside his bedroom window. He missed his house, the TV and videos, the bathtub, his mother's towels, the dried lavender that made the bathroom smell like the island of Hvar in June. She carried a vial of lavender oil in her nurse's smock and massaged it into his arms to relax him when fighter planes screeched low over the city. She had managed to lull the sick and wounded to sleep, but had no luck with her son. There was no relaxing in a bomb shelter. She told Luka to be patient, that it would be over soon, but he didn't believe her, because she had stopped wearing her watch.

It was her decision to stay. Luka had wanted to leave with the others, neighbors and friends, most of whom had fled north to refugee camps in Hungary. His mother told him he was too young to decide their fates.

"They'll have to kill us before they make us refugees," she said when the JNA, the mostly Serbian army or Chetniks (their derogatory nickname, much like *Ustasha* referred to the Croats) besieged the eastern Croatian town of Osijek in September. She and Luka watched ruefully as a swarm of armored vehicles, surface-to-air missiles, tanks, and antiaircraft batteries trundled through the road past her parents' farm, moving south and east into Bosnia. Luka dropped a bottle of milk, smashing the glass on the cement steps, the wild chickens squawking in the yard. The dogs barked at the drivers, mostly bewildered conscripts who gave them all the finger.

Luka glanced up at his mother. "It is not a parade, Mama."

"No, Luka. It's most certainly not."

His mother paced a lot, like she was doing now, the IV bag slung over her shoulder like a sack of sugar.

Luka crossed back from the door and sat cross-legged on the sleeping mat, watching his mother administer medicine to the wounded. She operated on autopilot here, her movements involuntary, like those of Luka's bus driver, who had been blinded by a grenade that exploded on the steps of their church. He had managed to drive with his eyes closed, knowing every stop for cigarettes and chocolate.

But unlike the bus driver, Elana Milanovich forbade herself to sit or to stop. Not since two bombs bombarded the hospital in early October, destroying the department of surgery and the operating theater. Only one exploded. The other crashed through several floors and landed on the foot of a bed of a wounded man, who survived. Elana had kept the mortar as a token, a sign that God was looking over her and her patients. She moved the infirm to the basement and kept them under her care. There were lives to be saved. And a city, too. She'd be damned before she gave up her view of the Danube or the stretch of sunflowers whose reflection painted the white walls in her kitchen yellow when the light was right. But the light had been wrong lately. Only firelight came from burning villages, then darkness.

Luka lifted his pillow off the sleeping mat and pulled out the transistor radio his mother had managed to save from the house. He tuned it, careful to keep it quiet. The news angered his mother, but he wanted to hear music, any music would do. He got mostly static, dead air, then switched to AM, finding one channel. A report warned of sniper nests in Zagreb. He was not familiar with snipers and figured his teachers had saved that unit for the fifth year science class. "Sniper nest." Curious words. He imagined huge colorful birds, flying peacocks, whose expansive wings shrouded entire cities in shadow. He wondered why somebody didn't shoot the birds if they were so scary.

"Turn it off, Luka."

He didn't have to look up. He saw his mother's white work shoes. The thick heels were smudged black from ash.

"Have you ever seen a sniper, Mama?"

"No," she said, taking the radio from him. She turned it over, banging the back side with the heel of her hand as if she were burping an infant. Two batteries popped out, and she dropped them in her pocket, where they clinked against the vial of lavender oil.

"Why'd you do that?"

"It's giving me a headache."

"But I didn't hear the music yet."

"Luka, enough! There is no more music."

Elana set the radio on the floor and covered the old man sleeping beside her son with a blanket. She crouched, touching the man's forehead with the back of her hand, then without waking him, she lifted his right wrist and unwound the bandages that had turned black from his blood.

"He said he'd help me find it."

"Find what?"

"My drum."

Elana sighed and tore off a strip of sterile gauze, the cotton fibers flittering in the dank air. She lifted the man's wrist to the penlight pressed between her lips and examined his wound. The man's skin was the color of a bruised pear.

"He said he knows where it is."

"Luka, please. He can hardly remember his name."

She set the man's wrist down, pressing two pills into the palm of his hand. She had taken the medicine from her own personal supply, waiting anxiously for the Red Cross to deliver more to the hospital. They expected an arrival any day, the request placed two months ago, trying to accompany the needs of hundreds of wounded civilians who had suffered injuries from the mortar and air assaults in September. The hospital registered an average of sixteen to eighty wounded per day for two weeks, a more manageable figure than the ninety-two wounded who arrived in early October, infecting the hospital with its present mode of pandemonium. There were obviously more pressing concerns, but Luka insisted.

"Ask him when he wakes up. He'll remember."

Elana folded the man's ashen fingers over the pills and turned, looking squarely at her son. "Even if he remembers, the streets are not safe."

"When will they be safe?"

"I don't know. The Serbs are still here."

"I want them to leave," Luka pleaded, tracing the smudge marks on the heel of her shoes. "Can't somebody tell them to go home?"

"They think this *is* their home."

"But they've never lived here."

"They want to, Luka. They will."

Elana's voice cracked. Luka looked up, watching the lump push against her throat like a beach pebble trying to dislodge itself from wet sand. Her eyes were blank as if her mind was far from the shelter, on a swim off the island of Hvar or a stroll above the stone walls of Dubrovnik.

"I miss it," Luka said.

"Me, too."

"You don't drum, Mama."

"I miss home," Elana said, fingering the curls on his head. The thick black hair reminded her of Alexander the Great. Her son Luka, the conqueror.

"The drum's out there," she said.

"You've seen it?"

"No, sweetie. Not yet. But I believe it."

"Somebody might take it."

"It's bad luck to steal a drum like that."

"Nobody knows it's bad luck."

"The drum will tell them."

Luka's face twisted with disappointment. "Let me walk with one of the guardsmen to find it."

Elana laughed, but Luka had not intended to joke. "For god's sake," she whispered, eyeing the armed men at the door. "They drive grocery trucks thinking they're tanks. They won't save you or find your drum." She tossed Luka the IV bag. "Play on this."

Luka caught the bag, gathering the liquid bulge between his fingers. "It feels like a boob," he said, disgusted, hurling it back. It was not a drum.

"A boob? How so?"

"Ratko's girlfriend let us feel her implants."

"Ratko's girlfriend is a Russian prostitute."

"Guess they make bad boobs in Russia."

"Guess so," Elana said, pinching the urge to laugh again. She glimpsed her late husband's wanderings in Luka's eyes, the innocence and sweetness. The loss was hers to carry through the years, carving her face with the lines of a woman who had loved once and passionately, but never again, reserving the rest for her son. She realized she would never have the power to protect Luka forever from the things that would go wrong in the world. It was as much her job as a mother to love her child as it was for the world to give him character, to shape him in ways beyond her control; and this was her torment and the risk she took as a parent in a world where war was possible.

Luka counted the tick marks he had drawn on his arms. "We've been here six weeks."

"I know, honey."

"I haven't played a real drum once."

"But you're safe, Luka. You should be so lucky."

"Do you feel lucky?"

"We survived."

"We're surviving, Mama. It's not over, is it?"

"Not yet," Elana said, wishing to tell him that the war had only just begun.

〜

Luka had made a promise. He would stay in the shelter until his mother returned from work, but he could think of nothing but the drum. His body ached for the rhythms, not the hollow tap of pencils on porcelain. The boy could not face the toilets again. He wanted to feel the skin and the body of the drum, hug it between his knees, pound out a beat that blistered his palms and made his heart explode. He wanted to drum outside, pump the sun into twilight, the moon into dawn. He wanted a way to forget everything he knew about why they were in the shelter.

Luka wanted to move. He stared at the old man sleeping on the mat beside him, whose lips puckered from snoring. Luka wondered if the old man wanted to move, too, if he moved in his dreams, which way, how far, and if he would ever wake again. Luka didn't understand how the man could sleep with his wrists messed up and all the babies screaming and the teenage couples making sucking sounds in the corners as if nobody could see or hear them. Luka had not slept since September, and he longed to exchange places with the old man, offering him his youth for a dose of sleep.

The old man fidgeted with the silver locket dangling from his neck. He clutched it every so often when his dreams turned, as if the locket were an oar he used to navigate the uncharted waters of a war that remained undeclared, still, after two months of bombardment and a summer of sporadic shelling that had shattered the front window of his barber shop and every mirror inside.

Luka leaned forward to get a better look at the locket, and, making sure nobody was watching him, he slowly opened it, surprised to find a lock of hair drop below the man's chin. He blew the strands with his breath.

"You like waking the dead?"

Luka snapped his eyes upward, seeing Ratko dressed in a guardsman uniform. He was surprised not only to be caught, but also to see the doughy punk rocker dressed in anything other than ripped jeans and studded leather. The purple mohawk had been shaved, the blond bristles sprouting from his scalp. A gun swung loosely from his shoulder like a guitar.

"Ratko?"

"The hair is his daughter's."

Luka flinched, moving back as Ratko crouched and stuffed the hair back into the locket. The old man continued to snore. Ratko tapped the man's shoulder with his clean fingernails. The black nail polish was missing.

"Lucky for him he sleeps."

"What are you doing?"

"We need your radio."

"I mean in the uniform."

"I'm saving Vukovar. What you do think?"

He held out his hand, and Luka passed him the radio. "It doesn't work. My mom took out the batteries."

Ratko examined the radio. He popped out a tape. "*Planet Drum*. Keep it safe."

Luka reached up for the cassette. He had played every day during the summer, trying to memorize the rudiments from Mickey Hart's latest and greatest album. Luka slid the tape inside his pillowcase and looked up at Ratko. "Do you really drive a grocery truck?"

"Bus. I drive a *bus*." Ratko straightened the collar on his shirt and stood erect, saluting Luka. He was tall and thick as an oak tree with ruddy cheeks and a crooked jaw that had been cracked more than once.

"What for? There's nobody left to drive."

Ratko looked insulted and pouted. "Guns, Luka. Bullets. Don't be such a dumb-ass. I volunteered to fight for Croatia. The Chetniks want to put Vukovar on a spit. Hasn't your mom told you anything?"

Luka stared at him, shaking his head, doubtful.

"Well she ought to," Ratko said. "You have a right to know what's happening. Don't you smell it in the air? Doesn't the ash burn your nose? Wake up, man. Vukovar will not be the Vukovar you know when you see it next. That is, if there's anything left of it."

Luka rolled his eyes. Ratko was always exaggerating. The only time he had told the truth was when he described the size of his Russian girlfriend's boobs. He seemed to be proud of the fact that they were fake. After all, he paid for them, selling imitation Levi's to Romanian gypsies on the black market in southern Hungary. How he got the Levi's or from whom had always been a mystery, something he refused to talk about with either Zoran or Luka. He said he had connections. He could get things.

"They let you outside?"

"Who?"

"Your boss."

"Our *commander*."

"Yeah. Him. Let you buy cigarettes and stuff?"

"Every now and then. We have shifts." Ratko stared at the boy, reading his face. It was the look his brother Zoran gave him when he wanted an adult magazine or X-rated videos. "What do you smoke?" Ratko asked.

"Smoke?"

"There's no guarantee. And you'll pay through the roof. But I'll see what I can do. Marlboros are out of the question. You'll have to try the cheaper kind. From Asia. Thai cigarettes. I may have a deal for Camels. But it's the kind with Turkish tobacco. You cool with that?"

"What?"

"Muslim tobacco."

"Huh?" Luka's mouth hung open. He was dizzy with Ratko's ramblings.

"Don't get me wrong. It's not like I have anything against them. I mean they're not Chetniks, for God's sake. They're not trying to kill us and destroy our homeland."

Luka stared, drumming his bottom lip with his thumb. "I don't smoke."

"What? You want brandy? Beer?"

"I want my drum. I left it on the street."

"You want me to let you *outside*?"

Luka nodded. "Just this once."

Ratko scratched the patchy goatee growing around his mouth, considering. Luka stared at the guardsman's watch, reading the bluish glow on the digital display, trusting there still would be light.

⌒

At four o'clock, Luka followed Ratko through a small corridor connecting the bomb shelter to a dark stairwell that led to the street. They passed the guardsmen's office. The door was slightly ajar, and Luka glimpsed his mother leaning against a filing cabinet and talking not to a doctor, but to a man with a machine gun who was dressed in camouflage. Luka had never seen a guardsman wearing camouflage, and as much as he was uncertain about who the man was, he was grateful for the distraction. Probably another dumb suitor trying to win his mother's heart, he thought. The man didn't seem barbaric or vile. He was drinking tea, after all. His mother was pretending to oblige the man's inquiries, whatever they concerned. In any case, she'd be preoccupied.

"Oh, shit."

"What?"

Luka stumbled onto the heals of Ratko. The guardsman pushed Luka against the wall and covered his mouth.

"See his armband?"

Luka nodded, squirming to free himself from Ratko.

"He's a Chetnik." Ratko lifted his hand from Luka's mouth.

"A Chetnik?"

"Yes. A Serb soldier."

"What's he doing with my mom?"

"I can tell you what he's not doing," he said, staring at the Serb soldier. Ratko felt a chill up his spine. No Serbs had ever been invited into the shelter, and Ratko could tell by the way the man was fondling the gun slung over his shoulder that Elana had not opened the door to him nor was she tending to his injuries.

The Chetnik appeared to have no injuries at all but looked at Elana as if he intended to inflict many on her and the patients in the shelter.

"Maybe this isn't such a good idea."

"What?"

Ratko fixed his gaze on the Serb and checked his watch. He had not been informed of any impending attacks, but his stomach quivered.

"He's just flirting," Luka said. "Everybody flirts with my mom. She's a nurse. She takes care of people. He probably wants attention."

"He'll get attention. Trust me." Ratko shifted his gaze, locking eyes with Luka. "I can't let you out in the street."

"What? Why not?"

"Don't argue."

"After all the sandwiches and the *prikle*? You ate my birthday gift, and now you say no?"

It had not been a simple task for Luka to convince Ratko to help. The cantankerous, punk-rock, black-market bureaucrat was already in a foul mood, heartsick over his girlfriend and the prosthetic breasts he missed. It took three *kulen,* local salami sandwiches prepared in the shelter's kitchen, for Luka to convince the guardsman that his request was worthy even though the drum had been left on the street two months ago. The chances of finding it, Ratko reminded him between puffs on his Thai cigarette, were slim to none. Luka countered with a small bag of *prikle,* Croatian fried dough balls coated with sugar. It was a birthday gift from the women who had managed to cook the fried dough over an electric double burner donated by one of the guardsmen's wives, not from the Red Cross, which had promised to deliver it two months ago. Admiring Luka's sacrifice, Ratko gave in and gladly accepted the fried dough, consuming it at once.

"You'll have to wear a uniform," Ratko had said with his mouth stuffed.

"Why?"

"So nobody asks where you're going."

Luka pulled the pants up over his jeans, rolling them at the ankles to keep from tripping.

Ratko had already considered calling the whole thing off. If anybody caught them, it would be him and the National Guardsmen, not Luka who would take the heat. He risked humiliation by overseeing such a negligible mission. Where were the heroics in supervising the rescue of a drum? He'd be the laughingstock of the guardsmen. Ratko had wished the operation had been more perilous from the start, but Luka was too innocent to want or wish for anything other than the drum. Drugs, alcohol, and porn never crossed the boy's mind. What appeared to be trouble for nothing had suddenly shifted.

Ratko grabbed Luka's shoulders and turned him around to watch the Serb soldier. "See his machine gun?"

Luka nodded.

"He could kill all of us if he wanted."

"He won't," Luka said. "Because he'd have nobody left to give him the attention he wants. Look. Are you going to let me out of here or what?"

"How badly do you want that drum?"

"How badly do you want to see your girl's fake boobs?"

"Luka."

"That bad. I know."

"You win, Luka. You win."

Luka smiled, eyes gleaming in the darkened hallway.

"Promise me you won't talk to the Chetniks."

"I'll be so fast, you won't even know I was gone."

"You better take off the uniform," Ratko said, unzipping the coat from Luka.

"Why? I kind of like it."

"You're too young to be a guardsman."

"I'm not too young to help somebody."

"You're saving a drum, Luka. Not a life."

"What's the difference?"

Luka sneezed. It was dusty in the stairwell, and they smelled urine and formaldehyde, making them both wonder about the rumors they heard that the kitchen had been converted into a morgue.

"You're sniper candy with the uniform," Ratko said, and unzipped the thick oil coat, letting Luka step away. The boy shivered. It was cold in the stairwell; the wind slipped under the door. Ratko held a small flashlight up to Luka's face, his eyes ringed from lack of light.

He pulled out a pair of sunglasses and handed them to Luka. "Don't take them off."

"They're too big," Luka said.

"Too bad. You haven't seen the sun in six weeks. You'll go blind."

Luka pushed up the huge sunglasses that had slid down his nose. His heart pounded. "Think Mickey Hart ever lost a drum?"

"Only if Jerry Garcia sat on it."

Luka's brow tightened. "It's not very professional to lose a drum."

"You're not a pro, Luka."

Ratko sighed, weary of indulging the boy's fantasies. He reached for the door, sliding his fingers over the latch, hesitant to open it too soon.

"Don't go any farther than the school. I don't want you wandering all over the streets with the Chetniks. I'd never survive your mother. She carries needles."

"She won't know."

"She'll know. Mothers know everything now. Get out of here. I'll wait until you come back."

Ratko opened the door and nudged Luka outside, flicking his thumb beneath the boy's chin. "School and back," he said.

"School and back."

Luka lowered himself to the street. He clasped the sunglasses, pressing them tight against his small face, half excited, half terrified to see snipers. He opened his eyes slowly, blinking away the sting, trying to adjust to the light, the images of Vukovar slowly taking shape.

Vukovar had been leveled, street by street, house by house, battered until nothing but a skeleton remained. Cars lay overturned, hoods open, engines and batteries stolen. Artillery had decimated entire blocks, reducing the concrete sidewalks to broken belts, buckled and studded with bullets. The entire street looked like the surface of the moon, gaping holes, scarred and pockmarked by mortar. Luka's eyes jumped from hole to hole, trying to reconstruct the lines of the city, rebuilding it from his memory. He recalled the streets first, the order of shops. The Jovic café. The Violic bakery and the bicycle shop in the back. He recognized the newsstand, awning shredded by artillery fire, the green canvas flapping in the wind. Only a single mailbox remained outside the post office, the building scorched. The red-and-white-striped pole outside the old man's barbershop had survived, but its cash register lay open, robbed and rusted on the sidewalk. Ratko was right. Vukovar was not the Vukovar he remembered.

A siren wailed in the distance. The pop of a machine gun echoed off a building. Luka stiffened, adjusting the sunglasses. He turned, seeing a JNA tank parked outside the hospital. The armed reservists smoked cigarettes, smashing empty beer bottles on the steps. He looked over at the soldiers by the tank, feeling their eyes on him. He turned up the collar of his sweater. *"School and back."* He could hear Ratko's order, but he knew the drum could be anywhere.

Luka could not remember the exact details of the rush to the shelter or when exactly he had dropped the drum. The Yugoslav Army had set fire to the villages outside Vukovar and were ad-

vancing toward the city center. Electricity, food, and water supplies had been cut off, and telephone lines were disconnected.
Tank traps wrapped in barbed wire had been set at the main in-
tersections of all the roads, but the Yugoslav Army managed to
come anyway to claim the oil-rich land. They had already wiped
the town of Kijevo off the map in late August, taking twelve hours
to clean the ground there, but Luka did not understand how the
ground could be clean with corpses strewn upon it. They were
everywhere. Not just in Kijevo, but on his street, too, tossed into
trucks by local gravediggers. One of the gravediggers, a tall, thin
man, forbade Luka to look at the bodies the day he and his
mother fled their neighborhood. He had covered Luka's eyes
with a handkerchief, but the boy had already looked.

Luka remembered the dismembered body. How the dead eyes
stared at him, strangely apologetic, as if they had done something
wrong and were forbidden to close. He did not want to see another body like it, and he wanted suddenly to run back to the
shelter. One knock and Ratko would let him in. One knock and
he'd be safe. But safety, he knew, was not his greatest concern. He
could not bear another day of the shelter's silence. He had nothing to lose now. He was old enough to walk the streets alone. He
didn't need a guardsman. He didn't need a gun.

Luka turned, hearing the shattering of glass. The soldiers
tossed empty bottles into the street, checking their watches. Luka
was not sure what they were waiting for but decided it would not
be him. He began to walk away from the shelter, negotiating his
way among the crater holes and rubble. There was nothing left of
the cars in the Opel dealership behind the school playground.
Even the doors had been stolen. Spray-painted across a trunk:
LONG LIVE SERBIA, the black words leading a trail of similar plati-
tudes to the school where the playground had been tagged with
OVE JE SRBIJA, "This is Serbia."

Luka walked to the edge of the basketball court, covering his
mouth. The court was flooded, and a foul metallic stench bub-

bled up from the puddles. A tattered Croatian flag blew defiantly from a pole. There was nothing familiar about the scene. Dangling from the rusted rim was a large doll, stripped of a dress, and the school mascot, a Dalmatian puppy tied by its hind legs, throat slit and bleeding. He had named it Miki.

Luka's chest tightened. He held his breath, feeling a warm tingling sensation on the inside of his thighs, then a numbing cold. He looked down, unable to control himself, wishing he could piss on the words instead: *This is Serbia.* They lied. This was not Serbia. This was not Croatia. Things like this did not happen in his town. Bad things happened in the movies, to people who deserved it. But this was not the movies. It was real.

"Miki?"

He lifted his eyes, expecting the puppy to wag its tail, but there was nothing, no hint of movement, only the wind pinning back its ears. He picked out a stone that had been wedged between the dog's front paw, then tossed it as hard as he could, hitting an empty soda can that rolled and rattled across the macadam.

The sunglasses slid down Luka's face, dropping into a puddle with his tears. When he bent down to pick them up, he saw in the reflection the butt of a rifle, recognizing instantly the Chetnik armband. He heard the click of a trigger and felt the cold metal pressed against his skull.

"Don't you know school's out?"

Luka turned slowly, lifting his eyes cautiously to the Serb soldier whose long fingers, clean and clipped, fondled the gun sight. He had stringy, ashen hair and smelled of alcohol. Stitch marks crossed his cheeks like train tracks. He pulled back the hammer.

Luka felt a sharp pinch in the back of his head and threw his eyes into the macadam, trying to relieve them of the light. The soldier lifted the sunglasses from the puddle and held them out to the boy.

"These yours?"

Luka nodded, squeezing his eyes closed, pawing the air with his hand. He searched for the sunglasses but felt only the cold puddle water dripping off them. He could not speak and felt as if his voice had slid into his stomach.

"I'm not suppose to take them off."

"There's nothing to see, boy."

The Serb soldier dropped the sunglasses behind his right boot, then lifting it, stomped once, crushing the frames beneath his heel. He scooped up the bits of plastic and sprinkled them over the boy's shoulder.

"Souvenirs," he said, slurring his speech.

Luka cowered, pressing his back into the basketball pole, wishing he could curl up and roll into one of the craters in the street.

The soldier pulled out a flask from his front coat pocket and unscrewed the lid. "Want a sip?"

Luka smelled the alcohol. His stomach churned.

"A boy like you shouldn't be on the street."

"I lost something."

Luka's voice was nothing more than a whisper. He remained crouched, terrified of standing, hoping the reservist would not see his wet jeans. His skin prickly and cold beneath the fabric.

"You lost something?"

Luka nodded.

The soldier gurgled the liquor as if he were standing over a sink, hiccupping between words. "There's nothing—left—to lose. Every—thing's been—taken."

"Then maybe you've seen it."

"What?"

"My drum." Luka held his hands over his face, looking through the slits between his fingers.

The soldier seemed genuinely interested, as if the boy had mentioned something he had forgotten, a pint of milk, perhaps, eggs, a loaf of bread, a game he hadn't played in a while. The soldier took out a cigarette and studied the boy.

"What kind of drum?"

Luka held out his hands, imagining it. "It's made from a human skull."

The soldier emptied the flask, head tilted, mouth open, shaking the excess on his tongue. "I've seen a lot of skulls, boy. Trust me. None of them were drums."

"Mine's special."

"I bet it is. Somebody was dumb enough to let you—"

A spray of automatic fire interrupted him. The reservist dropped the flask and yanked the boy to his knees, tearing a hole through his jeans. A shower of grenades rained on the school, the pillars in the old Baroque arcade crumbling.

"*Hadje!* Go!"

Luka followed the reservist and lay on his stomach inching across the macadam, his sweater soggy with mud, soaking up puddles. The young Serb, too drunk to load the magazine, passed the gun back to Luka.

"You do it."

"I don't know how."

"You will help me!"

A tear rolled down Luka's cheek, and the reservist reached out and slapped it as if it were a fly.

"Take it."

The soldier shoved the gun under the boy's chin, flipping over his hands, palms up, to receive the bullets, but Luka missed and the bullets scattered on the ground. His vision was still blurry, clouded by gun smoke, still sensitive to the light. Another round of automatic fire arched over them, igniting the roof of the school. The soldier continued to curse, spitting out the words, his fingers too limp to load the bullets himself.

Luka remained motionless, frozen in terror, transfixed by the dead dog swinging from the basketball hoop. The tail had been shot off and lay like a mangled rope by Luka's foot. He reached back to touch it, not quite believing it was real, the fur wet and sticky, warm from the blast. His fingers recoiled from the spongy flesh when a round of automatic fire peeled back the asphalt by Luka's hand, embedding shrapnel into his wrists.

The Serb slumped to the ground. His back had been shot, and he could not move. Blood oozed from the hole in his coat.

He grabbed Luka's ankle, digging his thumbnails into the flesh to keep the boy from twisting away. "You can't leave me here," he moaned.

"I'll get help. My mother's a nurse."

"She won't help a Serb."

Luka stared into the soldier's eyes. "She married one."

The reservist let go of Luka's ankle and reached out to touch the boy's cheek, softly this time, with concern. The boy shrank from him, flinching from the man's touch.

"I'm so sorry," he said. "You're one of us."

The soldier withdrew his hands from the boy's face and remained prostrate on the playground, separated by the stream of blood between them. There was no sign he would rise. MiG jets swooped over the block, crushing his words.

"Please. Help me."

Luka reached out and took the bullets scattered on the playground. He popped them into his mouth, tonguing the metal, then turned the pointed ends toward his teeth and swallowed them all.

꒜

Luka could not remember what happened next. His memory refused to give a shape or chronology to the events for the longest time. Somehow he had managed to drag the Serbian soldier's body for three kilometers, stumbling in his white blindness through the rubble and broken roof tiles only to realize the man was already dead when they reached the hospital. The soldier's face was blue.

It was dark when they arrived, the air glowing orange, thumping with artillery fire. A battery of JNA tanks blocked the street.

Luka remembered the hysteria, the swarms of sick and wounded fleeing from the hospital, how the Serb soldiers opened fire and shot a doctor in the head. He watched other Serb soldiers direct and divide the refugees from the bomb shelter. Men on one side, women and children on the other. He saw his mother and called out to her, but she could not hear him through the gunfire. She boarded a school bus and disappeared through a column of smoke. Luka stood there, unable to move for what seemed like hours, the only world he knew deserting him.

A Yugoslav Army tank stopped in front of him. He did not hear them coming. He didn't even hear the gunfire meant to shove him aside. One of the officers climbed out of the tank and shook Luka, screaming. But the boy heard nothing, watching the soldier's lips move, wondering what kind of candy he held under his tongue.

The officer screamed again. "I said are you a Croat or a Serb?"

Without thinking, Luka blurted the word. "Serb," he said.

"Then you can stay. This is your city now."

The Serb officer took a cigarette from his vest pocket and stuck it between Luka's lips. He climbed back into the tank and drove away, firing into the air the one bullet that had been intended for the boy had he been a Croat. He shot instead an empty bottle of plum brandy left on the street. After that, Luka remembered nothing but a silence more unbearable than any he had known in the shelter, a silence haunted by the old woman's words. *"Never let them tell you who you are."*

3

～

In his silence, Luka swore to remember nothing and no one, except his mother, which is why when the composer caught him breaking into his studio and demanded his name, the boy pointed to BECHSTEIN on the grand piano.

"Very well," Milan said, trying to compose himself. He had met the boy once before in Dubrovnik but did not expect to meet him again. Not tonight.

"Play. You know a bit about music."

Luka backed himself against the wall and into the shadow of a palm tree that arched over him from the street. He crunched bits of glass from the window, shifting nervously, taking in the room. It was large and spare, nothing but a grand piano and a single bed with rails, like a child's, and columns and columns of notebooks stacked higher than Luka's head. Empty prescription bottles lay haphazardly across the pillow where a white envelope slid out of the case. Dividing the room was a huge piece of fishing net bejeweled with sea glass that dangled from the ceiling and cast shadows on the walls when lightning flashed.

Centered above the bed was the only picture in the room, the framed portrait of a young woman with a child waving from what appeared to be a dark island festooned by cypress and pines. There was an eerie asceticism about the place, a loneliness and silence that begged to be broken, like a curse that had been forgotten but remained.

Luka dragged his eyes across the floor, lifting them slowly to the tall young man in the corner with the suitcase. The seams bulged, and where the zipper had broken, cracked leather straps had been pulled tightly over the panels securing the contents of whatever was inside. From the way the composer set the suitcase on the floor, holding the small of his back with his hand, Luka assumed he had packed the weight of the world.

"I'd like to hear Chopin before I leave," he said, watching for the signal, the beam of a flashlight across the studio. Nothing but lightning. Perhaps the boat was not leaving in the storm. He had not seen any movement in the harbor from his window, the waters of Fort Saint John empty and black, bearded with white caps from the *bura,* the hard wind that blew from the north, scouring the Dalmatian coast in winter. It would not be easy to get a boat out of the harbor, let alone move it across the sea to Italy in this weather. Milan had been uneasy about the arrangements, funneling money, a life savings, into the pockets of a stranger who had guaranteed the passage to Bari where he would take a train north to Austria, east to Hungary. Everything had been so hurried that he had no time to consider the legitimacy of the transaction. It could have been a hoax. He was not even sure that the camp in Hungary would accept him, a Serb, among the mostly Croatian refugees. In either case, the boy was certainly not the boatman. The boatman would have used the door.

Luka dropped the jackknife in his hand. Rain poured through the roof cankered with mortal holes and he could see storm clouds moving in on the moon. Water filled the cuffs of his pant legs and soaked his shoes, but he did not step out of the rain. He picked at the scab on his chin, cursing the turn of events. Shitty luck, he thought.

Chopin. He knew nothing of Chopin. Mickey Hart, sure. Gene Krupa. Buddy Rich, *Traps the Drum Wonder,* his hero. The pioneer of percussive possibilities. Luka knew nothing of classical music and could not for the life of him even pretend to play the piano. Not now. He could not play much of anything the way his hands were shaking.

Luka did not expect to find the composer here. He had assumed the old building was abandoned. The shutters had not been opened in the four weeks that he had been on the streets of Dubrovnik. His eyes had adjusted over the month, and he could see better than he could when he left Vukovar. He paid closer attention to the details in the dark now, and he figured whoever had been living in the building had fled before Christmas. Graffiti was the dead giveaway. CHETNIK had been spray-painted in red across the walls, the stones chipped from shrapnel. Broken eggshells and beer bottles littered the steps. It was a Serb house, and few Serbs, Luka knew, lived in Dubrovnik. Some had stayed and defended the city but many had left, not to join the Yugoslav Army or even to support it, but to escape it and save their lives. Dubrovnik was a target. And targets were targets. Bullets knew no difference between Croats or Serbs—or children, for that matter—which is why Luka moved at night, darkness his greatest protection.

He had found places to hide. It's not like Dubrovnik had been decimated like Vukovar. Hardly. The place had been hit hard and heavily damaged, but it had survived the seige. A good number of locals still lived there, and refugees from neighboring villages were living inside hotels. Luka wondered why anyone would live inside the hotels when they could have slept inside the old medieval towers with views of the sea. He figured everyone could have a room with a view if they could manage to live above the stone walls of the city. The forts had always been his first choice, but it was too cold to stay inside them. There were better bastions where he could live, and he cased the old town for weeks, discovering homes and apartments that had been left tidy, cabinets filled with canned goods, mostly corn and beans on which he had survived for months. He cleaned up after himself, wiped down

counters, and left IOU notes, promises to replace what he had
taken once his mom came, offering her services as a nurse or a
cook, recommending her cold cherry soup. But there were no
beans to eat here inside the composer's studio. No soup to make.
It didn't look like the composer could offer anything to eat or had
eaten much of anything himself. He was a waifish young man who
chewed thoughts, as he did now, pacing the room, consuming the
ideas that leapt across his mind.

In the darkness, Luka could see only half the man's face, split
by shadows and angles, long, hard lines drawn not by genetics but
by circumstance. He wore a white raincoat, collar turned up
against the cold. A cigarette burned between his lips. He managed to blow smoke from the side of his mouth without taking the
cigarette out, studying the boy, curious, not so much because the
boy had intruded, but because in the decade that he had lived and
worked in the studio, not a single person other than his mentor,
Anton, had ever dared to visit him there. Standing there now, at
the opposite wall in the shadows of a storm, was a child who had
violated the privacy and safety of his solitude.

The composer was not used to company. Visitors scared him,
although he had instincts for hospitality. He kept a set of cups and
saucers handy and clean in the studio. He knew how to brew
Turkish coffee, make tea, offer a biscuit. Fillet a fish if he ever got
close enough to the water to catch one. He knew, too, from growing up in a hotel, how to fold sheets, place a candy on a pillow,
fold the end of the toilet roll into a triangle. His mother had
taught him how to lavish visitors with Dalmatian charm, and he
could easily imitate her hospitality. His unease was not from lack-
ing the sophistication that came through experience and expo-
sure. He had been social, insisting once as a child on giving a
private piano recital for Tito, mistaking the ailing white-haired
politician for Saint Nicholas. But despite Milan's effort to use
music as a bridge between himself and the world, the composer
had never succeeded at putting people at ease. His chronic

seizures frightened people, and he did his best to avoid them when he wasn't teaching. He conducted business at night, when the streets were less congested, and even then stuck to alleys where there were no people to hurt. He did not trust himself. And he never invited anyone into his studio.

The last thing Milan wanted was to be blamed for the fate of Luka. He had not invited the boy here. He wanted nothing to do with him. Milan removed the cigarette from his mouth and cleared his throat.

"I won't help you. I don't owe you anything."

Lightning illuminated Luka's face. His hair wild, plastered to his head. He smelled wet and rotted, of fallow earth and trampled places, the smell of disgrace itself. His eyes were red and sunken, skin tight around the cheek and browbones. There was a certain vacuousness in his gaze and with it an irony, as if the boy had been filled with too many things, the wrong things.

Milan kept his distance. He wondered where the child in a boy his age could go, had gone, if there were places in the world where the lost souls of children could gather and find what they had lost, a place for which he himself had wished long ago. He knew the boy harbored unspoken strengths. Taboos, too.

༄

It had been an accident. Luka kept telling himself it was not his fault. He had never heard of the superstition. Lokrum was the beautiful wooded island of olive groves and Lebanese cedars shaved by the wind. The water was more blue than he had ever seen in his life and cleaner than most in the world. A chorus of cicadas sang from the trees and serenaded all who came to visit. The island was a paradise, a fifteen-minute boat-ride retreat from the urban bustle of Dubrovnik. Children swam and played all day unsupervised while their mothers gathered and fed wild peacocks that roamed the rocks. Lovers bathed nude on the western side, and newlyweds exchanged vows under the shade of the east. Ice cream stands and a restaurant offered lunch on special occasions, and tour groups hiked through the woods to the old monastery built by Richard the Lionheart, who, after surviving a shipwreck off its coast, vowed to erect a monument of gratitude to God for saving him and his crew. Lokrum was an unlikely place of concern. Apparently, nobody slept there, but those who did died the very next day.

Luka had missed the boat. Quite literally. Under normal circumstances during the spring and summer, boats from Dubrovnik left for the island on the hour, every hour, leaving it at seven o'clock each night. No tour boats had gone there since the air assaults. The Yugoslav Army had used the island as a test target. Only Dalmatian fishermen and locals with private boats dared to cross the waters to the island now. Their journeys were brief and prompt, always in the thick black waters of night. Luka would have never chosen the island knowing what he knew now. But that's the way of his luck, he thought. He had made choices, and in his choosing, he seemed to lose.

In choosing a place to hide for the night, Luka had boarded one of the boats in the harbor, a big red whale of a rig named *Elana*. A common name. A good name. If he could not be with his mother, he could hide on a boat named after her and fake his way to feeling safe. Luka was adept at convincing himself of the things he believed could be true. He had no idea that by the next morning, this morning, he would become part of the calamari crew driven by the cravings of diplomats who had come to assess war damage. Zarko, the captain, had caught Luka hiding behind a wall of life vests stuffed into a small closet in the galley.

"What are you doing?" he screamed at the boy.

"Waiting for Elana."

"Elana didn't invite you."

"She doesn't know I'm here."

"She does now."

The mercurial one-eyed fisherman yanked Luka out by the straps of his backpack and hurled a tangle of fishing net at him, the boat rocking in the wind. He shoved a hurricane lamp and matches into the boy's hand, casting him and the net aside on the island, demanding the boy repair it while he went about his fishing business. But the net was beyond repair, and Luka, who knew nothing of tying or untangling knots, took to exploring the dark island instead, charmed by its hidden pathways and botanical garden and the shadows cast by the hurricane lamp. He had peed behind a cluster of giant aloe plants whose spiky, waxy leaves seemed to roll like tongues that had been carved with the names of lovers. The plants spooked him. But it was the diary he spotted wedged into the base of the aloe plant that alarmed him most.

Luka spent the night sitting on the ground reading, learning the names of all the myrtle and eucalyptus trees planted there, their care and value and the names and questions of the more interesting tourists who had visited in 1983 when the diary was written. Through the pages, he followed the routine of a woman named Mirada, the caretaker of the botanical garden, who had apparently lived on the island with her husband and was exempt from its curse. How and why were not disclosed. There was a mysteriousness about her entries. The handwriting changed significantly from the beginning to the end, and marking the middle was a piece of composition paper crowded with musical notations that had been folded into a cross. No longer were the words the scatterings of a botanist. The handwriting was smaller, tighter, as if the thoughts somehow carried a bigger burden and needed more space. A story about two boys, brothers. Half brothers. There were ghosts between the lines, and it was this invisible part of the story, the silent story, that Luka wanted to know most. Why the brothers were fighting and why the caretaker did nothing when one of them drowned.

By the time Luka finished reading the diary, it was morning, dawn bleeding into the sky. The fishing boat had long since returned to the harbor. The boy assumed that Zarko and his crew were probably eating fried calamari with the diplomats and had forgotten about him. He wanted also to believe that Zarko was joking about the island's curse, telling him a fib the way the man in the red cardigan from the bomb shelter had told him about the location of his drum to keep his spirits up, to keep the boy smiling when the old man himself had forgotten how. Zarko did not seem like the kind of person who had the imagination to conceive of such a superstition; however, he seemed to possess the bitterness of a person who dug holes in his memories and filled them up with lies.

Either way, Zarko could not be trusted, and it was up to Luka to decipher the truth. Until now, Luka had eaten bullets, withstood showers of grenades, survived snipers and storms. He thought it was God's cruel joke to survive all that and die from sleeping on an island. Besides, he had not slept there. He could not sleep wondering when Zarko would return, if at all.

Zarko had not forgotten about the boy. He left him there to teach him a lesson about trespassing, as if he were an expert on it himself, leaving the boy no other choice but to stay overnight on the island with its grievances and ghosts. Luka had wandered to the rocks on the west side, staring into the black waters, thinking not about the boy who had drowned, but about Milan, the boy who had gotten away. Luka wondered how long Milan had lived, if he had lived at all, and if he had, the severity of the curse on his life for having spent a night there.

Standing there on the edge of Lokrum with the hurricane lamp burning in his hand, Luka had experienced the same feeling he had the day he left the bomb shelter. His best intentions had betrayed him again. And he would suffer the consequences. Death was a possibility. Who was he to believe a boy was exempt from anything? He was entitled to the terror and trauma of the world as much as its beauty. It was more of an accident to live than to die, he thought. And this was the dilemma of his surviving.

Luka did not run. Not yet. He had nowhere else to go. He could either stay on the island and die or climb into Zarko's boat and die in the city. He did not trust the men on the boat. They did not look like fishermen. They wore black oil coats, and he could see the whites of their cleric collars sucked against their necks. They swung lanterns of incense around him, quietly studying the boy in the dark. They wrapped him in a wool blanket and gave him warm soup from a thermos and hunks of white bread crusted with poppy seeds. When he finished, they pressed Swiss chocolate into his hands and asked him where he was going. They handled their question as if it could shatter, scaring him, and he pulled the blanket tight around his shoulders.

"I'm going home," he said, playing with the foil from the chocolate. He rolled it between his fingers.

"Where do you live?"

"Around. In the city."

Luka looked up, trying hard to keep the lie from exposing itself through his tears.

"Old town?"

"I have a place," Luka said. "With a piano."

They nodded, discrediting his story the way they tossed their glances at one another.

Zarko started up the motor, threw the boat into gear. "Enough," he snapped at them. "I promised you could see him. Not keep him. That's all."

They crossed in fifteen minutes the black waters of the sea to Saint John's harbor, the priests murmuring prayers, blessing the boy with safekeeping and salvation. There were twelve of them. He avoided their faces, counting their shoes instead. Apostles of war, he thought. They said nothing, just sang and prayed and hummed, touching the top of his head with their hands as if they had the power to heal the wounds they could not see.

When they arrived in the harbor, Zarko directed the priests to disembark and turn their backs while the boy went his separate

way. He demanded payment from the boy for his deliverance
from Lokrum and pointed to the diary that had fallen out of his
backpack during the crossing, pages open, soaked and stained
with salt water on the floorboards between Zarko's feet. Luka
shrugged. He kept his eye on the priests, backing out of the boat,
wondering if all of this was a setup for his capture. It wouldn't
really matter. It was his last night in Dubrovnik anyway. Luka answered without moving his eyes from the priests. The diary meant
nothing to him. He had found it. That's all.

"Take it," he said. "But there aren't pictures."

"I don't need pictures."

"You can read?"

One of the priests laughed. Another hushed him.

"Of course I can read. I read the Bible."

"I figured boob magazines."

Another priest gasped. "I don't need boobs!"

"Sure you do. Everybody needs boobs. Ratko says so."

"Who's Ratko?"

Luka stood on the stone jetty, stepping away from Zarko as he
stepped out of the boat.

"Somebody I used to know."

Luka felt his jaw stiffen. He threw his gaze at the fisherman's
boots. Zarko curled his lip, trying to smile, exposing a single
tooth that protruded, cockeyed, from his top gum. He patted the
boy on the shoulder, turning, waiting impatiently for the priests
to leave. They moved slowly across the stones in the square, dis-
appearing into the hallowed recesses of their monastery. Zarko
listened to the click of their heels grow distant. Luka listened to
his heart pound.

"You let them go," he said.

Zarko shook his head.

"I let *you* go."

"Why?"

"You remind me of Damir."

"Who's Damir?"

"Somebody I used to know."

Zarko tucked the diary inside the breast pocket of his coat and then pulled out two cigarettes, sticking one in the boy's mouth. He stared at him in the darkness. The boy appeared to be the same age as his son, forever nine when he died. Zarko had not had the fortune of rescuing Damir from Lokrum. He had received him, instead, inside a body bag. Ten years ago but still a looped memory. His son was the first thing he remembered every morning and the last thing he forgot before went to bed. He liked fishing at night because it kept him awake and safe from the sleep that tortured him with nightmares.

What Zarko wanted to catch from the sea were not the squid and calamari that filled his nets, but glimpses of the truth behind his son's drowning. He had waited ten years for a shred of evidence to convict Milan of the murder, finding nothing, until now. Everything he had ever needed to know had been penned inside the diary.

Zarko did not pray anymore, but he lifted his eyes to the night sky and made the sign of the cross now. He was thankful the boy had trespassed on his boat, feeling less guilty about leaving him on the island and even better about his decision not to turn him into the authorities. Zarko would not have benefited. He had no money to place a bet. He could not hear that well. The drumming had never bothered him.

He struck a match and lit the cigarette in his mouth, offering the flame to the boy, but Luka spit the cigarette out over the edge of the boat. It floated on the water with a pigeon feather.

"Why'd you do that!"

"I don't smoke. My mother will kill me."

"Who cares?" Zarko said, reaching over the boat, fishing for the cigarette. "You're going to die anyway. This war will kill every one of us."

He didn't mean today, but the boy thought he did.

Luka opened his eyes, feeling the composer's stare. He wanted
to die and be done with it, stand up to the curse like a man. This
is what he had come to do, alone. He had not intended for an audience and was unprepared to wait. He was not good at waiting
for much of anything, a haircut or his drum or his mother.
Seventy-three days since he had seen her last. He had made a
slash mark on his wrist for every day he had survived without her.
He thought about the bus in Vukovar, wondering where it had
taken her, why she had not yet come to find him.

Luka did not want to be angry with his mother, but he thought
about all the ways she could have found him here before now.
Why hadn't she heard the drumming? There was no mistaking it
was him. He played for her the rhythms he had played at his father's funeral, marching behind the casket on the way to the
cemetery. The rhythms had been their code, the secret language
of their hearts in conversation. For months after the funeral, Luka
had been silent, drumming his responses to the questions his
mother asked. Two taps for yes. One for no. Two for Dubrovnik.
Always two. His mother's dream. His mother's choice of refuge.
She had sung the word *Dubrovnik* into his ear as if by going there,
they would find themselves again. The Dubrovnik of his childhood dreams. The Dubrovnik where he first heard a live orches-
tra, where music began to matter most. Where sounds had
meaning and the power to heal. Where, for the first time, he
heard joy in his mother's laughter, as if the salt in the sea had
rubbed out the sarcasm that had made everything she had said
before sound coarse. It was here, too, where Luka spotted his first
octopus, dived for oysters, found pearls. His mother had told him
Dubrovnik was the crown of the Adriatic, a jewel dangling from
a necklace that the world had forgotten to wear. It was the world's
shame, she said, to abandon such beauty.

The composer motioned to him. "You'll catch your death.
Come sit."

Luka remained standing. He tilted his head toward the hole in the roof and opened his mouth to catch the hail on his tongue, oblivious of the composer. He grinned, amused by the game they had started, by the composer's quibbling. But the composer, more impatient than amused, had grown tired of the boy's refusal to respond. He had been kind. Anybody else would have marched the boy to the cops, but Milan wanted to give the boy a reason to stay.

⌒

For the longest time Milan did not believe the boy existed. Nobody did. Sure, they had heard him. He kept them awake, drove them to madness with the thumping and pumping of his drum. But nobody had really seen him. The back of his head occasionally. Wet footprints. His was the grace of transparency. Of shadows. He moved, like fate, through their lives undetected, unnoticed, the unsubstantiated phantom of their minds, which is why, when the composer met him for the first time, he believed the boy was a ghost.

It was late. The composer had left the radio station early, taking a shortcut home. It was not his routine to walk through the park beneath Pile Gate, the old moat that had been filled in and planted with an orchard where fallen tangerines covered the ground, infusing the air with citrus.

Milan crossed to the wall facing the water and sat on a bench to rest his back. He was exhausted from playing the piano, prodded by Anton to perform for Dubrovnik what he had only recently begun to play for himself, the hundreds of notebooks he had filled with the sound of blue. Color had ordered the composer's hand. Without color, he heard nothing. He filled notebooks with the sound of yellow and red. Purple. Green. Pink. The colors of the Adriatic coast. Like Liszt and Stravinsky, Kandinsky and Rimbaud, Milan shared the multisensory perceptions of synesthetes and, unfortunately, the seizures that about 4 percent of them endured. A synesthete experienced a union of sensations, associating shape with taste, smell with sound, sound

with color, and so forth. Milan's epilepsy resulted from these multisensory experiences caused by a temporal lesion in the brain.
The hallucinations, when triggered, repeated themselves involun-
tarily and could drive him to the brink of madness with their
vividness.

Anton had asked him over the radio to describe the sound of
blue. Milan said it was beyond words, for words failed him, and
he dismissed them as a waste of time. Music, he believed,
achieved everything that language could not. He had studied
music with a feverish intimacy he had never learned to replicate
in his personal life, as if the music knew him better than he knew
himself. Music was both his refuge and sanctuary. He had nothing else. He felt secure in the music and sheltered from the torment of seizures within the shades and shadows of blue. In his
wallet he carried not the photos of friends and lovers, but the
photocopied and reduced busts of Beethoven and Liszt, hungry
for their inspiration. He kept no lovers and, like pets or hobbies
prone to sucking time, believed they interfered with the music.
Milan's perfect composition consumed him, and he obliged its
gnawing, the beast he had never captured but spent his life trying
to tame.

"Blue is the opening and closing door to all that matters and
gives my life meaning," he said earlier in a live broadcast. Only in
the safety of the radio station, behind the glass walls of Anton's
recording studio, could he expose himself to Dubrovnik. Anton
asked him questions for which he had known too well the answers for years.

"Which composer do you identify with most?"

"Schubert."

"Schubert, really?"

"They say his pen was half ink. Half tears."

"Is sadness your inspiration?"

"Shadows. The part of us that scares us most."

Milan fixed his eyes on Anton. The bulb above them flickered.

Then the room went dark. They had lost power again. When the electricity was not restored, Anton dismissed Milan for the night. He had seemed nervous, not about the power loss—they were used to the blackouts by now—but by the composer's words. Lately, there had been a tension building between them. He rarely visited Anton's house anymore. And when he did, he kept his thoughts to himself, sat alone on the patio facing the dark island of Lokrum, lost in the holes of his memory. He insisted on sleeping on the couch instead of the bed in his room, too spooked by the ghosts of his childhood that lived there.

Shadows on the wall by the drawbridge caught his attention. Milan stood from the bench, alarmed by the clanging of bottles and the smashing of glass on stone. A group of young men his age moved out from the shadows of the orange trees and stood facing him. They hurled a small transistor radio at his feet. The battery case open, empty.

There were five of them. All drunk. Milan dug his nails into the back of the bench as they approached. *"Chetnik,"* they hissed. *"Chetnik."* He did not recognize their accent. It was northern, eastern. Perhaps Croatians from Bosnia-Herzegovina but they were not from Dubrovnik. Nobody from Dubrovnik called him Chetnik. That his name was Serbian was not an issue before the war. It was never a threat to him until now, until the radio show had made it public. Fuck, he thought. The irony of publicity.

They circled him, feeling through the pockets of his raincoat, taking out a pack of cigarettes.

"You mind?"

Milan said nothing, lowered his gaze. He stiffened, feeling their hands slip inside the flap of his coat, searching his breast pocket for the vial of barbiturates he carried. They pulled it out, popped the lid.

"Candy, boys?"

"Don't," Milan said. "They're too hard to find here."

"Medicine is hard to find anywhere."

They distributed the drugs among themselves, crunching them as if they were sugarcubes, unaware that the composer depended on the medication more than he did the music.

"A Chetnik doesn't deserve medicine. You didn't fight for Dubrovnik."

"I tried," he said. "I wanted to. But I can't fight."

"Can't you see who the enemy is?"

They pulled the glasses from his face and flung them on the ground, crushing the lenses beneath their shoes.

"The police won't give me a gun."

"Why? 'Cause you'll have a seizure?"

They laughed, amused, tossing the empty prescription bottle at Milan's shoes. They lit the cigarettes, staring at their frail contemporary with contempt, deciding who would take a turn with him first to prove to themselves that they were still men. They pissed on him the *slivovitz* that they blamed for their behavior, then left his body bloody and broken on the ground when they had finished.

The sound of a drum woke him.

The rhythm was unexpected. Milan blinked open an eye. The other was swollen shut, his head pressed with fluids. His kidneys ached where the men had kicked him. His tongue was swollen, too, and his mouth ached, fingers pulsing with the rhythms. He had no idea how long he had been there or if he had had a seizure, but he tasted no metal in his mouth. He breathed deeply, filling his lungs with the cool sea air, then exhaled, groping in the darkness for the remains of his glasses, nothing but bent wire frames. He lay on the ground, unable to see beyond the fog, listening to the drummer draw closer.

He felt as if someone were watching, luring him to the edge of something he could not see in the dark, a threshold to everything that awaited on the other side of the sound. An owl swooped down to the orange trees and flapped its wings as if to applaud the drumming. It was a seductive pulse. At first slow, duping the composer with its subtle complexity. And then, without warning, it exploded. No longer the dull repetition, the call and answer that had awakened Milan, but something far more extended with multiple meters graduating from three beats in one voice to two beats in another, then seven and four, fifteen and two. A second hand played a succession of even beats. *Ra-ta. Ra-ta. Ra-ta. Ra-ta-ta.* The drumming seized him with the severity of a migraine, his head in the vise of the rhythm. Each beat carved lines—barbed, charged wires of sound in his mind. He screamed for the drumming to stop, pleading mercy with the drummer, but he played defiantly louder, harder until the composer sat up.

Then the drumming stopped.

Milan hugged his knees to his chest, groaning, head still thumping with the primitive rhythms. His face was wet, streaked from tears and the silver shavings of fog that reflected in his eyes. He flung a tuft of hair from his fingers and rubbed the bald spot on his head.

"What do you want from me?"

The fog had lifted slightly, revealing a small boy who stood crouched with the drum in his lap. His wrists were bound with bandages that looked blue in the light. The boy leaned forward slowly, searching the darkness for the composer's eyes. They were bloodshot and glassy. He was dressed too well to be a soldier. And he was definitely not a priest. A washed-up singer, perhaps, with his bright teeth and shaggy beard. His front tooth was broken, his top lip fat and bleeding. He was alive.

"Leave me alone, boy!"

Milan reached for the boy's drum, wrestling it from his hands, wrenching it free. He held it up to the moonlight seeing that the boy's drum was no ordinary drum. It was a *damaru*. A human skull. It had the power to wake the dead. Milan dropped it immediately, and the boy, as if expecting this, held out his hands to catch it. He dug his fingernails into the seams in the bone, pressing the skull drum against his chest.

"It's not your fault," he said.

Milan stiffened. He whispered.

"What?"

"It's not your fault."

The boy raised his chin, turned his face toward the composer, offering it as if it were not his own. His eyes drifted as if he were not looking through them, but down from some place hovering over the park. It was as if in that moment, someone else spoke for him, through the drum. Milan reached out with his hand and gently touched the boy's head. He pushed himself off the ground but said nothing, not even good-bye, then quickly climbed the stairs to Pile Gate and crossed the bridge into the old town, his head throbbing. He wished it had been a hallucination, not the boy, that produced the drumming. For once in his life, the composer had wished for a seizure.

⌒

Luka's drumming possessed Milan. He had followed the boy for months, at night, hunting him not the way the priests and nuns had done, but with peregrine persistence, circling, swooping close when the boy least expected, hoping to seize his drum. No matter where he went, Milan felt the boy's presence, the dull thumping inside his head that refused to subside. They competed for silence. What obsessed one infuriated the other. What the boy wanted to forget, the composer needed to remember. It was as if encoded within the rhythms was the boy's only language. He spoke through the drum the things they had no words to say. Silence only amplified the dialectic between them.

But the drum was noise. And noise had no place in Milan's musical vocabulary. It's not that Anton had never taught him to play a drum. The music teacher insisted he learn to respect it, and he had, in the way he respected lightning. Both could strike and destroy. Drumming was a definitive action. It could stop time. Transfer it. Transcend it. The drum was the only instrument in which the player had no time to think about the mundane.

Thoughts did not drift. In fact, at times there were no thoughts at all, a clearing of the mind. Drumming was a way to forget, but the composer did not want to forget. He needed music to remember his past and defend him against everything that had gone wrong.

Some people believed it was the drumming, not the shelling itself, that shook loose the stones in the city walls and threatened their protection. They dreamed the boy had killed them. And then they dreamed of killing the boy, but these dreams, silly dreams, ended in the morning, and by noon they daydreamed of saving him instead.

But the composer wanted nothing to do with the salvation of the boy. In his dreams, Milan wrestled not the drum, but the rhythms from the boy's fingers until there were none. He believed the boy was more fugitive than refugee. The drum, his accomplice, had stolen his peace, his silence, the amniotic fluid of all sound, as if it was his right to possess it. Silence activated the composer's creative energy and his best ideas emerged when he was on the edge of sleep, making it a habit of teetering there, half-awake, treading lightly on the fragments of sound as if they were shards of glass. Sound, he believed, was a fragile thing. There was a husbandry about its conception and care. It had to be guarded and nurtured, coaxed and coddled, the cowering child of his mind. But the boy had trampled upon it, crushing it with the angst-ridden energy of a thief who ends up destroying the very thing he set out to steal. In this case, the music Milan had strived so hard to create despite the war. He was not the stereotypical composer, furiously penning a symphony as if it had been blown in from the sea. He recorded the voices *of* the sea. And until recently, he was not the composer who paced back and forth in his studio, cursing the blank page that held in contempt the notes he had in his head.

Without silence, ideas would float and collide, puncturing Milan's mind. He needed the dullness for his body to sink into the barely discernible posture that allowed the sounds to assemble and make sense. After the shelling had stopped, after the last building collapsed, the last fire had been extinguished, silence was all the composer had to reclaim the voices that sang in his head.

He had nothing to record now. He no longer heard the voices against the boy's untamed polyrhythms. Not that he refused to record them. Milan failed to keep up with the boy's pace. Extended meter had always troubled him, and he refused to write anything that implied its possibility. He panicked with five-four meter. It was too, too wild. It made his brain work overtime and demanded too much attention; however, he had caught himself tapping out the rhythms of the boy's drum when he *wasn't* writing, a problem with grave consequences.

The drumming, more than gunfire, induced Milan's seizures, doubling the frequency and duration since the boy had arrived in Dubrovnik. Milan had lost his bottom tooth, broken a jaw, and bruised six ribs from the convulsions, suffering more damage in two months than two years. He had increased his barbiturate intake while attempting to drown out the drumming. He played records so loud, he had blown the speakers then resorted to the use of a Walkman only to wear it out and the tapes it played. What Milan needed were not more tapes, another Walkman, or speakers. Milan needed to alleviate the burden of what Anton identified years ago as *horlust,* his hearing passion. The composer needed silence. But the boy never stopped.

Nobody knew how long the drumming would continue. The locals made bets on when it would stop, how long it would last, trading cigarettes and batteries, bullets and beer for boredom. The boy had given them something to do. Entire stables of underground bookies had emerged throughout Dubrovnik since the drumming had started. Milan was certain that one of the monasteries had initiated the bet, having placed one in the cloister garden himself, pressing into the hands of a hooded priest twenty deutsche marks, the only currency of value. Apparently, inspired war correspondents, bent on the perverse and not apologetic for it, had twisted the story into an account of a boy-run refugee casino that doled out spare blood and body parts. Nothing could have been further from the truth.

Milan knew the boy better than anyone else. He had taken the time to hunt him, not because he thought he could save him, but because he wanted to reclaim the silence and save *himself*. He wondered if the boy had it in him to continue much longer. On the one hand, he was curious about the boy's talents, on the other, they made him jealous. He envied Luka's endurance and concentration, especially now, in the aftermath of war. The boy seemed to possess the calm yet feral contemplation of a medicine man, pouncing on the rhythms, beating the drum as if he himself understood the magic of the instrument. Nothing could distract the boy. Nothing could tempt his focus, not even the shelling. It was as if Luka understood that the drum could generate a terror more powerful than the noise of war itself.

The boy held a privileged position. He was wanted and admired, secret and ingenious, mysterious and mythic. The stuff of legends. The people of Dubrovnik prayed for him. Nobody knew whose child he was, but wished in some way he was their own. Even the bookies. They believed he had protected them, occupying their battlefield with his drum. That the boy had parlayed with the enemy, as war drummers do, dispersing messages and making connections, was a contested rumor. But they were certain of this much. The boy's drumming, in the strangest way, had reestablished the order of their lives. Drumming preserved their sense of time, returning the past to the present. The boy had made their lives mean something after everything that had meant anything had been destroyed.

⌒

Luka stood by the composer's window, staring up at the clouds moving in on the moon. His clothes were soaked, and he felt the cold deep inside his bones. The rain turned to hail and bounced off the top of the piano, scattering like glass beads at the base. The composer crossed the room, dragging the overstuffed suitcase through the puddles that had collected on the floor. He set the suitcase against the piano and stood behind the bench, brushing off the keyboard with the back of his hand, waiting for the boy to begin.

"Hurry up. There's not much time," Milan said, and clapped, startling the boy.

Luka knocked the bookcase by the window, accidentally sending the stack of notebooks onto the floor. He stared incredulous at the heap of papers and rusted metal spirals. The notebooks lay opened, pages smudged with musical notes gathered like a clump of bees swarming the paper. Luka had never seen so much music, not even at school or in books. The notebooks, filled in every margin, had been stuffed with scraps of paper, receipts, napkins, matchbooks, used envelopes that held more notes. Luka crouched, fingering the pages, wondering if Mickey Hart had ever written as much music as this strange, skinny man. He squeezed his eyes shut, hoping that when he opened them, the composer and the piano would disappear. He was not about to play the piano. He had come to die and expected to collapse and expire on the floor any moment now. He stepped into the rain pouring through the roof, hoping to induce a cold of sorts, or the flu. Bronchitis. Encephalitis. Meningitis. Any *itis* would do, although he had never heard his mother mention anyone dying from an *itis* except meningitis, and his chances of contracting the bacteria were about as high as him falling asleep in his mother's lap tonight.

Luka opened his eyes and turned, hearing the click of heels on the stones in the street below the window. His stomach sank with the thought that the priests had followed him there, but they were too wrapped up in an odd contest he had seen before and studied. They lined up by the wall of the monastery cloister and tried to balance on the forehead of a slick stone gargoyle that jutted out a few inches above the street. He had seen local boys try before. Nobody could hold his balance for more than a few seconds. Not even the priests. It had been a week since they had blessed him on the boat, and Luka wondered if their prayers *had* saved him, if the incense had reversed the curse of Lokrum and if it did, how much he would owe them. He did not want to be indebted to anyone but himself. Not now. He would rather die than sit down at the piano. He would rather lose his balance and fall off the wall like the priests. He wondered what was taking the curse of Lokrum so long.

"You can play anything from Chopin. But I'd prefer to hear the Mazurka in A Minor. I'm sure you've heard it."

Milan sat down at the piano, sliding to the edge of the bench, leaving room for the boy. He turned, waiting for Luka to step away from the hail, but the boy fixed his gaze on the priests on the wall.

"Why do they fall so much?"

Milan shifted his eyes and looked out the window to a familiar sight. "They're not strong enough."

"They're stronger than me."

"Staying on that wall has nothing to do with strength or balance. It's about what you believe you can do," Milan said. "Listen, I'll play a bit if you've forgotten."

He played the first four measures almost painfully slow, one note at a time as he did with students who had never once touched a keyboard. He stretched out the already suspended introduction to Chopin's mazurka, accentuating its haunting tempo and emotional sheen. He favored Chopin's version of the typically robust dance song for the mystery of its introduction, finding it appropriate for the chance meeting with the boy. There was something melancholy about the piece, a yearning for the fragile sounds to begin again in the silence as if within them was the hope that Milan and the boy still shared.

"You know Chopin was only fourteen when he wrote it?"

The boy stared at him. He was shaking now. The sharp lines of his body revealed the edginess of his thoughts, his elbows bent at his sides, hands on hips. Lighting came through the window, casting shadows on the walls behind the boy, making him out to be a winged creature of sorts, the unwitting angel who shifted awkwardly in his dilemma.

"He was only a few years older than you."

Milan grazed the keys with his fingertips but did not play another note. He did not want to intimidate the boy with the boldness and shape of his fingers, the way they glided over the keys, giving the impression that playing the piece was effortless. Instead, he listened to the song play out in the chambers of his memory.

"Chopin loved rhythm," he said, hoping to draw the boy closer with his words. Luka stepped out of the rain.

"Rhythm was everything to him."

Luka swallowed and pushed up his sleeves, letting the backpack slip off his shoulders and dangle at the bend in his elbows. He paused, eyes fixed on the composer and slowly unwound the bandages from his wrists, exposing raw, tender flesh that had been recently wounded. Rain dripped from his fingers, and the composer, hoping the boy would dry his hands before he played, pulled out the handkerchief in his front pocket. He folded it into a triangle, then draping it over the keyboards, stood and stepped away from the bench, making a grand sweeping gesture with his hand to welcome the boy.

Luka walked slowly toward the piano and sat down. He took off the backpack and removed the red sweater, exposing bruised ribs and a bony chest pricked with goose bumps. The sweater was soggy and smelled of wet cats, and he flung it on the floor. He dropped the backpack between his feet, squeezing it with his bony ankles, feeling through the holes in his shoes, the cold metal of the pedals. He had never sat at a piano. He straightened himself and threw his shoulders back, lifted his chin, gazing down beneath the arch of his eyebrow. He felt as if he were in a church, unsure of the forces that resided inside it, unconvinced they had any power over that of his drum. Pianos could not wake the dead. Neither could churches.

"Play softly," Milan said. "Don't wake anybody."

Milan was concerned about the neighbors seeing him leave. He did not want to explain why he was taking the boat to Bari, fearful they would believe he had betrayed them at last. The Serb who had finally turned on them. The Serb who claimed it was not safe to stay. He did not want them to wake up from the water dripping through the floorboards and picking up a bucket by the door, crossed the floor and set it under the hole in the roof to collect the rain and the boy's jackknife. The blade was stained with blood.

"It's a good knife," he said, feeling the boy watch him. "But I'm no good at cutting things."

Luka watched him cross the floor, distrusting most of everything the man said. He believed the composer was playing some kind of game, testing him, teasing him with the knife, pressuring him to perform. It worked. He sat, slumped and defeated, staring at the keys, spooked by the way they glowed in the dark like the gleaming smile of a fairy-tale cat. He shivered. *This* was his death, he thought.

He fingered the cigarette burn on middle C, digging his thumb into it as if it were the hole into which he could escape. The immensity and the burden of the piano terrified him, the big black stone pressed against his lie. All along, he expected to die like the Yugoslav soldier, turn blue and stop breathing. Instead, his breaths were long and slow, lungs expanding like an accordion inside his chest. He had never breathed as deeply until now, and he could taste in the air the rain and the storm and the sea, the taste of tears themselves, as if all the world's dead were crying for him because they knew he would not join them. Something in life wanted him to survive.

His heart pounded and his head throbbed. He pressed on the right-hand keys with his left hand, fingers crawling over the black keys as if to find higher ground from the sprawling white spaces of sound, the polished black plain that swallowed him whole.

Thunder shook the building, and the boy grabbed on to the lip of the piano, feeling the rumble move through it, vibrating the strings. He slid his fingers off the lid and found the keys again, spreading his fingers, poised to play as if it suddenly struck him how to do so. He scooted forward on the bench to reach the pedals, pressing them both at once, lifting his feet up and down, heels to toes, as if he were pumping a tire, inflating the piano with his will to play. Milan stood by the door and watched, captivated by the boy's expressions, face twisted by confusion, making some kind of decision, drawing a conclusion in the dark. It was not only the boy's vulnerability in that moment, but also his resolve that Milan recognized as his own. The boy wanted to connect with something that would not betray him.

Suddenly a light flashed across the studio. Once. Twice. Three times. The signal for Milan to leave. Luka froze at the piano, fingers poised, watching Milan in the reflection, the slow twist of the doorknob, the hinges creaking as it opened slowly to the darkness in the hall. From the staircase, the flashlight beamed across the studio, shining directly on the boy's head.

A woman's voice whispered, "We almost left without you." Milan turned to her, smelling jasmine. He recognized the voice. "Mirada?"

She turned off the flashlight, and the two embraced, silhouettes on the threshold of the composer's studio. Milan dug into his pocket and tossed a key to the boy. The tinny thump of brass on wood. The boy reached down and picked it up, turning the key in the moonlight.

"There's a door," he said. "Use it next time."

The boy nodded and with the same impulse, reached into his backpack and stood with the drum, arms outstretched, offering it to the composer, negotiating with him at the crossroads of his faith, thanking him for the things he would never fully understand. They stared at each other in the darkness. The rain had stopped and washed the room with a stillness that the composer had never experienced before tonight. And now the boy had somehow given him what he had wanted all along. The boy offered him silence, but Milan could not take the drum from him now. He did not want it. He lifted the suitcase and stepped over the threshold into the hallway, closing the door behind him, feeling for the first time a sense of relief. The dead, *his* dead, did not need waking.

4

Sara waited for the music to play again as it did every night from the boathouse. The violin seduced her from her sleep, encouraging her to cross the river and seek it. But she did not trust the ice and listened instead from the bridges of Csokhid, making it a habit of crossing them at night as if the music would make more sense to her in the darkness. A voice in the music haunted her, and she wondered if the player had heard it, too, using the violin as a means to exorcise it. She did not believe in ghosts but detected a woman's voice submerged beneath the notes as if she were singing underwater. Sara was surprised she carried the song so well, suspecting it was a way to fight the silence in the camp. She yearned for the crunch of snow, the straining of the bow, welcoming any break from the refugees' silence. She studied their windows best from the bridges, seeing who was up, how they, too, managed to pass the time and violate its most quiet hours.

The silence unnerved them all. It hung like a thick smoke between their breaths. They had stopped speaking not only to themselves, but also to Sara. It's not that they didn't like her. They chose silence to protect her. She was younger than most of them, and they felt responsible for keeping her at the camp. They did not want to spook her or burden her with things a girl like her, they presumed, had no business knowing and no way of relating to. They needed her to remain ignorant of their past, of their shame. She was a tall but slender girl with narrow shoulders and did not appear to be strong enough to carry much of anything other than her attitude and sense of adventure. They liked her youth and energy. They liked the fire in her hair, the perfect teeth, the smile she shared every day, and the beauty that reminded them of what they had once possessed. They liked her unconditional willingness to please them. Distract them. Turn their attention to something else. She introduced them to films they had never seen, films she had loved in college, screening every Friday night the Merchant Ivory production of E. M. Forster's *A Room with a View*. She was surprised that most of the refugees had already seen *Easy Rider* and could quote Jack Nicholson and Dennis Hopper committing the actors' lines to memory as if they were lyrics to a rock song. Some of them had memorized entire scenes and performed in English class when they had grown tired of the lessons. They were smart and eager to learn more. The books in her room were not enough, and she had boxes sent, having written to her church the day she discovered the refugees had burned their books for fuel—furniture, too—when electricity had been cut in Vukovar. She had built for them towers of entertainment, indulging the refugees with escape as if she had mastered the craft herself.

Sara had grown on them, her affection and concern genuine. They liked the sound of her voice, the hope and confidence soothing. She did not condescend because she was a native speaker, but sat quietly deferential, giving them the chance to speak first. She understood their hesitation, experiencing it herself, not wanting to push them or make them feel uncomfortable. She insisted they sit in circles, as she had done in her own English classes, emphasizing the importance of conversation. The problem was finding something to talk about. The mundane and trivial seemed offensive. Each of the refugees, she sensed, had suffered enough to write a book, but rather than share their experiences, they shrank inside the cages of their memory. They had withdrawn slowly but deliberately, unsure of how to be who they had become since they crossed into the camp.

In eight weeks, the refugees had abandoned language for something that could speak for them, opting for silence instead. There was no use in learning a new language or mastering a language they had already learned. Fluency was no goal. They had their own language and wanted to speak it, whispering against Gabor's strict orders to use only English in the camp. It's not that he could penalize them or even that he wanted to. He encouraged the refugees with rewards. He had devised a merit system, rewarding the children who sang Hungarian folk songs in English with Danish cookies from the dust-covered tins in his office. Or chocolates when his own daughters had not depleted the supply. At the end of every hallway hung a list of the names of refugees who had managed to go an entire day speaking English. Gabor allowed those with the most points to eat first on Tuesday. Thursdays he reversed the shower order, saving hot water for those who could recite, from memory, the rules of the camp. Sunday mornings he solicited volunteers to read Scripture when he was too hungover to read the Bible himself. He whistled more Psalms than folk songs. There was a skip in his voice, a playful trill in his tongue when he used English, as if the language itself were a bridge to another life he wished to live. A life that extended beyond the bridges of Csokhid. English fed the illusion of his fantasies. It gave him hope. And hope was all he could guarantee anyone, including himself.

For the most part, Gabor took pride in his fluency and the accent he fashioned from Larry Hagman, having watched enough episodes of *Dallas* to work as an understudy for J. R. Gabor wanted the refugees to speak like he did, encouraging their mimicry. He believed he had set a good example by speaking English to the staff when he could have spoken Hungarian. When he was feeling extra generous or happened to be in good spirits, usually when the Red Cross made deliveries or when he got paid, he delivered bottles of wine to the most advanced English speakers, teenagers, earning their respect and affection. But after they had consumed the wine and allowed their tongues to soften, coping with Gabor's foolhardy tactics to improve their English, they practiced in front of him, speaking loudly and quickly the things he could not comprehend.

The truth is they wanted to speak their own tongue. Eat their own food. Sleep in their own beds. The refugees had no intention of finding a better life, and that was one of the hardest things for Sara to understand. Not every refugee wanted to find another country. They had a country once, and they wanted it back. Most of them wanted to go home. They dreamed of starting over, of course not in Vukovar, but elsewhere in Croatia. Istria. Dalmatia. The islands. No paradise in the West compared to its coastline and the blue waters that rivaled the rest of the world's as the cleanest. They had as much of the West as they wanted. Even under Tito, they had watched *Star Trek* and listened to the Rolling Stones. English, like German, was a part of their culture. It was no novelty but a prerequisite to their connection with the rest of the world. Their tongues bore holes through the Communist Bloc long before it crumbled.

Sara's students were mostly intermediate and advanced, and they sailed through present tense and present progressive. She had laughed out loud when they opened to the unit on present perfect, accidentally spilling coffee on the textbook, the pages stained and crinkled now from her folly. She had no control over the nervous eruption, the spasm that tickled her throat and nearly choked her. Where was the perfection in the present? The only perfection she had witnessed since her arrival was the way in which the refugees wrestled the demons of denial, believing that the less they spoke about what happened, the less it mattered. But there was nothing safe about silence. Even Sara knew that.

In the beginning, she had instructed them to use only the present tense. Gabor's rule number five. The refugees had no choice
but to abandon the past. Their new language promised a bridge
to the golden opportunities that awaited on the flip side of their
tongue. Knowledge of English was more than a means to leaving
the camp but a way to live through each day, to pass the time
quickly, harmlessly, brainlessly, numb. English had become a
game show, and Sara was the host. Round robin, role play. Name
that idiom: Catch on. Cut the mustard. Up one's alley. Run in the
family. Short on something. Get over it. Upper crust. On the ball.
Have a ball. Go bananas. Smart cookie, which the local staff upon
overhearing the word burst into hysterics, *kuki,* slang for "penis"
in Hungarian.

In one memorable lesson, Sara walked over to a student
squeezed between the headphones of a Walkman. He was drawing guns with pencils and pens, his canvas spilling from his notebook to the desk. The pages were filled with not pistols but
sizable weapons, semiautomatics and Uzis. When she knocked on
the desk, the student looked up, his casual glance dismissing her.

"What are you doing?" she asked.

"Putting the world on hold."

He held eye contact long enough for Sara to feel her cheeks
burn, to understand the anguish of his boredom, identifying it in
herself first.

She had nothing more to teach them. Her job, futile. Class size
diminished by the day. Half a dozen. Sometimes less. And never
any consistency. She would wait forty-five minutes to teach for fifteen, depending on who showed up. They refused to do homework, claiming they couldn't concentrate, failing to memorize
vocabulary lists of words they would never use. *Porter. Bellman.
Butler.* The textbooks were worn, the pages yellowed, of interest
it seemed only to the older men, the drunk who rocked back and
forth, staring at the text with colorless eyes.

She did not teach much. Two days at most. Tuesday and Thursdays, and even then her schedule was interrupted too many times to call it a schedule at all. On the rare occasion that the students attended class, their minds wandered. Only the pornography of war kept their attention, eyes glued to the television in the recreation room as if at any moment the newscasters would announce that the war had ended. But the war had only moved east, spreading its twentieth-century psoriasis. January 9. The Serbian Republic of Bosnia-Herzegovina forms. February 26. The Serbs and Croats meet in Graz, Austria, denying conspiracy against the Muslims. They propose population transfers, setting up Bureaus for Population Exchange, agents for ethnic cleansing. The point of the war.

The refugees from Vukovar had clung to the conviction that the war would end soon. Nobody warned them to blink a few times, to turn the channel, to turn it off. They would wait five years. It seemed that they had been there that long already. Time dragged. The days were too long, the nights longer. The silence got louder the longer they refused to speak. Where there had been no walls, new ones emerged and grew higher, invisible bricks of words separating them. The refugees had managed to gather the silence around them, pulling it close against their hearts and throats as if it were the worn wool blankets that had been offered the night of their arrival. High on the hill above Csokhid and the great plain that rolled to the east, the refugees had sunken below the earth in their grief, not anticipating that they would return.

They lived together suspended in a stupor eclipsing anything that resembled real life because Life as they knew it had been put on hold. They waited and worried about waiting. They waited to hear of their missing husbands and brothers, fathers who had disappeared on the buses that day. They waited for proof of the mass graves because the idea was impossible to comprehend. How could a mass grave fit beneath the hills and meadows where they took picnics and fell in love? They waited to live again, but the silence prevented them from living at all.

Nobody slept. There was no real sleep and no true waking, only a teetering on the edge of consciousness. Even Gabor, on his most spirited days, seemed drowsy. He napped. The Swedish woman napped. Sara napped. She dozed off in her own classes with the rest of the students, hypnotized by the ticking of the wall clock and their refusal to speak. The silence had changed her in little ways already. It made her nervous, gnawed at her stomach. She ate less. Worried more. Smoked. Smoking gave herself something to do when she would have been sleeping. She did not blame them or blame herself for the vices she used to cope. How could they expect her to sleep?

Sara envied those who managed to surrender to their collective exhaustion. She would often find the refugees collapsed in the laundry room, heaps of half a dozen curled like cats against each other lulled by the spin of the washer. She admired their resourcefulness. They abandoned their beds for the places of greatest noise, the clatter of the kitchen, the nursery where even the wailing of infants was more comforting than the eerie stillness in the hallways. Late at night, when she had been on the phone with her parents, she heard whisperings in the darkened stairwell, refugees who had gathered to speak Croatian, remaining faceless in the confession of their pain and rage. In the mornings, when the sun crossed the stairs, she had found the stones wet with their spit, as if they had spoken out against the silence and wanted desperately to be caught and relieved of their burden.

Sara was not sure that the hospital that the camp had once been was as quiet as the refugees had made it now. By entering it, they honored unspoken vows. They kept to themselves and remained strangers, cramped inside the miniature universes of their rooms. They worked together to clean, to establish the order of things but they did not speak when they worked. They shared civilities at first. Greetings, news of the war. But over the course of weeks and months they rarely gathered for conversation and instead shuffled around each other as if they were stuck too long at a bus station in a blizzard waiting for the storm to pass, for the roads to clear. But the only road intended for the passage of refugees was an impassable road that seemed to end here. They knew better than to gather anywhere, because in their gathering they would share what happened and would invite it to happen again. And to speak of the past would be to make it real, and that was too big a burden for a refugee who wished only to forget it.

Like the refugees, Sara's life had become intensely quiet in a way that had nothing to do with solitude. Long gone was the solitude of study and simple reflection from the recesses of a college library. There was nothing simple about the complexity of the camp. She had no syllabus to follow here, no formula for achievement, no guarantee that she would succeed. In many ways, the camp had failed her already. She felt not only lonely, but also alone. For as long as she could remember, she'd had no problems spending time by herself. She was the one who went to movies on weekends when everyone else partied on campus. She took jobs where there was little supervision, working as a security guard in the campus theater for three years, a florist for one. She was disciplined, her worst critic, her own boss. She did not do well taking orders from others, especially when she could do their jobs better, which in most instances she could.

But at the camp, she seemed to be struggling more than the refugees themselves. They were surviving it better than she. They had each other. They had support. Sure, there were moments when Sara made connections with them outside the classroom. The women who stopped in the hallways to squeeze her hand, locking bony fingers, asking her how *she* was doing. Sara was amazed by their selflessness. They were determined to offer her comfort when they had no way of accepting it themselves. There would be no comfort as long as they remained at the camp, in limbo, wives or widows (nobody could say or dared to speculate), but it was this limbo that fostered their community and allowed them to connect despite the silence.

Even the Swedish woman seemed to have formed close ties with the local staff, speaking Hungarian with them, dating the cook. She had not reached out to Sara the way Sara had expected and instead observed the subtle changes taking place inside her as if Sara, not the refugees, epitomized the paradigm of loneliness; To admit loneliness was to capitulate the need for a connection with somebody other than herself as it had been in the past. Connecting scared Sara. The last thing she wanted to do now was to connect to that other side of herself that seemed to grow louder the longer she remained silent. She no longer felt safe with this part of herself provoked by the camp, the side that was more of a stranger to her than the refugees themselves. She was not sure she wanted to recognize the girl who lived inside her, beside the woman she had become. Harvard's rejection, she knew, was an excuse for her own surrender. But it was too early for her to admit that yet, too painful to remember the details. She had always prided herself on organization and often thought of consulting on the side. She was good at keeping things in compartments, and she kept locked in her mind safe deposit boxes of pain and regret.

She absorbed the isolation of the camp as she had learned to do with that of her campus, losing herself in its legend of greatness. She lost herself in the beauty and history of Csokhid, too, studying the fluted towers of the castle, rapt by its fairy tale. She imagined the princesses who lived there in safety, isolated from the dangers of the world, their innocence preserved from the outside's perversity. She imagined the dances held on the patios, the many festivals that had for centuries breathed life into the region and reminded it of the glory days of its past, before the Turkish invasion, before the Nazis had assaulted it. She had spent a great deal of time exploring Csokhid, implored by Gabor to know where she had been. He wanted Sara to acquire a taste for the area and to associate it with more than the bitterness of the camp.

Gabor had insisted that Sara accompany him on several field trips, at first with his wife and the Swedish woman until they made fun of his need to impress Sara with his knowledge of the history of the place, which he often got wrong. He had taken her alone to Mohacs, to the festival of the masks, shared bitter spirits and fish stew. He had also spoiled her with trips to his family's wine cellar, loading her arms with bottles of red wine, even though she didn't drink, and homemade sausages that hung from the ceilings. He had taken her to Pec to see the mosque and to the farms south of Lake Balaton teeming with Lipizzaners, insisting she take lessons and enjoy herself. She had gladly accepted the invitations despite the rumors that circulated when she returned to the camp. She liked horses but preferred to spend her time exploring the vine-draped hills overlooking the camp where she considered exactly how she would tell Gabor it was time to leave.

And so Sara came to the river seeking the comfort of the violin, driven by her need to move away from the camp, away from the loneliest part of herself that resided there. The music had stopped abruptly in the middle of a song. It was unusual for the player to take a break much less pause during the evening sessions. Sara found it daunting that he had the energy to sustain hours of playing, unfazed it seemed by his own lack of sleep. She often wondered whether or not he played for her. He seemed to follow her with his music, accompanying her nightly walks as if he intended to keep her company. He had a habit of playing louder the closer she got, but she found it ironic that he stopped now when she stood closest to the boathouse.

The silence seized her. She felt her throat tighten. The hairs rising on her arms and neck. A cold wind blew down from the castle, sweeping snow dust around her. Dark clouds feathered the moon and gathered in thick bands across the sky. There would be more snow. She stepped down from the bridge and followed a path through the frozen slush, passing chocolate wrappers and empty wine bottles, the shimmer of moonlight on the foil and glass.

Sara stood a few feet from the boathouse in the shadow of an oak tree, the trunk carved by the names of lovers. Stray mittens and gloves, lost and found, dangled from the thin branches and from the thicker ones, ice skates hung by shredded laces and rotated slowly as if displayed inside a thrift-store window. It pleased Sara to see the refugees had used the donations, practically wearing the blades dull. Skating had become their salvation, and they spent most of their time here, imploring Sara to join them. But Sara did not skate. She paced the frozen bank, watching them carve figure eights. She did not trust the ice would hold her.

The frayed tail of a rope swing grazed the back of her hand, startling her. She reached out and caught it, pulling too hard, her neck cold with the snow that had shaken loose and slid inside her scarf. She froze, not from the chill, but from what she glimpsed beyond the flicker of the candle inside the boathouse, the player collapsed on the floor.

She slipped, running toward the door, skinning her hand on the chipped stone threshold. She grabbed the handle and shook loose the latch that had been closed over the lock and pushed back the door. A taper candle burned from a small holder in front of the player, splayed prone with his cheek turned against the floor.

He did not see Sara. In fact, he did not see much of anything in the periphery, his gaze directed toward the candle flame, pupils reduced to pinpoints, retaining a blankness as if he were staring through the fire, trying to keep in his sight everything on the floor—hundreds of notebooks of various sizes and colors opened to pages crammed with musical notes. He had smeared the notes on the page pinned beneath his chin, his left hand wrapped around the pen that had drawn them.

A cold wind blew across the room, but the player's face glistened. He was sweating, but there was no heat in the boathouse, the windowpanes frosted from the inside. He jerked his head once, then three times before his body began to convulse as if he had been let loose to flop around the floor like some windup doll.

His face drooped to the left as if the skin had turned to clay or melting wax, the texture shifting with his startled expressions. His tongue hung out of his mouth, and strings of spit dangled from his lips, doglike, sloppy with no regard to the fact that he was drooling all over the music. It was as if his jaw possessed the only consciousness, pinning what he valued most to the floor, away from his own hands that inadvertently crushed the violin and snapped the bow.

Sara had never witnessed a seizure. She stiffened, watching helplessly as the young man flailed on the floor. Everything happened so fast. His head inched closer to the taper candle, and without thinking, she ran to it and blew it out, unable to kick away the empty wine bottle before his fist smashed through it. She dropped to her knees and shrugged off her jacket, sliding it beneath the young man's head, gathering in her fingers his damp hair and neck. She leaned forward, trying to catch the fist that pounded the floor like a jackhammer locked in habit. She brushed away the bits of broken glass, unable to arrest the tongue that dangled, licking the floor. She knew better than to stick anything in his mouth, fearing she would lose her fingers. Basic first aid. She could not speculate if the player had epilepsy, but permitted the energy to unleash itself and let the seizure run its course.

He swerved his hand and smacked her lip unknowingly, drawing blood; she did not flinch or move but waited with him while his body flailed on the boathouse floor. She held his wrist, feeling the warmth of his medical bracelet, unable to read his condition in Serbo-Croatian. She felt his breath on her arm and squeezed him tightly as if the harder she held him, the sooner the seizure would end. It was a long two minutes, but not the longest in her life. She had suffered a longer minute before this one. She cradled his head with her other hand, fingers entangled with his dark curls, wet and sticking to his forehead, the dead weight of him in her lap.

⤙

Epilepsy was the composer's carnival of afflictions, holding him at the mercy of the unpredictable forces inside him. It was a process of disintegration. He was capable of doing anything, unleashing a strength quite contrary to his willowy frame. The episodes made him remorseful, wishing for once he could act right in public.

That he had been suspected of killing his half brother was not news. The case had been dismissed as an accident. Two boys fighting. One wins. The other loses. A tragedy, of course. Nobody took the time to investigate what happened on the island of Lokrum until now, but it was too late. The story circulated a decade later as if it had occurred only yesterday. It was the kind of talk that once cycled through rumor, becomes accepted myth. It's not that people wanted somebody to blame. They wanted to keep telling the story, seduced by its mystery.

"Maybe he killed his mother, too," they would say tracing with their finger the rims of empty cappuccino cups. *"There was no reason for her to commit suicide, not with her looks. She had every man in Dubrovnik chasing her. I'd be chasing her, too. Ever see her calves? Longest legs in the Balkans. Beautiful woman. And she was a Serb! Good heavens, the Lord works in mysterious ways."*

⤙

When the seizure ended, Milan let go of Sara's hand and looked up, eyes wide, spooked, following the arch of the beams across the boathouse ceiling. He was confused, trying to orient himself in the darkness. The shapes and colors of the room were unintelligible. He did not know where he was, unable to familiarize himself with the moment that preceded the seizure. He padded the floor with his hand, dragged his fingers over the wire spiral of the notebook, feeling his stomach sink when he gathered the broken strings of the violin instead. He had hoped he had not destroyed the instrument but knew better than to believe he had spared anything or anyone from his violence. The splintered wood of the neck poked at his thigh through his jeans, and he tongued the roof of his mouth, tasting metal. It was a bittersweet relief. He knew instantly what had happened.

His heart pounded, and he felt exhausted. He rubbed his face, massaging the muscles, pushing his cheeks into place. It was his first seizure since he arrived in the camp. Up to this point, Milan's face had healed. No longer were his cheeks blued with bruises. He looked healthier than he had been in Dubrovnik despite the lack of sun. He had been careful with his medication, never missing a dose. He did not want the other refugees to know about his condition and bought Dilatin at a local pharmacy rather than order it through the Swedish woman and the Red Cross. He had no idea what had triggered the seizure this time. He had honored his routine as best as he could in the camp. He ate alone. Avoided crowds. Kept to himself. And wrote. There was nothing overstimulating about the monochrome environs, no bright colors to induce his synesthesia. Milan wondered if this is why he had suffered only one seizure since he had arrived. He drew in a deep breath and exhaled slowly, gaining consciousness, letting his mind shake off the numbness as if it had fallen asleep like an arm or a foot.

Milan did not lift his head from the woman's lap and shifted only his gaze to the shadows on the wall, seeing her silhouette next to his in the moonlight. He recognized the long thick curls draping the English teacher's back, the sad slouch in her shoulders, the way he identified her at night from the other refugees who crossed the bridges, too, listening to his music. Sara was easiest to identify. She always walked alone. One night Milan noticed a group of refugees had stopped her on the bridge to offer cigarettes, the secret code of embers flickering between them. Sara shared a quick smoke but continued on her way as if she were too afraid to stop for long. Milan sensed it was not the cold that kept Sara moving but some-

thing he felt every time they had passed each other in the hallways of the camp, a coldness pressed between them, like a
ghost. It was as if Milan's presence reminded Sara of something she had tried her best to avoid. She abandoned his eyes,
throwing her gaze into the shine of the linoleum, deliberately
stepping out of his way, either to let him pass in front of her or
to let herself pass first. They had never spoken. She did not re-
cruit him for English classes, omitting his name from the original roster. She seemed to do everything she could to make
sure he didn't attend, changing class times on several occasions and switching locations once.

Sara played a game, keeping Milan at bay during the day, yet
desperately sought his music at night as if only in the darkness
could she reveal herself to him, slowly, on her own terms. He had
caught her once, fast asleep, in the hallway outside his room. She
had been listening again. He did not take offense and covered her
with the blanket from his bed. He did not believe *The Sound of
Blue* had bored her but transported her mind instead to a restful
place beyond the quiet anxiety of the camp. She did not return
the blanket. He had found it folded on a cot in the nurse's station
where she napped.

It was Sara who followed Milan the first night he left the camp
to play in the boathouse, crossing the bridge behind him in the
snow. She had waited outside until dawn, crouched inside a boat
stranded on the embankment. Her breath gave her away in the
dark. Milan had said nothing, refusing to call out to her, to call
her bluff. He played knowing it was his playing, not him, that
kept her there. She had fallen under his charm, and the myth of
it amused him. Like Orpheus, he played to pull her out of her
hiding place and into the world of the living.

In the strangest of ways, Sara was Milan's gauge. He measured the efficacy of his music against her reactions, having never
before seen the expression of a listener. The radio show in
Dubrovnik was the closest he had ever been to a live audience.

He had not experienced the pleasure of watching the magic of a stanza part lips and bring tears to reluctant eyes. Sara validated his power. Behind the closed doors of the boathouse, Milan watched the hardness in her face and throat soften, her eyes brighten, moods shifting with the stars over Csokhid. His music delivered her from some place deep inside her heart, plucking out the stones wedged there. He saw in her reactions the holiness of a person struggling to understand her relationship to the world.

⌐ᗡ

Sara had given Milan the chance to touch and change a stranger with his music. She had given him a chance to be more than a refugee. They both knew what was happening but said nothing as the weeks passed. Sara made no effort to acknowledge their relationship. She appeared to want to be near him only when there was music. Without it, she fled into the corners of the camp, making herself hard to find when he searched for her, wanting private English lessons. He could not handle a group without risking the humiliation of a seizure. Milan wanted her instruction alone, but she had assumed he already spoke English. He sensed she had assumed too many things, the wrong things about him. He was older but not by much. They were different, he knew that, but equally vulnerable, sharing the same relationship to the camp. Surrounded by the refugees, they were both alone.

There were times Milan wanted to surrender the violin and join Sara during her nightly walks, to get to know her in a different context beyond their awkward encounters, but he did not trust the person he would become if he stopped playing. He did not trust she would want to know him without the music. The music protected him. It gave him an identity, extending his status far beyond the limitations imposed on the other refugees. Milan needed to play as long as Sara and the other refugees needed to listen. It became his job. The payment, respect, and omission from the questions they reserved—wondering who he was, what he had done to survive. Why he, a Serb at twenty-six, wasn't dead. Besides the teenagers, he was the only male in the camp under the age of forty. His youth put him at a great disadvantage, making him culpable for the horrors he was incapable of imagining, for all the things the refugees had suffered before they had crossed into the camp.

Milan withheld his name and his story, remaining anonymous to everyone but Gabor and the English teacher. The thought occurred to him more than once that perhaps he didn't deserve to be there. Not that he wanted to go back. Not yet. Not after everything he had risked securing the boat ride to Bari, leaving Anton and the boy, hoping one day that both of them would find a way to forgive him. He had refused to speak with the translators, fearing they would question the legitimacy of his trauma and dismiss him, concluding it was irrelevant to that of the other refugees, the *real* refugees. In a way, they would be right. He had not left Croatia for the same reasons. The asylum he sought had nothing to do with the war and everything to do with the silences extending beyond it, but these things he kept to himself along with the secrets of his past.

Dubrovnik was occupied and surrounded by the Yugoslav Army, but it had not been destroyed like Vukovar. People still lived in Dubrovnik during the war and despite it. Buildings had been destroyed, but lives had been spared. Fewer than one hundred civilians had died since the attacks in the fall. The people had food. They ate grilled fish. Baked bread in gas ovens. Cooked pasta with salt water. Dubrovnik had not suffered the way Vukovar had, the way the Bosnians of Mostar, Sarajevo, and Srebrenica would suffer still. And for this Milan did not believe he belonged with its survivors.

Milan gladly took the graveyard shift, deliberately resting in the day when he was least likely to have a confrontation with the other men in his room, or worse have a seizure in front of them, giving them more reasons, he believed, to hate him. He played for them not to break the silence but as a result of finding it again. He abandoned Croatia for the anonymity afforded by the camp. He could be anyone here. Somebody who mattered. Milan had a chance of exposing something other than his seizures, hoping his concern and consideration would be enough.

Until now.

He sat up, feeling his face burn. He brushed back the hair from his forehead, locking eyes with Sara. She had not closed her mouth yet, her bottom lip swollen and open. Blood dribbled down her chin, splattering the notebook. Neither moved. They were stuck staring in awe and horror. Milan had never seen Sara's face like that from any music he had played, and he was uncertain what her expression conveyed now. It made him uncomfortable. He did not want to know how her lip had come to bleed, unable to bear the truth if he had hit her.

He pushed himself off the floor, feeling his back quiver. His neck and arms were sore, muscles and tendons aching. He glimpsed a view of himself from the reflection in the front window of the boathouse, seeing a bruise crown his head, which tomorrow, he knew, would ripen like a plum. His nose was bleeding and he pressed the crook of his elbow against it, smelling Sara on his sleeve. Cigarettes and chocolate milk. Until now, a phantom scent in the hallways. Sara was the last person he wanted to witness his seizures. He had the urge to run from her, to leap from the boathouse and abandon the music, willing the ice to melt so that he could float down the river far away from the humiliation.

Instead, he pulled a handkerchief from his pants pocket and turned, sitting on the floor in front of Sara, surprising both of them. She stiffened when he reached out to dab the blood from her chin, noticing for the first time the small scar that crossed it. It was an old scar, the skin white and crinkled. He touched it gently with the tip of his index finger, watching the skin spring back. Sara shrank from his touch, but her shrinking did not deter him from wanting to help her more. He folded a corner of the handkerchief over her bottom lip and pressed it with his thumb, his touch gentle and tender. He held the cloth against her longer than she needed, until sunrise washed the boathouse with the pink light of morning and he was certain that she would not bleed again.

⌒

They gathered the notebooks and the pieces of the violin, crossing the bridge to the camp in silence, meeting Gabor at the door. He stood behind the glass, wearing a new jumpsuit from PUMA, the red nylon pants bright and tight around his legs. He appeared to be a lost if not disfigured action hero, squeezed into a role he was unfit to play. It was not yet noon, and already his face glimmered with oils, fingerprints and smudge marks from the glass door distorting it. He sipped from the American-flag mug he had given to Sara, spilling tea on the floor. He had not expected to unlock the doors for Sara. She had a key.

He fingered the lock and studied Sara's lip, the key chain hooked around his pinky, pointing at Milan. "What happened?"

Milan spoke quickly, a tone of apology and strained regret, trying to explain in Croatian.

Gabor flicked his hand, dismissing him, and unlocked the door. He had no patience for the banal and barked when he spoke. "English! Please. How many times do I have to tell you people? We speak English here."

Milan stiffened. Gabor's hot breath curled into the cold and greeted him, the smell of cheese *kifli* drifting up from the crescent-shaped roll sticking out of his pocket. He fingered the top, breaking it off. It dropped on the floor by his heel, and he bent down and picked it up, popping it into his mouth.

"You missed breakfast. They made *palacinta.*"

Sara shrugged, indifferent. Gabor drew his head back, much like a rooster stepping around horseshit. He knew Sara loved *palacinta,* the paper-thin Hungarian pancakes that reminded her, she had said, of crepes. He had designated Saturdays as pancake days, having first learned of the tradition from watching *Dallas.* J. R. had surprised Victoria Principal with breakfast in bed, although that part of the tradition Gabor forgot to share when he had told his wife and children about it.

"We're in time for lunch," Sara said.

"Lunch? You have classes. Your students are waiting."

"What students?"

"Sara. It's Tuesday."

Gabor scowled, eyes narrowed by his own petulance as if he were more upset about seeing Sara with Milan than by her negligence and irresponsibility. He tapped his foot against the weatherstripping on the door, sliding his fingers over the lock. He looked out at the boathouse, determined to put a lock on it, too. Already groups of refugees had gathered on the river to skate, the blades reflecting the sun. Sara met his gaze in the glass.

"The river can teach them more," Sara said.

"It can't teach them English."

Gabor stepped back from the door, out of the sun. The icicles hung like spears from the roof, dripping water onto the sidewalks, catching the light as they fell. Sara stared at him, hard, defiant, remembering the Canadian's warning. *"My job is to translate their past. Your job is to help them forget it. You teach the present tense."*

"English is not what they want," she said.

"Perhaps. But it's what they need."

Sara wanted to ask him, *What do you know about what they need?* but said nothing and stood still.

Gabor stepped aside, his arm grazing the stack of notebooks in Sara's arms. He tossed her a curious look. "What's that?"

"Homework."

"Yours or his?"

"His," she said, and pressed them against Milan's chest, directing him with a quick shift of her eyes to leave her now. He locked eyes with her for a moment and said something in Croatian that she could not understand. An attempt to make her laugh, perhaps, because he smiled when he finished speaking. The color had returned to his cheeks, and his eyes were brighter, light blue like round mints in the light coming through the door. He gathered the notebooks in both arms and made his way down the hallway, aware that Gabor and Sara were watching him, both for different reasons.

When Milan had disappeared around the corner, Gabor turned to Sara. "I'm not paying you to give private lessons."

"Of course not. He's giving *me* lessons."

Gabor stared at her, trying to assemble the sarcasm.

"Lessons in what?"

"Listening."

Gabor tapped the floor with his shoe. He batted his eyes, incredulous, volleying between the ghost of Milan and Sara, feeling left out and fractured by his futile attempt to understand the conspiracy of their meeting. Until now, Gabor had never seen Sara alone with any of the refugees. She had heeded his warning and stayed away from them. Her job was not to be their friend. He had reminded her time after time. Her job was to give them hope, but he wondered what kind of hope, if any, they were giving her now. She seemed in better spirits, her tongue sharper and more defensive than usual, *serrated* he'd say, like a bread knife. Her words sliced into him.

"He's a good man," she said.

"He's not well."

"He means well."

Gabor's eyes narrowed to pinpoints. "Are you okay?"

She shrugged and let out a caustic laugh. "Yeah. Sure. I'm okay, Gabor. You're okay, too. Right? You sleep. You eat. Life goes on for you. But him," she said pointing down the hall. "He's not okay. The others? I'm not sure if they're okay either. And this? *This* is definitely not okay."

She marched over to a pair of children's sneakers propped against the radiator to dry. They were pink with glitter stars on the ankle. The soles were worn and hung off the toe, flopping backward like drooping tongues melting in the heat. It infuriated Sara to see that such basic needs had not been met at the camp besides shelter and food. She wondered what Gabor did all day, what he had checked off the list from his clipboard. At times there had not been enough toilet paper, and the refugees had been taking napkins and paper towels with them, stuffing their pockets with extra from the kitchen, causing a shortage there, too. The latest crisis was more harrowing. The women, naturally, began to menstruate together, and sanitary supplies had become scarce. It was a problem Gabor had not anticipated. He was shocked, if not appalled, to learn of this biochemical phenomenon. His daughters were too young. His wife never mentioned it, and he had no sisters. He rattled his hand, waving it as if he were extinguishing a small fire as Sara explained. It was Gabor who remained breathless and beaded with sweat when she finished.

Gabor promised to order supplies. Two months ago. He wondered why the bleach had run out and why the sheets and towels, which had once been white (he cursed them for being so) looked darker and darker as the weeks progressed. Sara had shared her own supplies and had written for more when Gabor's promise had been broken, hoping her family would splurge on industrial boxes of tampons, not feeling the least bit guilty about the gross consumption, because she knew every single item would be used. She had taken it upon herself to identify deficiencies in the supplies and kept lists of the things Gabor had overlooked, spending more time in the storage room than the classroom. In keeping track of what the refugees needed, Sara was trying to preserve their dignity. She did not believe they should have to reuse anything other than a plastic cup.

Sara lifted the pink sneaker off the radiator and tossed it across the hallway to the wall on the other side. The sole fell off with a definitive thud, rending the shoe useless. It should have been repaired long ago, not to mention the condition of the foot that had worn it. She imagined blisters, corns, calluses, scrunched toes. The rounded shoulders of the child too embarrassed to look down at her feet, who instead of moving forward stood still.

"Where are the other shoes?"

Gabor shrugged. "What shoes?"

Sara believed he didn't care, not that he didn't know. His apathy, poison. The irony unnerved her. It was as if the only person Gabor truly cared about was Sara, making sure it was her sheets that stayed whitest, her food hottest, her clothes cleanest, her room the warmest, although she never slept there and he knew it. He had folded back the sheets once, discovering, to his shock, the chocolates he had left for her the night of her arrival. The wrappers had curled in the heat. He did not leave chocolates for the refugees, or gifts of any kind, unless of course they earned them by speaking English and speaking it well. He treated the refugees no better or worse than unexpected guests who overstayed their welcome, possessing an air of authority and arrogance that suggested he could, at any moment, revoke that welcome. The old women rolled their eyes, stepping out of his way when he passed. He disliked them most because their language skills, in his mind, were hopeless. He had no way of placing the old women anywhere, here or elsewhere, clearly not in Germany where he had begun to negotiate, for a small fee, jobs in a Volkswagen plant outside Leipzig. He focused on the big picture. Moving the refugees beyond the camps and Hungary. Shoes were not a priority when they had skates to wear.

Gabor marched over to the pink shoe and picked both it and the sole off the floor.

"We can fix it."

"With what? Glue?" Sara stared, incredulous.

He was thinking just that, eyebrow twitching. He nodded, brows furrowed with his better intentions. He spoke with his best Texan twang, twirling the crescent-shape *kifli* around his finger as if it were a pistol then shoving it into his mouth. "Things come apart. But they can go back together."

He fit the sole to the shoe, but it was so warped, neither fit the other. He wiggled the rubber around the bottom, securing the heel with this thumb, and Sara could see the desperation in his eyes to prove that he was right. But he was wrong. They both knew it. To what degree Sara could only imagine and feared because she did not want to know why it had taken Gabor so long to do anything about the shoe problem, let alone the other problems in the camp.

Sara had written months ago to her church, seeking donations from rummage sales—women and children's clothing and shoes, toiletries, books, videos. In addition to putting Iraq on the bulletin, the church now included Croatia and the refugees that Sara mentioned she taught, surprising her parents most of all when they read it during the service on Ash Wednesday. Strategic planning. Perfect timing. Before her father could chide her or demand an explanation over the phone, he praised her instead after receiving heartfelt congratulations from the congregation, who after greeting the shiny-headed minister, stood in line to shake Robert Foster's hand. Father of Sara Foster. The girl who was going to Harvard. The girl they believed in more than her father ever could. Her mother stood by his side and said nothing, her mind clouded, recalling the many phone calls they had had since Christmas. She felt a slight pinch of disappointment in her heart because for so long she had imagined her daughter riding a bicycle through Budapest, teaching the sons and daughters of ambassadors. She had nodded politely when the passersby lauded her for inspiring Sara to travel to Hungary, but Sara's mother could not for the life of her identify Csokhid on the map. But they received the approval of the community, and that's all they needed to approve of Sara's decision themselves. To make it worthy. To make it all right.

Soon the secretary of the church started to send Sara newsletters along with *Newsweek,* marking pages on the war in Iraq, highlighting information that might be relevant to her cousin Mark's position with the Chemical Corps, making no mention of the bloodbath flooding the land one hour south of Sara. Mark's name continued to be listed, the congregation deep in prayer over his well-being months after he had returned. The mention of the refugees and Yugoslavia was listed last, almost as a side note.

Gabor shoved the pieces of the shoe into his pocket. He sipped from the mug, fingering the hand-painted stars, thoughtfully doling out his words as if they were meant to make Sara feel better. "The shoes will come."

"When?"

"It's hard to say. The mail is slow."

"Then why do letters take only a week?"

"Letters don't go through customs."

"Damn it, Gabor. They're not drugs. Or guns! How much inspection does a box of shoes need to get to the people who need them most? I don't understand you people. I don't understand any of this. The church sent them at the end of January. It's almost March."

She was furious now, cheeks flushed with blood. Two children, twin girls, had poked their heads out of one of the rooms. The door slammed behind them, returning the silence to the hallway. Only the buzzing of the fluorescent bulbs in the ceiling. The chill of the boathouse had worked its way into Sara's bones, and only now, by the dry heat of the radiator, was she beginning to thaw, feeling the tingle of blood in her fingers and toes.

Gabor picked the crumbs from his lips, flicking off flakes of *kifli*. He sucked the rest from his teeth and drummed his bottom lip, studying Sara's, still concerned over the swelling. "You must be patient, Sara. This is not America."

She pressed her gaze against his. "I never said it was."

"But you expect it to be."

Sara pressed her lips, feeling her jaw stiffen. Her lip stung, and she could see the swelling when she glanced down, a fuzzy protrusion. But she did not flinch or carry in her face the pain she felt from the injury—Milan's accidental, Gabor's intentional. Gabor had a habit of patronizing her, presuming that she could not possibly understand the politics of running the camp. How and why the funding worked its way in drips and drops, percolating from the pot of bureaucracy in Budapest. But it didn't take a genius in economics to understand the basic premise. Everything was slow here: Mail. Meals. Medicine. Change.

Even the buses in Csokhid defied their schedules. On the rare occasion they arrived, they took forever to get anywhere, the drivers turning in to various villages for eggs and sundries, not because the destinations were on the route but because the drivers wanted to stop. Fifteen kilometers could take two hours, depending on the driver, his moods and cravings a variable Sara often considered, opting instead to walk. The aggravation was not worth it. She would rather be cold and tired than wait, but she admired the patience of the locals who endured public transportation. According to Gabor, most people had been waiting at least five years to buy a car, settling on a fiberglass Trabant or if their ship really arrived, a Ford Fiesta. How Gabor decided to sell his grandmother's jewelry for a down payment on a blue Mercedes and found the money to finance it was another story. The point is that even Gabor dreamed of moving faster, faster perhaps than the buses and mail, to be on time for once in his life. For what remained a question, but he sensed a quickening. He needed the speed of a schedule to administer his ego, which is why he honored the militant routine of the camp, moving through the daily programs at a brisk pace, hoping that he could foster new habits and replace old ones, including his own.

Gabor told Sara that people there weren't used to schedules, but she didn't believe him, because that's all they knew for forty years under Communism until the Berlin Wall fell. Fragments of the regime remained, residues that stained the mindset of everyone. It made people like Gabor find excuses for everything and accountable for nothing. Even if the shoes and clothes had arrived, Sara would not have been surprised if the boxes sat unopened in some back room to which only Gabor had the key.

Sara stepped away from Gabor. She was feeling nauseated, smelling the coffee and cheese *kifli* on his breath.

He pointed to her face, his own expression twisted. "Your lip."

"What about it?"

"It's big."

She nodded, reading his face. He wanted an answer. "I slipped on the ice."

"You don't skate."

"Maybe I should learn," she said, shifting her gaze out the window to the refugees on the river. "I'm not the only teacher here. You should give them a chance."

She moved past him, but he held out his hand, taking her elbow. He gripped her tightly, but his warning was not intended for her. "If he ever hurts you—"

Sara yanked her elbow from his grip. "He didn't," she said.

"I'll kill him."

The radiator kicked in, an aggravating ticking as if a fight of some kind had broken out inside it.

"What?"

Gabor nodded but did not repeat himself. She heard him, and the steeliness of his words struck her as he intended. He unzipped the front of his jumpsuit and fingered the cross dangling from the gold chain at his neck, the skin pink and moist, nicked by a razor.

Sara stared incredulous, not wanting to believe the threat. Gabor waved the stubby finger of his right hand, trying to offset the shaking in his body. A sudden darkness seemed to gather around him in the hallway under the fluorescent lights, his face split by the shadow of Sara. She studied him calmly, understanding that in his desperate attempt to protect her, he had scared her more than in the moment he had chosen her over the other teachers for the camp. She had never questioned his intentions until now, assuming he knew she would work harder because she had the least experience. She assumed wrong. There was something else in Gabor's voice, a plan plucked between the harshness of his vocal cords, the booming bass in his tone. Gabor had momentarily abandoned his cheery Hungarian-Texan twang for a voice that sounded as if it brokered darker deals, irrevocable and illegitimate transactions that battled his quarrel with the world.

"He's a Serb," he blurted.

"I thought he was from Dubrovnik."

"He *lived* there. But he was born in Belgrade. Once a Serb, always a Serb."

Sara swallowed the word like a pill that had gone down the wrong tube. Her eyes narrowed, and she shook her head as if she knew, but she did not know and she was not sure it mattered whether or not Milan was a Croat or a Serb.

"He's my friend," she said.

A cold wind rattled the front doors. Gabor zipped up his jacket. "There are no friends here, remember?"

"Rule number thirteen?"

Gabor's smile flattened. Sara stepped away from the radiator. Her jeans, soggy with snow, had become crisp from the heat, and her calves were burning.

"You don't even know him," she said.

"And you do?" Gabor let out a caustic laugh. Sometimes he could not believe the audacity of idealism.

"I know he wouldn't hurt me."

"Not yet."

Sara watched his lip curl, from amusement or disgust, she was uncertain.

Gabor continued, lips snarled. He spoke with his hands behind his back. "Rumor has it he killed a man."

"Who?"

"A Croat. His half brother." Gabor jabbed a finger in the air and continued. "Don't look so surprised. That's the way it is with these people. Serb blood."

Sara's throat tightened. She recalled Milan's slender fingers. They were the hands of a musician. An artist. They were the hands that created not destroyed. She could not believe Milan was capable of using them in any other way, and she wondered what the difference was between the hand of a Croat and a Serb. They could both hold and let things go.

Gabor turned and crossed the hallway to his office, his hand over the knob. "Everybody takes something from somebody here," he said. "Don't let it be your life. Nothing's worth that. You don't get paid enough."

He closed the door, leaving Sara alone in the hallway. The silence returned and hung thicker than coal smoke. The twins, who had obviously been eavesdropping, cracked open their door to see the English teacher, wondering why her eyes were bloodshot when she passed them, her face twisted with the irony of James Brown's "Payback" playing from a radio.

"Good morning, Ms. Foster. How are you today?"

"I'm fine, thank you."

Sara smiled for the girls despite herself and walked toward the laundry room, relieved to find it empty. She closed the door behind her and stepped inside, sinking into a pile of sheets and towels, too tired to care they were filthy and stained. She permitted herself to cry against the spinning of the washer for all the things split and swelling inside her, not only her lip, but her heart, as well.

꙳

She found the Swedish woman sorting mail on the bed. It was dark again. Night. The usual bottle of wine open and empty by nine. The TV was on, the VCR running a video of *Thelma & Louise* in Hungarian. The nurse spent most of her time watching movies since Sara had given her the VCR. Sara didn't want it in her room. She figured the refugees could use the distraction from whatever pain, real or imagined, they presented, seeking another bandage or aspirin, or any combination of a bedside manner the nurse guaranteed them. She kept a jar of salty licorice in the shape of small fish by the bed. It was empty now, the glass pawed by the many fingers that had handled it that week.

The Swedish woman, taking one look at Sara's puffy eyes and swollen lip, set the mail aside and lifted the lid off the jar, offering licorice and a tissue.

"It's free. And Gabor only touched it once."

Sara forced a smile and laughed quietly. Her voice hoarse. She was getting used to smiling despite herself. She dabbed her eyes with the tissue, smearing mascara on her cheek. She took the licorice and popped it in her mouth. No sooner did she begin to chew than she spit it on the floor.

"What the hell?"

"Tastes like ammonia, eh?"

Sara scraped her tongue with her front teeth, trying to remove the bitterness. "You call that candy? It could clean a toilet!"

"Works like a charm."

"It's horrible."

"Sure. But it makes everything else taste better."

The Swedish woman smiled, teeth gleaming blue from the flicker of the TV. She was proud of herself. The trick had worked on Sara, too, keeping the tears at bay. She soaked a cotton ball with peroxide from the bottle on the shelf behind her where a small Swedish flag stuck out of a blue vase beside a button that read YOU CAN TELL A SWEDE. BUT YOU CAN'T TELL 'EM MUCH.

"He finally got to you."

Sara nodded.

"His music," she said. "It keeps me awake."

"Not Milan. Gabor."

She handed the wet cotton to Sara, curious. Nine weeks. No tears. The camp had not yet broken her, unlike the other teachers who had come and gone. Something had hardened in Sara. The girl was stronger than the Swedish woman thought, determined, it seemed, to stay in control, to fight her tears and only then in the privacy of her own company, much as she herself did. She knew Sara smoked not because she liked it or was even addicted to the tobacco. Not now. Not after two months. She smoked because it kept her from crying. It was hard to smoke and cry at the same time. She had tried it once and choked.

The Swedish woman dabbed Sara's lip with peroxide, wiping away dried blood on the cotton. "Rough day?"

"It's becoming a habit." Sara sat on the edge of the cot the Swedish woman had set up for the nights when she wasn't crossing the bridges, listening to the music.

"He's jealous," she said.

"Who?"

"Gabor."

"Of what?"

"He wants you to pay attention to *him*. Not Milan."

Sara scratched her neck, pricked with goose bumps. "I don't owe him a thing for bringing me to this hellhole."

"That's the point."

The Swedish woman looked down at Sara. The girl's face was twisted with frustration, pinched, it seemed, by every indignity she had witnessed or endured at the camp. That she would blame Gabor was natural. She had done so herself.

"He owes *you*," the Swedish woman said.

"For what?"

"Staying."

"What's that got to do with paying attention to him?"

"He wants to know you appreciate what he's done to make you comfortable. To keep you here."

Sara laughed. "That's perfect logic. Ass-backwards as everything else. Have you taken a whiff of the hallway lately? They've pissed on the plants and that rubber palm tree. I've seen better behavior in a zoo. At least a zoo is worth the price of admission. Don't hold your breath on me staying."

"It's not about endurance, Sara."

"Oh, yeah? Then what is it? What keeps *you* here?"

"Respect."

Sara dunked the word back into her throat as if it were a stone. She could not believe the Swedish woman had not learned the same lesson. "Whose? The refugees?"

"Yours."

The Swedish woman locked eyes with Sara. She took out a cigarette and sat on the bed opposite Sara, picking at the tobacco. Her nails, glossy with red polish, galloped nervously across her lap.

"The truth is we stay because it makes us feel good. We both know we can't expect respect from the refugees. Most of them wouldn't be caught dead volunteering here or anywhere if you asked them. They don't understand why people like you and me leave perfectly safe countries, good lives, lovers, and jobs to end up in places like this. Of our own volition. The reward? A shot of self-respect. Most of them had it before they crossed the bridge. They didn't need to give up something or leave their countries thinking they could save the world. You see, we're here for us. Not them. All this altruistic bullshit. I never bought it."

"You help people here. I don't."

"Depends. Anybody can do my job. It doesn't take Mother Teresa to work at a refugee camp."

"They need you."

"Sometimes. I guess. I help them with their wounds," she said, then whispered, "but they're really helping me with mine. They heal the wounds I don't see."

Sara picked bits of cotton off her lip. She lay on the cot and stared up at the TV, watching the movie. "I don't know why you're worried about respect. You chose to be here. I didn't."

"But you're a teacher. That's respectable."

"How? I don't even know what I teach. Or who."

"Maybe the only person you're suppose to teach here is yourself," the Swede said, offering another cotton ball. Sara waved it away, rolling on her side, reaching into the Swedish woman's pocket for a lighter and cigarettes. The Swedish woman said nothing. They had developed this ritual, sharing things without speaking, a hairbrush, ponytail holders, a pot of lip gloss. Clothes. It was as if they wanted to share what they had with each other, knowing they could never share enough with the refugees. They had both been blessed by the privileges of their passports and had in many ways shared the guilt of having too much. They did not speak about home life. Nothing more than cold facts. They withheld the details, trying instead to inflate the fiction of the life inside the camp, a life more real, it seemed, than the one they had left behind.

Sara tossed the cotton ball into the trash can beneath the Swedish woman's desk. "How long did it take to get used to the nights?"

"I'm still trying. It's been four years."

"I'll be lucky if I make four months."

The Swedish woman replaced the lid on the glass jar, setting it on the shelf, blowing dust off it. "You might surprise yourself."

Sara leaned back into the pillow, the down goose feathers bunching like a soft hand behind her head. She blew smoke across her chest, watching it curl into the dim light of the bulb overhead. The Swedish woman turned up the volume on the TV. The Hungarian voices sounded off, too high-pitched for the low, sultry tones of Geena Davis and Susan Sarandon, whose throats, rubbed raw by Wild Turkey, had grown coarser with curse words. It was the middle of the movie, Louise at the wheel of a mint-green '66 T-bird convertible, racing down the freeway after Thelma robbed a convenience store.

The Swedish woman clapped. "Must be something to be on the run. I don't know any women like that. Do you?"

Sara nodded. The movie had been released during Sara's junior year. As much as she loved to see movies alone, she feared it was the male-basher everyone criticized. The head of Women's Studies made it mandatory and part of the final exam for everyone in the department, even those like Sara who opted to take the course as an elective. But Sara aced the exam. She understood Thelma's journey. It was complex in its simplicity, which is why she believed nobody had understood it. Callie Khouri didn't write a male-basher. She wrote a story about a woman surviving. Sara had cut off the sleeves of every T-shirt she owned after seeing the movie, starting a small fad on campus. She never intended to make survival a trend. It deserved more permanence.

The Swedish woman turned to Sara. "What's it like in Texas?"

"Big. Hot." Sara nodded.

"You like it?"

"It's home, right?"

The Swedish women puckered. "Takes a special person for heat." The Swedish woman took out her cigarette and exhaled, waving the letter opener in her hand as if to move the smoke around. "It's really that hot?"

"Scorching."

The Swedish woman pointed to the TV. "No wonder Louise hates Texas."

Sara flicked the lighter, trying to get it to work. No matter how many times she tried, there was no flame. The Swedish woman took it and lighted it instead. Sara leaned into the flame, drawing in the smoke when the Swedish woman pointed to the boxes beneath Sara's cot. Her finger jabbed the air, accusatory and curious.

Two boxes sat unopened beneath the sagging mattress. A third had arrived today as the others had the last week of the month. Each box was postmarked from Fort Bragg, North Carolina. Care packages from the PX. American-flag stickers covered the brown paper with smiley faces drawn in pen.

"If you don't open them, Gabor will."

"You can have them."

Sara sucked on the cigarette. The Swedish woman could see the hollows of her cheekbones. They sloped elegantly down her face but looked bruised in the light. The Swedish woman took the boxes from the bed, propped them on her lap, picking at the packing tape. "Three packages in three months. That's a record. Your father must care a great deal about you."

"Mark's my cousin."

The Swedish woman shook the boxes, rattling the pastel Styrofoam peanuts Mark always used to pack them.

"They're heavy," she said. "I can tell a lot of care went into them."

"Depends on what kind of care."

"You kidding? Trust me, Sara. A care package is a gift around here. A rare gift. Don't let the refugees catch you with anything unopened. They'll start to wonder. Think you're spoiled or ungrateful or something. The only packages I've received here are bags of frozen blood from the Red Cross. Not exactly *care packages*."

Sara turned, taking a compact mirror from the milk crate beside the cot. She opened it and studied her lip, picking at the scab forming. She needed ice and stood. "Go ahead. Open them."

"Aren't you curious?"

"I know what he sent."

Sara looked into the mirror, seeing the boxes balanced on each of the Swedish woman's knees. Mark had been sending care packages to her every month since she had left for college. A new destination would not change their content. Mark had sent German chocolates from his posting in Munich, advent calendars with marzipan and chocolate figures behind each window in December. Spices from the Middle East. Jumbo jelly beans from San Antonio with pot holders the shape of Texas. But Sara didn't cook. Not when she was studying. When Mark remembered where she was in the semester, he stuffed the boxes with macaroni and cheese, packets of hot cocoa and instant oatmeal—apple cinnamon, Sara's favorite. Everything was instant inside the boxes, and what Mark wanted in return for his care was Sara's instant approval. She knew the packages Mark sent every month, every year, were not sealed with care but apology.

Sara snapped the mirror shut. "Take it. Take everything."

She felt her lip burn, swelling. She motioned to the Swedish woman to open the boxes and instead of watching, shifted her gaze to Geena Davis driving circles around some beer-bellied trucker who had honked, cat calling from the window of his tractor trailer, mud flaps glittering with metallic Playboy insignia.

The Swedish woman hesitated, then seeing Sara gesture with her hand, she sliced through the packing tape with the letter opener, popping open the boxes. They had been packed so tightly that the foam peanuts jumped out and scattered on the floor. The Swedish woman dumped the contents on the bed. The usual. Everything Sara had expected. And a letter. Sara didn't turn to see.

"You're not even curious?"

"I'm not a big fan of surprises." Sara felt the thick envelope at her back.

"He wrote you."

The Swedish woman pressed the hard card against her, insisting Sara at least turn to take it, but she remained motionless, eyes fixed not on the TV, but on the pastel peanuts littering the floor. She searched for something lost.

"Aren't you going to read it?"

Sara turned. She took the letter opener from the Swedish woman but instead of using it, tore off the top with her fingers, leaving prints on the paper, expensive ivory linen stationery. She pulled out the card. An invitation to Mark's wedding. She read the announcement over and over as if she were not getting it the first time, the words blurry. She used her finger, tracing the loops in the calligraphy, making out the date and place of the ceremony. West Point in July. He wrote a postscript.

Would she be his woman of honor?

"What is it?" the Swedish woman asked, searching Sara's eyes. They had clouded over, more puffy than the moment she walked into the room. "Looks like an invitation."

Sara nodded. She bit her lip, out of habit, not feeling anything this time. Her body numb with the news. "Mark's getting married."

She blurted the words, firing them from her tongue with a hot breath still bitter from the salty licorice.

"A wedding? You act like somebody died."

"Not yet," Sara whispered, moving toward the door, the jumble of thoughts churning in her stomach, making her steps heavy and slow. She paused at the threshold, feeling the hot, dry air move past her from the radiator.

"Heat," she said, and glanced one last time at Louise.

The Swedish woman looked up at the screen then back at Sara, whose face had drained, the already pale skin nearly alabaster in the light. Sara forced the words.

"The heat is not why Louise hates Texas."

～

Sara unlocked the doors of her closet to find sneakers with soles not yet outworn and left the camp running with her pockets full of money. She stayed on the east side of the river, passing the refugees, refusing their offers to join them skating, following instead a sinuous path through Csokhid, beyond stranded gondolas and boats, abandoned restaurants and cafés, awnings studded with icicles. It was as if the whole town were frozen in its slumber and Sara ran faster, louder, wanting desperately to wake it up, if not for the people who lived there, then for herself.

The sun had slid into the hills, stretching Sara's shadow across the ice in the river. She raced the silence, trying to outrun it, to shake it loose from her ears, but she carried it with her even when the camp appeared as a small box on the hill. She raced herself, snapping frozen stalks of dead grasses like glass tubes beneath her feet. She felt heavy, sluggish, impacted by the sense of another world closing in on her. A world both unfamiliar and uninhabited, no more lived in than her room.

She had not exercised in three months, and her lungs felt as if they were expanding, exploding, expelling all the blackness she had sucked into them. Her legs throbbed, too, pounding the earth, filling with lactic acid. She wore only her jeans and a thin cotton sweater, wishing for once to numb herself with the cold, to freeze the turmoil in her heart. She felt at her back the edge of Mark's invitation dig into her. She had not expected to receive the invitation now. Not yet. Mark had met the woman in Iraq. A nurse in his division who neutralized the burns of chemical warfare. It's not that Sara didn't approve of her. She hardly knew the woman. She seemed nice enough. She had a nice smile. Came from a nice town outside Boston suitable for a nice Irish Catholic family. Her name was Michelle. Youngest of six. Mark had described her in letters and sent photos that did not match. Pictures ready-framed with magnets on the back reserved for refrigerators or filing cabinets, places of highest visibility, places that had the power to remind. Sara's remained empty. She had not pulled the photos from their boxes. Mark had sent enough to fill a small album. When Sara asked to see the photos Mark had sent to her parents, they pointed to a single postcard taped to the center of the freezer. Sara wondered why Mark had made her the recipient of the photos for no other reason, perhaps, than his fiancée looked just like her, only brunette.

Would she be his woman of honor? Sara Foster, the only woman, the first in her family to be a groom's woman. She would stand beside the cadets from West Point, saluting her cousin's new life and bride, the woman who would make him honorable. There was a perverse audacity about the request, and it seized her left side with a cramp.

Sara stood by the river, trying to catch her breath. Her legs shook as if the ground kept moving, but she was standing still, her breaths exposing her in the dark. The taillights of a stranded Trabant blinked red from a snowbank, windows fogged from the breath of lovers. U2 played from the car radio. A song of love and regret off *Joshua Tree.* Unspoken apologies. Unheeded concerns. Mark loved this album.

Sara squeezed her hands, trying to get the blood to circulate, the thump of the bass in her fingers and toes. She felt a quickening in her heart, a series of contractions, quick and tight. The song triggered something familiar and comforting despite the pain. She had felt this before, but in a lesser degree when she received the rejection letter from Harvard. She had stood beneath the halos of a streetlamp in the rain, watching her dream dissolve through the paper. She had felt then as she did now, unbalanced and lost, yet hopeful that she would recover with a lie. She believed only a fool accepted defeat. She kept her wits about her. Her chin up. She had moved forward with no regard to the consequences of lying, unharmed, unchanged. But Mark's request triggered everything the lie didn't. It shifted the center of her spirit, knocked her to the edge of something she was afraid to enter.

For weeks now, Sara had made concessions, confessing to herself the true reasons she had come to teach English, not believing anymore that it was entirely Harvard's fault. Her need to leave her country, her family, and the systems that expected so much of her had little to do with acceptance into law school and everything to do with the rejection of her past. Disillusionment had served a function. Sara had begun to look beneath the lie, turn it inside out, see it for what it was. She felt a gradual split. Some unsolicited force at the camp had amplified the inner voices she had silenced. The constant chatter unnerved her, and no matter how hard she tried, she could not remove herself. Speed was no defense. She could not outrun the voices now.

She felt as if her heart would explode, suddenly and unexpectedly outgrowing its chambers, divesting itself from whatever had stunted it, the stony memory still lodged there.

She looked out across the river, wishing for the island of her childhood and a chance to talk to her grandfather one more time. She wanted to hear from him that everything would be okay. She wanted to take comfort in his rituals, to wake to the smell of bacon and eggs from the double burner in the fishing cabin. In the mornings, he would sit in his swim trunks on the edge of the dock with his coffee, waiting for Sara to join him and cross the river to watch the sun rise from a small island he had named after her. He told her that every girl should have an island. He had carved her name into a maple tree that he planted there because it matched the color of her hair. Then he made her a crown of red leaves and placed it on her head and made the island hers. He told her the island would always hear her heart when she forgot to listen and that it was as much her gift to visit the island throughout her life as it was her duty to remember why she was there. On the anniversaries of his death, Sara had made a ritual of crossing the river to the island at night to sit under the maple tree and watch the river flow, feeling safe in the darkness from the things she did not want to see in the light but heard inside her heart.

She cursed the light that slipped inside the sliver of moon, shining, outspoken against the stars. Standing there on the frozen bank, Sara knew no other place for her heart to hide than in the darkness of Hungary. She had been given one too many nights to think about what she would lose when she met herself alone, unannounced, springing like a cat from the feral shadows of secrets. It was here by the river that Sara Foster felt closest to a language she could still not reach but trusted was hers to speak.

Sara grabbed her throat and pressed down on the skin, hoping to keep herself from getting sick. The smell of sulfur oozed from pockets in the river where locals had broken through the ice to soak in mineral baths. She hated the smell, not because it reminded her of rotten eggs, but because it smelled of fireworks. Celebrations of any kind unnerved her. Sara picked up a stone by her foot and tossed it into a hole in the river, half terrifying herself when a small fox slid across the ice and jumped through the bushes beside her. The animal, although injured and hopping on its hind leg, hurried past, looking back as if it expected her to follow.

She ran after the fox to the hill overlooking the train station, where it nosed its way through snow drifts to a camp of gypsies sleeping in a huddle beside the tracks. Coal smoke had thickened the horizon and stubbed out the moon, making it difficult for her to see. Sara post-holed, knee-high, jeans soaked, each step an eternity to the next. She stopped by the boxcars where the gypsies breathed dreams, breaths rising above the great plain.

The fox circled them, sniffing, turning over an empty jar of pickled sweet peppers. He found nothing but stood looking up at Sara. Food was not his reason for being there. He took off, hearing the bark of a German shepherd that paced the platform of the station, leaving Sara alone with the gypsies as if he knew she needed to find them.

Sara had heard the gypsies play music from the train station, violins and accordions conducting the symphony of strangers passing through Csokhid. They came from Bucharest to hustle socks they had stuffed inside duffle bags that doubled as pillows, keeping their heads above the snow, hands covered with one of many pairs they hoped to sell in the morning. But Sara had no need for socks. It was the violin she wanted. She needed music to lose herself within the soft walls of the notes where she had no name, no past. She knew that each time she had listened to Milan play, she reinvented herself with a new face and a new language. How she would manage to take the violin, even if the gypsies accepted her money, was a matter complicated by the fact that gypsies, she believed, depended on music more than they did on money to survive.

She studied their faces, dark skin wrapped in wool. The Asian eyes sloped with lines that aged them young. One hundred kilometers from Bucharest. One thousand years from India. She could not tell from their hands whether or not they were fortune-tellers or beggars, coppersmiths or fruit pickers. Musicians, yes. An accordion tucked beneath an arm. A tambourine propped against hips, heels stacked against each other, soles touching, each a bookend to the other. She marveled at the way they slept, lashes fluttering and laced with frost, holding hands, wrapped in the cocoons of their safety and truth. Theirs was the embodiment of humility and danger, a life exhausted by their quest for refuge. They were passionate survivors.

She approached them slowly, cautiously, unprepared to explain herself if they should wake. They did not move. Their breaths curled into the cold night air. The German shepherd barked against the movement he smelled but could not see behind the boxcars. Sara paused, wondering if the dog would find her first. Her heart pounded. She did not have much time. She moved closer to the youngest, a boy whose tiny fingers were wrapped around the neck of the violin. A bow lay beside him on the ground.

Sara dug inside her front coat pocket and took out the money, rolling it into a thick wad—the only money she had brought with her to the camp. Roughly one thousand dollars. She crouched in front of the boy and pried his fingers gently from the violin, replacing it with the wad of bills. He opened his eyes and for a moment Sara believed he would scream, but he drifted back to sleep. Sara folded the boy's hand against his chest and took the violin and bow in her own, zipping them inside her coat, unabashed by the act. It was the first time she had stolen anything. The gypsies, she believed, would understand.

↬

Milan climbed through the window in the hallway to the fire escape and stood looking out over the river, wondering when Sara would return. He had seen her from his window leave the camp running. Storm clouds had gathered around the moon, and already flurries softened the twilight. In the air, the smell of *porklot*—stewed onions, peppers, and fish—drifted up from the vents in the kitchen. Milan's stomach growled, but he had no appetite. The seizure still nauseated him. He cursed himself for destroying not only the violin, but also his chances of knowing the girl fully. He could not bear anymore to guess who she was, why she needed his music, but without it she had no reason to see him again. They would resume their anonymity, passing in the hallways without speaking, abandoning the incident in the boathouse to the darker reveries of silence.

It's not that Milan wanted Sara to remember. He would have liked for both of them to forget the seizure, wanting instead to remember the way it felt when he opened his eyes and saw her staring not through or even beyond him like the others who strained themselves to glimpse the demons that possessed him in those lost minutes. He wanted to remember what it felt like to have someone see *him* not an epileptic. Not a freak. In the boathouse, Milan felt visible for the first time in his life. Where sound had made him visible to others who would never see him, the English teacher with the fire in her hair and sad slouch in her shoulders saw what he wanted to see in himself. A man wounded and alone and in need of a connection that music could not provide.

Until now, Milan believed music promised the only true intimacy, but he could not shake the girl's face from his mind. The look in her eyes, wide and spooked and brimming with tears, when he held the cloth over her lip, as if he reminded her of someone she once knew but had not seen in a long time and could not believe she was seeing again in the boathouse. Her body went limp after trembling in a way he presumed had matched his own, and he wondered if he had inadvertently transferred the energy of the seizure to her, or if she had solicited it for some unknown reason. In the darkness, he watched the light in the white of her eyes flicker and fade and felt in her heavy uneven breaths the burden of something that had collapsed inside her. Her lips had gone cold when he touched them, shriveling like flat, blue raisins beneath his fingers, already too warm with her blood to let go.

He had gone to the Red Cross station to check in on her late in the afternoon. The Swedish woman, eyeing him suspiciously, if not without a scowl that made her curious, said she didn't expect to see Sara until the next morning. "I figured she'd be with you."

Milan stared. The words meant nothing in English. The nurse made a gesture, cradling under her chin an invisible violin, playing it with her hand. Milan shook his head and lay on Sara's pillow the bracelet he had braided from the strings of the bow. He wanted to ask the nurse where Sara had gone, hoping that she was not running away from him.

Sara had not shrunk from him in the boathouse the way she had inside the camp, and her shrinking only provoked him to prove her wrong. He followed her to prove that he was incapable of harming her. In their game of cat and mouse, they established a strange dynamic; by avoiding him, she endorsed his power over her, a power he himself was too aware he possessed. She was afraid of him the way children and cats are afraid of things they can't see but sense like ghosts and storms gathering in the distance. His presence, although unwitting, seemed to precipitate a series of events, moments that still scraped and scarred her heart with their cruelties, large and small. He wondered if the heart of the English teacher had been spun from glass, not believing for a moment that the steeliness she seemed to possess around him was not a defense against everything that had made her delicate and fragile. It was as if Milan had caught her in an inescapable moment of vulnerability. Whatever she was running from, he believed he triggered. Whatever he had done, he wanted to undo and make right.

Milan lifted his eyes to the moon, the light already compromised by clouds, hoping Sara would find her way home in the dark. If she did not return by midnight, he would go out to search for her. The flurries fell heavier now, sticking to the cold metal of the fire escape. He climbed through the window and closed it against the wood smoke, hearing an argument in the hallway. Two women, one in a skirt, the other in sweatpants, struggled with a cardboard box bulging with housewares. A small boy in bare feet and threadbare underwear stood under the fire extinguisher, biting his fingers, watching the glass of a picture frame shatter around him on the floor. It was an old photo, sepia-toned with sloppy borders, the image of a happy village family. The women cursed each other and instead of picking up the child, launched into a tirade, trying to find fault. They did not see Milan approach from behind, coming from the opposite end of the hallway, but when he picked up the boy to lift him above the glass, they turned and shrieked, dropping the rest of the box, vases and lamps breaking. The boy began to cry, struggling in Milan's arms, striking him in the shoulder with his fist. Milan quickly set the boy on the floor where there was no glass but did not move quickly enough to avoid the women who had begun to strike him, too. They lashed his back, cursing him, calling him Chetnik. The boy, eyeing a piece of the vase, ran to it, scooping it up, and threw it at Milan's head, grazing his neck, drawing blood. Milan held his hand over the small wound, trying to stave off the flailing arms of the women who had slapped him so many times that their own hands were stinging and numb, voices hoarse from screaming.

"Don't take my son," they repeated in unison as if they had rehearsed it too many times before an unwitting audience. Their voices broke, and when they could no longer scream their plea, they cried it instead.

Milan offered his hand. "I'm only trying to help."

"We don't want your help," the boy hissed, aware he had broken Gabor's rule by speaking Croatian. He clung to his mother's legs, wiping his face in the flaps of her skirt. She smoothed his blond hair and the scar running the length of his back, the skin raw and recently wounded from a bullet or knife, Milan was unsure.

The woman in sweatpants dropped to her knees, raking her fingers through the broken heirlooms with the kind of anguish reserved for mourning. She waved the photo in the air like a flag, eyes dark and glaring, drilled into Milan.

"You Serbs don't know when to stop."

She spoke with a clipped accent, words slicing the air between them. The boy, wary, stepped aside, reaching for his aunt's hand. He stared at Milan with a defiance that reminded Milan of his own, the way he used to look at Zarko for all the ways he had betrayed him. Milan wondered if he had given Luka a photo of himself before he left him at the piano, would he glower like the boy did now? Milan lowered his head, feeling the accusatory stares of the women trying to make him culpable for the things he wished he could not imagine but knew too well had caused the Croats to hate the Serbs. He knew then neither side would win the war.

"What's the problem?"

Milan turned, seeing Gabor approaching with a broom. The women launched into hysterics, pointing fingers. Milan stood still, absorbing the accusation. There was nothing else he could do. The women spoke English, earning Gabor's immediate sympathies.

Gabor shoved the broom at Milan. "When you're done, see me in my office."

He pointed to the door where an American flag had been hung next to the shape of Texas. He didn't need to point. Milan understood him without understanding his language. He recognized Gabor's door because it always remained closed.

Gabor spoke calmly to the women. *"Csokolom,"* he said, greeting them with the Hungarian endearment that translated into "kiss your hand." He lifted the woman off the floor, scooping the boy into an embrace. The boy grabbed the gold cross on Gabor's necklace, staring with a sullen anger. He did not believe it was real or had the power to do much of anything but dangle, indifferent, from the director's neck. The boy began to sob softly, and Gabor, wanting nothing to do with tears or trials, dug into the pocket of his sweatpants and pulled out a chocolate as if it were a bone he kept handy for unruly animals.

"Cho-co-late," he said slowly in English, withholding it from the boy until he repeated him.

"Cho-co-late," the boy repeated, and opened his mouth. Gabor dropped the chocolate on his tongue. The boy's mother reached out and took Gabor's hand in her own and kissed it, bending almost imperceptibly into a curtsy. Gabor gestured for her to follow, directing her and her sister into the stairwell, leaving Milan with the mess on the floor.

Milan began to sweep, the glass scraping the silence. He could not blame Gabor for his apathy. The man, like him, was not interested in the truth. What mattered was to whom it belonged, and they would both shed blood to decide it.

⌇

He set the broom against the wall and closed the door. A young woman, not much older than himself, looked up from Gabor's desk, quickly closing the file of photographs she had been hunched over studying. She wore reading glasses, her blue eyes bloodshot as if she had been there awhile. He recognized her face. She was a poised, striking woman, tall, with high cheekbones and a long, elegant nose that made him uncertain that she was a model, not a nurse from Vukovar who shared a room down the hall with two attorneys, a chemist, and a professor, a common arrangement in the camp. Many of the refugees had been professionals, but they were learning the ropes of becoming professional refugees. The woman with the reading glasses was never without a legal pad or counsel and had taken copious notes on the one beneath her elbow. Her hand slowed but did not stop when Milan entered, as if she could not afford to lose the evidence she had gathered.

"Gabor wanted to see me."

"Yes. He'll be back in a minute," Elana said, gesturing for Milan to take a seat on the split leather club chair in the corner. She had spoken Croatian, and he smiled, relieved to know that they could momentarily indulge themselves with their native language. Milan crossed the room and sat in the chair, the leather squeaking beneath him. Cigarette smoke curled around a lightbulb in the ceiling that cast shadows of brandy bottles and Stetson hats on Gabor's desk, the shadows more prominent than his trophies.

"You work here?"

Elana continued to write. "He needed me to translate," she said.

"I hope he's paying you."

"He can't. It's against the rules."

Milan fingered the brass buttons on the side of the chair, feeling a cigarette burn that reminded him of the piano in his study. He roved the certificates on the walls looking for a reason to respect the man who resided here. "Gabor doesn't strike me as the kind of person who follows the rules."

Elana looked up and laughed. He saw in her quick smile a sadness that lingered in the flatness of her lips as if they had not moved in such a way for a long time. She pulled a pencil from the thick twist in her hair and tapped the edge of the desk. "He pays me in other ways," she said.

"I bet he does."

"It's not like that," she said, pointing to the file. "I get access to this when he's not around."

Milan watched the smile fade. "You looking for somebody?"

"Aren't we all?"

She picked at her hands, raw and chapped as if she had worked too long with a scouring agent or bleach, trying to clean the things that could no longer be brightened.

The door opened, and Gabor, hearing them laugh again, looked agitated, his face pinched by their amusement. Before Gabor could notice, Elana slid the file inside the notebook and lifted both from the desk. She pushed the chair back and stood for Gabor. He marched toward her, suspicious, turning right side up a brandy snifter she had flipped over, capturing a small spider inside the glass. He smashed the spider with the heel of his hand then flicked the dead insect with his finger into the trash. He unzipped his sweatsuit jacket, draping it neatly over the back of the chair and, brushing off the cat hairs on the seat, sat.

"Are they okay?" Milan spoke first. He could not stand the way Gabor was staring at him, anticipating something he could not foresee building between them.

Elana translated. Gabor stared, incredulous. "Who? The women?" he asked.

Elana spoke to Milan. Milan nodded. "Yes. Of course."

Gabor leaned back in the chair, inflating his chest. He pulled out of the desk drawer a half-eaten *Pick* salami and sliced through it with a letter opener, stabbing it, offering a slice to Elana. She shook her head, repulsed, and shifted on her feet. There was nowhere for her to sit, and she stood between them. Milan, noticing, offered the chair, but Gabor objected.

"She's a nurse. She's used to standing," he said. "Besides, this won't take long."

Elana translated for Milan, lowering her chin ever so slightly to acknowledge his courtesy, trying hard to hold back the urge to

challenge the director. Elana did not strike Milan as a person easily defeated or insulted, but Gabor's offense had obviously unnerved her. The veins in her neck throbbed, blood bubbling with
his effrontery. She clasped her hands tightly against her abdomen,
pressing against the nerve he struck. There was something familiar about her long, slender fingers, and Milan wondered if she
had ever taken piano lessons from him, perhaps on a vacation to
Dubrovnik or a week at the summer music camp. He remembered the hands of his students better than the names and faces,
but it was her face this time that struck him most. Something in
her eyes, both haunted and hopeful, made him believe they had
met before.

Milan turned his gaze to the director, who had slid a pair of
keys across the desk. "I found you a job."

"A job?" Milan brightened. He sat up in the chair. He was uncertain of how to react, the news completely opposite of what he
had expected. He had requested the use of a piano to teach at the
camp, hoping eventually to teach at the local schools. He did not
need to speak another language to teach. He could teach music
with music. Gabor had seemed genuinely interested in helping
him, but that was three months ago. Gabor's interest in Milan
waned weekly. Milan sensed a rivalry between them, as if his
music threatened the director's power and position. That Gabor
should display such goodwill now made Milan wonder if perhaps
his judgment of the director had been too harsh.

"You found a piano?"

Elana translated, waiting for Gabor to respond. He shook his
head, unbending a paper clip into a hook. "The job has nothing
to do with music."

When the woman translated, Milan listened intently, trying to
ascertain from Gabor's gestures what exactly he was saying.
Gabor spoke quickly to Elana, telling her Milan's job had everything to do with security reasons. He could not afford to have a
Serb at the camp. He said too many of the Croats had already

complained about Milan, but she knew better because she had recorded most of the complaints in a notebook and voiced them herself. The truth was that the refugees wanted Milan to play inside the camp not the boathouse.

Elana translated only one question for Milan, searching for his eyes in the smoky haze. "Do you like bread?"

Milan nodded. "Of course I like bread. Everybody likes bread. Is that all he wanted to know? If I like bread?"

He stared at her, waiting. Something shifted in her face, sudden dread, as if she were withholding the rest of the translation from him.

She nodded. "Can you make bread?"

Milan chuckled. The idea amused him. "I'm a musician. Not a baker."

Milan looked up at Gabor while the woman translated. Gabor mumbled in Hungarian then spoke English. "He'll learn. The job starts tonight."

Gabor held out the key, waiting.

"What's the key about?"

Milan locked eyes with Elana. She did not answer. She did not have the heart to tell him the truth but gave nothing away in her face. She offered a perfunctory smile.

"You're lucky," she said. "You get paid to leave."

Milan shifted his eyes to Gabor, who had already turned his back to pick up the long scroll of paper spitting from the fax machine. No one spoke, the only sound the paper crumpling in Gabor's lap. Elana crossed to the door before Milan could get there first, picking up the broom that had fallen across the threshold. She sat it upright against the wall and opened the door, ushering in the silence and the cold, damp air from the hallway.

Milan pushed himself up from the chair and crossed to the desk. He stared first at Gabor's back waiting for him to turn, then threw his gaze at the key when the director refused. It was a long brass key, tarnished and worn in such a way that Milan was un-

certain it could open any door at all. It seemed to be the kind of
key for doors rarely used, the kind that remained closed more
often than open. He wondered how long the director had kept
the key in his pocket. If he had always kept it there but had
waited for the opportunity, right or wrong, to give it to Milan. He
wondered if Gabor's intention from the start had been for him to
leave, if he had crossed his name off the list of refugees as he was
doing now from the scroll spewing from the fax machine. How
many names had Gabor determined deserved a bed in the camp?
He wondered who you had to be to earn Gabor's sympathies,
searching Elana's face for another explanation because nothing in
his mind seemed plausible. If he couldn't find refuge in a refugee
camp, where the hell would he go?

Milan took the key and moved toward the door, fixing his gaze
on the notebook in Elena's hand and the file hidden inside it. He
spoke Croatian loudly, defiant, hoping Gabor would understand
everything he meant.

"He doesn't deserve your help," he said.

Elana lifted her hand from the doorknob. "You must understand—"

Milan flicked his eyes at the notebook, disgusted. "That file
must be worth something."

"It is," she said. "I'm searching for my son."

↩

They took Milan's suitcase and patted his body, searching for
guns and knives, and finding nothing but the bottle of barbiturates, gave him an apron and a bar of soap and told him to wash
his hands in the basin, the pipes were frozen. He pulled the key
from the lock and shut the door behind him, staring incredulous
at the workers bent over, oblivious, fists clenched and punching
wads of dough. They swarmed the various stations, pressed
against each other, beaded with sweat as if they were in a gym not
a bakery. They listened to the Rolling Stones from a cassette
player perched in the window, singing along to *Tattoo You,* half of

them tone-deaf, voices as outworn as the tape. They wore faded
jeans and T-shirts, the sleeves cut off. Their arms were branded
with the Chetnik insignia, muscles bulging with scars that shone
in the light, making them appear more like convicts than the conscripts they were.

They spoke Serbian.

"What? Never seen a Chetnik before?"

The young man who had taken the suitcase snapped his fingers under Milan's chin. Milan took off his hat and flicked the
snow from the rim. He noticed the young man had no tattoos or
scars of any kind, but imprinted in his eyes was a rage reserved for
those whose innocence had been compromised without consent.
He seemed angry not for the sake of the emotion itself but because he did not know how else to be. He asked Milan to call him
Ivan even though it was not his real name, he said, as if he had
shamed it. His voice was gruff, scratched by cigarette smoke and
the kind of liquor that could harden even the softest spirit. He
slapped Milan gently on both cheeks, left then right, and left
again as if he had momentarily forgotten how to greet his coun-
trymen with the customary kiss of the Balkans. A slap worked just
as well to express endearment these days.

"Welcome to the jungle," Ivan said, looking out the window,
seeing the taillights of Gabor's Mercedes beat against the snow as
he pulled away from the bakery.

"The guy must love you."

"Who? Gabor?"

Ivan jabbed an elbow into Milan's side. "Yeah. Tough love."

"Love is not what I had in mind," Milan said.

"You must've done something right."

Ivan gestured to the suitcase. "He let you keep your things."

"He took yours?"

"Sold everything we had so we wouldn't buy drugs."

He laughed at the thought, then looked again at the suitcase.
"Lucky you didn't bring any valuables."

Ivan pressed the bar of soap harder into Milan's hand and squeezed his shoulder, directing him to the storage room at the back of the bakery. Milan stepped away from the suitcase, slowly, reluctant to turn his back on it too soon, not knowing if the young man would open it.

Ivan, sensing his reticence, waved his hand. "Go on. It's okay."

"I'd like to take it with me."

"Let it go, man."

"Where do we sleep?"

Ivan lifted his eyes, pointing to the exposed floor joists in the ceiling, the wood sagging. "I'll take it upstairs," he offered.

"You sure? It's heavy."

"Relax, man. I can handle it."

Milan pushed the suitcase along the wall, out of the way of the workers, setting his hat over the handle. He didn't trust that Ivan could carry it up the stairs without help. Milan was used to the weight but not the pain, and he rubbed his lower back when he stood. Ivan stared, inquisitive.

"The hell you carrying in there? A dead body?"

Milan nodded. "Almost."

Ivan smiled, toothless, lips leveled by the sobriety of Milan's response. "Shit. Keep it shut," he said, eyes bugged with an overdose of adrenaline. "We've seen too many bodies."

Milan followed the footprints along the floorboards stamped with flour, avoiding the men who followed him with their eyes. They were young, younger than himself, mostly boys who he was uncertain had lost their virginity. They were thin and cagey and moved about the bakery like wounded birds, hopping on crutches, appendages taped and bandaged. An amputee punched the dough with the stub of his right arm with such blatant abandon that Milan wondered if the boy were trying to recover the feelings he had lost. He jabbed the table even after the dough had been pushed off it accidentally by the man working beside him. A man with a broken leg hobbled by, using his crutches like giant tongs to pick up the dough. He smashed it against the stub of the amputee's arm and stuck a cigarette between his lips, lighting it for the obvious right-hander who had not yet mastered flicking the lighter with his left. They and the others said little, dancing around each other in the dim light of the bakery, performing their odd black ballet, heads bobbing, lips in sync with the lyrics of Mick Jagger blasting from the cassette player. They worked with a feverish pitch, the music turned up, as if by kneading the dough, they were attempting to reshape a part of themselves they wished to change forever.

They had traveled as troops six miles along the Highway of Brotherhood and Unity from Belgrade to Vukovar, not because they wanted to or saw the honor in the journey, but because they did not have a choice. Others had volunteered, the ones who jeered and cajoled them from the tanks they drove through their neighborhoods to pillage and plunder places and people they had no reason to hate before the war. The conscripts had been picked up along the way, plucked off the streets, young and ripe and impressionable. Perfect troops to promulgate Serbian President Milosevic's campaign of ethnic cleansing. Even if they had never heard the term and could not for the life of them wrap their minds around the concept, the intention of the war was to teach them and eventually make it understood and necessary. Where they had never held a gun, they learned overnight. Where they had never killed a human being, the act became as routine as cleaning a magazine to reload more bullets. It was easy to teach a conscript as long as the conscript came without a conscience. But it was a difficult task to convince college students and professionals to decapitate their neighbors, mutilate old men, rape their wives, and torch churches and schools and buildings that had for so long been the pride of Yugoslavian heritage. Slaughter had not been what they sought when they left their villages for an education, and their professors in Belgrade would have agreed, but too many had been killed to comment. And so these young men stood by in a smoky haze of gunfire watching their friends who resisted the call of the Yugoslav Army shot and killed in the streets.

Survival had shamed them. The young men working in the bakery, safe and warm under its roof, had left many people dead and wounded in Vukovar, making them no better than the men who had conscripted them. This they knew and could not change or escape its haunting. They divided the survivors in the bomb shelter, women and children from the men and boys. They forced them to choose Serbia or Croatia as their homeland, then under the orders of the Yugoslav Army, massacred the men who remained, burying them in mass graves outside the city. One of the conscripts, their friend and classmate who would have become a veterinarian, jumped into the pit of corpses before a bulldozer dumped two tons of earth on top as if it were filling a pothole. Apparently he had been forced at gunpoint by a fellow conscript to slit the throat of a Dalmatian puppy and hang it from the rim of a basketball net while its owner, a small girl in a navy pea coat, stood on the playground and watched.

With nightfall came a burden of grief that consumed the young men, not only for their friend who had died, but also for the others who died with him and those who would soon die at their hands. The two dozen conscripts who knew him had made a decision to dodge the draft in his honor. *"Fuck him,"* they said in his memory, cursing Milosevic's campaign of ethnic cleansing and his plan for a Greater Serbia. *"Fuck Serbia. Fuck Croatia. Fuck Yugoslavia."*

They abandoned the tanks and crossed minefields in the snow, running for sixteen hours until they crossed into Hungary. They had been picked up by a trucker from the northern town of Eger, whose passenger was a prostitute from Sophia. She sang to them the Bulgarian rendition of Patsy Cline from the window that opened to the cab. They rode in the back, mounting casks of *Egri Bikavar,* Bull's Blood wine, sharing a huge pot of homemade goulash that the trucker's wife had made for the trip as if she knew he expected company on the road. The trucker delivered the prostitute as promised to Gabor then, at the director's request, drove the conscripts to the bakery when Gabor refused to offer them a bed at the camp. They had been promised food and board in exchange for the bread they would make for him. The conscripts, gracious for a second chance, did not question the fact that most of the bread they had baked was never consumed by the people of Csokhid but disappeared mysteriously before daylight. The bread might not have been eaten, but it was being used.

Milan felt his way in the dark to the storage room, the windows fogged by steam. Hundreds of loaves of warm bread gleamed from the racks like swollen silver bullets in the moonlight. Milan stood next to the window, looking out over the river. The large wooden wheel of the mill sat frozen, cloaked by the naked limbs of willow trees that swayed like skeletons turned loose in the wind.

He pulled out a small stepladder beneath the window and climbed it, bracing himself against the frame. He took the bar of soap and carefully wrote his name backwards in huge block letters across the glass. He did not care much if the men could read it. He wanted Sara to know where he was if she happened to pass the bakery and look up. She had not returned to the camp when he left with Gabor that night, and he had no way of knowing if Gabor would tell her where he had gone and why. He wanted to say good-bye and had checked the nurse's station, finding the Swedish woman and the cook asleep on the floor, arms and limbs entangled in a blanket. No sign of Sara. Where her boots usually thawed, the floor was dry. The bracelet he had made from the bow remained on her pillow. Curled on the cot was the girl in the navy pea coat who visited every night for a story. She had fallen asleep waiting, hands still clutching the book about a hedgehog. Milan covered her with the blanket. It was unlike Sara to abandon the girl.

Milan stepped down from the ladder, seeing in the reflection of the glass something fly across the bakery. The radio had been turned down. There was the chatter of speculation, the men taking bets on something, hooting, hollering, laughing. Milan walked back through the storage room, seeing out of the corner of his eye the very object being tossed through the flour dust—one of his notebooks. It was when he heard the sound of paper tearing from the spiral binding that he began to run.

Ivan was chasing the notebooks from station to station, slipping on the flour-dusted floor, trying to retrieve them. In his attempt to carry the suitcase up the stairs to the loft, the zipper had busted and the hundreds of notebooks stuffed inside fell out, sliding down the stairs. He had tried to retrieve as many notebooks as possible, gathering in his arms a stack of twenty at best, trying to stave off the curiosity of the others. He turned to Milan, offering an apologetic look, sneering at the others who had already abandoned their dough, surrounding Milan for a game of monkey in the middle, making the bakery grounds for the poorest sportsmanship.

Even at the camp, the compositions had remained safe. None of the refugees seemed interested in the suitcase, even when it was opened and they had a chance to see for themselves. Paper and notes. Nothing like drugs or money they had fashioned in their minds when they first saw it. Milan had been careful not to leave the music for too long, lugging it with him when he took his meals alone and ate in the stairwell, flipping through the pages, listening. He had not once anticipated a public flogging of his life's work, not even in Dubrovnik. He stood helpless, eyes volleying the notebooks as they were tossed over his head from one man to the other, the pages sticky with dough and stamped with flour handprints. They flipped through them, looking up every now and then at Milan as if they could not believe he had written the notes himself. He reached up and caught a notebook sailing over his head and dropping to his knees, ripped out the pages one by one, shredding them in halves and quarters until each of the men had stopped.

Ivan ran around to the workstations, collecting the notebooks and delivered them in piles to Milan. "It's okay. They don't mean any harm."

Milan looked up, eyes dilated. He fingered through the bits of paper, the black notes like confetti. Suspended in the air with the smell of yeast was a collective burden he shared with the conscripts. Ivan had seen every one of the workers break at some point, but he had not seen a display of passion as poignant as the composer's.

"You're welcome here. We've all killed somebody."

Milan turned his head. He could barely make out the shapes of the men, crutches and limbs blurred. "I killed none," he said, stacking the notebooks in no particular order, but to order the chaos of the moment.

He looked past the young man, panning the faces of the others who stared expectant if not disappointed by his response. He pressed a notebook against his chest, removing himself from the conscripts' shame. Unlike them, Milan expected forgiveness. He had not killed a man, not exactly, but he had let his brother die. And that was as good a reason as any, he believed, to seek refuge from the past.

༄

Ivan offered to buy the first bottle. The conscripts bought the rest until the wine sweetened the bitterness between them and they were certain that Milan understood his initiation into the vagaries of life inside the bakery. They sat together inside a wine cellar dug into a hillside on the edge of town where locals gathered to hear the owner play piano. It was crowded with men. The Virgin Mary stared down on them from a calendar that hung cockeyed from the wall. The walls were damp and covered with moss and coins that had been pressed into them by those who believed that if the money stuck, they would be back again for more spirits and good times.

A tall blind man, playing an accordian, worked his way around the cellar, lungs expanding like the instrument itself, ribs poking through his shirt when he breathed. The owner of the place got up from the piano and pranced around with a glass wine thief as long as his legs, brandishing it as if it were the wand he needed to cast a spell on his patrons, sensing the tension in the air already. The folk music did not seem to pacify them. They were a surly international crew, tongues twisted with Russian more than Magyar, brows knitted by the intensity of meeting here not for pleasure but for business. Most of them were red-faced and drunk, eyeing each other suspiciously, trying to decipher the odds of deception.

Milan was not surprised to find Gabor of all people, sitting at the center table, presiding over this unlikely summit between the Russians and Hungarians. Milan figured after forty years under Communism, the locals would want nothing to do with red stars and sickles. But Gabor seemed to enjoy the company. He conversed fluently in Russian with an ease that suggested they had been old classmates who had met for a weekend away from their wives. He was in the middle of a joke he liked to tell that illustrated the common image Hungarians held about themselves. "When the carriage comes down the street, it is only the Hungarian that stands there and gets splashed with mud." He could not finish the joke, startled out of the punch line when he saw Milan. He stopped and held his chin, directing his gaze as if he intended to bore holes through the composer. The accordion player stopped, certain from the way Gabor looked at the frail young man, there would be trouble. Gabor stood and squeezed his way through the tables, standing between Milan and the piano.

He spoke instead to Ivan. "I told you not to bring them down here."

"But there's nothing to drink at the bakery."

"I'm not paying you to drink."

"You're not paying us at all, Gabor, remember?"

Gabor sucked in his cheeks, feeling the eyes of the Russians, seizing the opportunity to entertain them, if not impress them with his power over his employees. He spoke English to the Serbs. "Do you know he's a composer?"

Ivan nodded, shifting an apologetic stare to Milan. "Yes. We know now."

"Have you ever heard him play?"

"No. He broke his violin."

"That's too bad. He's very good. So good in fact, the English teacher has fallen in love with him. Ask him if he wants to play for us. Maybe we'll fall in love, too."

"He's drunk, Gabor."

"Perfect. We can have ourselves a little dance."

Ivan turned to Milan and spoke Serbo-Croatian. "He wants you to play."

"Fuck him."

"No thanks," Ivan said, and lowered his voice. "Look, I know you're tired and angry at all of us after what happened today, but I swear to you, you'll never suffer another minute in that bakery if you just do what he asks."

"Why doesn't he play?"

Milan stared at the piano, feeling ill and hot from the wine and the dread of public performance.

"Gabor's got as much talent for music as he does for dressing. That guy wouldn't know how to play if God showed him how. His playing is not the point."

"What is?"

"Those men over there."

"What about them?"

"We work for them. Not Gabor."

"What are you talking about?"

"They own the bakery."

"The hell does that have to do with me playing?"

"They own you, too. They're giving us all refuge."

"Christ," Milan said.

Ivan locked eyes with him, pleading a look that suggested he would explain everything later, but not now.

"Just one song, Milan. Anything you want."

Milan pushed himself up from the table and walked to the piano, pulling out the bench. He did not sit yet but stared at the keys with the same scorn and helplessness as he had years ago under Zarko's direction. Zarko had made the same request. One song. *"Anything you want,"* he had said.

Milan sat on the bench, sensing Gabor's impatience. He watched the director's reflection in the folds of the lid as he had seen the face of his mother's boss twenty years ago. They wore the same expression of impatience and petulance. The story was the same but only the scene was different. Instead of throngs of Russians who crowded the wine cellar, tourists and businessmen had filled the lobby of the hotel Zarko managed and Eva cleaned, eager to hear the boy play. It was Milan's way of thanking them for the exotic bouquets and perfumes they left for his mother from cities she had never gone. The gifts had made her smile, but they did not bring her true happiness. Eva did not smile much since her husband's death. Happiness was hearing her son play, and so Milan assumed the role of making her smile, at least once a day, with the songs he heard in his head.

He performed the sounds of blue from memory not from sight. He could not read music. He could read only comic strips at the age of six, yet Zarko insisted he play Chopin's Etude in C Minor, flinging the sheet at Milan in front of the hotel guests. Milan had frozen. The notes seemed to melt off the page and slide into the cracks between the keys. The music had run everywhere but where Milan had wanted it to run, into a nice neat line that made sense. Milan had not even known which way to hold the music, and Zarko had no trouble showing him, turning right-side up the sheet that Milan had set horizontally on the music stand. Zarko slapped him for making the stupid mistake, believing the

boy should have known better. After all, he was a musician. And real musicians could read music.

Milan, he concluded, was not a real musician. When Milan slipped into a seizure from the blow to his head, Zarko concluded he was not fit for much of anything at all. To call the boy talented was a fictional convenience, he thought. He slammed the lid on his fingers and dismissed him from the lobby, charging him later for the performance he failed to give.

Staring at Gabor in the lid of the piano, Milan refused to suffer the same humiliation and shut the lid over the keys himself.

He turned to Ivan. "Tell him I quit."

"You can't quit. Where will you go?"

"Home."

Milan stood from the piano and crossed to the door, leaving the conscripts to their drunken stupor. Most of them were unaware of the tension in the room and started to sing a song about a hedgehog and a rabbit. He handed the key to the bakery back to Gabor, but Gabor was too stunned to respond. He simply started to sing, driving the composer away with his stale breath and tone deafness.

Ivan followed Milan out of the wine cellar but stopped him by a bread truck parked beside a snowdrift. The license plate was Serbian. "Wait. You need to see something."

Ivan opened the back door, revealing trays of bread. The windows were fogged with steam. He pulled one of the largest loaves off the rack and handed it to Milan. He offered it oddly from the palm of his hand to drive home the point that they were not really employed as bakers. Ivan lifted the top half where the crust had been sliced, revealing that most of the bread had been removed and replaced with the long barrel of a semiautomatic rifle.

⌒

Sara expected to find a hair on the pillow case, a slight dent in the sheet; any sign of Milan would do. The sheets, cold to the touch, were pulled tightly around the mattress with no evidence that a body had ever been there. The bed appeared to be clean and awaiting a new refugee. Sara had seen Vera the "clean woman" walk out of the room with a bundle of old sheets. She returned a week later. The mattress had remained bare and empty, the plastic cover shining like a scar in Milan's absence. Sara faced the other beds, made but empty. She knew very little of the men who slept here apart from the clues they left. Prayer beads hung on the walls above the beds, rugs rolled tightly at the end of mattresses, shoes lined against the walls. She had no idea if the men knew Milan was gone or if they cared. People came and went through the camp. After all, it was a camp. It was not their home. One day they would all be leaving.

"He left."

Sara turned, seeing Gabor struggling to maneuver a middle-aged man in a wheelchair through the door. He was a good-looking man, with full lips, a chiseled jaw, and broad Balkan shoulders designed to carry burdens. He had no legs. Black wool socks had been stretched over the stubs. Gabor squeezed the man through the opening, accidentally jamming his thumb between the wheel and doorframe.

"Shit. They sure don't make it easy to help."

He popped the man through the doorjamb, but the man, understanding English, took it upon himself to wheel to the bed. He lifted himself out of the chair and dived onto the mattress, groaning.

"Sara. Misko. Misko. Sara."

Sara nodded, holding out her hand, exposing on her wrist the bracelet Milan had made for her.

"Welcome to Csokhid. Nice to meet you."

"Fuck you," Misko said, and rolled onto his side.

Sara turned, startled.

Gabor waved his hand. "He's medicated."

"Medicated?"

"War photographer. Went to Bosnia on assignment. Lost his

legs *and* his mind. Can't get a complete sentence out of him but when he speaks, he's got a very good vocabulary. Lots of curse words I didn't know. Maybe he can help you?"

"I know how to curse in English, thanks."

Gabor moved past her and set a bottle of medication beside the photographer. He had already fallen asleep. "Teaching, Sara. I figure you could use some help."

"I'm fine on my own."

"Don't you want a colleague?"

Sara laughed. "For what? To correct papers? Have a talent show?"

"Sure. We could use some entertainment around here."

Sara stared hard. Her voice was cold and void of the sweetness associated with her laughter. "We had it. You took him away," she said.

Gabor turned his back and covered the photographer with a blanket.

"Where is Milan? It's been a week."

"I told you. He left."

"Where did he go?"

"Didn't he tell you?" Gabor parked the wheelchair at the end of the bed and snapped the brakes in place. He turned, face earnest with surprise.

Sara locked eyes with him. "You know Milan doesn't speak English," she said.

"Still? I'm surprised, Sara. You've had such good results with the other students."

"Tell me where he is."

Gabor stepped closer and leaned into her face, seeing himself in the watery world of Sara's eyes. The skin on her neck and cheeks burned red, and her hands were trembling, shaking the plastic bag that dangled from her forearm. Her passion surprised him. She had not taken any particular interest in the other refugees except for the girl in the navy pea coat who came to her every night for a story. But the girl did not threaten Gabor. Nor did her relationship with the Swedish woman. The connection between Sara and Milan knotted his stomach with a disappointment he had never known.

He did not want to hate the composer. In all honesty, Milan had caused little trouble at the camp. He ate by himself. He kept to himself. He abided by all the rules except for the rule of language, and on several occasions had to be reminded to speak English or not to speak at all. Gabor was not even sure he believed the rumors about the composer's past. He seemed too young, too naïve to have ever killed anybody, and he couldn't imagine the man with a gun despite its importance in his culture. Gabor did not hate Milan for being a Serb either. He might have been born in Belgrade, but he came from Dubrovnik. He was a true Dalmatian; however, Gabor wanted to mitigate the tension at the camp, preferring to keep the Croats and Serbs separated in his perfect world, the only world he could create and control.

What Gabor hated about Milan had nothing to do with ethnicity, nationality, age, or experience. He hated the refugee's music because it provided for Sara in ways he could not. Sara needed the music. She did not need Gabor and had left no indication of her gratitude for the things he had done to make her comfortable, to remind her of the status she held over the others at the camp. She confused him lately. The more he tried to applaud her efforts, the more she disappointed him by failing to teach. Her work ethic clashed with the credential she had submitted when she applied for the job. Granted she harbored resentment toward him for taking her from the school in Budapest to teach in the camp. He could handle her disdain and believed it would be only temporary. He thought he had won her over by offering her opportunities to travel, but she refused to accompany him anymore and left him alone on the long drives to his family's wine cellar to contemplate how he could earn back the girl's good graces. He wondered if the opposite tactic would work and considered offending her, scaring her into obeying him and respecting him again.

She was crying now, silent, and wiped the tears from her cheeks, embarrassed that she had cried in front of him. "He was sick," she said.

"They all are. In some way or another." Gabor threw his gaze at the war correspondent who had dozed off to sleep and was snoring.

"He has seizures," she said, rubbing her eyes. "I think he has epilepsy. That medical bracelet he wears. You've read it. You must know."

Gabor backed up and shrugged. "Seemed healthy to me when I dropped him off at the train station."

"Where would he go?"

"Germany. He's got relatives there."

"Or not. He's a Serb."

She knew there had been no trains at the station and the ones that were scheduled to arrive had been delayed by the blizzard, the worst to hit southeastern Europe in a decade, but Gabor failed to consider inclement weather, history, or much of any logic when he fashioned his lies. Serbs would never go to Germany for refuge. The Germans had recognized Croatia's independence. And a Serb from Croatia would have too much explaining to do to evoke their sympathies.

Gabor, reading the accusation in Sara's eyes, threw his gaze at the plastic bag in her hands. She had tried to find the appropriate time to present the violin to Milan, without drawing any attention to herself or the gift. She carried it wrapped in newspapers inside the bag.

"You still carrying that thing around?"

"Gabor don't—"

He slid the bag off her forearm and opened it, peeling back layers of newspaper, revealing the violin to himself for the first time. He crumpled the paper into a ball, tossing it onto the floor.

He said nothing at first, but whistled, holding the violin up to the light, turning it slowly, inspecting it as if he understood its value. "What a pity he forgot it. I'll send it to him."

"You can't. It's mine." Sara reached out and put her hand on the neck, her stare threatening.

"He gave you his violin?"

Gabor let go. He stared at her, stunned and dejected, thrusting his hands in his pockets. Sara tucked the violin under her arm and turned abruptly, refusing to give Gabor the satisfaction of saying no, that Milan had not given her the violin, that the violin was not the point.

〜

Sara paced the river restless and full of his memory. If she could not listen to the music directly, she would try her best to remember the voice within it, tormented by its accuracy and clarity against the snow. The silence at the camp resounded louder and longer with each week that passed in Milan's absence. It had been two months, but the music had managed to loop itself in her mind. She recalled the voice more clearly than the details of his face, too distracted by the skaters who called out to her, inviting her into their dance on ice.

It was Easter. Gabor had dressed in a bunny outfit and was busy escorting refugees to the boathouse for an Easter-egg hunt. The ice glittered with the gold foil of chocolate coins he had scattered that morning in the snow, imbuing the river with the ethereal glow of heaven. Everything about the river that day suggested safety, and for the first time since the refugees had crossed into the camp, Sara sensed a delirious happiness about them as if the holiday marked a point of no return. They skated with abandon if not recklessness, unaware of the popping and hissing of the ice, the sun higher, burning longer. They assured Sara that she didn't need to know how to skate to join them and could walk if she wanted. She stood in a tangle of frozen reeds by the bank and politely declined with a flick of her hand. But they booed and hissed and stomped on the ice to prove its thickness. Even in spring, they assured her the ice would hold her. Sooner or later, they teased, she would have to join them.

"It's your turn."

Sara felt a massive fur paw on her shoulder and turned, seeing Gabor taking off his bunny mask. His nose was raw and red and dripping. He wiped it with the fur on his sleeve and handed her the skates. They were in poor shape with shredded laces and blades as sharp as the edge of a table. That they could dig into anything other than mud would have surprised her.

"I'm fine watching," Sara said.

"You always watch."

"There's a lot to see."

"Sara, it's Easter. Have some fun."

She stared at the bunny mask, trying hard not to laugh. Gabor the sudden philanthropist, an immaculate fiction of the camp. She did not trust his gestures any more than she trusted the river was completely frozen.

"I'm having fun."

"Yes. Like a clown at a funeral. I thought American girls were fun."

"We are. We can be."

"But you are a mud in stick."

"A stick-in-the-mud?"

Gabor shoved the skates at Sara, stuffing a chocolate bunny beneath his tongue. A group of refugees, mostly teenagers, formed a train and skated past them, spraying them both with ice shavings.

"Now that. That is fun."

Gabor waved, smiling, revealing bits of chocolate between his teeth. He pulled the bunny mask down around his face and negotiated the slippery bank in his own skates, stepping onto the ice to chase them. He yelped, gleeful, gliding with them under one of the bridges.

Sara waited until all the refugees had joined the train and only when she was certain they had skated as far as the river was frozen did she bend down and try on the skates. It was too muddy to run today and she set her sneakers aside, slipping inside the skates. She wiggled her toes, feeling a draft where the leather had been punctured. She retied the laces, pulling them tight around her ankles and paused, noticing a familiar tag hanging off the heel. Her mother's writing. Her name scribbled with a grease pencil. She fingered the tag and smiled, amused that her feet had not grown since junior high school. She had grown two inches taller through high school and college, but her feet had remained stunted. No matter how far she wanted to step, it seemed her feet would remain the same. Of all the skates Gabor had found in the heap of donations, he had returned to Sara her own. She traced her initials etched along the blade, remembering they were Mark's gift to her. Her mother came from the south and had never learned to skate. Her father claimed to have lost his balance in Vietnam. It was her cousin Mark who taught her to skate on the river by their family's fishing cabin. He respected the river and the ice and taught her the perils of both. After the canoes were cleaned and hung under the cabin and the inner tubes deflated and the coolers emptied of beer, Mark longed for the freezing of not only the river but also the memories of summer. He taught Sara it was as much the nature of ice to preserve and to protect the delicate life under the river as it was to keep frozen the things that should never move. Mark gave Sara skates to navigate the fragile world of ice and to know its perfect silence.

Sara tucked the frayed laces beneath the worn tongue of the skates and moved slowly through the reeds to the river. Bloated bits of moss and grass floated on the water where the ice had melted closest to the bank. Traces of Gabor's blades had vanished, leaving no evidence that he had stepped onto the river to skate. It occurred to Sara that she had never once watched how the refugees actually got from the bank to the river, especially now that signs had been posted warning of thawing ice. She did not know where to step and did not trust Gabor's path and walked slowly, trying to balance herself on the skates, searching the bank for a place where the ice was thickest. She found a small patch, not more than a meter wide around the docks and held onto the posts, crawling hand over hand, making her way to the ice.

She dug her nails into the wood, terrified of letting go. Her heart pounded. She knew how to skate. She had been a good skater but was surprised that it evoked such fear in her now. She looked up, suddenly self-conscious, feeling as if somebody were watching her from the bridge. A cold wind hissed through the willow trees, but there was no one there. It was quiet and still. Snow started to fall again, powdering the riverbank and the roof of the boathouse. The refugees would be back soon, cold. Sara did not want them to see her, and she stood quickly, remembering to keep her knees slightly bent. She slid each foot forward and back, testing the blades and her balance, talking herself into letting go.

She took a deep breath and pushed herself off the dock, feeling a sharp pain in her ankles. She kept her knees knocked, fighting the urge to fall, and glided slowly to the center of the river into the shadow of the bridge.

She lifted her arms, fingers fanned with snow and unlocked her knees, slowly standing, tucking her chin, allowing her body to turn. She closed her eyes and spun slowly at first, finding her center, then lowered herself closer to the ice. Her heart pounded, and she spun faster to its beating, growing deliriously dizzy and disoriented. She felt the light change, as if a cloud had passed over the sun, and opened her eyes, seeing within the shadow of the bridge the shape of a man looking down on her.

The man lifted his hat and nodded. Sara lifted her arm but did not wave, her body suddenly stiff, overcome by the numbness of the spinning. She did not need to look up at the bridge to recognize the face in the shadow. She knew the dark curls and had held them once between her fingers.

"Sara?"

She looked up at the bridge, expecting to see Milan, but he had already climbed down the bank and was walking across the ice toward her crunching snow beneath his boots. His shadow stretched long over the ice and reached her first, his head at her feet, then beyond her until he stood above her, statuary, searching her face. She had not lifted her eyes to see him, distrusting her imagination as if by looking too soon, he would disappear. And she would have rather not seen him at all than to know she would not see him again. She had tried not to miss him. She had tried to pretend their meeting had not mattered.

She fixed her eyes on his boots, the flour handprints on his pants and coat. He reached into his front pocket and pulled out a loaf of challah bread bejeweled with raisins and dried fruit. He took her arm and cradled the bread in the crook of her elbow, catching on the crust the tear that had slid down her nose.

He leaned in slowly and slid his chin over her head, taking her into his embrace. She felt so small to him now trembling. He knew it was not only her body he held but also all the pain that remained wordless and locked inside her. They did not speak. They had no use for conventional language except to obey the grammar of pain, if only for their own safety. Until now it was the wonder of his freedom, not his safety, that sustained Milan the first month at the bakery. He accepted the key and the money from Gabor with a new attitude, overwhelmed by the possibility of his freedom. He had no identity. He could be anyone. He could be no one. He could be healthy. He could change his name, his hair, his clothes, his posture, but not his past. He wanted to be who he had become when he met Sara. He wanted to hold her as he held her now because Sara made him feel safe. It was Sara, not the camp nor the conscripts, who had offered him refuge.

He pulled her closer but said nothing, snow erasing their shadows. They remained still, his finger tracing her lip and the ghost of the wound that remained. She reached up and caught his hand, lifting it off her face, squeezing the warmth in his fingers before letting go. She stepped back to see him for the first time since he had left the camp. She followed the contours of his bruises, her gaze insistent, determined to find an answer to the blue of his face. He was thinner than he had been when they first met, his jawline and cheekbones more pronounced, but it was the fragments of something deep inside that concerned her most, as if the edge at which he lived had chipped and chiseled the softest places in his body.

She wanted to know where he had been. What he had eaten if anything. Had he slept? Could he sleep? Was it possible to sleep without the music? Because she had not and would not sleep until she heard the music again. She felt the lump in her throat, the urge to scream. Part of her wanted him to leave, to stop reminding her of what she did not want to need. She came to believe he had the power to alter the course of her life, if he had not already. He had touched her and changed her with his music. It had found a way to her heart, reshaping it, changing forever the way she listened.

Milan had reawakened thoughts and feelings, memories that Sara had stifled. She needed him to help her remember everything she had wanted to forget, but she resented her dependence on the music. She felt ashamed that she consumed it as Gabor hoarded English, stuffing herself with the things she needed most to survive.

Sara skated around Milan, defiant, bringing color to her cheeks. It was late, the ice washed pink with sunset, blanketed by snow that continued to fall heavy and fast. She circled Milan once more then stopped, hearing Gabor and the refugees' laughter draw nearer, as if they were privy to a joke that only the river could tell. Sara's heart beat faster as they approached. She did not want Gabor to see her with Milan and panicked, skating off

across the river, searching through the snow for the post of the
dock that would lead her safely to the bank.

It was too white, and she could not distinguish the sky from
the river or see to the other side. She slowed down to wipe her
face, lashes clumped with snowflakes. She dug her skate into the
ice to stop, trying to steady herself, feeling a shift as the ice started
to break. She drew in a breath, unable to scream. Her lungs and
throat tightened, body pricked with adrenaline. Her mind raced,
not with rational thought but the higher order of emotion,
flushed with the terror that she was losing control. There was no
solid ground, nothing to hold, no way to reverse the course of
things. Change loomed sudden and catastrophic. She was falling
through the ice but could do nothing. No thoughts. No breath.
Hands thrust in the sky as if to climb into the white, groping for
a ladder above the darkness.

It was a left foot that plunged into the water first. Then a calf.
A knee. Her right foot. Ankles, toes sinking. Jeans sucked to her
thighs, coat inflated, pockets filled with water. The river conducted its electric current of cold, leaching the heat from her
body, piercing hips and navel, nipples pricked against her
sweater, spine needled. The muscles in her back and neck tingled,
and she felt at the base of her skull a sharpness as if the chill had
drilled into her brain, forging the deepest recesses to shock the
memory into motion. An acute listening, more automatic than
screaming or even breathing, seized her as if she had suddenly
tuned herself to hear more deeply the voices submerged under
water. She heard the refugees' laughter again as her body, com-
fortably numb, slid completely into the river. It was only here, beneath the surface, where Sara felt safe enough to unseal the
memory. She trusted the hand that held her now would not let go.

⤸

It took two signals. He lifted the damp hair off her neck and
kissed her shoulder. She did not move. He twisted her hair into a
rope, squeezing the water from the river over the pillowcase. She

moved, rolling forward to give them space. It was unlike Mark to snuggle. He said he got too hot, even when it rained. He made her sleep on the top bunk, where she could read by the light on the log. He told her to be brave in the storm, to count the seconds between thunder. She counted now the space between the thunder in her heart, feeling his teeth bite the strap of her bathing suit. He told her he was chewing stars earlier from the canoe, but now, lying on top of her, he said nothing at all.

He had been acting strange all day. She thought he was nervous. The senator would be joining them to celebrate Mark's appointment to West Point. There was nothing to be nervous about. The senator played horseshoes. Their fathers would entertain him. Their mothers had made enough potato salad to feed an army, they said, amused by the irony. Sara had been assigned the windows and spent the morning on the roof of the cabin, cleaning spider webs from the skylights. She couldn't understand why the windows had to be cleaned or why the senator would care to look up at them. She wanted to swim instead. Her mother scolded her for being selfish, that this was Mark's day and she should be happy for Mark. She was. Mark knew it. She had made him a photo collage to take to West Point so he wouldn't forget their summers at the river. It occurred to her that her mother was right. Maybe she had been selfish. She wanted Mark to remember her, not the river, most of all. And he would. But not the way she wanted.

She could not see his face in the dark. Only the fireworks outside glimmered in his eye. Flashes of silver and blue, scattered jewels in the sky, eclipsed the darker moons orbiting Mark. She wanted to be brave, but his stare made her nervous. It was unlike Mark not to speak when he looked at her that way, and she was not sure what it meant or why he refused to lift his eyes to the stars beyond the skylight. He focused on the body beneath the swimsuit, the small breasts that had worked their way to the surface, the boyish hips suddenly rounder. His cousin Sara blossoming. Even at thirteen, she had still not recognized her own beauty. He worried that she might never see the woman she was becoming when he was gone, as if it were his duty to show her now. He traced the stripes across her suit with his fingers, connecting the stars one by one like notes as if he intended to play a song on her body.

A warm breeze blew back the curtain above them, ushering in the scent of the apple pipe their grandfather smoked from the porch swing outside. She could hear the flick of his lighter, the tap of a thumb packing the pipe with tobacco. The slow, thorough folding of the pouch, the creak of the porch swing.

"I'm hungry," Sara said, and sat up on her elbows, moving away from Mark, his chest still warm from the sun.

"In a minute."

"We're missing the fireworks."

Her stomach growled. They had swum through dinner. She wanted the cheeseburger left on the grill. Her father had forgotten about it, absorbed in horseshoes, brother versus brother, vying for the ringer, the thud of steel in sand, the clanking of empty beer cans, the fizzle of sparklers dying. The senator's voice arched over them, definitive, eloquent, praising the Fosters like a soap box preacher. Mark would bring the family great honor, he said. More important, Mark would make the country proud.

"Do they have fireworks at West Point?"

"Yes," Mark said, but there was sadness in his voice, and he spoke to her as if he were sorry. He had not let go of her hair, still twisted like a rope in his fingers.

It felt right in its strange way, like a compliment. The kissing gentle at first. Mark's lips on her shoulders and cheeks. He moved over her softly, quietly, slipping his hand inside her suit. She brushed it away, thinking it had been a mistake. They had been close before. Their bodies were no strangers. They had bathed together as children. She knew his body. The galaxy of moles on his back and neck. The bulk of his shoulders and chest from wrestling. She read over the years the network of veins in his arms and legs as if they intended to map his strength. He was taller than her father and his own, well over six feet, with hands that could palm a basketball before he was twelve. He split apples without a knife. His best trick, he said.

It felt like a trick now, his hand inside her suit, fingers pressed against her thighs still wet from the river. A Coke bottle exploded against the cabin from the fireworks, the bygone prank of a brother. Sara tried to wiggle herself out of Mark's embrace, but he bit her lip and stuffed the twist of hair inside her mouth and told her to be still. She nodded, eyes wide, floating above her own body, arms and hands limp as dolls flung over the edge of the bed. She opened her mouth but could not find the words to speak. She knew no language for the pain. Even if she wanted to scream, she refused to let anyone hear her. The shift in her voice was obvious. Silence had struck a deal with her conscience. She wanted to believe that silence would free her, that silence was wiser than truth. Sara Foster wanted to believe that silence would forget, but silence would remember everything.

⟿

It was Milan's hand she felt first when she woke in the morning. He sat beside her, barely drinking coffee, the cup shaking in his right hand. With his left hand, he held Sara, refusing to let go and surrender to the seizure threatening him. He had carried Sara from the river, his body still galvanized by the icy water, fingers and toes numb. He refused to let Gabor or the other refugees help him and staggered with Sara over the bridge, entering the camp alone. There had been a moment when they were both sinking, pinioned by a sheet of ice that had broken free, trapping them under the river. He had held Sara's face in his hand, thumb and forefinger pressed tight against her cheeks, trying to get her to focus, but she had already closed her eyes. He screamed through the water, calling her name until he could not hear himself and could no longer breathe. He had been unable to see above the ice, and just as he thought they might both drown, Milan felt with a foot a sunken post, and stepping on it, dragged her body over the dock, his fingers locked with her own.

The blades of Sara's skates had torn his pants and slashed his shins, the floor splattered with blood and river water. The Swedish woman offered him a cigarette, but he refused, eyes fixed on the goose bumps pricking Sara's neck, the pallid lips. He pulled tighter the wool blanket wrapped around her body. She had already gone through a dozen blankets, her body sucking in the heat from the dryer. She was still cold and shivering, and every now and then she opened her eyes, staring at the ceiling, vacuous, as if she had not quite returned from wherever she had gone since he had pulled her from the river.

Her eyes stung, swollen, and it was only when Milan reached out to dab the tears on her cheek that she realized she was still crying. She had not let go of Milan's hand and squeezed it, turning her face into the crook of his arm. Her mind lingered in a place five thousand miles from the camp, and she was unable to bring it any closer, afraid of revealing the residue of its shame. She did not want to forget too soon what had taken eight years to remember. She was not one to trust memory, her own or anyone else's, but she could not deny the indelible details. She had forgotten nothing. The taste of the apple pipe lingered in her mouth, and her ears popped with fireworks.

She felt the refugees, the room warm with their body heat. They carried the smell of chocolate and Easter eggs on their shirts and coats, breath stale with coffee that wired them to stay up all night. Word had traveled quickly, and the hallway buzzed for hours with concern over Sara's accident. It was the first time she had heard voices in the camp louder than a whisper, and she was pleased to hear the refugees speak their native language. It amused Sara to think that her own misfortune had permitted them to return to themselves, if only for a moment. A good excuse, she thought, for falling from grace.

Gabor, who had not yet taken off the bunny suit, delivered a floor heater and set it beside the cot where Sara lay. He searched the wall for a socket that worked but finding none, paced the room with a brandy snifter, unable to stave off the crowd of refugees who had gathered around the English teacher and blocked the door. He moved around Milan as if he were not there, unimpressed by his heroic deed. He grumbled in English, agitated that Milan had not let go of Sara's hand. He refused to look away, frustrated that he could not determine whose grasp was tighter or who had reached out first. He did not want to believe that Milan had saved Sara. He had tried to skate past Milan and get to her first but had stumbled over the bunny suit. His cheek was swollen from the fall, and he was uncertain now if Milan acted unfairly, perhaps tripping him. Milan had foiled his plan to rescue Sara, and he would pay.

The nurse from Vukovar made her way through the crowd with a tray of hot tea and fresh *popogas,* small biscuits baked with shredded cheese. She paused in front of Milan, locking eyes with him, nodding once to welcome him back.

She lowered the tray and her voice and spoke in Croatian. "You need to leave the bakery."

"You always deliver good news?"

"I'm serious. It's not safe."

"Jesus. What is?"

Milan lifted Sara's hair off the pillowcase and squeezed the excess water on a towel. He did not turn to Elana, but reached out and took a biscuit, eyes fixed on Sara's face, waiting for her eyes to open again.

The nurse from Vukovar leaned closer to Milan. "Don't wait for her."

Milan shifted his eyes, feeling Elana's breath on his neck. She continued, her voice barely audible.

"You have a choice that we don't. You still have a home in Dubrovnik. Go home, Milan."

She held his gaze, trying to tell him more, but Gabor inter-rupted, stepping between them, pawing the *popogas* with the bunny suit.

He cleared his throat. "Are we speaking English? I don't hear English."

"Happy Easter," Milan said, and lifted his gaze to the director. He knew what it meant in English.

"You speak English now?"

Elana cleared her own throat. "No. But he saved your teacher."

She met his gaze with disdain and stepped back into the crowd, carrying the tray high above her head, offering the tea and biscuits as if she were serving hope.

"Good afternoon, Gabor."

The girl in the navy pea coat negotiated the puddles of river water and made her way to Sara's side, staring up at the director with a dimpled grin.

"Is Sara teaching today?"

The girl spoke perfect English. Her accent almost undistin-guished. Gabor nodded and reached out to the girl, removing lint from her collar.

"Will Sara tell a story?"

Gabor looked down at Sara. She had opened her eyes. He spoke loudly as if she could not hear.

"She wants you to tell a story, Sara."

The girl with the navy pea coat slid the book under Sara's arm then sat cross-legged on the floor, staring up at her, daring the English teacher to speak.

Sara remained motionless, gaze fixed on the long crack in the ceiling as if she had fallen through it, not the ice, to land among the living dead. She felt a heaviness as if the missing parts of her had suddenly found their places inside her body. The return had exhausted her. She did not want to tell stories. Not now. Not again. She felt as if every story she had ever known had suddenly become her own. She could no longer separate herself from the characters or the plight of any other stranger. For the first time Sara felt connected to them. Their conflict related directly to her own. The story of the refugees was never hers to learn. She had known it all along.

She turned to the girl. "I'll need some water first."

"Don't you think you've had enough?" The Swedish woman, on vigilant standby, smiled, relieved to hear her voice. She passed the glass to Milan and he parted Sara's lips, giving her a drink.

When she was finished, she sat up slowly and opened the book. The girl in the navy pea coat stood, the room and hallway suddenly quiet when Sara began to read. They did not recognize the sound of her voice at first. Her words were garbled and unfounded as if her voice were trying to find itself. It was only when she lifted her eyes to meet theirs that they noticed the shift. Confidence gathered in her tone, and she no longer worked against herself to defer the things she needed to say. Her voice had been charged with the grace of suffering. She wanted to know what had happened to the refugees and was no longer afraid to ask. Their story was her story. Universal. Complete. What Sara Foster had come to teach the refugees she had taught herself.

⌒

Sara and Milan broke the lock on the boathouse at midnight and stumbled inside, drunk on Bull's Blood and cheap champagne. It was warmer under the cloud cover and smelled of melting snow and earth. A few drops of rain had begun to fall, dabbing at the boathouse windows.

Sara closed the door, peering through an eye in the wood, making sure they were alone. She had been followed earlier. The refugees had refused to leave her, rotating in shifts through the day, bringing her more stories to read. It was as if her voice had permitted them to hear their own, and they continued to listen to one another's stories long after she had stopped reading. A levy had broken in their throats, flushing the silence of the camp, permitting conversation to extend beyond its stairwells.

When they had finally exhausted themselves and left for dinner, Sara stuffed a blanket with dirty sheets to make it look like she was sleeping and led Milan through the hallway with the bag she had kept for him under the cot. He followed her path through the moonlight, crossing the bridge, pausing on the other side to listen to the river. They leaned over their reflections, pressed against each other. Neither spoke. Their reverence was not so much for the power of the river, but for the resolve of the ice that had broken free.

They had entered the boathouse with a reckless levity, stumbling over cans of varnish and paint from a boat that had been stripped and flipped over on the floor. There was no place to sit. Gabor, in his paranoia, had taken all the furniture and boarded up the windows, too cheap to use a lock no stronger than one for a suitcase. He had shut off the electricity too, leaving them in darkness. Milan could hardly find his way to Sara, who had climbed on top of the boat and sat waiting, arms outstretched with the bag. Her eyes smiled and swept across him with the vague hope that he would play.

Milan did not sit. He stood in front of Sara as if they were meeting for the first time. The warmth of her eyes relaxed him, and he saw in the qualities of her face a woman whose courage to trust a stranger had released him from his greatest fear. She was the first person in his life who had been helped, not hurt, by his strength. She had taught him unwittingly to know his power and to use it in a way that would not shame him. Her quality of openness was different from that of anyone he knew, and his heart turned over when she smiled as if he were the only person who mattered.

He reached out and slid the bag off her arm.

"*Hvala,*" he said, thanking her.

The bag was lighter than he imagined. Milan had only

glimpsed the bundle of newspaper, thinking that perhaps it was more wine. They had drunk enough already. He had passed off the rest of the bottles to the refugees who had come to celebrate with Sara, much to Gabor's consternation. They finished a dozen or more bottles, willing to share the hard-earned rewards they had accumulated from Gabor for speaking English. When Milan passed the bottle of Gabor's family wine to him, having not taken his medication since he left the bakery, the director stormed out of the room as if he had been offered poison. Alcohol was not something Milan needed. He didn't care if he had offended Gabor by giving it back, but he did not want to disappoint Sara. He would accept the gift. The conscripts would enjoy it. Maybe they would leave him alone.

He reached into the bag and stiffened. It was not a bottle he gripped now, but the neck of something familiar, the strings pressed against his thumb, the smell of resin rubbing him with a sense of calm. He tore off the newspaper revealing the violin, and stood staring, unable to speak. His lungs tightened. The rush of air escaped in a gasp. Milan was rarely the recipient of a true gift, and he had few occasions to give anything other than his music. The last gift he had been given was his mother's wedding ring the day she was buried. He was six years old. Anton had been careful not to spoil him and gave him the gift of silence, allowing him to listen to the music in his head. But Sara unexpectedly had returned to him his life. She unzipped her coat and reached down the back of her sweater to pull out the bow, waving it in front of him as if it were the wand they both needed to forget this place.

The air moved beneath the bow, the smell of dust and mold stirred up in the dark. Milan caught the bow between his fingers, each of them holding the opposite end, feeling a charge. Sara let go first, encouraging him with her hand and the look in her eyes. There was something custodial about her gaze, as if her offer were conditional. Sara hungered for his music as one hungers for touch.

"Will you play?"

Milan understood her inflection, the supplication in her voice. He set the bow on the top of the boat, hesitant to establish a connection to it. He had never played for a private audience. He traced the body of the violin with his finger, roaming its curves in the dark, imagining Sara. He was uncertain if he could play for her alone. He would have rather played *her*.

Anton had told him once that the greatest instrument in the world is the body of a woman, which is why so many things resemble her shape. That God had created women with such precision to carry the perfect pitch in their voice. Attuning oneself with that voice, he advised, could enable a person to glimpse the secrets of the universe. He said women resonated with the sound of life and that it was the eternal plight of man to try and emulate that sound, which is why, he explained, a man plays an instrument as if he were making love to it, because he was, and would be forever, trying to love it so it would love him back. Anton told him this desire was so intense, it could drive a man mad. Milan had believed him because it was his mother he had wanted to touch with the music. He had spent his life composing what he believed was the sound of her voice, the sound of blue, what he heard when he looked into the water. Since she had died, music was the only dialogue Milan could share with her, what Anton called the language of wombs.

It suddenly dawned on Milan that Sara knew nothing of his past, of his condition, of the reasons for his refuge, nor did he know anything about her own. It was too late for trivia. Details seemed irrelevant and would not make her reasons matter. Pain was enough. She had already conveyed to him the things that words had failed. Her accident had permitted them not only to recognize each other, but also to trust their silence as the necessary and appropriate portal to their meeting now. He slid the medical bracelet off his wrist and slipped it into the pocket of his trench coat as if he were depositing the seed of a voluntary secret.

Then he took the bow and propped the violin beneath his chin and began to play, offering his past to Sara.

He spoke through the violin of the things language had destroyed. His music had recently taken the shape of his dreams, and he played now, certain of its power to restore. Milan wanted to wash away the sounds of war, of prejudices, of everything that had prevented him from loving and being loved. He played first to thank Sara and then to touch her with the intensity and intimacy of sound. He believed the sound of blue was a safe place, a place with no boundaries, no sides, no hate. It took shape in his mind, absorbing him in its drama all over again, his personal confession entangled between the notes. The music did not avoid dissonance but was fueled by pain, retaining a self-renewing madness where his struggles could reside. At the darkest center was the song of a child, alone, scared, trying to make sense of his place in the world where there was no safety and no guarantee that anyone would ever hear him or care to listen.

His were the rhythms of healing. He played as if he were assembling for the first time the pieces of their hearts into one discernible whole. He repeated the song through the night, wanting to hold the look in Sara's eyes long after they would say good-bye. He needed repetition to prove his goodness to her. He wanted to straighten the sad slouch in her shoulders, brighten her eyes, remove whatever had haunted her when she fell through the ice. His music had no power to destroy her past but it could shift her relationship to it, as it had his own. The songs transposed pain rather than mitigating it, allowing it to enter the world again in the form of love. He played for Sara, suddenly aware that his music, like love, was an event of the soul. The sound of blue had permitted perfect strangers to turn toward each other in one measured moment of refuge.

⌒

Sara's peace had come with a price. She had fallen in love with a song. She wanted nothing else and nobody to touch her now and had waited two weeks to hear it again. She had found in the music a precise safety she had never known and desired to be curled inside it forever, as if the music were the womb of the world. She wanted to be left alone to explore its resonating chamber, but this place was not permanent and not without its perils. She could not hide forever. Sooner or later the music would exact its toll. Until now it hadn't mattered to her that she had lived a lie, but the music had moved her beyond the walls of her defenses and confronted her with the choice to honor the life that remained on the other side of her memory.

She clutched the phone in her hand, waiting in the staircase of the camp. It was dark, but she did not bother to turn on the light, knowing it would go off. She had not spoken to her family since the accident.

A woman picked up and cleared her throat. It was Michelle. She spoke above the screech of a siren that passed on the street. "Hello?"

Sara fingered the receiver. It smelled of aftershave. "Michelle, it's Sara."

"Hello? I can't hear you."

Sara could barely lift her voice above a whisper. "Sara Foster."

"Sara. Sara! My god. How are you? Are you okay?"

Michelle sounded sincere, albeit shocked at this hour. Four thirty East Coast time. Sara didn't bother to look at her watch. Impulse, not consideration, drove her to dial and then hang up. She could not find the words to answer Michelle. Only *older* came to mind. It was not Michelle's voice that spooked her. It was the man snoring beside her. Sara did not want Mark to ask her the same question. She wasn't prepared to answer him honestly. Not now. Not yet.

She placed the phone on the receiver and walked through the hallway and paused, seeing beyond the front doors of the camp Gabor gathered around a group of young men with a suitcase. They were wearing white aprons, and their pants were dusted with handprints. They talked frantically, waving their arms around, pointing at Sara. They swung at Gabor, and he picked up the suitcase and lugged it up the steps of the camp.

He was sweating when Sara met him at the door. "Don't you ever sleep?" he asked.

"I'm not tired."

"Christ. No wonder."

Gabor pulled out a handkerchief from his pocket and dabbed under his chin and forehead. His hands were shaking, and he seemed distracted. "You should sleep," he said.

He reached out and touched her cheek.

"You're losing color."

"I'm fine, Gabor."

"You need another sweater? I have more."

"My sweater's fine."

"It's old."

He hooked his finger in a tear at the shoulder seam, inspecting the quality of the garment, as if he had made it himself and was embarrassed at the shoddy workmanship. He had been acting peculiar ever since the accident, treating Sara as if she were more of an invalid than the amputees. She appreciated his concern but did not like his doting and tried her best to avoid it, pinching herself to bring the blood to her cheeks and appear healthier than she felt. But Gabor knew better. She was quieter than she had ever been, distant if not aloof. She had grown paler, wandering around the camp, pressed against the windows, staring out at the river, waiting for Milan to cross the bridge.

Gabor set the suitcase on the floor. He flipped the handle with his thumb, back and forth, staring at Sara.

"You going somewhere?" she asked.

"Not yet."

"Whose bag is it?"

"Milan's."

Sara directed her gaze past him through the doors. Her eyes brightened. "He's coming back?"

Elana had told her about the bakery. Sara took a bus to the edge of Csokhid to see it but walked home, trying to digest everything she had learned. The young men living there had made her so uncomfortable that she had no desire for the tour they offered. Sara wanted to know if Milan was working, but they laughed and said he hadn't worked in a week. They weren't sure where he had gone and presumed he had met a girl. He had talked about her in his dreams, they said, pointing to Sara, identifying her as the girl with the fire in her hair.

"He's gone," Gabor said. He chewed his bottom lip, tearing off a bit of dry skin.

Sara eyed him suspiciously. "Where. Germany?"

Gabor straightened. "No, Sara."

"He never went to Germany."

The disappointment in her voice unnerved him, and he felt the blood coursing through the veins in his neck.

Sara glimpsed for the first time the scramble inside Gabor, his confidence crumbling. He could hardly maintain eye contact and shifted his gaze to the blinking lights on the palm tree. The baby Jesus had been replaced with a wood carved figure of the crucifixion.

"He's not coming back, Sara."

"He came back before."

Gabor crouched, the fabric of his pants gathering in a bunch at his knees. He lay the suitcase on its side and unzipped it, lifting the cover to reveal the hundreds of notebooks inside.

Sara huffed, unimpressed. "We need clothes not notebooks here." She was disgusted by the timing. It had taken five months for school supplies to reach the camp.

"The music is not for the refugees."

Gabor took one of the notebooks and opened it, tracing the letters in the title. He didn't understand Elana when she had translated the words, thinking at first she meant the color of blue, not the sound of blue. He didn't think it made sense. Elana told him it was not meant for him to understand. Gabor passed the notebook to Sara. She stared, incredulous, tracing the jumble of musical notes with her finger, not wanting to believe what she knew was true.

"He left *The Sound of Blue* for you."

"What?"

"He calls his music *The Sound of Blue*."

"You didn't steal it?"

Gabor dropped his voice, stunned by her accusation. The music had no meaning to him. He wanted to prove to her that he was incapable of such a petty crime and pulled his fist out of his pocket, unfolding a letter first then his fingers, revealing a pair of eyeglasses, the frames bent, lenses split. He took Sara's hand and pressed the letter into her palm, depositing the pieces of the glasses on top. The rims were covered with mud, and she could see grass stuck at the bend in the frame. Gabor held her arm. She was shaking and stiffened, feeling a rod drive deep into her heart.

She curled her fingers over the letter. "Where is he, Gabor?"

"I don't know, Sara. Nobody does. Those young men found the glasses by the river this morning."

Those young men are conscripts, she thought. Those young men have killed people.

Gabor scratched the stubble on his chin. He had not shaved or slept in days, eyes bloodshot and bruised from lack of sleep. His forehead was carved with the lines of worry and what appeared to be genuine concern, but Sara did not want to believe him. A lie would have hurt less than the truth. Gabor zipped the suitcase shut then carried it to Sara's room and slid it under the cot. He could not bear to see her cry and left her alone in the hallway with a letter whose words had no meaning to him.

〜

Sara searched the camp for the nurse from Vukovar, hoping she could translate. There was not much written. Only a few sentences, penmanship hurried, sloppy as if it were written by a man on the run. The nurse's roommates directed Sara down the hallway to the bathroom, rolling their eyes. They were surprised Sara of all people didn't know Elana's routine by now. Sara was the only other person in the camp who slept as little as the nurse.

Sara paused in the doorway, watching Elana bent over the sink, wringing excess water from a white T-shirt. The lights were off, and a candle flickered from the shelf above the sink, rosary beads dangling, a crucifix made from the broken blades of ice skates. Elana mumbled prayers, hanging the child's T-shirt on a wash line strung across the bathroom crowded with other small T-shirts and pairs of boy's underwear. Same size. Same threadbare condition. The T-shirts were so thin that Sara could see the nurse's face through them as if she were a ghost. She turned, startled, hearing Sara close the door and unfold the letter.

"I didn't mean to scare you."

Elana turned off the sink and flicked water from her fingers, wiping them on the sides of her jeans. She spoke English. Her accent softened the language and made it easy to listen. "What are you doing up?" she asked Sara.

"Worrying."

"That makes two of us." Elana lifted her chin, eyeing the letter. "Good news I hope."

"I don't know. I can't read it."

"Who's it from?"

"Milan."

"Love letter?"

Elana's eyes beamed, and she ducked beneath the wash line, crossing toward Sara, meeting her like a teenager in a high school bathroom who skipped class to share gossip and the woes of womanhood. She took the letter from Sara, reaching behind her to turn on the light. She read it once, then again, making sense of the message, uncertain how much Sara needed to know.

Sara picked her fingers, nervous. "I don't want to know if it's bad."

Elana nodded, throwing her gaze into the cracks between the tiles as if they contained the words she needed to translate. "He wants to thank you."

"Thank *me*?"

"You helped him."

Elana read from the letter:

> *By the time you get this, I will be gone, but you will not be forgotten. I will carry for the rest of my life the burden of regret for not saying good-bye. Perhaps it is because I fear that if I saw you again, I would never leave you until you left me. And you will leave, you must leave, because this is not your home. We will all leave at some point, but saying good-bye is not a useful word in any language. There are no good-byes really and no true endings. I should like to say hello to you instead because my life has only just begun. Before we met I believed I could go anywhere in this world and still be a stranger because I had no country. But you took me to a place I did not have the courage to wish for. I did not find refuge at this camp. I found it in you.*

Elana looked up, folding the letter, handing it back to Sara. She dabbed the tears staining Sara's cheek, her fingers smelling of bleach. Sara covered her eyes with her hands, embarrassed, biting back the urge to scream. She did not understand the tone of the letter. There were too many questions raised, too many answers she believed she would never know.

Her jaw stiffened, and she squeezed the words through her teeth. "What about the music?"

"He wants you to keep it."

"Why?"

Elana paused, glancing down at the letter. She folded her elbows, bracing herself and Sara against the truth. "It's the only way you could leave with *him*."

Sara slapped the wall, turning off the light, leaving them in darkness again with the flicker of the candle. It was too bright, too much to see. She turned her back to the mirror, crushing the letter inside her fist and hurled it against the stall door.

Her voice broke. "You helped *me*!"

She pounded the door and slunk onto the floor, clutching her knees to her chest. "I was suppose to thank you," she said over and over until her voice grew hoarse.

The nurse approached her slowly and picked up the letter, uncrumpling it, smoothing it against her arm. She spoke calmly, trying to get Sara to breathe. "When did he write it?"

Sara rocked back and forth on the bathroom floor. A cold draft blew down from the window around her ankles. She lifted her eyes. They stung even in the darkness.

"I don't know. Nobody's seen him since the accident."

"What about the bakery?"

"I went again this week. He wasn't there."

"Does Gabor know?"

"Gabor gave me the suitcase."

Elana swallowed, crossing herself. She held out a hand and lifted Sara off the floor. "Get up. You'll catch your death down there."

She led Sara to the sink and dipped her hands in the basin of bleach and water where the boy's T-shirts were soaking next to a Wonder Woman T-shirt. Elena hadn't noticed before because Sara rarely smiled, but she glimpsed in the mirror one of two dimples hidden inside her cheeks.

"One of my heroes," Sara said.

"Me, too. I never believed she could lose her power. Lucky find. I bought it at the market."

"In Csokhid?"

"Somebody was selling old clothes from their car."

"Guess that's a theme around here."

"Selling clothes from a car?"

"Giving away the things that matter."

Sara threw her gaze into the sink, rinsed her hands under the faucet. The spigots spit chunks of rust from the pipes, but she had grown used to it by now and did not flinch, her mind drifting. Elana clipped the Wonder Woman T-shirt on the clothesline above Sara's head.

"What are you going to do with the music?"

Sara turned off the water and leaned against the sink, bracing herself against the inevitable answer. She could not keep the music. It was not hers. "Take it back where it belongs."

"Where? Dubrovnik?"

Sara nodded. Elana laughed at the absurdity, but her lips quickly flattened. She read in Sara's face a determination she had not seen before, not even when she attempted to get the refugees to memorize an original poem in English. She had spent one month preparing for a public reading only to find out at the last minute Gabor forbid them to speak about the war.

"You can't just go to Dubrovnik, Sara."

"Why not?"

"Because it's not safe yet."

"And this place is? I want to know what happened. Did he ever talk to you?"

"Yes. We spoke a few times."

"Why did he leave Dubrovnik?"

"He's a Serb, Sara."

"So?"

"Any Serb knows it's not the wisest decision to stay in Croatia no matter how long they lived there. Just like no sane Croat would take chances living in Serbia."

Sara locked eyes with her. "I don't believe he came because of the war."

"What?"

"He came for refuge."

Elana brushed the hair from her eyes and laughed. "What's the difference?"

"You don't have to escape a war to be a refugee."

Sara crossed her arms against her chest, feeling the draft from the window. The nurse stared, inquisitive, handing Sara a towel. "You love him, don't you?"

Sara said nothing and dried her hands, refusing to acknowledge the question. She scanned the clothesline.

"You love him, too."

"I don't love Milan," Elana said.

Sara poked one of the boy's T-shirts with her finger. "Your son. I thought I knew all the kids here."

"You do."

"I've never met your son," Sara said.

It was the nurse this time who threw her gaze into the sink and the dirty T-shirts soiled with fresh grass stains. She sighed and let out a breath, her thin shoulders rising and falling beneath her blouse, suddenly exhausted, the veins in her forehead more pronounced.

"Where is he?" Sara asked.

"I don't know."

"You don't know?"

Sara swallowed, feeling her stomach knot, knowing too well the answers to the questions she had not yet asked. She did want to know the name of Elana's son, because she could not bear his reality, that he had, at one time, worn all the T-shirts hanging above them, playing, singing, living his life as a child. Sara asked nothing more about the boy, not even how Elana and he were separated or why. She remembered the Swedish woman's rule to avoid details, that details can be deadly, the one rule Sara obeyed.

Sara took one step toward Elana and reached out to embrace her, hugging as sisters do after a long separation. She recalled the moment she had met the nurse, the woman with the child's suitcase decorated with dancing bear stickers from the Grateful Dead.

Sara understood now why Elana had held on to the walnut tree outside the front door of the camp, reluctant to uproot her past. She felt Elana's heart pound, her body heavy with regret. Sara lifted her eyes to the boy's clothes, wondering if by honoring this ritual the nurse had somehow restored the emptiness of her son, as if by filling the huge cavity in her heart she had made God more real and had kept her son alive.

∽

Sara walked along the river, passing local fishermen who smoked, the bank muddy and sucking her feet into the earth. The river was brown and swollen, the great plain soaked in spring. She stood by a willow tree and waved to the fishermen. They had gotten to know her over the weeks, not because she wanted to join them fishing, but because she wanted them to tell her all they had caught.

"Csok hol?"

"Csok hol, csokolom."

Many fish. That's all she wanted to hear. When they offered her the fish in their buckets, she declined, pacing the bank behind them, scanning the river with an eagle eye. They had offered her an apple box on which to sit, sensing she was not interested in the fish they had caught but the other things that had not yet surfaced. These men with the fur caps pulled down around their faces reminded her of her grandfather, and she felt comforted by their tiny gestures to welcome her with this rite of spring. She could tell them she taught English at the refugee camp but could not tell them much else, her Hungarian limited to civilities and formal greetings. She was relieved they could not speak to each other because she did not want to explain to them her reasons for watching the river.

It had been three weeks since Milan's disappearance. No word from the men at the bakery. No word from the local police. She had met with several officers, trying her best to explain to them that a man had been missing. When she told them he was a Serb from Croatia, they wished her good luck, then asked her, in English, to teach them the rules of American baseball. She left the station and did not return. She avoided Gabor's daily updates and tore up the notes he had left on her pillow, distrusting his sincere effort to locate Milan. Apparently Gabor had received a tip from the police in Dubrovnik about a local disc jockey, an older man named Anton, who had worked and lived with Milan. They told him Milan had no parents, no family. And no, they had not been killed in the war. He was made famous not for the music he wrote but for the reason why he composed it in the first place. From what they knew, Milan had been an orphan most of his life. His father had been killed. His mother had drowned. They weren't so sure Milan had not caused both of their deaths. He was dangerous, they said, and confirmed the rumor that he had killed a man.

The fishermen knew nothing of this, although they could sense that Sara was deeply troubled. Dark clouds had gathered over the river, and a heavy rain began to fall. The fishermen collected their rods and tackle boxes and ran to the road, lifting a small white Trabant out of the mud. They called out to Sara and offered a ride; they were going to the market to sell the fish, would she like to come?

She understood their gesture, pointing excitedly to the fish, making the money signal by rubbing their fingers together. They honked when she did not budge, waving their arms frantically when lightning flashed and struck the roof of the boathouse. Sara prodded through the mud to the road and climbed inside the car before the next jolt of lightning struck the willow tree where she had been standing. She closed the door with the flap of her coat stuck in the jamb, and the fishermen took off, flipping on the radio to folk songs.

They parked behind a series of flower stands and vegetable stalls draped with garlands of red pepper and garlic. The market was busy and festive despite the storm. Local villagers squeezed themselves against the aisles, hoarding the dry places, stepping away from the rain gushing over the awnings. The children of farmers who had come to help played games of chicken, daring each other to step into the storm. The air crackled with electricity.

Sara climbed out of the car, following the fishermen through the market. They gave her a newspaper to cover herself, and she pulled it over her face, feeling her cheeks burn when she passed the gypsy family. They did not see her, too frantic salvaging socks and stuffing them inside the duffle bags. The fishermen paused in front of a mobile café, offering to buy Sara coffee and a croissant, but she was too distracted to drink or eat anything.

Sara saw behind the flower stand Gabor's blue Mercedes and the girl with the navy pea coat shoving his daughters against it. The girl shrieked.

"Excuse me."

Sara dropped the newspaper on the ground and stepped into the rain, working her way through the stands toward the car. She did not take her eye off the girl with the navy pea coat who had grabbed what appeared to be a necklace around the oldest daughter's neck. She pulled her to the ground into a puddle that had formed over a drainage ditch clogged with cherry blossoms and broken twigs. The girl lay helpless, pinching a bloody nose.

The girl in the navy pea coat looked up, half relieved half terrified to see Sara. Her face was scratched, and she had sunk her teeth into her fists, silencing herself, too embittered to cry. Sara crouched beside her, lifting Gabor's daughter out of the ditch. The girl's eyes were glazed and dry, too traumatized to cry.

"What happened?"

Both girls understood her question and began to shout at each other, soliciting curious passersby who crowded into the narrow space between the Mercedes and a bread truck, volleying for position, not to help, but to watch the fight continue as if they had waited all morning for a spectacle. Sara tried to stave them off, holding up her hand. She knew only one word in Hungarian more powerful then the worst curse word in English and taking a deep breath, shouted *Kus!* above the girls' argument. The girls stared at her with huge eyes, baffled by Sara's perfect pronunciation of what translated into *"Shut the fuck up."* It worked. The passersby got very quiet and slowly dispersed. Sara lifted her face to the sky, grateful for the rain that fell harder now and drove away the crowd. Gabor's daughter stared dumbfounded, still numbed by Sara's vulgarity.

Sara directed the question to the girl in the navy pea coat. "What happened?"

The girl spoke in Croatian, quickly, breathless. She poured out her language as if a great dam had been broken, cheeks flooded with tears. She lifted her eyes to Sara, begging compassion, her hand clenched and shaking.

"Give me your hand."

The girl lifted her hand reluctantly, hoping she could trust the look in Sara's eyes. Sara lifted the girl's fingers, one by one, revealing in her palm the gold locket she had worn the first day of the camp. Sara rubbed the girl's initials engraved on the heart.

"Your puppy?"

The girl nodded, wiping her drippy nose into the crook of her arm. She looked on, expectant, as Sara opened the locket. The girl gasped. The picture of the Dalmatian puppy had been replaced with a photo of Gabor and his family. Sara turned to the oldest daughter whose sister was wiping the blood from her nose with her sleeve. Both girls held Sara's gaze, neither speaking, waiting it seemed for a judgment of sorts. But there would be no judgment.

Sara's stomach churned. Gabor had stolen the locket from under the girl's nose the first day of the camp as if it were his right to help himself because he had agreed to help her. That he should endow his position with dirty privileges did not surprise Sara now. Gabor's twisted logic and morality had been merely harmless, a pathetic attempt, she had thought, to exert his power and control over the refugees and herself. But it was not the locket that sickened Sara most.

She stood, clenching the locket in her fist when she looked into the trunk of the Mercedes. Stacked in piles as neat as a department store were women's and children's clothes, patterns and brands she recognized because they had been her own and those of her neighbors and friends and family. Elana's Wonder Woman T-shirt suddenly made sense. She wondered what other items she could recall from her own wardrobe and tore through the clothes, checking labels, identifying brands that had not yet reached the former Communist Bloc. The jeans were gone, of course. They earned the highest price. The refugees had requested jeans, but they would not be wearing jeans or any items in the trunk.

Sara fingered through sweaters and skirts, feeling duped, manipulated, taken for granted. All this time she believed that customs was taking too long. Gabor assured her that the clothes would arrive. He had asked for her patience. She had backed off, gave customs time, and waited. Gabor delivered the ice skates, making it appear they had arrived in another shipment. Sara opened the box herself, trusting the clothes would arrive soon thereafter. And they had. But not the way she intended. The only person to benefit from the donations was Gabor, and Sara was uncertain that he had the heart to share anything that wasn't stolen.

Gabor's oldest daughter remained on the ground, quietly sobbing, cowering by the rear wheel as if she knew, before Sara did, the significance of the clothes in the trunk—the clothes her father had told her and her sister to sell, the money of which had been stuffed under his seat. Gabor had needed an airline ticket but had refused to tell the girls where he was taking them, promising it was a surprise. They had never been on a plane, and the idea of travel excited them. They were told not to tell their mother. The trip was only for a father and his daughters. They were to sell the clothes on Tuesdays, because Sara taught English Tuesdays. She would not be at the market Tuesdays and would not see the clothes. But it was too late. Sara clenched her fist, the locket pressed against her palm and stepped closer, hovering above the trunk of the Mercedes.

Sara slammed the trunk. She took the hand of the girl with the navy pea coat and looked down on Gabor's daughter. Sara tried to find the words to explain to the sisters that the locket was not theirs but belonged to the girl in the pea coat. She wanted them to know this girl had nothing left of her world other than this tiny piece of gold. Sara took the girl's hand and walked toward the bus stop to wait in the rain for a bus, she hoped, that would take as long as possible to deliver them to the refugee camp.

↜

Sara did not knock. She opened the door of Gabor's office and crossed the room, dropping the locket into Gabor's lap. His back was toward the door and he was hunched over the fax machine, the room thick with smoke from the cigarette burning in a large glass ashtray. The Stetson hat had been dusted and taken off the bookshelf, sitting prominently on the desk next to Gabor's passport. Plane tickets lay beside two cuff links molded into the shape of Texas.

Gabor turned, catching the chain of the locket between his fingers. He let the fax machine spit pages of photos, more refugees crossing the border. He seemed uninterested now that Sara stood between him and the smoke, demanding an explanation. She did not bring any clothes from the trunk. She didn't need them to make her point and waited for Gabor to speak first.

"Things get lost," he said.

"It wasn't lost. It was never lost."

Gabor took the cigarette. It had burned to a stub, but he smoked it anyway. "It's not like you think," he said.

Sara shifted her eyes to the floor, seeing the faces of the refugees from the fax machine. Gabor pushed the pins on his cuff links and lowered his voice.

"I found it."

"You stole it."

"She shouldn't be reminded of her past!" Gabor cried.

"Why? You think it will go away if she ignores it?"

Sara pulled the cigarette from Gabor's mouth and stamped it out on the desk, burning a small hole in the thin maple veneer, wishing it could have been his heart.

Gabor straightened, the chair creaking. He locked eyes with Sara, seeing for the first time not sadness nor frustration. Rage rippled through her face and neck, and he swore he could hear her heart pounding against the ticking of the wall clock.

Sara picked the locket off the desk and opened it, peeling out the photo of Gabor's family. She tore it in half and deposited the pieces into the ashtray, feeling neither shame nor regret for her choice. She dug in her pocket and pulled out the front key to the camp and lay it on the desk beside the cuff links, wondering how many other English teachers had done the same.

"I'm quiting," she said.

"Quiting?"

Gabor sat up, his neck red with surprise. He chuckled, nervous. Quitting seemed a preposterous choice for Sara. She was not the kind of girl who quit. Gabor rubbed the twitch from his eye.

"You're quitting because I took some old necklace?"

Sara shook her head defiantly. "No."

"Because I lied about Milan?"

"No. I'm quitting because *I lied.*"

"You lied?"

Sara picked up the tickets from the desk, reading the destination: Dallas, Texas. Jesus, she thought, recalling the flight attendant's first warning to doubt what she saw in the great plain of Hungary. But she didn't doubt any of Gabor's reasons for hiring her. He had never needed an English teacher, at least not for the camp at Csokhid. He wanted a Texan, somebody he would know, somebody who would owe him the same hospitality and make him feel comfortable in a land he had never been, nor would ever be, a land so foreign that it existed only in the avenues of his mind. The Texas he had wanted to visit was not the Texas Sara knew. She stared at Gabor, the portly man in a jumpsuit, the lone action hero who had delivered her to this dark place in order to rescue her from it. She understood the complexity of his affection and doting. He could take as much as he gave to her. And he had given her a lot because he expected as much in return. It was not her youth or access to the mind she possessed that he wanted. He wanted Sara to deliver him to a new life, a life he truly believed existed and had fashioned for himself watching reruns of *Dallas.* Gabor had faith in the refuge he imagined she could offer him in America. He could start over. Build a business. Build his honor. Seeing him now, Sara recognized the unstable facade of a man who composed a life of illusion.

Gabor swallowed. His mouth was dry, and he unscrewed the lid on the *palinka,* pouring himself a glass. He did not bother to wipe off the spider's leg still stuck to the rim and raised the snifter to his lips, hands trembling, throat clenched, choking off the urge to cry. He drank the brandy in one sip, chin wet with dribble. He seemed so small and alone to Sara in the ring of his dark carnival, cowering in the chair, shrinking from the glare she willed herself to soften. Sara actually felt sorry for him, and she wondered how it was possible to forgive his fantasy, realizing what Gabor deemed precious was more precious than truth. It wouldn't matter to him now or later that she lied.

"I'm not a teacher," she said. "I never was."

It was then she glimpsed the photo of herself that she had seen photocopied and tacked to the bathroom wall. Gabor had kept on his desk the original photo inside the envelope from which it had been sent. The return address was from Fort Bragg, North Carolina, written in Mark's tiny block print. Neat, pressed, as if between the words he still had something to hide.

Sara turned and crossed to the door, closing it on the absurdity one last time, seeing Gabor slumped across the desk with a hand on the Stetson.

~

The refugees had cut Sara's hair, dividing the six-inch pieces among themselves, trusting she would return. They had gathered in the nurse's station, arguing over her safety, trying to convince her not to cross the border, that there would be nothing in Croatia that she needed or could possibly want. She listened to them but dismissed their caution, unwilling to compromise. She did not believe the fisherman who had found a white raincoat floating in the river. The refugees delivered it to her, trusting she would have the sense to accept Milan's inevitable death, but she denied any connection to the composer. There were a lot of white raincoats in the world. She refused to believe this one belonged to Milan. It was too dirty, she said.

"Did you see the way he kept his bed?"

When she began to give away all the things Mark had sent over the months, the refugees had no choice but to accept that she was leaving. They sat with her quietly the last night, singing songs she had taught them, dancing as they did the first night. They insisted Sara take a picture of herself with each of them. She had only enough film for one picture, and it was with the nurse from Vukovar. Elana stood with her now on the platform of the train station, listening to the gypsies play an accordion, unwittingly serenading Sara's departure. The music reminded Sara of everything she had not understood about Milan but was determined to learn. She stood with his suitcase and a backpack, staring down the tracks at her shadow, trusting they would meet again.

5

〜

Sara followed Mirada through the streets of Dubrovnik, lugging the suitcase and backpack, trying to keep up with the old woman. The sun had set behind Fort Bokar, the huge stone coronet on the hill that separated the old town from the newer neighborhoods of Dubrovnik. Men in uniforms swept rooms in the fort, preparing stages for the upcoming music festival. They waved their brooms at Mirada, and Mirada waved back, crossing the drawbridge above the old moat, passing beneath a semicircular tower where the city's patron Saint Blaise stood guard since the sixteenth century. Beyond the second arch, children gathered around the Italian masterpiece Onofrio's Fountain, a huge circle of medieval faces etched in stone. The children sang under the direction of nuns.

"Orphans," Mirada said, slipping into a blackened alley. Sara turned sideways to fit the suitcase and backpack through, chasing Mirada up a narrow flight of stone stairs to Prijeko Street, passing the old synagogue, the second oldest in Europe. Mirada made the sign of the cross at every blackened wall and crumbled roof, setting upright potted plants of rosemary and lavender, lining them along the steps of her neighbors.

"Very sorry," she said, taking full responsibility as if she were apologizing for a messy kitchen, a stack of dishes that had sat too long in her sink. Chaos betrayed the strict uniformity of Dubrovnik. Never before 1991 had the city been attacked, staving off foreign invasion for thousands of years. It was a mercantile power, the paradigm of diplomacy, at once its own republic. Now sandbags and planks had been placed strategically over doorways and fountains. Street lanterns swung in the breeze, impatient for glass and electricity.

"Shit."

Sara tripped on a cobblestone, smacking her hand against the wall of a corner store Mirada had entered. Schoolboys stood outside unloading pallets of fresh figs from a hand truck.

"You walk fast."

Sara set the suitcase down and turned, seeing the boy who spoke. In any other country, he would have been a high school student, eighteen, tall and thin, wearing a soccer jersey. He was an amputee and balanced on his right leg.

"We're in a hurry," Sara said, although she didn't know why. She wiped the hair from her face and shook the sting out of her hand. The student stared at her, shoulders scrunched around his ears where the skin was slashed and scarred.

"You see sniper?" he asked in English knowing she was not from there because of her red hair and fair skin.

Sara turned.

"What?"

"We walk only fast when snipers watch."

"Are they?"

She didn't want to know, but the student looked at his leg, grinning, as if he had outwitted them by surviving.

"They *always* watch."

He looked up, shooting a finger in the air, pointing at Mount Srđ rising to the east of Dubrovnik. He tossed a handful of figs to Sara. She reached out and caught them, the skins warm and soft between her fingers.

"Thank you."

"Cigarette?" he asked, cupping his hands.

"I don't smoke," she said although she wanted to. She would have done anything for a cigarette but had vowed to stop when she left the camp. She didn't have to talk when she smoked. She didn't want to talk now.

"No smoke?"

"No smoke."

The student's eyes opened wide, incredulous. "Where from you?"

"Far away," Sara said softly, feeling like she stood on the other side of the moon.

"How far?"

"Too far."

They stared at each other, neither budging. Sara smiled. She didn't want to speak anymore, reveal anything to the student. She could have been English. French. Irish. Swiss. Canadian. Right then she wanted to be anything but American. The accent was always a dead giveaway, and she had learned to speak slower, without as many colloquialisms or verbal phrases, taking out the local color, numbing her tongue with the monosyllabic. In the last five months, she had learned the art of saying everything without words. A gesture meant more than a sentence in any language. She smiled a lot. There was diplomacy in a smile.

"Nice hair," the student said.

"Thank you."

"I see?"

He hopped toward her and reaching out, lifted a curl from her shoulder, red hair the object of intrigue to the Balkan people.

Mirada walked out of the store with a loaf of bread and cheese. She barked, cursing the boy in Croatian. He immediately dropped Sara's hair, the curl heavy and warm against her neck like the breath of a warning.

⟿

Sara had followed the old woman from the bus stop, trusting her more than the other pensioners vying for business. Mirada had not pushed Sara. The old woman stood by a pear tree in bloom, watching, waiting for Sara to make eye contact with her. Mirada nodded once, recognizing not the girl, but the suitcase. Sara nodded back, closing the deal. Mirada was one of many widows gathered at the bus stop to meet backpackers seeking the comforts of the Dalmatian Coast, travelers naïve enough to believe the war had passed over Dubrovnik.

Sara had stood with the suitcase on a shrapnel-studded sidewalk, sharing a grilled ham sandwich with a young Czech couple she had met on the bus.

"You students?" the vendor asked.

"No," Sara said, realizing it was the first time somebody had asked her this since graduation. She wished she could have said yes, that the safety and security of an ivy-draped campus awaited her return.

"Don't you know there's a war going on here?"

Sara nodded, reloaded the sandwich with sweet peppers, but the Czech couple swallowed and spoke emphatically.

"We know."

"So what? You thought you'd visit?"

The Czechs answered in unison, rehearsed, as if they'd been asked this question a thousand times in two days and had already grown weary of it.

"We thought it'd be cheaper with the war."

Sara turned and stared at them.

The street vendor shook his head, offering a napkin. "What a bargain," he said.

The Czech couple grinned, proud of their frugal trip to the Balkan Riviera. The cerulean dream of the Adriatic was all theirs, and you could see it in their eyes, begging the vendor to offer tips on where to eat, what to do, which islands he loved the most, if Corfu was worth the twenty-four-hour ferry ride or if the six-hour boat to Bari, Italy, would allow them to buy more shoes.

The vendor ignored them and looked at Sara, trusting she was wiser. "You, too?"

Sara looked up embarrassed, playing with the handle on the suitcase. She had rehearsed the many ways she could explain the story along the bus ride, but no sooner would a thought emerge when the bus banked sharply to the shoulder, dodging pieces of mortar or boulders that had slid into the road after an explosion. The bus drivers drove at night without headlights to avoid sniper fire. No speed limit. No stopping. Sara traveled eighteen hours tucked into a ball, wedged between the seats. Plastic Fanta bottles with the lids cut off lined a crate at the back of the bus for those who dared to urinate. The Czech couple managed to take advantage of the small luxury, cheering quietly when they did not splatter the floor. It was a game to them, the mastery of which came not from skill but the willingness to risk. But Sara had already taken her risks crossing the border into Croatia.

The vendor stared at her, waiting for an answer.

"I thought the war was over here."

The street vendor arched an eyebrow and scanned Mount Srđ, the rocky outcrop above the city where the Yugoslav Army, mostly Serbs and Serbian Montenegrins had taken over Napoléon's Fort, blasting to bits the huge cross there.

"The war just began," he said, and laughed.

Sara played with the straps on her backpack, confused. The shelling had stopped in Dubrovnik, but the war had moved north and east into the mountains of Bosnia-Herzegovina. She knew the Yugoslav Army continued to occupy the resort town of Cavtat and Konavle, the Dalmatian pastoral south of Dubrovnik. The Croats who lived there had fled into the old town, seeking refuge in local hotels, but the city appeared to be quiet and safe. The last missile hit the old town in December but now in May, repairs had already started. Some of the roofs had been patched. You could still see the scarred buildings, the holes in the walls, the pockmarked streets where bits of shrapnel peeled back the pavement, but life, although far from normal, had resumed. The outdoor market was small but fairly busy. Advertisements for the summer music festival had been posted around town, and in the air lavender drifted through courtyards. The streets were wet with salt water dripping from bikinis hung out to dry. It was Mediterranean, hot and sultry. Hardly a setting for a fight of any kind.

Sara finished the sandwich and crumpled the waxed paper into a ball, tossing it into a wire basket beside the street vendor. The Czech couple unzipped the back pocket of Sara's backpack and deposited a card with the telephone number of their pension. The street vendor saw it and laughed.

"Good luck calling," he said.

"Don't the phones work?"

"You'll be lucky if you get soap."

The vendor lifted his eyes to the telephone poles on the street. The wires had been shredded, dangling like leather fringe from an outworn folk costume. The Czech couple rolled their eyes, gathering their backpacks to board the bullet-riddled shuttle bus that had pulled into the parking lot.

"You have friends here?"

Sara nodded.

"You do?"

The Czechs wanted the address, hoping for a free meal or a room, but she didn't have an address.

"Your friends Croats?"

Sara shifted, pressing her heel against the curb. "Serb."

"Give a call," they said unfazed. "We go dancing."

Sara waved while they boarded the bus.

"Your friend Serb?"

Sara turned to the vendor. He shot her a look of perfidy, as if by mentioning the word *Serb* she had breached an intimacy. Serbs were the minority in Croatian Dalmatia, especially in the Catholic city of Dubrovnik.

"He was," she said, feeling her throat tighten. She turned the toe of her shoe into the sidewalk.

"He Croat now?"

The vendor laughed at the absurdity, lips flattening when Sara locked eyes with him. There was a desperation about the girl, and he could tell she was trying hard to fight the tears welling in her eyes.

"He was a student of mine."

"Student? *You* teacher?"

"English teacher," Sara said, surprising herself. "In Hungary." She had not intended to tell anyone here.

The vendor wiped the corner of his mouth as if he had left a bit of food but had not been eating. He stirred a trough of pickled onions, his jaw tightening. "We speak English," he snapped. "We do not need English lessons. We need country."

Sara stared at him, nodding. She understood his anger and frustration, how her job had offended his integrity and intelligence. She wondered where he had come from. Which village on the map had been burned? If his village was big enough for a map, if it mattered. She knew the heart of a cartographer suffered politics, that the street vendor's village, wherever it was or had been, could vanish without warning or compromise in the Balkans. That the vendor found refuge along the Adriatic coast, especially Dubrovnik, was not surprising. Refugees from the coastal hamlet of Cavtat, formerly Epidaurum, settled the city in ancient times. Its motto *libertas* welcomed those who believed in freedom.

"Your Serb friend. Here he lived?"

"His whole life."

"No home for Serb," the vendor said.

Sara followed the street vendor's gaze toward the bus driver who stood outside tossing a bucket of rainwater on the windshield. The residents of Dubrovnik had learned to collect rainwater as priests collect alms, bathing once a week at most. Clean windows, a luxury in war. The vendor's sharp eyes softened, voice calm but pained.

"Tell him things very dirty now."

Sara nodded, silent. She'd be lying if she said yes. The vendor gave her another sandwich, wrapped it in paper, his hands refusing payment. Sara smiled, searching for the right words to thank him, wish the refugee well, but nothing in her native language seemed appropriate.

～

It was dark and still. The limestone streets, worn smooth by a thousand years of foot traffic, looked wet under the streetlamps. Moonbeams leapt off roof tiles, seduced by the hypnotic rhythms of a drum beating somewhere within the old city walls. At the top of every flight of stairs, Mirada, smoking, grabbed the railing and heaved, twisting a certain weariness into the wrought iron.

"Oh, my Got," she said, catching her breath. "You hear?"

"What?"

"The drum."

Sara nodded, setting the suitcase down again. She rubbed her shoulders, her neck knotted from the backpack.

"Nobody sleep. He play *all* night."

"Who?"

Mirada jabbed the air with her finger. "Little boy. We try to catch him. Take him to nuns, but always he runs."

"Why? What's he doing?"

"Waiting for war to end," she said taking out the cigarette. "But war never ends. Even when finish."

Mirada thumped the rhythms against the cigarette, dropping ash on the stoop outside her house. It was a moderate villa overlooking the Adriatic in the tony neighborhood of Ploce on a hill at the southern end of Dubrovnik. From the balcony, the wooded island of Lokrum rose from the sea, the palm trees black against the light.

"My home," she said, pointing to Lokrum.

"You lived there?"

"I work many years there. Best years."

"Doing what?"

"My husband and me. We keep botanical garden and monastery. Very special. I take you. You see."

"I'd like that," Sara said.

Mirada pushed up the huge glasses that had slid down her nose in the heat. She studied Sara, considering what it meant to let her inside her home. Her eyes held crescent moons that made them look like they were smiling.

Sara did not look away too soon, aware that Mirada had not yet taken her eyes off her face, waiting for the moment when Mirada trusted herself to trust her, a friend of a Serb. Mirada spoke a scattered English but understood enough of the exchange between the street vendor and Sara. She knew why the girl was there. Mirada was defensive and proud of her city, the kind of Dalmatian who discriminated against those who did not regard Dubrovnik in the same way, but Sara had already grown enchanted by Dubrovnik without ever having been there.

Sara had never heard about Dubrovnik until she met Milan. It's not like she'd forgotten or mixed up the name. She had read about Belgrade when she studied World War I. Most people knew about the assassination of the Archduke Ferdinand, but she was more familiar with Yugos. Her father, a Ford man, poked fun of cars that weren't made in America. He threatened her with a used Yugo if she didn't pass the driver's license test on the first try. But Yugoslavia, the Balkans, had made an impression on her. It was something of a dream, this place tucked against the edge of the world, a fairy tale with a tragic twist of fate.

Mirada finished her cigarette and tossed the butt into the planter. She dug between fingers of rosemary and pulled out a key, offering it to Sara. Sara opened her hand but did not reach out, still hesitant to accept the key. The old woman smiled, childlike, her front tooth missing.

"Go," Mirada said.

The old woman waved her hand at the door, moved not by excitement but relief. Sara wiggled the key in the lock, boring past rust that had accumulated. The door was old and heavy and covered in peeling green paint. She opened it slowly, pushing against a stack of mail that spilled from the letter slot. There were bills and letters, and even though it was late May, unopened Christmas cards. Moonlight flooded the hallway, exposing flower arrangements crammed along the walls. Mirada turned on the light, revealing the decayed petals of roses and carnations. It smelled sour and moldy, of old flower water, the smell of death itself.

Mirada stepped inside first, fingering the silken bows and ribbons that had faded in the light. She paused before a framed photograph of a young woman hanging from the wall. The young woman sat on what appeared to be the ruins of an old monastery, her body in profile, swollen and pregnant. Her legs, long and lean and brown with sun, dangled over the edge as if she wanted to jump.

"Lokrum," Mirada said, fixing her eyes on the photo.

Sara turned, startled out of her concentration.

"The island?"

Mirada nodded, bending over to pick dead leaves from a vase of carnations. Painted on the vase was the portrait of an older man, a husband perhaps, or a brother wearing a Croatian National Guardsman uniform. Red, white, and blue ribbons trailed from the neck of the vase, and Mirada tied them each into knots, her fingers shaking. She took the rosary beads tucked inside her blouse and kneeled, mumbling prayers, gesturing for Sara to join her.

Sara stood at the door, unable to move, eyes fixed on the picture of the young woman in the island monastery. There was something sharp and pained about the look in her eyes. She possessed nothing of the glow of an expectant mother and appeared to be bursting not with life, but death. Sara felt a chill and turned, hearing the door creak open. It was obvious that Mirada had not been home in God knew how long or where she had gone during the siege. She wasn't sure if Mirada needed her money or companionship more by taking her in as a houseguest. Sara bent down and gathered the mail, feeling the grit of sand on the envelopes, and something smooth and metallic, an empty bullet shell that had slipped inside the slot. She stood and offered the bundle of mail to Mirada, who had managed to push herself off the floor and stood bracing herself against the wall.

"Your Christmas cards."

"Leave them," she said. "I don't want to know."

Sara nodded, compliant, setting the stack of letters neatly against the wall. She pointed to her shoes, feeling self-conscious, wondering if Mirada wanted her to take them off, but the old woman shook her head offended.

"Please, keep."

"They're dirty."

Mirada jabbed the air with a bony thumb, insistent. "Death walk on my floor."

Sara nodded, feeling her stomach tighten.

"Passport, please."

Mirada held out her hand, abiding by Croatian law to report all guests to the local police department. Sara lifted her T-shirt and pulled out the money belt tucked inside her jeans. She felt the weight of Mirada's eyes, anticipating exactly how Western she was. She handed her the passport. Mirada took it and traced the gold letters, the wings of the eagle. She opened to Sara's picture and held it up against her face. Her hair had been pulled into a ponytail, her face fuller, now long and thin. Mirada ran her finger under Sara's cheekbones, tracing the hollows.

Mirada took her hand away and flipped through the pages. They were blank except for the first page where a Hungarian visa had been pasted over a German stamp. Mirada opened a drawer and pulled out a small tablet, writing down Sara's name and number. She made a strange gesture, the passport between her hands, one on top, the other palm up, offering it with the slightest bow. Sara slipped it back into the money pouch, the sound of Velcro officiating its importance and power. The tearing that separated Sara, the American, from Mirada, the Croat.

Sara hated that sound and looked up, her eyes rueful in the dying light of the hall lamp. Mirada said nothing and lifted the suitcase.

"Let me help you," Sara said.

Mirada waved her away. She gripped the suitcase with ease, holding it lengthwise with her palm flat, supporting the belly, her other hand free to grip the side and walk through the doorway as if she had grown accustomed to carrying heavy things. She set the suitcase in front of the closet and opened the door, pushing back a rack of men's clothes— suits and dress pants—making room for Sara. She paused, crossing herself with two fingers, speaking to Sara in Croatian as if the young woman were an old friend that she hadn't seen in a long time. She pointed out hand-woven tapestries, offering a towel embroidered with red tulips and a cross, then crouched, fingers poised over the zipper of the suitcase, ready to open it.

"No," Sara said. "Please leave it."

Mirada lifted her hand from the zipper and nodded. She stood and stepped back from the suitcase, leaving it on the floor.

Sara stared helpless, heart pounding. "I'll do it myself, thank you."

"As you wish."

"I'm sorry. I just—I'm tired."

Sara set the backpack on the ground. She didn't want her clothes to hang in the closet, wondering whose clothes hung on the racks. A husband's. A son's perhaps. A son-in-law's.

A warm wind blew back the shutters, inviting palm fronds through the slats, poking the side of the house like stiff fingers. Sara closed the closet door, her hand over the knob. She locked eyes with Mirada, politely declining the old woman's hospitality. Mirada moved to the dresser by the bed and opened the drawers. She set three candles and a box of matches on the nightstand then turned and walked out the door.

Sara kicked off her sneakers and sat on the bed, taking in the room. It was clean and freshly painted an eggshell blue with a mural of a jungle climbing one wall. Sara wondered if Mirada had planned for a guest and expected a grandson or nephew to arrive any day. Bits of sea glass bejeweled a fishing net that hung from the ceiling, giving the room a storybook feeling like Max's dream in *Where the Wild Things Are*. A collection of seashells and smooth, round pebbles crowded a small circular table by the window where the stubs of white candles had melted onto the cloth. Various crucifixes had been shaped and fashioned out of the branches of olive trees, and a large wreath of laurel leaves crowned the table.

Sara lay on the bed, overcome by an eerie sense of calm, as if she had just woken up. Her life had suddenly assumed the essence of a dream. She was in it, yet this life she had known for the last five months was anything but normal, riddled with characters and places she would know once but forever. There was no past or future to her days, just the presence of a perfect song that played in her memory.

The drum continued to beat. Sara wondered how long the boy would play, if his playing could outlast the war. She crossed to the window, pulling the shutters closed, sliding the latch into place to protect her from not only the sound but also from everything that had gone wrong. She knew the risk of being there. She looked out through the slats across the ripples of the sea, haunted by a blue she had not yet seen but had come to understand. She reached out as if to touch the water, making the sign of the cross with two fingers and a thumb, the way she was taught a Serb would pray to make things right.

⌐

Ghosts threatened Sara's dreams. She swam beneath a fishing boat, staring up at the driver, a young woman whose hands reached out, trying to pull her into the stern. She had no sensation of falling, just floating, suspended between two blue worlds as if the boat were not floating on water but on clouds. Every time Sara reached out to hold the young woman's hands, they shattered into hundreds of black dots and fell into the water, assembling like a school of fish. In the last dream, Sara dived deep and chased them, realizing they were not black dots but musical notes that had come undone.

She woke with the sheets soaked and twisted around her body. Even with her eyes closed, she could not shake the woman's face from her mind, and she realized it was the face of the woman in the photo. She threw back the sheets and taking the candle and matches, made her way in the dark to the hallway, hoping not to wake Mirada. She lighted the candle, trying to glimpse beyond the frame the place this young woman wanted to go. In the photo, the shadow of a child, a boy, crossed the woman's back. He stood behind the stone column of what appeared to be a monastery, as if he, too, had caught her in this moment of quiet contemplation but remained hidden in the shadows from the photographer. Sara traced the woman's face with her finger and the sad slope in her shoulders, recognizing the posture as her own. Sara was not the kind of person duped by happenstance, but lately everyone who had come into her life had taken on an eerie similarity the way strangers conjure images of the dead long after they have passed.

Sara blew out the candle and walked down the hall to her room, charged by the drum. There was a sadness and despair about the rhythms that matched those in her heart, yet she felt a strange release when she listened. There was a fluidity about the rhythm, a certain gravity she detected as if the boy's drumming sought the place that needed it most like water or love. The drumming seemed to deliver her, momentarily, from her grief, and she trusted her instinct to follow it. She dressed in the dark and slipped outside, feeling her way through the blue-black darkness down the steps to the harbor.

↩

A long, wiry man with a crop of silver hair tied neatly into a ponytail dangled his legs over the dock. The mooring of a sunken fishing boat draped his ankles like a snake, charmed by the notes he breathed into the saxophone, accompanied by the drumming from somewhere above the city walls. He paused but did not turn, feeling Sara, studying her reflection in the water. She sat beside the man without asking, permitting herself to this private concert by the sea as if she had known about it all along. She searched the black waters, her lips turned down with his song, as if she, too, knew the source of his mourning.

The sputter of a calamari boat interrupted the music. The man looked up, gesturing to the fishermen across the harbor, hoping they would stop and allow him to finish, but they smoked and belched folk songs from the stern. The men were oblivious of his communion, and he surrendered the saxophone, laying it to rest on his thigh, the sun rising slowly, warming the brass.

Sara clapped, and the man turned to her, smiling. "Thank you."

He spoke English, knowing before the girl spoke that she was not from there. His first guess was Ireland, from the flaming head of hair. "The sea no clap for me," he said.

"You play every day?"

He nodded, speaking like he played. His words galloped, chasing each other in disjointed rhythms. "When I can. He steal my show."

He glanced up at the walls behind him, surprised the drumming had suddenly stopped.

"I'll applaud for both of you."

"Very well," he said, extending his hand.

Sara reached out to shake it, surprised by the grip in his fingers. He had huge hands, scarred and nicked by fishing hooks that had gotten their way. His hands were those of a man who held many things but let go of those that no longer served him.

"Anton Vidovic."

"Sara Foster."

"You like music?"

"I don't know much about it. That's why I'm here."

"Nothing to know," Anton said, throwing his gaze into the water. "Music is feeling, but you pay price."

Sara turned, fixing her eyes on the old man. "Better than not feeling, right?"

Anton turned to Sara, curious by the girl's inquiry, her intelligent eyes, probing. He had not seen a tourist in Dubrovnik since the summer. It had been nine months, the tavern empty, bottles drained mostly by war correspondents. He had interviewed a few, drunk, on his radio show. She appeared too naïve to be a journalist.

"You come for music festival?"

Sara nodded. "More or less. It's a special year."

"Yes. War year."

Anton lifted his gaze to a falcon flying overhead, its caw interrupting him.

"Not safe year to travel here. You crazy girl."

Sara forced herself to smile. Her eyes held a sadness that her smile did not, and Anton reached out, taking her hand. She did not flinch from his touch.

"So far from home," he said.

Sara lifted her eyes to meet his, reading the arch in his eyebrow. Anton possessed a warmth and generosity of spirit, paternal in its instinct, yet youthful, even capricious. She felt as if she had already met him. Her fingers softened in his grip, and he squeezed her gently, leaving no marks this time.

"This is the only place I'm suppose to be," she said.

"Croatia?"

"Dubrovnik."

He nodded, smiling, impressed that she understood the difference. Because there was a difference. Dubrovnik was not Croatia as most travelers knew it. And Croatia was not Dubrovnik, but another strand of the Balkans entirely, with its own stories and ghosts. It was a place that lingered on the edge of things, a sliver of land locked between the mountains and the sea, the periphery of the politics of the world and in many ways the edge where it met its deepest truths and plunged into darkness because of them.

"Why Dubrovnik?"

Sara paused, considering what it meant to tell him the truth. She could think of a million other reasons why she had chosen the city. The Mediterranean gaiety. Renaissance spirit. The warm sea. Its walls. The magic of its summers. If she told Anton the truth, she would commit herself to him, but it was too late. She already shared his past.

"I want to hear *The Sound of Blue,*" she said, dipping her heels in the water, salt stinging the open blisters.

Anton stared at her, unable to speak, jaw stiff with her words. He could not detect the source of her accent, aware she withheld it from him. Her words were soft and shapeless as if she were afraid to commit to them, afraid of saying too much.

◞

Sara and Anton climbed the Jesuit Steps, silent, their long shadows chasing pigeons that scavenged crumbs from the cherry strudel they shared. The smell of cigarettes and coffee drifted down from the courtyard where city workers salvaged bricks from a blast at the church. Sara paused at a statue of the Virgin Mary. Her eyes had been gouged out by sniper fire, and her hands were blown off. They lay on the ground, palms up, poised as if she wished to collect something, hope perhaps, the alms of war.

Anton spoke first, his accent on the first and third words. He seemed agitated and nervous, his voice low, eyes shifting to the workers. "How do you find me?"

"I didn't. Csikos Gabor did."

Anton stiffened. He had refused to speak to the refugee camp director, unwilling to deny Milan's sudden disappearance from Dubrovnik. Anton had lied to Gabor, as he had to the police, assuring them all that Milan was still in town, preparing his testimony for the trial.

"I don't know him."

Sara locked eyes with Anton. "He said he spoke with you."

"Are you lawyer?"

Sara lifted her chin, feeing the weight of the word, the ring of it in her ear. *Lawyer.* It sounded tinny and hollow now, its richness an affect of tone and tongue. Her words came sharp and hard with the lie that preceded them.

"No. I'm not a lawyer," she said. "I'm a teacher."

"How do you know this man Gabor?"

"I taught English at the camp. He said Milan lived with you for ten years. What happened to his parents?"

Anton stared at her. "You ask a lot of questions."

"I'm a teacher."

Sara followed Anton behind the church and into an alley where two boys played basketball from a hoop drilled into the stone wall.

"His father die in Yugo factory near Belgrade."

"What?"

Anton winked, indifferent. "Anticommunists have most original obituary in Yugoslavia. I still wait for mine."

Sara lowered her eyes, noticing for the first time the tattoo on Anton's arm: there were no pictures, only numbers. He unfolded his cuff and pulled down the sleeve, averting the pity in her eyes.

"Do not feel sorry. My choice," he said. "And my choice to take care of Milan. I respect his mother's politics. She raised the boy right."

"What happened to her?"

Anton turned, catching the ball. He hurled it back at the boys.

They waved, but Anton shifted his gaze, eyeing the blackened roof of the monestary. "Killed," he said.

"How?"

Anton lowered his eyes to Sara. "She drown."

"Oh, my god."

"Many people drown here," he said.

The children ran past them, giggling, tossing the ball at a cat that had leapt off the wall above Anton.

"Were you his guardian?"

"No."

"You took care of him after his mother died."

Anton reached out and scooped up the cat. It was gray and thin and had no more than a stub for a tail. He rubbed the cat's ear, triggering more of a groan than a purr.

"We had no paper, nothing legal. He was too young to make decision for himself. *These* tall when he stand up straight," Anton said, holding his hand by his hip. "Nobody would look after him with his condition."

"But you looked out for him instead?"

"As much as he let me. But you must see. Milan would choose to die first before he let me or anyone help him."

"Why?"

"He never believe he deserve it."

Sara locked eyes with Anton, studying him closely, searching for any indication that he was culpable for Milan's plight. She was impatient to lash him with accusations, not once believing the composer had chosen to leave Dubrovnik. She walked ahead of Anton, climbing a stack of sandbags to the walkway on top of the city walls, anxious to get a view of the sea. Anton caught up with her, finding her crouched, peering through a loophole.

"He was hiding," she said. "Wasn't he?"

"Hiding?"

"From whatever it is he left here."

"He left nothing," Anton snapped. "Except me." He ground out the bitterness with his words.

Sara turned. She read the confusion and anger, the sadness bagged beneath his eyes. "Why didn't you help him?"

"I tell you. He don't let me help."

"Why not? He could have stayed here."

"He tell you this?"

"He told me nothing," she said. "We never spoke. Not really. We didn't understand each other that way." She pressed her lips against the warm stone.

Anton reached out to touch her shoulder. "You must see. I spend whole life helping Milan. He leave *me*. Boom. One day he go."

"He must have left for a good reason."

"Nobody tell him to leave, Sara."

"How many Serbs have stayed here? Would you?"

Anton shook his head. "Is he safe?"

"Why did you stay?"

"Tell me he is safe."

"I don't know!" Sara said. Her words, full of apology, tumbled from her tongue. She turned and gripped the wall.

"I thought he'd be here by now."

Anton softened his voice. "Milan always late. You learn that first. The only time composer keeps is in music he writes, yes?"

"He's not late, Anton."

"He took bus? With you?"

Sara looked past him, at the sea, as if all the answers Anton needed were out there. She shifted at the wall, staring beyond the sunken fishing boats, searching for a net to catch the pain, to sink it, too, but she knew there was nothing that would make this any easier for Anton. She pulled out a small envelope from the money belt tucked inside her pants and stood, taking Anton's hand. His fingers had turned suddenly cold, and she uncurled them, dumping a bent wire frame and two lenses into his palm. He stared at the metal, reshaping it in his mind, seeing the eyes that had once looked up at him through the glass. He leaned against the wall, needing support, tracing the initials M.V. etched into the frame. He swallowed, breath shallow, intending neither to cry nor scream but to trap the pain inside his lungs.

He whispered. "How could he not be safe?"

Sara braced herself against the questions she read in the dull flat line of Anton's mouth. He shook his head defiantly, unable to find the logic. She reached out to touch the old man's shoulder, trying to comfort him, but he withdrew, gaze fixed on the shadow of himself on the wall, wishing it had been Milan beside him, not the woman with the fire in her hair and heart.

Anton lifted his eyes to the sky and made the sign of the cross, fingers taciturn, frustrated over the futility of prayer. His forehead rippled with wrinkles, trying to make sense of the pieces in his hand. He curled his fingers around the bent wire, unfolding it with his thumb, then popping the lenses into place, folded the rims as if he were crossing the arms of the dead.

～

Anton had no more words for the young woman and excused himself for the evening. He ambled through the streets, disoriented, stumbling through a sea of broken roof tiles. The news registered as the dull ache in his neck. He wished he would bump into Milan, pen in one hand, notebook in the other. He did not want to believe they had already said good-bye. The story was not meant to go like this. The composer was suppose to survive *him*.

Anton walked Prijeko Street, passing a man older than himself draped by fishing overalls who swept the sidewalk, performing the dance of insomniacs, the ritual for those haunted by the sounds of war. Sleep was a luxury to few in Dubrovnik. Anton was not the only person who had trouble passing the nights. It had been five months since the last bomb had fallen, but he could hear the blasts looped in his memory. He had found ways to pass the time. Play saxophone. Polish silverware. Run the radio show, rebroadcasting Milan's performances before he had left

Dubrovnik. Anton missed the shows. He cherished that time the most, despite the war, watching Milan slip into a peaceful existence as if his music absorbed all the troubles of the world.

He stopped outside the radio station and removed the sandbags stacked against the front door. He was surprised to find one of the bags had been opened, the sand spilling on the cobblestones. Stuffed inside the bag was a child's white T-shirt and a shrunken red wool sweater. The collar had come unraveled, leaving a misshapen scoop neck, the sleeves rolled, stuffed with candied figs. Tucked inside the sweater was a set of pencils, none of them sharpened, the erasers worn, rounded at the tips. Anton dug deeper into the bag, pulling out a trading card of Ryan Giggs, the famous Welsh soccer star of Manchester United. Whoever's card it was drew a curly mustache on the young man's mouth and a machine gun in his hand. Beyond that, Anton retrieved the lavender wrapper of a Cadbury chocolate bar and a mass of crumpled newspapers wrapped around a round, heavy object. He pushed back the papers and paused, astounded by what he held in his hand, a grenade with the pin in place.

"Jesus God," he said. "They never stop."

Anton set the grenade on the ground and reloaded the bag, hands shaking, taking all of it to the local police station. It was the last thing he wanted to do, wishing instead to start his day over without the news from the woman from the camp. He refused to call her Sara again until he could consider her a friend. Her news had unnerved him, and he had done nothing but drink since he left her above the city walls. He was drunk now on plum brandy, but he needed no sobering to recognize a grenade.

He stumbled through the doors of the police station, their temporary headquarters once a basement café where academics and artists had been known to gather. It was a bohemian nest, adorned with photos of the Rolling Stones and paintings of Bette Davis rendered in oil. Black-and-white images of famous musicians had been signed and hung in succession according to the summer they had performed in Dubrovnik's music festival. The owner, Danilo, had a sense of humor and had taken the time to mount mortar that had landed in the kitchen sink but had not exploded. Written as a headline across the base of the mount: SERB ADVANCES. The officers were playing a game of rummy, cards yellow from cigarette smoke that hung from the ceiling. They stopped, surprised to see the old man waiting at the door, hand outstretched and shaking with the grenade.

"Hell of a time to make a confession, Anton."

Anton stiffened. "Confession?"

Anton was not sure what kind of pranks the police were in the mood for tonight. One could never tell exactly how they spent their time and he was not entirely convinced they wouldn't accuse him of possessing a weapon. After all, he was Milan's teacher, a friend of a Serb. The police were known to look for any excuse to alleviate their boredom.

The youngest policeman, early twenties, pushed back his chair and caned his way to Anton, taking the grenade. "Sit down, old man."

Anton slid into the booth closest to the door, needing air. The officer lowered his voice, sharing with Anton what had fueled the fire of recent gossip.

"Milan ever tell you somebody kept a diary of the day Damir Babic drowned?"

"No. He never told me about the diary."

"Zarko got it from some kid who found it off Lokrum a few months ago."

"When?"

"December. Cover was blown off by a bullet, otherwise the thing reads clear as a window. Milan read it."

"He did?"

"Christmas. He never told you?"

Anton pressed his lips together. Everything was slowly beginning to unfold, making sense in a way that made logic too painful.

The last time he saw Milan was Christmas day at the radio station to record a live performance of *The Sound of Blue*. Milan had never mentioned the diary and wondered why Zarko had accompanied him into the studio, impatient for him to finish. Milan had lived for one year with his mother in the hotel Zarko managed before they moved to Lokrum. Milan was six. He had avoided Zarko most of his life. He despised the man but feared him more than anything. He was the man who had made Milan's seizures public, humiliating him in front of strangers, tourists, and locals who would gather in the hotel lobby to hear the boy play. Zarko collected the money for the performances, never once giving Milan or his mother a portion of the proceeds, which is why it was strange to see Zarko in the radio station, offering Milan money for what Anton presumed to be an old debt that had never been and could never be settled. Zarko had never been to the station, and he waited for Milan, clutching a small black book in his hand. Anton thought it was the Bible, but it had been the diary found on Lokrum. Milan had been exceptionally nervous during the performance, and Anton wondered now if Milan knew it would be his last.

The officer took out a cigarette and continued. "I told Milan the diary could only help his case if he ever shows up for the trial. You do remember that much."

Anton clenched his fist. "I remember. He'll be there."

"Good. He's got a lot of remembering to do himself. Zarko's son didn't exactly drown, if you know what I mean."

Anton stared, expectant, trying hard to keep a straight face, revealing nothing. His throat tightened.

"Don't look so surprised, old man. Not now. Not after all the shit we've seen around here. This is nothing. More like a good drama. Entertainment." The younger officer held up the grenade. "Where did you get it?"

"I found it."

The officer laughed. "In Milan's freezer?"

Anton pressed himself against the curve of the booth, the

wood sticky on his back. "No. Outside the radio station. With this."

Anton held out the stuffed sandbag, shoving it across the table to the officer. He was convinced the officer had booby-trapped Milan's apartment, hoping the composer would take off his own hand and render himself as disabled as the former soccer pro. Anton could not get a straight answer from anybody, police officers or neighbors alike, about the suspected vandals in Milan's apartment. He did not believe they were the band of teenagers who had been caught earlier for raiding a Serb restaurant, only to pass out from the dozens of bottles of plum brandy they had consumed. The grenade that had been hidden in Milan's freezer was not the prank of a teenager, but of somebody older, an insidious move to right a wrong that had long since been relevant to the composer.

The young officer fixed his eyes on Anton, searching the sandbag with his fingers. He laid the child's sweater and pencils on the table, keeping the trading card of Ryan Giggs for himself, rubbing off the mustache with his thumb.

"I'll be damned," he said.

Anton said nothing, wishing for once not to contradict the young officer. True, he thought. "Take a look at this."

Two other officers got up from the table and crossed to the booth with the cards still in their hands, unable to trust each other not to cheat. They stood behind the young officer and fingered through the belongings on the table, holding up the small T-shirt, looking for the tag where a laundry pen had written the name LUKA on the label. They were most surprised by the pack of pencils.

"Surprised he forgot his drumsticks."

Anton looked up. "I play saxophone. Not drums."

"Not you, old man. The kid."

"What kid?"

The young officer rapped on the table with this knuckles,

making a drumming sound. "The kid who found the diary. The drummer boy."

Anton stared incredulous at the pencils, making sense of the news. One of the officers who had left returned with a canvas bag. He held it with both hands, his bony arms bulging beneath the weight. He pulled out a pile of clothes, a pair of jeans, other T-shirts, boy's underwear, and a flak jacket too big for a child.

"Kid's been leaving his clothes everywhere with the heat. Probably running around stark naked by now."

Anton lifted the flak jacket off the table, wondering how a boy could carry lead that weighed almost half of him.

"You've seen him?"

The older officer nodded.

"Some nuns spotted him at Onofrio's Fountain last week. Bold little boy. Tried the spouts for water. Left a toothbrush there when he saw them sneak up from behind. Kid's got legs. A gazelle, I say. Just as wild, too, with the street smarts of a criminal."

The older officer spun the grenade on the table.

"We have a composite now." The other officer took out his wallet and unfolded a copy of the boy's cartoonlike image. The only accurate feature was the boy's curly dark hair.

"You recognize him?"

Anton shook his head, massaging his temples. "Only the drumming."

"Rumor has it he found the diary on Lokrum."

Anton straightened, sobered by the news, the buzz of plum brandy waning. "Makes you want to kill him," he said, speech slurred.

The officer studied Anton, curious. The disc jockey had been a loyal patron of the tavern for years. He had lost weight, eyes bloodshot, rivers of worry on his nose from too much booze.

"How you holding up, Anton?"

"It's been quiet. Too quiet."

"You got the drumming," the officer said, hopeful, trying to make the old man break a smile. Anton picked at the space in his wristwatch where a link was missing. He slid out of the booth and stood, grateful for the officer's hand to keep him balanced. He was light-headed and warm.

"Thanks for stopping by."

"Anytime," Anton said, turning to the younger officer. "When I find more, I'll be sure to toss them your way."

The young officer grunted. He was in no mood. "Don't forget to pull the pin first."

Anton stepped away from the young officer and crossed to the door, but the policeman stayed on his heels, opening the door for him. He leaned in and whispered.

"Any word from Milan?"

Anton turned. The sharp black eyes of the officer pierced him, probing for answers.

"No," Anton said, refusing to share the news with the police. He did not want to see their satisfaction, knowing they had not killed the Serb composer themselves.

↤

Anton emptied the last bottle of Jack Daniel's, drowning the young police officer's words. He passed out at the desk of his studio, snoring, saxophone between his knees, legs entangled by a fishing net he had dragged inside to repair.

"Anton. Wake up."

The front window rattled. Anton batted the air with his hand, content to let the cats curled around his neck resettle on his lap.

"I need your help, Anton."

The bartender opened one eye and stared at the ceiling, recognizing instantly the voice that called out to him from the other side of the door. He stiffened, rising slowly, blood thick with booze. He stretched his fingers, accidentally knocking the empty bottle to the floor. It did not break but rolled to the door.

"Open up!"

Anton rubbed his eyes, lifting his gaze to the wall clock behind him. It was only 3:23 in the morning but when he turned and looked at the front of the radio station, light flooded the floor, casting a network of shadows through the cane-backed chairs lining the studio window. It was daylight outside, the air crisp with autumn, the shadows long and stretched over the cobblestones.

"Anton, you awake?"

Anton growled, flicking away floating cat hairs with his index finger, unaware he was dreaming about his past.

"You think I'm awake?

Anton pushed himself off the seat, knees cracking, and crossed the floor, stumbling past a grand piano and the series of microphones standing beside it. He turned the dead bolt in the door.

"Read the sign," Anton whispered. "On Air."

"Just one drink."

Anton tapped the glass with an admonishing finger. "You won't find the muse in a bottle here."

"Fuck the muse."

"I tried," Anton said. "Which is why I play saxophone and you compose. Go home and sleep."

Milan slouched beneath the station door, the awning fluttering in the wind. He leaned, not against the door, but as he always did pressed against sounds. He had a habit of listening with one ear to daily noise, idle chatter, cat calls, doorbells, horns, but tuned in with the other ear to the sounds that mattered most, to music and voices, the movements in his heart. He chewed nervously on a pen cap, studying the door, his pale blue eyes wide and wild with their self-absorbed passions. He fingered the buttons on his coat, waiting anxiously for Anton to unlatch the lock as if its opening would free him from his torment.

"When's the last time you slept?"

Milan glowered at the joke. "That's the point, Anton. I don't."

"Then go home and write. Make yourself useful. You know how many calls I'm getting asking you to play again?"

Anton knew the composer did not need to drink, but to vent the vexing creative process that seemed, as of late, to induce his seizures. He needed music, not alcohol, not with the half dozen barbiturates prescribed to control the epilepsy. But it was too late. The composer did not sleep, increasing his chances for a seizure by half. His nutrition was far from preventative, especially during peak creative periods. He survived on ham sandwiches and candied figs, craving salt and sugar. He believed that sugar spiked creative impulses and salt sustained them, distilling the essence of a tear into both. He had convinced himself that musicians could survive on tears alone, the only physical evidence of pure emotion, the essence of music itself.

From glimpsing the willowy body through the white rain coat, it appeared to Anton that Milan's most recent diet consisted only of emotion, his body withered and ravaged by war. The composer was thinner, the veins in his neck and forehead more pronounced, blue rivers mapping his worry. His hair was a tangle of dark curls making him appear to be more of the madman everyone wanted to believe he was, the aggressive scientist of sound. He faced a deadline for the summer music festival, which only made him more anxious and demanding of himself. He would go days without eating until he got the music right. And he hadn't gotten the music right, not yet, blaming the war.

Who knows how long it would take him. He was stubborn. His worst critic even as a child, driven more by fear than ambition. Getting the music right meant gaining control of the seizures, and Milan would do just about anything, save killing himself, to ensure that safety. At ten years old, he refused to speak to anyone until he could perform, from memory, with the perfect pitch, intensity, time, and timbre, Chopin's piano Etude in C Minor, the *Revolutionary Etude* of 1832. He bled his fingers trying to master the torrent of piano runs, determined to match the *appassionato* melody Chopin had intended, willing his fingers to set the keys aflame for the explosive ending. He learned to wrap his fingers with masking tape to keep the keys from sticking with blood. The piece was short, the form simple, yet it took Milan a year to perfect, a year without the formal abuses he had adopted later in his life.

Milan approached composing with the same austerity and deprivation in which he played. When Anton had advised him to practice scales three times a day, Milan practiced ten. Nothing was too much. Nothing overwhelmed him. He had made it a habit of climbing the Jesuit Steps, reciting chord progressions, committing them to memory. He hungered for pain and if need be would starve himself of everything but his passions. He said the hollowing of his insides made his hearing sharper, not to mention his temper. At twenty-six, he possessed the energy and enthusiasm of a child and the petulance of a teenager. It wasn't enough to complete a composition. Milan wanted to write the *perfect* composition, proclaiming to know at the ripe age of six precisely what it was because it played in his head.

Anton advised Milan to take it easy on himself, to lift the self-imposed sanctions. Looking at him now, he saw the face of a musician surviving on petty vices, cigarettes and fettered passions.

"You're listening too hard."

"It's hard to listen. All I hear are explosions."

"That's all you *remember* hearing. Give yourself a chance to get used to the silence."

Anton shifted his eyes to the composer's hands. They fumbled with the buttons on his shirt.

"Milan? You hear me?"

Milan nodded. "Yes. You hear *me*? One drink."

He shifted his eyes to the door, anticipating Anton's fingers would turn back the dead lock. Anton gasped, making the sign of the cross with two fingers.

"Don't even think about it. Your blood is a minefield with all those pills."

Milan nodded. "True. The blood of a Croat and Serb makes no ground for a picnic."

Anton lowered his voice, hissing. "You are crazy man, Milan. I don't want to make jokes with you. No drinking. Not now. What if you fall down the stairs? Or tumble to death from the city walls? I am too old to scrape you off the streets. What would Anton have left? Nothing but a bucket and hose."

"Anton, stop. I'm no good at flattery."

Anton flicked the glass with his fingers, incensed. His face strained, veins popping in his neck the way they did when he played Benny Goodman on the saxophone.

"I had another seizure, Anton."

Anton dragged his pinkie down the window, slowly, smudging the glass with the word. "What? When?"

"Yesterday. And the day before. Clusters."

"How many episodes?"

"Like clockwork," Milan said, snapping his finger. He turned his cheek toward the window, the bruise glazed from striking it, unconsciously, against the rails of his bed. He was prone to tonic-clonic seizures, having bitten his tongue in half as a child only to have it sewn together by his mother, not the nurses, who were made too anxious by Milan's condition to help him.

"There's no way I can perform in the festival."

"That's six months from now."

Anton's pupils shriveled like little raisins when he pressed his face against the window, looking out into the empty street. National Guardsmen armed with guns patrolled the sidewalk, escorting a group of United Nations delegates to an armored vehicle parked across from the station.

"It will be too late," Milan said.

"To late for what?"

Milan produced a letter from his coat, pressing it against the window for Anton to read the subpoena.

"I have to testify," he said.

"Testify?"

"They're reinvestigating Damir's death."

"Why? Because Zarko's bribing them?"

"Because I'm an adult now. If they put me under oath, I have to tell the truth."

Milan chewed his bottom lip, waiting for Anton to give in and open the door, but the old man said nothing, face pinched with sudden dread. He lifted his finger as if to say something, then dropped the shade. He walked back to the piano and lay on the bench as if he had never moved from it. He closed his eyes and slept long and hard for a day, hearing not the drum, but the beating of his heart louder than any bomb.

↬

Sara watched the play of the sea from the city walls, drawn into the blueness. She wondered how many times Milan had walked above these same walls, if the walls, not Anton, held the mystery behind Milan's music. She regretted her decision to tell Anton about Milan. The old man did not need to suffer any more bad news, and she was uncertain if telling him had moved her closer to understanding the voice within *The Sound of Blue*. Sara leached every last bit of hope from Anton and he looked withered when he left.

A group of Croatian National Guardsmen approached Sara, boots clicking against the stone, guns slung around shoulders and hips, bandoliers strapped across chests. It was windy, and Sara had not heard them above the waves. They spoke in Croatian, pointing fingers, insisting she move from the walls. Sara detected the alarm in their voice, but before she could stand, they had already ushered her to the stairs, impatient for her descent to safer ground.

Sara stepped away from the shadows of the guardsmen into a small church whose doors had not been sandbagged. She did not like the way the men had followed her so closely, rushing her away from the walls. She was not entirely certain their willingness to es-

cort her had anything to do with her safety. They seemed amused
by her, if not smitten and intrigued. Sara was not a religious person and did not admire churches the way most people did when
they traveled, but something about the small stone building felt
welcoming, cool inside, relieving her of the heat and the guardsmen on the street.

Sara walked down the aisles, feeling awkward, staring at the
nuns, heads bowed, reverent, muttering prayers of faith and forgiveness. Sara did not want to disturb them or draw more attention to herself. She slipped inside the dark confessional,
feeling safer. It was not the guardsmen she wanted to avoid
really but the acceptance of Milan's death. She wanted to ask for
his deliverance if only for her own. She needed to believe he was
still alive, not because she wanted to see him again, but because
she needed to hear his music. She knew better than to waste her
breath praying for petty things, but she believed if she could
hear the music again, she would understand completely the
voice within it. It was the voice that had delivered her from
Hungary, the voice that kept her awake and alive and she
wanted to know why.

She leaned against the confessional, the wood sweating beneath her back as if it knew the futility of her prayer. She barely
uttered a word when something caught her eye through the slit in
the confessional door. The nuns had gathered in the front pews,
embroiled in an argument, passing around what appeared to be a
composite of a boy. One of them stood, gesticulating wildly, accidentally loosening her habit to the floor. The nuns were too busy
racing to the confessional to pick it up.

They pounded on the door, breathing heavy, voices garbled as
if their mouths had been filled with lighter fluid, throats jammed
with matches for the fire they were about to set with words. The
spoke in Croatian.

"You cannot run forever. You come out here right this minute.
We know you're in there."

Sara understood only the fury in their tone and braced herself against the walls of the confessional.

"God will punish you, young man. You've caused enough trouble in this town, and you will suffer."

The nuns rapped their thick knuckles against the door. It felt like a pack of animals outside, and Sara had no idea what she did to merit such commotion. She had not seen any signs outside the church, not that she could read them, but she could at least understand the context of a sign that seemed unusual or out of place. Perhaps the church was off-limits to visitors like her. Maybe they knew she didn't believe in the kind of God they did. She wasn't Catholic, but she had crossed herself the way a Serb did and wondered now if all her sins, known and unknown, were somehow exacting their toll.

Sara lifted the curtain over the screen, hearing a gasp. She was startled to see not a priest, but a young boy staring back at her with wide, wild, insistent eyes. They shared mutual surprise. Sara looked away first, lowering her gaze, gathering the boy in her sight. He was smaller than the largeness of his stare. He wore torn jeans and sat with his knees to chest, bracing himself against the wrath of the nuns. He was thin and bare chested, chest glistening and bronzed from the sun. In any other country and context, he could have been a young diver or fisherman. He had about him the sparkle and spirit of an indigenous soul. He did not appear to belong in the church. There was something of the devil cooped up inside the boy, and he looked as if he were about to explode. His chin quivered when he spoke, whispering his plea in Croatian. Sara understood nothing but the desperation in his voice. The nuns knocked again, their rapping louder, harder, shaking the confessional.

"You are an orphan. You belong with us."

The boy crossed himself, eyes still fixed on Sara, curious. There was something about the way she looked at him that told him she was not from there. He took a deep breath and quietly unlatched the hook from the confessional door, slipping outside seemingly undetected. He was about to lift the drum off the seat when one of the nuns lurched forward from behind a statue of Saint Paul. She was not much taller than the boy himself and cornered him, his arms outstretched, fingers grazing the base of the drum, still stuck on the bench inside the confessional. The nun spoke quickly, eyebrows arched in consternation and awe at having discovered him. She moved closer, reaching for his hand. Luka's heart pounded, knowing his only two choices were to take the drum and be caught, or seize the opportunity to run. He stomped on her foot once, not hard, but not lightly, enough to make her scream, then scurried past her and out the back door of the church.

She limped around to the front of the confessional where the other nuns swung open the door on Sara's side. They stared dumbfounded, sorely disappointed to find the woman with the red curls, not the boy with the black. The nuns muttered blessings when she stood and stepped outside the confessional, walking passed them into the aisle. She slid into a pew to sit for hours until the streetlamps shone through the stained glass and the church was dark and empty. When Sara was certain that she was alone, she walked back to the confessional and took the drum the boy had left as if it were the confession he had intended to make to her, not to God.

⌒

Luka sat crouched inside the well of Onofrio's Fountain, catching his breath, cursing himself for leaving the drum in the church. Stupid move, he thought, probably the worst move since he left the bomb shelter in Vukovar. Oddly enough, somebody else was playing it now, and they were horrible. Whoever played the drum had no sense of rhythm and banged it with the force of fists pounding a table. It pained Luka to hear the drum abused this way, but he was grateful for the noise, for the sound, even if it cost him. He couldn't bear the silence. Not even for a night.

Without the drum, Luka was rootless and lost in his wandering. He needed it to speak. The boy's entire world was composed of the rhythms that matched the words in his heart, and he wanted desperately for someone else to hear them. Not that they would rush the rhythms.

He was hungry and heated, body perspired from the confessional. Until now, it had been a good hiding place when the priests had nodded off in the cellars of their parishes as they did every day after lunch. Luka hadn't expected the nuns. They usually sang at the orphanage at night, abandoning their search for him for roughly two hours before they reassembled in pairs and scoured the alleys, following the beating of the drum well into the morning. Luka wondered why the nuns cared so much, why his capture had become a game to the priests, too, as if saving him would grant them all clemency and a ticket to heaven.

They were not quick enough, not smart enough, and always failed to catch him. Luka would feel them coming, their hurry vibrating the stones. He had learned to take naps standing up and was quite proud of his ability to dream in broom closets and empty pantries. He knew every abandoned dwelling in Dubrovnik and took advantage of the ash bedding that softened its stone floors. He had learned, too, of the bakery whose back door was forever unlocked for the policeman who was in love with the baker. Whenever they stepped into the toilet to kiss, Luka reached around to the trash can by the door and took a misshapen loaf of bread, feeling less guilty about taking something that had already been thrown away. Once he found a bag of chocolates and thought somebody had made a mistake. He took only half, leaving the rest on the counter, fingerprints included, which the police had no qualms about collecting to use as evidence for the boy's arrest. Everybody wanted a reason to capture him. But it was not him they wanted. He suspected they wanted his drum. But he did not have his drum and wished to redirect them to the person who did.

The priests approached Luka slowly, black soldiers draped with garlic and guns. He had nestled himself behind the sandbags but was uncertain that they did not see him. He faked sleep, hands pressed against his stomach to hush the growling. If he could steal the garlic bulbs, he'd eat them whole with the skins and roots, paper pearls in his mouth, better than prayers, he thought. He smelled incense. Oranges. The musk of funerals. Holy men arched over him. He counted twelve pairs of sandals, seeing slash marks where broken tiles had scraped their ankles and toes.

The priests reached out to the spouts, murmuring blessings as if their touch might bring water, eyes trained on the sky, searching for tracers, wondering when mortar would strike again. The priests had been warned once by Saint Blaise of an impending attack in the sixteenth century, and they asked their patron saint to watch over them now. History had taught them to trust their premonitions. The city had taken its share of hits, and it could not afford to lose any more life. Their hands had grown weary, and they refused to offer their youth to the ground. The cemeteries were already too crowded.

Luka held his breath, craned his neck, trying to make himself smaller, unseen. The priests circled the fountain then broke off one by one, hearing the drum, but before they took off in search of it, they ran to the gargoyle on the monastery wall and tried again to keep their balance, hands outstretched on the stones. Nobody held it for long. One of the priests missed the gargoyle's forehead entirely and ran straight into the wall, chipping his tooth. He slunk into an alley, wincing, while the others took off in search of the drum. Luka held his breath, trying to trap the giggle in his throat. The nuns were running out of the church now, each one chasing the other, habits flapping in the warm wind that blew in from the sea. Nobody had found the drum when they returned one hour later, empty-handed and defeated.

Much to Luka's surprise, the drumming continued, pumping

the moon into the midnight sky. He peered through the sandbags, watching the lights go off in the apartments, waiting for Dubrovnik to sleep. He listened for the buzz of snores until he felt it was safe to leave the fountain in search of his own drum. Luka waited longer than he needed, thinking at first the nuns and priests had played a trick on him, but when he saw them slip into the only tavern still open, he knew they had retired for the night.

Luka lowered himself to the street and ran into the closest alley, moving sideways through shadows, keeping his back to the wall. He paused at the synagogue, waiting for the man with the broom to sweep past him. He was convinced the old man was blind and did not consider the possibility of him sleepwalking. In any case, he seemed disinterested in the boy. It felt safe for Luka to pass him and follow the drumming through the city's south gate, Pile. It was from the drawbridge where Luka stood looking down on a graveyard of fishing boats seeing the woman with the red hair playing his drum. His shadow cast itself over her, and she turned, looking up at him as if she had been waiting. He took the stairs and crossed under the bridge, walking toward her, sitting on the boat until she had finished. She stood, relieved, but said nothing, walking away from the drum, leaving the boy to the business of his survival.

~

Sara slowly climbed the stone stairs to Mirada's pension, the air thick with humidity and portent. Her body felt heavy and not entirely her own, invaded by a virus perhaps, and she wondered if it had been something she ate. She stood on the deck outside her room and opened the door, intending to sleep, but it was too hot, the room already stuffy with the heat from the oven. Even at this late hour, the kitchen window was open and she heard Mirada pounding dough, exacerbating Sara's headache. She had experienced migraines once when she studied for the law school exam, but she recognized the symptoms now, the nausea and the pressure drilling into the top of her skull. Her head throbbed with the rhythms of the drum, and she found it odd that the moment she began to play it, she felt a tingling sensation, almost electric, as if she had stood too close to a live wire and risked shocking herself.

Sara had never played a drum. Not the kind of drum the boy had left in the confessional. She was impressed by its antiquity and condition. The boy obviously took good care of it. At first she thought the drum was made of plastic until she ran her fingers along the seams, realizing they were not made from a machine but were the indentations of bone, specifically a skull. The base of the skull had been decorated with a silk brocade and glass beads that reminded her of something from India or Indonesia, not the Balkans. The most significant difference of this drum from any other drums that Sara was aware existed was that it could be shaken like a rattle. It was when she shook the skull drum that the migraine began.

She fell into the rhythm slowly but easily, not because she had it in her, but because the rhythm was finding its way into *her*. She continued to play the drum despite the blatant pain it was causing. The definitive action of the drumming itself allowed her mind to pause, to forget momentarily everything. She could let go of the worry and the grief over Milan. She could block all the warning signs that her safety had been threatened by crossing into Croatia. The rhythms flushed all the tension in her body. She felt calm, riding the rhythms as if they were taking her to the place she needed to go, not back to the refugee camp, but home. At first there was a sadness to the rhythms, as if the boy's drumming still lingered there. She felt drawn into the life of the drum and in a strange way, believed the drum was connecting her to someone she did not know but felt through her body. It was as if Sara wasn't playing the drum at all but had unwittingly allowed somebody to play through her.

Sara was surprised that it took more energy for her not to drum than to stop when the boy found her. The drumming had

made her feel more alive than she had in months, if not years. Most important, the drum made her feel safe, and she was unwilling to let go too soon. The boy allowed her to finish, as if he understood what she needed.

She wanted to listen to the waves on the beach now, hoping they would mitigate the migraine. She closed the door to the pension, leaving Mirada to her rituals, hoping to find Anton again by the harbor. The sun was rising over Mount Srđ and she could hear construction workers hammering roof tiles into place before the heat got too intense. Only a few fishermen had started out, the dark blue waters calm.

Sara walked out on the jetty, finding the place where Anton had played and sat. She rolled up the cuffs of her pants and dipped her feet into the water as she had done yesterday. She was unaware that anything had changed about the scene until she shifted her gaze into the water, seeing the body of a woman drifting beneath the surface. The woman was young, twenty-something, wearing a colorful dress and a wreath of flowers around her head, her hair long and blond. Sara thought the woman was swimming.

Sara splashed the water with her foot, trying to get a reaction from the woman. The body did not move. Sara splashed again. Still, no movement. She searched the water for air bubbles. Nothing but dull ripples. She could not believe the woman had drowned. The woman's body was not bloated and the muscles in her arms and legs were well-defined giving her the appearance of a dancer or athlete. There was a grace about this woman in the way she held herself fixed in the pose as if it were the way she wanted to be remembered most. Sara called out, waving her arms to the fishermen. The body needed to be pulled out of the water. She could not will herself to reach down and touch it when it flipped over exposing the woman's face. Sara stopped waving her arms. She did not need the fishermen. She stared helplessly at the woman, unable to shake the image of her face when she suddenly disappeared, leaving only Sara's shadow in her place.

⌒

Mirada had not intended to snoop. She wanted to be a proper Dalmatian host. Make the girl comfortable. Welcome her. Spoil her with the things that would make her trip memorable. She had stayed up all night cooking, not once taking for granted an evening when the electricity worked. She had not yet settled into the routine of surviving and as much as she wanted to believe the war had passed over Dubrovnik, she did not. Too many families continued to give her business, taking them to Bari in her late husband's boat. She had secured the trip for hundreds of people and at the request of a local woman who served as president of the local Red Cross, had taken orphans and other refugee children to host families in Italy. Mirada was not sure how many more trips the boat had in her. It was old. But she was older, trying to make the most of the time they both had left. She had hoped to rent the room to correspondents, securing a more stable income, but there was something about the young woman with the red hair that provoked her to choose her without ever asking her name or purpose.

Mirada was cleaning, washing the floor, trying to air out Sara's room when she stumbled onto the suitcase. She had wondered what the young woman had brought with her. The bag had been heavy and she assumed, filled with books. It had been dark when they entered the house and she had not recognized the suitcase until now. She leaned the wet mop against the wall, leaving enough dry space on the floor to lay the suitcase down. She unzipped it and lifted the lid, slowly, with anticipation.

Mirada dropped to her knees, crossing herself, unable to take the rosary beads from her pocket. She did not have to open the notebooks to know what was inside. She heard the music already in her head. In every way the suitcase contained the things that had been forgotten but never properly buried. She gathered a pile of notebooks in her arms and pressed her face against the pages, reminded of the boy who had filled them on Lokrum and the man who had given them away. The mop slid away from the wall and crashed on the floor, but Mirada did not move and sat slumped against the suitcase, hugging not the notebooks themselves, but the boy still trapped inside them.

⇜

It was the first time Anton had opened the wine cellar since Milan had left, ripping off the planks nailed over the door at Sara's request. She knew nothing of the space but had promised she would leave Anton alone if he told her everything he knew about *The Sound of Blue*. She had met him in the square panicked, breathless. She carried in her face the look of the haunted. Something had gotten into her, and he was not sure if it was the same woman looking out from her eyes. He had been drinking, yes, and he had a hangover, but he glimpsed something strange and dark in the way she held his gaze. He was unshaved, and he wondered if his growth had frightened her. No doubt, something had spooked Sara. She followed him too closely to the wine cellar, leaving no space for his own anxiety. He was not prepared to open the door now but figured it was worth the trouble if it meant Sara would leave sooner than later.

In his haste to pry off the planks nailed over the doorway, the wood splintered in his fingers, puncturing his palm with a nail. He felt nothing, his head still throbbed from a hangover, numb by the odd dream. His thoughts were fuzzy. He could not remember the last time he heard himself think, his mind far from lucid. He blamed the drumming, but Sara dared not tell him it was her, not the boy, with the drum last night. Milan grumbled through his teeth.

"He will drive us mad. Believe me."

"He's harmless," Sara said.

Anton snapped his eyes on her. "That boy wakes the dead."

Sara stopped, face twisted with consternation. Her eyes were sharp, probing Anton to continue.

"No lie. People say he plays a *damaru*."

"A what?"

"A Tibetan prayer drum."

"I've never heard of it."

"Not many people know it. It's made from a human skull. Whoever plays it wakes the dead."

Sara's throat tightened. She curled her hands into fists and stuffed them inside her pockets, not yet willing to ask Anton about the woman she had seen in the water. She was uncertain at this point if she saw anyone at all and tried to rationalize. It was hot. Hallucinations were common in the heat. People saw things.

"What? You don't believe me?"

"I do," she said. "I believe he wakes the dead."

"What happened to you last night?"

Sara looked up. "What do you mean?"

"You look ruffled. Like you went somewhere."

Sara nodded. "I did," she said, and meant it, but could not tell him where, because part of her, she felt, had not yet returned.

"You need to watch where you go around here."

Anton eyed her cautiously, unsure if she would listen. She had about her a conviction that he believed could lead a person like her into dark places, but no matter how many warnings the young woman received, she would do what she needed to do. He knew that. Nobody in their right mind would have crossed the border into a war-torn country to hear music. But he knew Sara understood the power behind it, which is why he led her into the wine cellar now, the crush of glass beneath their heels. Anton flicked on a small flashlight and paused by the wine racks, startled to find the place had been looted. Every last bottle of wine had been stolen, and the floor had been stamped with the footprints of a child. A small portal window on the wall facing the sea had been smashed with what appeared to be a crowbar, the stone sills cracked and flaking. A broken padlock lay on the floor like a lost lure, blue in the light coming through the window.

Anton crossed the cellar to the broken lock, kicking it across the floor to Sara.

"Son of *beech*," he said. "They take everything."

Anton crouched beneath the cask closest to him. He lay on his back and felt the belly of the barrel, sliding under it to unscrew a small trapdoor, yanking out the remains of a cassette tape. He gathered the unruly tape in his hand and slid out from under the cask, pushing himself up from the floor. He wiped his face with the back of his sleeve, cheeks fury-red, and hurled the crumpled mess at Sara.

"That's all that's left."

"Of what?"

"Milan's last recording."

Anton stormed across the cellar floor to the circular window, looking up at Mount Srđ, the scrub and sage blackened by artillery fire. He took a deep breath, then exhaled loudly, scaring away the pigeons on the roof.

"Shame on you! Shame on all of you!"

He shouted at the ghosts of conscripts and drunken soldiers who had burned the monastery library, destroying thirty thousand books, ten thousand musical compositions. And now this. Twelve cassette tapes with *The Sound of Blue,* the musical masterpiece that he believed had the power to reverse the course of history, unsow the seeds of the civil war and unite, not destroy Yugoslavia. Anton shouted at the government that had turned its back forsaking everyone who had not chosen war. He shouted at Slobodan Milosevic and his nationalism, at everyone who had taken sides and in doing so, chose to hate. He shouted at the boy, wishing he would stop the drumming and find his peace. He shouted at all of this and more, at the things he regretted most about the war, but mostly he shouted at himself.

He beat his hand against the windowsill, outraged against the injustice, wondering who could have possibly known about the wine cask. He cursed himself for thinking the recording would be safer here than in the radio station. He had hoped the recent vandals, bored and angry Bosnian-Croat teenagers who had already burned Milan's apartment in the name of nationalism, would believe there was nothing left to destroy. He turned, eyes wide.

"What will we do without the music?" Anton's eyes filled with tears. He grabbed Sara's shoulder and squeezed her as if she had the power to prove him wrong.

She searched his eyes. "There's nothing else left?"

"Just the recording. The tapes. He took everything else that mattered," he said, voice pinched with despair.

Anton turned from the wine cask and prodded through the darkness, feeling Sara close behind him. He stopped at the door, confessing to a stranger the only truth he knew. "The music was his only defense."

⤳

Mirada was gone when Sara returned. The house was dark, the windows bruised with twilight. One place setting remained on the counter with a bowl of pasta and calamari and a note she could not read. The table was crowded with photos and dirty rags, the glass and frames cleaned. Sara glanced down the hall seeing the large squares on the wall where the paint had not faded, hooks empty within them. She was surprised to find the photo of the woman still hanging. The rest of the walls were empty. It looked like Mirada had stripped the place. The old flowers were gone, and the floor had been scrubbed with ammonia and water, exacerbating the headache Sara still suffered.

She took the bowl from the counter and carried it with her into the hallway, grateful. Sara did not expect Mirada to cook for her but gladly accepted the hospitality. The food was fresh and better than anything she had eaten in the refugee camp. Sausage had complicated her system, and she no longer could stomach the smell of cabbage or any dish prepared with paprika. She was tired of telling people her constitution was weak. She felt better after a few bites but paused when she passed the photo of the woman, feeling suddenly nauseated.

Sara stood in the blue light of the hall, transfixed by the fate sealed in the woman's gaze. She had not noticed before in the candlelight, but the woman's eyes glowed with a kind of conviction that befalls apology or regret.

Sara set the bowl on the floor and lifted the photo off the wall. She flipped it over, hoping to find a name, and finding none, began to unscrew the frame, hoping to find a form of identification on the photo itself. She pulled back the hard cardboard backing and stiffened, feeling the hair rise on her arms and neck.

Pressed between the cardboard and the photo was a yellowed piece of notebook paper drawn with musical notes, the fragment of a composition. She quickly put the picture together, screwing the frame into place, then lifted the photo and hung it on the red square on the wall. It was not the young woman in the photo that interested Sara as much as the music hidden behind her face. Sara took the piece of composition to her room and quickly unzipped the suitcase, taking out one of the notebooks, comparing the handwriting to confirm her suspicions. She held her breath and exhaled fully, emptying herself of everything that had led her to this moment. The Swedish woman's warning still taunted her but had not yet divined its wisdom: *"The minute you open your heart to a refugee, you suffer everything they have suffered and more."*

⌇

Luka found a used razor in the composer's medicine cabinet, and standing on a chair to see his face in the mirror, shaved his head. The black curls had given him away too many times, and he could not afford to be recognized again. Things were getting too close. The nuns had scared him enough to commit himself to changing his appearance. He refused to let them tell him who he was. He recalled the old woman's voice from the bomb shelter, understanding her warning for the first time. It was not important that Luka know the difference between a Croat or a Serb but that he distinguish himself from other children who had no parents. Luka had a mother. She was coming. She was late. She would be there one day. He was no orphan, no matter what the nuns had decided. Luka believed that if it would help to keep the nuns away by *appearing* to be an orphan, then he would gladly sacrifice the curls on his head that his mother had sworn made him look like Alexander the Great.

He felt in a way like he was preparing for a battle now. He had never shaved in his life but had watched the men in the bomb shelter, often directing their hands in the dim light, tracing with his own hand the smooth skin that remained when their faces were clean. He had watched his mother and the other nurses shave the heads of wounded soldiers before the bullets were extracted. Apparently his mother was the only nurse who could stomach the operations and performed them herself when the doctor was too busy with amputations. Luka had learned to shave carefully with the precision of a surgeon, leaving fewer nicks than his mother had ever left on the Yugoslav soldiers. He did not believe her mistakes were accidents.

Long dark curls filled the sink but he did not bother to wash them down the drain. He glanced over at the window, seeing the sunset. He was late. The war correspondents had not taken kindly to his tardiness, especially when it meant they had to wait for him in places most people avoided. He changed locations every time, not trusting they would not follow him back to the composer's studio. He rushed to the window and looked out over the skeleton of the monastery, trying to see anyone he recognized. Stray cats milled about a rusted box spring but the place was empty. The reporters had left, but Luka knew where he would find them.

Luka entered the bar from the alley, sneaking in the back door, propped open for cigarette smoke and noise. An old Dalmatian slept curled against the door and watched the boy, wary. Luka had trained himself to carry pieces of pastries for all the dogs he believed to be problems here. Most of them were too shell-shocked now to react to much of anything other than food. Luka dug into his pocket and tore off a piece of week-old cherry strudel, the crust stale, filling chewy. He tossed the bit to the dog, and the dog lurched forward, snapping it with his gums. He lifted his head for Luka to scratch, letting him pass undisturbed.

It was dark inside and crowded. Luka recognized the reporters' backs and shoulders, thick with flak jackets that they refused to remove, even now, months after the shelling had stopped. Luka thought they were crazy to wear them in the heat and he told them that. They told him he was crazy for riding his bicycle from Vukovar to Dubrovnik. They were all crazy, Luka concluded, for wanting to write about any of this, especially him. His story intrigued them, and he offered it in parts, for a price. He earned two phone calls for the bicycle-ride story. For everything else Luka told them about the bomb shelter in Vukovar, they owed him one phone call to the embassy in Zagreb to inquire about his mother. Luka knew the war correspondents had mobile phones that worked when the other lines didn't, and he was determined to make use of the connection, never knowing when it would be cut again, or worse, completely severed. He did not have to leave his name when he called. They recognized his voice and the brisk rhythms of his questions. Had anyone seen the nurse from Vukovar? She carried vials of lavender oil. She traveled on a bus when she left the shelter. She was not tall but not short. And she was beautiful. The embassy told him the same thing every time. They knew a lot of nurses but they had not seen the nurse from Vukovar. He could call again next week.

It was next week. Luka needed to call. The reporters owed him for his testimonies and he was there to collect. They were shelling peanuts and pistachios, tossing them to the floor where mangy cats licked salt from the shells. A group of local musicians, including the bartender himself, played guitars, singing strange songs about leaving their hearts in San Francisco. Most of the people in the bar had heard the song and were singing along. Luka thought it was a stupid song, and he could think of a lot of other places where people had left their hearts, but those were places most people had never been or couldn't remember and didn't have a place in their hearts to hold.

The bartender, a tall man named Ivo, set down his guitar to re-braid his ponytail and flirt with a woman with red hair who sat at the bar with her back to Luka. He did not need to see her face to recognize her instantly. Luka was surprised to see her there. He didn't expect to see her in a bar. She seemed very upset, the way she drank, three glasses empty on the bar top. Luka figured that's the reason she was in the confessional. She probably drank too much and needed God to forgive her. He figured God was busy, because there were a lot of people who drank too much and now with the war everyone seemed to be drinking more.

The woman's speech was slurred, and she leaned against a man with a Canadian flag on his shirt. Everybody wore flags from everywhere, it seemed, except from the country they were in. Luka had not seen anyone with a Croatian flag on their clothes except for National Guardsmen. The flag hadn't become a fashion statement yet, but it had become a statement whenever the Yugoslav Army shredded it. A frayed flag hung on the wall opposite the bar, capturing Luka in its reflection from the mirror.

Nobody had noticed him yet, too rapt by the latest news to look down. They were watching a live broadcast from the TV above the bar, the reception blurry. The bartender fixed the antenna with aluminum foil and turned up the volume. The reporter announced that the Yugoslav Army had withdrawn from the western part of the commune they had occupied since October. The area of Slano was freed but the occupiers had stolen several paintings from Saint Jerome's convent. The Yugoslav Army had also left the island of Mjlet. The crowd at the bar cheered and everybody raised their glasses, toasting what they honestly believed to be the beginning of the end of the occupation.

Dubrovnik would have its summer. Dubrovnik would have its music festival.

Luka climbed onto a stool at the end of the bar, waiting for the man with the Canadian flag to finish his story but after eavesdropping for a moment, he realized the man was not telling a story at all. Luka understood most of what the man said in English because he spoke like the men in the movies.

"It's been quite a mind fuck, eh?"

The woman with red hair nodded. She dabbed her eyes. Luka could not tell if she were crying or laughing. She smiled, but it didn't look real. It looked waxy and dead.

"Don't be so hard on yourself. You did your job."

Sara nodded. She slid her glass across the counter. The bartender filled it with ice. He whispered in Croatian and winked, sliding the glass back to her.

"You've had enough, lady."

Sara took a chip of ice and ran it over her lip. She turned to the Canadian.

"I didn't really teach them much about the present tense, if that's what you want to know."

"But you helped them."

Sara looked up. Her eyes were bloodshot. "No. They helped me."

"To forget the past?"

"To remember it."

The Canadian took his cigarette and smoked, eyeing her curiously. She had changed a lot from the time they had met. He never expected to bump into her here, but he wasn't surprised. The worlds of a translator collided more often than he preferred. There were people he had met he would have liked to forget but had seen too much. It was usually the people he had met once and wished to see again that never crossed his path. Sara, he thought, had been the former. He hadn't liked the young woman he met on the tarmac. She was too soft. Too naïve with the most inflated sense of entitlement he had ever witnessed in one of the teachers.

Typical American, he thought. He had judged her, and he was wrong. She had developed an awareness and edge in the last five months that made her complicated and sexy.

"You got a story you need translated?"

Sara ran her finger around the rim of the glass, blowing wisps of hair from her eyes.

"Still working on it."

"This Serb friend. He is a friend, right?"

Sara shifted her eyes. "Yes. *Friend*."

The Canadian leaned closer, whispering. "You asked him what happened, didn't you?"

"I'm asking," she said.

"That's why you're here?"

Sara looked around the room. There was something wild and manic about the energy of the war correspondents, and she noticed not one of them wore a wedding ring. Their lives were in peril, jeopardized by the passion to hunt the stories that mattered most to the world. Of all people Sara thought, they could understand her obsession with truth. The Canadian caught her gaze.

"I can't go home until I know," she said.

The Canadian laughed, reading the fire in her eyes. "He's not just a friend, is he?"

"Yes."

"Don't tell me you fell in love."

"No."

"No you won't tell me? Or no you're not in love?"

Sara threw her gaze into the tumbler of ice, feeling her face burn. The Canadian pushed the glass out of her sight line and dumped some ice into his own. A few chips spilled onto the bar, melting immediately in the heat. The Canadian shoved the glass, half-empty, to Sara.

"Don't expect anyone to tell you the truth here."

"How do you know?"

"I don't," he said. "I just listen."

believed to be problems here. Most of them were too shell-shocked now to react to much of anything other than food. Luka dug into his pocket and tore off a piece of week-old cherry strudel, the crust stale, filling chewy. He tossed the bit to the dog, and the dog lurched forward, snapping it with his gums. He lifted his head for Luka to scratch, letting him pass undisturbed.

It was dark inside and crowded. Luka recognized the reporters' backs and shoulders, thick with flak jackets that they refused to remove, even now, months after the shelling had stopped. Luka thought they were crazy to wear them in the heat and he told them that. They told him he was crazy for riding his bicycle from Vukovar to Dubrovnik. They were all crazy, Luka concluded, for wanting to write about any of this, especially him. His story intrigued them, and he offered it in parts, for a price. He earned two phone calls for the bicycle-ride story. For everything else Luka told them about the bomb shelter in Vukovar, they owed him one phone call to the embassy in Zagreb to inquire about his mother. Luka knew the war correspondents had mobile phones that worked when the other lines didn't, and he was determined to make use of the connection, never knowing when it would be cut again, or worse, completely severed. He did not have to leave his name when he called. They recognized his voice and the brisk rhythms of his questions. Had anyone seen the nurse from Vukovar? She carried vials of lavender oil. She traveled on a bus when she left the shelter. She was not tall but not short. And she was beautiful. The embassy told him the same thing every time. They knew a lot of nurses but they had not seen the nurse from Vukovar. He could call again next week.

It was next week. Luka needed to call. The reporters owed him for his testimonies and he was there to collect. They were shelling peanuts and pistachios, tossing them to the floor where mangy cats licked salt from the shells. A group of local musicians, including the bartender himself, played guitars, singing strange songs about leaving their hearts in San Francisco. Most of the people in the bar had heard the song and were singing along. Luka thought it was a stupid song, and he could think of a lot of other places where people had left their hearts, but those were places most people had never been or couldn't remember and didn't have a place in their hearts to hold.

The bartender, a tall man named Ivo, set down his guitar to re-braid his ponytail and flirt with a woman with red hair who sat at the bar with her back to Luka. He did not need to see her face to recognize her instantly. Luka was surprised to see her there. He didn't expect to see her in a bar. She seemed very upset, the way she drank, three glasses empty on the bar top. Luka figured that's the reason she was in the confessional. She probably drank too much and needed God to forgive her. He figured God was busy, because there were a lot of people who drank too much and now with the war everyone seemed to be drinking more.

The woman's speech was slurred, and she leaned against a man with a Canadian flag on his shirt. Everybody wore flags from everywhere, it seemed, except from the country they were in. Luka had not seen anyone with a Croatian flag on their clothes except for National Guardsmen. The flag hadn't become a fashion statement yet, but it had become a statement whenever the Yugoslav Army shredded it. A frayed flag hung on the wall opposite the bar, capturing Luka in its reflection from the mirror.

Nobody had noticed him yet, too rapt by the latest news to look down. They were watching a live broadcast from the TV above the bar, the reception blurry. The bartender fixed the antenna with aluminum foil and turned up the volume. The reporter announced that the Yugoslav Army had withdrawn from the western part of the commune they had occupied since October. The area of Slano was freed but the occupiers had stolen several paintings from Saint Jerome's convent. The Yugoslav Army had also left the island of Mjlet. The crowd at the bar cheered and everybody raised their glasses, toasting what they honestly believed to be the beginning of the end of the occupation.

porters who were whispering among themselves, the mood suddenly sober as if they were trying to impress not each other but the boy.

"Ask them why they're really here."

"For his story?" Sara asked, incredulous.

"Chance to win the Pulitzer."

"If they win because of me, we split all money."

The Canadian winked at Sara then glanced down at Luka. He was holding out the phone, reluctant to return it. His face sagged with disappointment.

"Didn't you get through?"

"I got through."

"What'd they say?"

"No word."

"They didn't answer?"

"They do not find her."

"Have you asked the police?"

Luka lifted his eyes slowly to Sara.

"The police?"

Sara nodded. She held her eyes on the boy and for a moment, he believed she had asked a good question from the tone of her voice, but when the words registered, he knew better. *Police,* he thought, was the ugliest word.

"I cannot go to police."

"Why not?"

"They take me."

"Take you where?"

"They take me to orphanage."

"What's wrong with the orphanage? They'll take care of you there."

"I know," he said, looking at Sara as if she were a monster. Didn't she know? Didn't she understand? He had somebody to take care of him. She was coming. She was late.

"I have to pee," he said.

Luka negotiated his way through the crowd to the bathroom. He pushed open the door and slid the lock over the latch, taking deep breaths, slowing his thoughts. He dabbed his eyes, angry at himself and the correspondents for pushing him into this place. It was his idea to share his story. He had found them. And he had found trouble. He slapped the wall. Everything was beyond the power of the police now, only the war correspondents could help him but not if he turned to the police for help. They would ask too much, and he believed there was more safety in silence.

People always wanted to know where his mother was, not Luka's account of what happened to her or where he believed she was. He told them what he saw, what he remembered, but they accused him of lying. They said he was in denial. Denial. They kept repeating the word and it aggravated him. Luka remembered everything after a while and could deny nothing. He wasn't sure if the UN officer who happened to drive into Vukovar had heard him correctly. He spoke slowly, using the best English he knew, giving him details, pointing out the buildings that had burned, asking why it happened if the men with the blue helmets were in the area keeping the peace. But what peace? Keeping the peace *was* the lie. He did not trust the peacekeepers. They didn't listen. The UN officer tossed him a pack of chewing gum from his truck. The officer advised him to stay on the road, to stay out of the fields. Watch out for land mines, he said, but Luka didn't understand the translation. Nobody watched land mines unless they were crazy. Luka told him there were more land mines in the fields anyway. Bones, he said. Mass graves. The UN officer adjusted his helmet, threw the truck into reverse, and drove away. He had said he was sorry, that he couldn't do anything except warn the boy. Luka traced the tire marks with his eyes, wishing *he* could have been the warning and suddenly turn red like the fires that had burned his city, the kind of red that made most people stop and wonder what went wrong.

The Canadian knocked on the bathroom stall. "You okay, kid?"

"I am fine. Go away."

"You can't sleep in the bathroom."

Luka lifted the latch and pushed open the door. He rubbed his eyes and followed the Canadian back to the bar. The woman with the red hair was drinking a Coke from a thick bottle that looked as old as the bar itself.

"You want a sandwich?"

"Why?"

Luka stared suspiciously at the Canadian. He never offered him food. Only the mobile phone. Food was not part of their agreement. He could find his own food.

"Stay awhile. Finish your story."

"Why?"

"Why not?"

Luka gestured to the phone.

"I am finish. I do not need to call again. They say same thing every time."

"But your story's getting good."

Luka stared at him, eyes narrowed to sharp points. "Why do you care?"

"People should know."

"That you translate and you write?"

Luka stared at the war correspondents. The bar was completely silent. The bartender had snapped off the TV. A few men drank, and he heard the hardness of their swallow, fully aware he had offended them.

"Is that what you care about? My story? Your name? You are no better than men with blue helmets."

The Canadian reached out with his arm, trying to touch the boy but he shrugged him off his shoulder.

"We want to help you."

"Then believe me," Luka said.

"We do."

"What do you believe?"

The war correspondents stared helplessly, racking their numbed minds for the right words.

"See? Nobody believe me."

"I do," Sara said.

Luka turned, stunned.

"You believe I make lie."

Sara shook her head and fixed her eyes on the boy. "I believe your mother is alive," she said.

Luka pressed his lips together, squeezing back the urge to cry. His eyes filled with tears, and he turned and ran through the bar to the back door, letting himself outside before he could believe she was wrong.

⌐

Mirada knocked on the door of Anton's house then let herself inside. The shutters were closed and muffled, the sound of waves crashing against the cliffs. She had always loved this house by the sea and could see it from Lokrum, the clay roof tiles stark against the cypress surrounding the property. She had wished to live in a house like it long ago but had settled on the humble dwelling offered to her in the botanical garden. It pained her to see the house unkempt. Empty liquor bottles crowded the kitchen table and she stumbled over a fishing net tangled on the floor. The place was dank and smelled of old fish and seawater. If it weren't for the saxophone propped against a chair by the window, Mirada would have believed Anton had already left. She was surprised he had not left the house sooner and was uncertain how much longer he would stay in Dubrovnik. She pulled back the shutter over the sink, hearing a crash, seeing the old man hunched over a grave, building a fire pit with stones that had washed up on the beach.

Mirada waved from the window. "Are you hungry?"

"Depends."

"I made *prikle*."

Anton tossed another stone into the fire pit, ignoring her. He looked up again smelling the *prikle,* seeing Mirada from the long flight of steps leading down to the cove.

"Can I come down?"

"Why?"

"I want to talk to you. I haven't seen you in months."

"That's not my fault. I haven't gone anywhere."

Anton lifted another rock and hurled it at an incoming tide. He saw out of the corner of his eye the old woman turning, setting the bag of *prikle* by the gate. "I didn't come for a lecture, old man. I came to be your friend, but you make it easier to be your enemy."

"You never come to see me. You come for Eva."

"Well I came for you today. Surprise."

Mirada was halfway up the stairs. "Wait. Don't go, yet."

Anton negotiated his way in black rubber boots over a pile of driftwood to the gate at the end of the stairs. He didn't want tourists finding their way to Eva's grave and had kept the gate locked through the years, giving only Milan the key despite Mirada's many requests to have one, too. Anton was uncertain if he wanted to let her through. He was in no mood to talk or visit. Or be friends. Not now. What was the use in being friends with a neighbor who deserted Dubrovnik and her late husband's will to fight for freedom? Her husband and Anton had shared jail time for anticommunist activities under Tito. Anton could never fathom why the man married Mirada. She loved Tito. It made him sick. However, despite her politics, Anton could eat the old woman's baked goods. He dug into his fishing overalls and pulled the key from the pocket in his bib. Mirada walked back down to the gate, reading his face.

"I'll only be your friend for a minute. I promise."

Anton turned the key and pulled open the gate, taking flakes of green paint in his hand. Mirada smiled and lifted the bag of *prikle* from the step. Anton stared suspiciously.

"Prikle?"

"Fresh this morning."

"It's not Christmas or Milan's birthday."

"Consider yourself lucky. You could thank me."

Mirada stepped through the gate. She was a tiny woman, no higher than Anton's chest and barely that.

"The only other time you bake is when something bothers you. There's trouble."

"There's always trouble, Anton."

Mirada turned and pressed the bag against his chest, then walked past him and stepped down to the cove, finding her way to the grave. She took a small wreath of plastic roses she had worn around her wrist and laid it on top of the headstone, retying the bow that had come undone, hoping Eva would forgive the frugality and delinquency. Mirada had not been to the grave since the shelling had started, too afraid of getting hit on the hill closest to the Yugoslav Army and the gunboats waiting in the sea. It was God's gift that Anton's house was still standing, but she believed it was Eva, not God, who watched over it. She picked up a few bullet shells on the beach and tossed them into the water.

Anton walked up behind her.

"It will blow into the sea."

He reached out to the wreath, intending to move it from the grave, but Mirada grabbed his elbow.

"Leave it," she said. "God knows there are worse things in those waters."

"Yes. Like boats that leave in the night."

Mirada turned to Anton, following him away from the grave with his words. He stood at the edge of the water, watching a wave curl over his boot. He did not turn.

"Why didn't you tell me Milan was leaving?"

"I made a promise."

"To make my life hell?"

"Milan didn't want you to know."

"He could have said good-bye."

"That's the point. He didn't want to say good-bye. He'll come back, Anton. He wants to come home."

Anton pressed his lips together, tasting the salt and the sea. It was not yet noon and already his neck burned from the sun arching over the cove, reflecting off the water. He fingered the eyeglasses inside his pocket, feeling the bent wires of the rims, the shattered lenses. He could not tell Mirada that it was too late. Milan, he believed, would not be coming back at all.

"You think he left for the right reasons?"

Mirada stepped away from the water. "He's an adult now, Anton. He makes his own decisions. There's no use judging them."

Anton raised his voice. "I'm not the one judging. That jury will decide, and they'll think he's guilty because he left."

"What's the difference? Everyone blamed him before he left. Milan spent his whole life guilty. That trial won't make a damn bit of difference to any of us. What's done is done. You know that as well as me unless you're willing to risk Eva's honor, and no justice is worth that."

Anton looked past her, past the idle gunboats to the island rising from the blue waters, the cicadas chasing spirits from the trees.

"That trial has me thinking too much."

"Have you ever stopped thinking about it?"

Anton pushed up his sleeves, arms perspired. "How often do you think about it?

Mirada splashed her face with seawater. "You and Milan aren't the only ones haunted."

"Why? You still see Damir?"

Mirada nodded, tasting salt on her lips. "Every day I look out the window. Every time I see the island. Every time I see the water. But I don't even need the water. Blue is enough to trigger the details. That boy is always there in the blue. Even Eva. Especially Eva."

Anton turned to her. "How much have you told the police about the diary?"

"Nothing. I've been gone."

"That's convenient."

"I thought you'd be gone, too."

"Why did you come back, Mirada?"

"Why do any of us come back? This is our home. It might have gone to shit. But it's still ours."

Anton shifted, following with his eye a school of fish glittering like a million gold coins in the water as if they were the wishes he needed to change things now. "How much did Milan pay you for the boat ride?"

"None of your business."

"Milan *is* my business."

"Maybe that's the trouble," Mirada said. Anton was surprised to see her eyes were red and swollen. Her left cheek was wet and there was a resilience about the tear that lingered there the way a raindrop clings to a leaf.

"If you must know, he paid me nothing."

"You took him for free?"

"Yes. I wanted him to be free. To leave this place, the torment, once and for all. He deserves that much. You must let him go, too," Mirada said and turned back to the grave, grazing the rough-hewn stone with her finger.

"Eva would want that."

She kissed the stone. "You can't protect him forever."

"I can try," Anton said. There was anger in his voice, and he wished Mirada would leave. She pushed herself away from the grave, picking up two small pieces of driftwood and made a cross, propping it against the base.

"He did the right thing, you know?"

"Leaving me?"

"Letting that boy die," she whispered.

"He didn't, Mirada."

Mirada studied the old man's shadow, fixated on the permanency of it. The waves washed over the blackness, yet never pulled it back into the sea.

"He died, Anton. I saw everything. I saw Damir drown before you got there. I know what happened. Milan didn't kill anybody. The jury will know that much."

"It's in the diary?"

"Yes. Everything's in the diary. Milan was having a seizure. He didn't know what has happening. How could he have possibly hurt the boy?"

"He had no reason to help him."

Anton fixed his eyes on the island. He felt the weight of Mirada's stare. He did not turn to look at her.

"What do *you* remember?" she asked, uncertain she wanted to know the answers. The truth seemed unbearable after all these years. She thought she had recorded the story, but the story was wrong. Anton confirmed it.

"I remember Milan's eyes when I pulled him into the boat. They weren't dilated. He wasn't having a seizure."

Anton turned seeing Mirada's face, crestfallen. She felt within her body a sudden numbness as if she had been poisoned by the the old man's candor.

"Milan let his own brother drown?"

"No. Damir was breathing when I found him. I pulled Milan into the boat first."

"I don't understand," Mirada said, although she understood completely. She did not want to understand or believe what she knew to be true now.

"Damir reached for my hand," Anton said. "He wanted me to help him. But I didn't. I could never. Not after Eva."

"You didn't take his hand?"

"I took the oar," Anton said, voice cracking with the confession. "When I turned, Milan's hand was already there. I had to pry his fingers off the wood. That oar still bears his nail marks."

Mirada stared, incredulous. She could barely speak: "Damir was ten years old."

"Ten years too old."

Mirada stiffened, needled by the old man's lack of remorse for the hand he did not take and the life he did.

"Milan always knew it was you?"

Anton nodded, rubbing the heat from his fingers. "Milan left Dubrovnik not because he was a Serb. Not because he needed freedom," he said, looking out to the water. "He had all the freedom he wanted here. Milan left because he didn't want to tell the truth. He wanted to save *me* from the jury, not him."

Mirada crouched, gripping the headstone. Her heart pounded. She would have never agreed to take Milan on the boat to Bari if she had known what really happened that day on the island. If only he knew that it wasn't his fault. Nothing was his fault, not Damir's death or Eva's. What Anton had done for Milan, she knew Milan would have done for Eva. Damir would have died either way, she thought, facing the grave to fix the pieces of the cross that had already slipped away with prayers that remained unanswered.

⌇

Anton had warned Sara to stay out of the building but she could not resist the urge to know where the composer had lived and worked. If the Canadian translator was right, she no longer needed to ask questions but to find answers. Anton had prohibited her from exploring the property, not for safety, but out of respect for Milan's wish to refuse visitors, fearful of what his flat would reveal about his condition to those who could never fully understand it. Just as Milan did not want to frighten strangers, Anton did not want them, especially Sara, to confirm or spread more rumors.

Sara stood in the courtyard, climbing a trellis of hibiscus with her eyes to the second floor of the flat, surprised to see the shutters open. The walls had been gouged by gunfire and spray-painted with graffiti curses. CHETNIK in black, blue, and red. The house maintained a certain limpness without a roof, window and doorframes sloped and sagging as if they carried Milan's sadness.

Everything about the building indicated Sara should turn and walk away. An eerie stillness hung over it. The heat heavy, sky smudged with dark clouds since the morning. Sara had woken hungover, smelling cigarette smoke in her hair and fingers, skin sweating bourbon she had consumed to stave off her urge to mourn for Milan and the predicament she had created for both of them. She refused to fall for the Canadian's sympathy, no matter how well-intentioned he appeared to be. He had offered to walk her home. She walked home alone finding a group of Mirada's neighbors gathered in the street to inspect the gaping hole above the left rear wheel of a Volkswagen Golf. They pulled bullets from the tires, speculating that the shots had been intended to hit the gas tank. They offered a bullet to Sara for good luck, a sign from God, they said, that they were all being watched. Sara took the bullet and slept with it beneath her pillow, certain they were being watched through the scope of a gun.

She was being watched now by the old woman hanging clothes on a line from the next house. She barked something at Sara then darted inside, slamming the shutters shut when the rain began. Sara opened the gate and crossed through a garden to the door. Most of the flowers had been uprooted, the garden in disarray, but a ring of blue irises had pushed its way through the soil, surviving the vandals who had tried to eradicate Milan as if his roots were the weeds they were not strong enough to pull.

Sara paused at the door, the rain pelting the chipped paint, blue flakes falling to the stones by her feet. She noticed that most of the doors and shutters in Dubrovnik were painted a strict green, but Milan's were blue. Not the blue of yachts or sidewalk cafés but the cerulean blue of the Adriatic, as if the composer could not get enough of it. She reached out to the knob, hearing a saucer drop on the floor inside, wondering if a bird had discovered the flat after the fire.

She opened the door slowly and stepped inside. She walked carefully, following the floor joists, not entirely trusting the charred wood could support much of anything. She lowered her head beneath the many mobiles of sea glass and broken mirrors that hung from the ceiling. The flat was narrow, two rooms joined at a right angle with a network of windows that overlooked the Adriatic. It was stark with nothing but cryptic notations of words and musical notes penned into the walls imbuing them with a kind of mysterious poetry. The only furniture remaining was a black grand piano, a bed framed by steel rails that resembled more of a cage and a table carved of pearwood. Strewn on the floor below the table were a scattering of small notebooks that had shaken loose from a coffee can.

Sara stared at the table, eyes glazed, trying to make out the musical score etched into the wood, at the history drawn with the composer's pen. She figured Milan had spent most of his life hovered over this table, loving more than anything the sanctuary and safety of it, the only place he could wrestle the sounds from his head and find peace. She imagined it was the ship that took him to places nobody else dared to go, a place, perhaps, with no borders.

She pulled out the chair and sat at the table, tracing with her fingers the notes in the wood. Milan had signed his name in several places. The handwriting had changed with each signature, getting smaller, tighter, more refined, matching the stage of his talents, she thought, not once considering that Milan was trying to make himself unseen. Sara pressed her thumb against what appeared to be Milan's thumbprint, feeling a heaviness in her heart. She realized she might be the last person to sit at this table and understand what it had done for Milan and for those who had ever listened to his music. The music, she believed, was his blessing as much as it was his curse, holding him hostage as much as it had released him, but she could not yet understand why.

Sara lowered her mouth against the notes on the table, wishing she could kiss instead the hand that had made them. The wood was warm and perspired in the heat and she rubbed her lips against it, suddenly choked with grief. She felt a tightness in her chest and she wept, the table shaking from her body. She turned her cheek, staring at her reflection in the sea glass and broken mirrors, realizing she had not yet cried as she cried now for Milan. She lifted her eyes to the closet, seeing hanging from a rusted hook, a series of white raincoats that matched the one the fishermen had found floating in the river. Her eyes burned, and she turned her head, unable to look at them any longer, seeing Milan's body wrapped inside them, the violin under his chin, curls damp against his forehead when he played. He had worn the raincoat every day, even when it was sunny, as if the elements were the only things he needed protection against.

Sara wished it could be that simple, that whatever had driven Milan from Dubrovnik and out of the camp could be summarized, understood, digested. But Milan's story, like her own, was no simple tale. There was nothing simple about refuge, hers or anybody's, and she felt in her heart the hole burned in Milan's absence. Her body ached not for his touch as much as what she felt when his music touched her. She wanted desperately to be touched again by his playing, to feel what her body had not felt in years, her spirit actually inside it and resting. The music had given her a place to go and recover and she needed that safety now, distrusting anyone who was watching out for her here, where it felt like the edge of the world.

She had thought many times of destroying the music and the memory of Milan. As much as her body ached for the sound of blue, it burned with an anger she had never associated with it until now. The music was a cruel gift, she thought. Milan had left her everything that mattered to him and the burden of understanding why.

She thought that by coming here she would feel closer to him, but she could not feel further from him now. He was everywhere in Dubrovnik, his ghost on every stairwell and street corner, reminding her of how little they knew of each other. Their connection at the camp had been brief but enough to last a lifetime, and she wept for everything left unspoken between them and for the language they would never share. She wondered how much he would remember of her, how he interpreted their meeting, if it meant as much to him. They had met and parted in silence, and if she could do only one thing that mattered for the rest of her life, she was determined to break that silence, with or without his music. She wiped her cheeks, dragging her wet fingers across the table, collecting ash, then drew a cross on her forehead and prayed for Milan, trying to find a way in her heart to accept the chance that he was gone forever.

"The minute you open your heart to a refugee, you suffer everything they have suffered." She owned the lesson now and scorned it more than her darkest memory.

Rain blew in through the window where the shutters had been open, and Sara got up from the table to shut them. She stopped at the bathroom, dumbfounded, seeing wedged in the jamb, soaked with rain, the boy's drum and a pencil. She bent over to pick up the drum and stepped into the bathroom, finding the boy with the shaved head slumped against the toilet. She had no idea how long he had been there, all day perhaps. His eyes were closed, and she reached out to him, his body hot with fever. She scooped the boy up in her arms and carried him through the composer's studio and out the door into the rain to find a better shelter for them both.

᠊᠊᠊᠊

In his fever dream, Luka saw fire. He stood in the nave of the church with a can of gasoline. It was full and heavy as if the weight of the world had been distilled and splashed inside the tin. His eyes flickered with the red light burning inside the flame that hung by a chain above the baptismal fountain. Everything in the church was in its place as it had been in his memory. The satin skirt pressed around the altar, Communion wafers covered in lace.

The church was the last building in his neighborhood to survive until now. It boasted an impressive history but no architectural significance. Local folklore embellished the story of the altar being made from the same oak tree that had been carved into the reliquary of Saint John's arm. The organ, too, had been painted with gold melted from medieval times. The former president, Tito, had played it once when Luka's mother was pregnant, the first time she had felt the boy kick, stirred, she believed, by the music.

Standing there in the silence, Luka recalled the drone of the pipes, feeling them in his stomach. He heard the laughter of brides, the cries of babies baptized, the trickle of water running off their foreheads. He walked slowly down the aisle, listening to whispered confessions, his own seeking forgiveness and repentance from a God he had never seen but believed lived among the squirrels in the belfry.

Luka lifted his gaze to the vaulted ceiling. The diagonal buttress, keystone, and transverse arches all wood. The church would burn quickly. The reservist had not lied about that. He stood outside with the boy's drum, waiting for Luka to finish what he himself had no courage to do.

"It wasn't *my* idea," he said to Luka, his cigarette shaking between his fingers. He dropped bits of dried tobacco on the boy's head, pushing him inside the church.

"I don't want to do it. Don't make me do it."

"For Christ's sake, boy. It's a job. A fucking job."

Luka stared at the drum. Somebody had placed it on the front steps of the church, having found it in the street the day he fled his house to the bomb shelter. He cursed himself now for recognizing it, wishing he would have left it buried in the snow. The reservist had no idea what it was until Luka told him, but the reservist seemed to like it a lot more now that he could use it against the boy.

"You burn the church. I give you the drum."

Luka stared at him, seeing before he had even struck the first match a fire in the reservist's eyes, his face twisted with hate. It was not hate that compelled Luka to follow his orders but the love he had for the drum.

Luka began at the pulpit, splashing the pews first working his way toward the back of the church, his eyes glazed with tears. It was not so much the pews and altars and relics he wished to spare, but the stories he had made up from the stained glass windows, of saints and saviors who lived in worlds where things were good and right.

The boy could barely see when he reached the door, his breaths shallow, the gas fumes burning his lungs. His wet hands shook but he managed to light a match, and rather than toss it into the aisle, dropped the flame at his feet, hoping it would be him who burned, not the church.

He choked on the smoke, eyes burning, following the scorch dance of flames. Saint John's arm fell first. The flaming appendage dropped into the pulpit igniting the Bible that lay open on the podium. The flames climbed the north side of the church, devouring the ridge beams and rafters. Luka wanted to call out to the God in the belfry and tell him to fly, but he could barely breathe, his lungs too tight, wheezing. He smelled burning hair not realizing it was his own, then snuffing the fire with cupped hands, ran out the door. He collapsed on the steps, slipping into unconsciousness, fixing his eyes on a panel of stained glass, where a faceless angel flew out of the window before it exploded from the heat.

⌐

Sara dabbed the boy's face. The nuns stood behind her, silently watching, each one passing Luka's drum to the other, studying it in the dim light of a candle. The power had gone out in the storm. Thunder shook the building, and they flinched, not quite trusting it had come from the sky.

The nuns huddled around the boy, saying little, still stymied by his rescue. They had no idea how the woman with the red hair had managed to get Luka to comply and deliver him, finally, to the orphanage where he belonged. The nuns spoke little English, and Sara could not explain to them that there was no magic involved. She had stumbled upon him as she had his drum and this odd dream.

A group of boys from the orphanage had crept into the doorway, tiny faces scrunched in worry, behooved by the midnight spectacle. Everybody was up past curfew, including the nuns. They turned and snapped their fingers, hissing. The children scattered for the priests from the Dominican and Franciscan monasteries, who, having heard about the capture, wrestled themselves from the first night of sleep to meet the boy who had disturbed it for so long.

The priests gathered in two queues as if their teams had unwittingly come together for a truce. They were not quite ready to congratulate the woman with the red hair for finding the boy with the drum. They did not want to admit she had won. They had wanted to win, as if in finding the boy themselves, they could settle an age old dispute, not between each other, but with God about the consistency of their prayers.

Anton shuffled into the room behind the priests carrying a slender rectangular box the length of his forearm. He was groggy and grumpy, perturbed that he could not sleep now *without* the drum, wishing the boy would make up his mind. Even one day without the drumming had already sent waves of concern through the city. Rumors circulated. The boy had found one last grenade. The boy had been kidnapped. The boy had drowned. In any case, even Anton was relieved to see that the boy was sick and silent but had not disappeared or died.

Anton crossed the infirmary, passing rows of beds that until six months ago had been empty. He did not speak to Sara but lay the box over the boy's chest, hoping that when he woke, it would be the first thing he saw and would find comfort in its contents. Anton stepped back and fixed his gaze on Sara, stern, his shadow looming over her.

"I hear you find him in Milan's."

Sara looked up, seeing the disappointment on his face.

"I fell asleep."

"You lose hat or head if you sleep too long here."

Sara bit her lip, feeling suddenly foolish, younger than the boy in the bed. She squeezed the cloth over a basin of water that the nuns had delivered. The liquid was soft, silky with oils, smelling of sea salts and lavender.

"I'm sorry, Anton. I should have gone with you."

"Not with me. Never should you go."

"But I found him."

Anton nodded. "Yes. But you are not first."

He stared at the trace of the cross on her forehead. She had forgotten it was there and reached up, self-consciously rubbing it off with the back of her wrist.

"You pray—" he said.

"Sometimes."

"No. You pray like a Croat."

Anton was unimpressed and turned, walking to the window, taking a seat along the cloistered wall of the orphanage, watching Sara from a distance. He wondered how cruel it was that the universe had riddled his life with strangers who would change him forever. That what he did right now could affect his meeting with them in ten days or ten years. He did not like knowing that every one of his actions counted in the grand scheme of things. He did not want to believe that every meeting mattered, but he knew better. Sitting there staring at Sara and the boy, Anton knew his life was the sum of even the briefest of meetings he had known. He had never found comfort in the way they challenged his thinking, or the way they forced him to looked at himself in the mirror afterwards. He did not like the power behind these meetings, because he believed they exacted too much from him. He thought it was a mistake to expect people to change, just as it was a mistake to expect too much of forgiveness. It was not that Anton had people to forgive; he was the person to whom the forgiving was done.

He gripped the rails of the chair as if they held his past, wishing not to alter it, or worse, change his future.

"He's waking up," he said out loud, thinking to himself, *he's waking us up.*

The boy's eyes twitched and Sara lay the cloth over them, hoping he would rest longer. He woke suddenly and brushed the cloth away with his hand, staring up at the nuns and priests who hovered over him as wide-eyed and spooked as himself. They began to talk at once, mouths moving in slow motion, voices building to a dissonant crescendo. It reminded him of a bad movie, and he pulled the sheet up over his face, blocking the barrage of questions. Where was he from? How long did it take him to get there? Was he tired? What had he eaten? Was he hungry now? Was he in pain? Did he really take bread from the bakery, and if he did, God would forgive him. When they were finished, Luka slowly lowered the sheet, eyes darting, panicked.

Sara took the drum from one of the nuns and handed it to the boy. He braced himself against the headboard, clutching the drum so tight against his chest that his knuckles turned white. Anton got up from the chair and walked to the bed, handing the box to Luka. The boy stared at him, suspicious, lifting the lid slowly to reveal two drumsticks Anton had carved from a walnut tree.

Luka ran his fingers against the smooth curves and holding them under his nose, smelled the wood. He pressed them to his lips and kissed the tips, then gently set them on top of the drum, squeezing it tightly between his knees.

The nuns tried to talk to him now, trying to reason, lowering their voices this time, telling him he had done the right thing by coming there. That he was a silly boy for going so long without proper shelter. That he had scared them. That his drumming had kept them up at night and that wasn't the right way for a boy to live, keeping people from their sleep. They told him they wanted to help. They had a bed for him, with other boys his age, girls, too, who understood things that none of them, not even the nuns knew themselves. They would educate him and cook him good meals, teach him to swim in the sea, toss him soccer balls and basketballs, the remote for the TV. When it worked. They promised him a new life at the orphanage.

Luka looked up at Sara, pleading in Croatian, but it was Anton who translated for her. The boy explained in one breathless sentence that he had missed the bus that his mother had boarded and chased the road on a bicycle for forty days believing she was on her way to Dubrovnik and that he did not need help from anyone, thank you, because the bus was late that's all, and his mother was alive and coming to find him and that's why he could not stay here now or ever because he was not an orphan, and please would they not make him stop playing his drum even if it kept them up at night because he needed to play loud and long for his mother to hear him and find him.

The boy sucked in a breath. Sara turned to Anton, whose face drooped, crestfallen.

"What did he say?"

"He missed the bus."

"What bus?"

"The one that took his mother."

A hushed silence fell over the room. The nuns lowered their voices now and moved to the other side negotiating with the priests, finding a way to break the news to the boy that this was a phase in his thinking, in his recovery. They had met too many children like Luka who believed they would see their parents

again, kids who spent their days waiting on the edge of a playground scanning the crowds of passersby for faces that looked familiar. Yet nobody turned for the children clinging to the edges
of the orphanage.

"What are they saying?" Sara asked.

Anton touched his lip with his finger. He was not convinced a
boy Luka's age did not know even a little English. Luka watched
them, anticipating.

"They want him to stay but he say he is no orphan."

Anton rolled his eyes, but Sara cocked her head, discerning
the truth in the statement. She turned to the boy, watching her as
he did in the confessional.

"Maybe he's right."

The nuns, seeing the boy looking at Sara, walked back to him,
having settled their dispute. They told Anton that the matter was
solved, that Sara was the only adult the boy seemed to respond to.

"They want you to stay with him."

"Here? I can't stay here."

"They will give you a room and meals."

"For how long?"

"Until his mother arrive. In bus or in coffin, whatever come
first."

Sara looked down at the boy. He threw his eyes into the drum,
burying his head in his arms, wiping his nose in the crook of his
elbow. The nuns and priests waited for an answer, their hands
folded and clasped, thumbs picking nervously at one another.
They had no other resort. They refused to turn a child loose. God
would never forgive them.

Sara turned to Anton. "He's just a boy. I don't know how to
help him."

"Let him tell you."

"What?"

"His story. Maybe he just needs somebody to listen."

Luka had not removed his gaze from Sara.

"He trusts you," Anton said.

"He doesn't even know me."

"He look you the way Milan look me once."

Sara lifted her gaze to Anton. "What does he see?"

"Hope."

But it was not hope the boy saw. Luka would have liked to see the reflection of a bird or a plane. He stiffened. Flickering in the whites of Sara's eyes was the glow of green and orange from the sky outside. It reminded Luka of fireworks, but he knew better. Thunder shook the building again, this time blowing out the window, glass exploding across the room. The nuns and priests shrieked and raced for cover under the beds, shouting at Sara and Anton to cover the boy themselves. But Luka, recognizing the screech of tracers, ran to the window with his drum. He began to beat the drum with a rage none of them had ever witnessed, merciless, as if he believed the drum could stop a bullet.

~

Luka was wrong. Artillery had struck the orphanage, leaving a gaping hole in the wall with a view of the two-hundred-bed mobile hospital that had arrived from Denmark. The orphanage suffered no direct casualties, but three boys had been electrocuted, and one girl was killed the next day when a live power line fell through the roof of the room they shared. One of the priests who had tried to help lay with his hand over his chest, eyes wide and spooked, mouth gaping as if he were trying to sing away the heart attack. Luka wrestled himself from Sara's grip, rushing over to close the priest's mouth when bits of plaster dropped from the ceiling. He did not want the priest to choke, but the man was already dead.

Another blast shook the building from a gunboat that exploded in the harbor, bruising the spring sky with smoke. Sirens blasted loud and incessantly throughout the city, exacerbating the pandemonium that had seized it overnight. Nobody had expected another attack. There had been no warning from any patron saint or from the president of Croatia. Luka ran to the hole in the wall, looking into the square where war correspondents filmed the damage done to the Rector's Palace and the Church of Saint Blaise.

As much as Luka did not want to stay in the orphanage, he wished to escape the heat of the fires that burned everywhere else. It was already too hot without the fires. He found relief with Sara and the others in a dank basement shelter crowded with mannequins and costumes used for the summer theater. The details only exploited the already perverted fiction of the predicament. Luka had ended up where he began, in a shelter underground, but he was uncertain the costume shop, with its ornate stone frescoes and vaulted ceiling, would protect them for long. The nuns knew little of tending to wounds, and there were no nurses in the crowd. They were always coming up short when they counted heads, and for a while Luka believed they had never learned to count correctly. In any case, nothing was making much sense. Luka lay with the other children on a crumpled-up theater curtain spread on the floor, drifting in and out of consciousness, unaware that he, too, had been hit, his head bloody and wound covered with gauze.

He recognized only the Canadian and Sara standing over him, arguing. The Canadian's arm was in a sling, and he was tearing off pieces of gauze, handing them to Sara. Sara crouched and propped the boy's neck against her knee to clean his head with a rag. Her long curls hung over him, hiding her face while she worked, reminding him of the faceless angel in his dream. For a moment Luka did not believe he had moved from the bed. Perhaps he had dreamed the attacks. He gathered the theater curtain in his hand, wrestling the sting from his head wound. He had no idea how long he had lain on the ground, what day it was, what time. Fresh blood splattered across the Canadian's shoe. Luka did not know it dripped from his own head.

The Canadian was cursing, unable to make a connection with

the mobile phone from the basement shelter. He had been trying to contact the United Nations High Commissioner for Refugees, who had delivered twenty-seven tons of food to refugees and displaced people of Dubrovnik: 23,600 persons exactly. The commissioner was leaving in the afternoon and taking people with him. It was June 1. According to the radio, the attack was only the beginning of a brutal wave of summer attacks intended to keep tourists from visiting Dubrovnik and promulgating international sympathy.

"Maybe the commissioner already left," Sara said.

"He's waiting for both of us."

"For you."

"Don't you have the money?"

"I have enough. It's not about the money."

"Of course not, fuck, Sara!"

The Canadian lowered his voice, a hiss more than a whisper, aware the nuns had heard him cursing in front of the children and had no inhibitions reprimanding him.

"You can't stay here," he said.

"I'm not finished."

"Are you crazy? No refugee is worth your life."

Sara wrapped clean gauze around Luka's forehead. "I can't leave him."

"He's not your son."

"That's the point. He's somebody else's."

"My god. You honestly believe his mother is alive?"

"I do. I meant what I said the other night."

"Do you believe everybody wakes up from the dead?"

The Canadian wiped the blood from his own head, flinging it onto the stone floor. He rubbed his neck, feeling everything inside him tighten. He could not believe the tenacity of the woman, her naïve belief in heroics. Didn't she know? There would be no heroes in this war, and she would not be one of them, even if there were. He stared down at the boy, wishing he had never agreed to translate his story, but the boy had convinced him, if anything, that he was worth a few phone calls. He believed the boy could convince anybody to help him get what he needed. The story of his mother was good. Very good. Sure, it tugged on a few heart-strings, but it was nothing more than a prank pulled off with the prowess of a gypsy child. The kid was a pro.

"He's a storyteller, Sara. He'll have you eating out of his hands before all of this is said and done. He may be young, but he's smart. He'll manipulate you and leave you for dead. Is that what you want?"

"I want to help him," she said.

"And I want to help you."

"Then bring me the suitcase before you leave."

"Sara!"

"I'll only ask once. We both need the music now."

Luka opened his eyes, watching her. There were tears sliding down her cheek, and she slapped them away with the back of her wrist. She dug in her pocket, offering the key to Mirada's pension.

The Canadian reached out and grabbed her hand, giving it one swift shake, letting the key fall to the floor with a deadening ring. "Open you're heart too wide, it'll split."

He grabbed the bloody gauze from the floor and stood, wiping his sweaty brow, then walked away with the vaguest hope that Sara would realize her mistake and follow him.

⌒

Sara stayed by Luka for a week. Neither speaking, too shocked to show any real emotion, too numb to discuss the attacks or to acknowledge them at all. Nothing to do but wait and see and listen and survive. Every escape plan proved futile, and calling family crossed her mind like an inappropriate and ineffective joke. The phone lines were dead anyway. What would she say? Nobody could help her now. Nobody would believe her. She hardly believed herself. She did not want to know the details of the attacks. She did not want to confirm a war had broken out around her.

She censored her thoughts. She censored her heart. She fought the urge to cry. She did not want the boy to see her like this when she knew he had suffered more. The kind of fear that gripped Sara was different from what she had experienced on the tarmac five months ago. She knew the outcome and was terrified now. She would either live or die. Her test was not about getting through a winter at a refugee camp. Her test was to survive and keep the boy alive.

Sara could not remember anything clearly since the first bomb had fallen. She lived in a moment like that after a car accident, where the mind lingers indefinitely, playing over and over the events leading up to it but not recalling the accident itself. The gap remained huge and black, without detail or evidence to conclude any of this was real. It was as if Sara's mind clung to a ledge, terrified to let go and trust there was something on the other side to catch her fall. She and the others wandered around each other in the basement of the orphanage, sharing meals from a camp stove, pots of pasta boiled with salted seawater. Anton was their go-between, day and night, safety and peril. The old man took turns with the priests, delivering food from the shipment left by the United Nations. Apparently fights had broken out in the streets over donations sold in local shops, the owners profiting over the misfortune of their neighbors. The nuns and priests were outraged when they heard this and protested with candle vigils and prayers, seeking redemption for all the ways the war was leaching everything good from them.

Everything changed June 8. No longer could the nuns afford the protection of prayer alone. When the second attack hit Dubrovnik's old town, they agreed to spare the children and send them on a boat to Italy, where a sister orphanage outside Bari offered beds.

The nuns instructed the children not to waste time packing. "Take your life, not your belongings," they said, holding their own suitcases, ushering the children through the front door

with barely their shoes on. The nuns had spent the morning trying to convince Luka he was going with them, but he refused to
listen and hid from everyone but Sara. Luka stood at the front
door with the drum, watching with disdain the other children
climb into the van. He did not want to ride with the orphans
now or ever.

Sara crouched and locked eyes with him. "You'll be safer with
them," she said.

Luka thought her eyes looked like two small worlds, and he
watched in the reflection other orphans swinging from a tire that
hung from an oak tree in the courtyard. As much as he wanted to
play with them, he was not like them.

"I can't go," he said.

"You can't or you won't?"

Luka turned, startled to find the head nun standing over him.
The orphans from the courtyard had been ushered inside the van.
There was commotion among the driver and the other nuns, who
argued about where the children should sit. It was agreed they
would ride only on the right side, not the left where the gas tank
was a target for snipers.

"Luka, we're waiting."

Luka clutched the drum and backed out of her shadow. "I stay
here."

He used English, trying to distance himself further from the
nun, knowing she understood very little of what he said. The nun
spoke quickly in Croatian, her tongue a swift force against his
heart.

Luka looked up at Sara, pleading. "I can't leave now."

"You must. You are an orphan," the nun said.

"Do not tell me who I am!"

Luka leaned against the door, pressing his fingers against the ash
coating the panels. The air was thick with smoke from the fires still
smoldering from the Rector's Palace and the Church of Saint Blaise.
He squinted, trying to make eye contact with the nun. The woman

was flustered and spoke again, this time to Sara. Sara looked down at Luka, helpless, needing him to translate. He understood.

"Do you stay?" Luka asked her.

"I'm not going to Bari."

"You go home?"

"No," she said. "Not yet."

"She wants to know if you stay here. With me."

Sara shifted at the door. She pretended to look resigned, that the boy's request had not fazed her like the pinch in her heart that had worked its way to her throat, grabbing her tongue, withholding the right words, the rational words that would form her answer. It did not strike her that another force had already answered for her, making her struggle with the boy matter. She looked up at the nun and nodded, forcing a smile. She wondered if Mirada would take the boy in for a while. She would pay for him. He could sleep on the floor.

Sara glanced up at the hill at Mirada's pension and felt her stomach sink. The villa had no roof and barely a frame remained. Where the balcony had been, twisted steel rods pierced the empty space. Fire had reduced the villa to a charred skeleton, the sky thick with smoke from the date palm that smoldered in Mirada's garden. It was the first time Sara had stepped outside the orphanage since the attacks began. She could not believe the damage.

"You can stay with me."

Sara looked up, startled to hear Anton's voice.

"Until you come to your senses and go home."

Anton stood at the gate with bags of groceries. He stared dumbfounded at the nun and spoke in Croatian. There had been no talk of evacuation.

"You're leaving, too?" he asked.

The head nun squeezed herself through the gate, taking one of the bags of groceries from Anton. He surrendered the food, too appalled by her decision.

"If you leave, you help the Serbs to win."

"We'll let God decide who wins," she said, and climbed into the van, crossing herself, praying for the salvation of the drummer boy and the woman with the red hair. She thought the old man was hopeless and shut the door.

Sara walked up to Anton, Luka following closely behind her. He refused to take her hand, even when he felt safest, eyes locked on the van until it disappeared down the road. Sara had not moved her eyes off the hill behind Ploce.

"Her house. . . ," she said, unable to finish.

"It burned three days ago."

"All of it?"

"She lost everything."

Sara covered her face with her hands, biting the edge of her thumb and the scream blistering inside for the music she would have no chance to save. She imagined the suitcase burning, the music and notebooks as ash. She could find no words for the next question, unable to bear the old woman's fate.

She drew in a long, deep breath before she spoke. "Mirada's not. Is she—?"

"Waiting to see you. Come with me."

Sara reached for the gate, steadying herself, letting go of her breath. She walked beside Anton in silence, the boy between them sounding out the rhythms to a requiem on his drum. They passed the hotels Argentina and Excelsior, where war correspondents, hearing the drum, watched them from the windows as if they were a parade of the living dead. National Guardsmen waved them off the road, a sniper zone, but they continued, prodding through the rubble and their anxiety. The road between the orphanage and Anton's house seemed like the longest road in the world, and Sara believed that the heat rising from it would destroy her heart before the snipers would ever get their chance.

⌒

Mirada heard the drumming and rushed to meet them at the front door, hands outstretched with blackened rosary beads. She kissed Sara's forehead and cheeks, crossing herself repeatedly, mumbling over and over a prayer of thanksgiving for seeing the young woman alive. She looked down at the boy, running her hand over the bristles of hair, reading the bewilderment in Anton's eyes. He set the bag of groceries on the step, and massaged his hand where the plastic handles had cut off the circulation, leaving thick red marks along his fingers.

"They took the children to Bari."

Mirada glanced up at Mount Srđ, narrowing her eyes. "They're not finished, are they?"

"The nuns? Oh, they're done. Trust me. That woman had the audacity to take a bag of groceries from me. I waited four hours for this shit."

Anton opened the bag, revealing several packages of pasta, cans of corn, and stewed tomatoes, the only items left from the United Nations delivery. Everything else was gone, including the bottled water. The people of Dubrovnik would have to wait now every other day for water and still risk their lives getting it.

Mirada looked up, disgusted, her words defying her. "They had no choice. They're doing their best."

"They could stay like the rest of us," Anton snapped. "Who else will defend Dubrovnik? I'd rather be dead before the Chetniks occupy my house or this city."

He picked up the bag and stormed through the door. Mirada gestured for Sara and Luka to follow, but Anton turned and stopped the boy at the door.

"Leave the drum outside," he said.

Sara paused in the hallway, understanding Anton's intention from the wide, spooked eyes of the boy. Luka lowered the drum, reluctant to let go.

"I know about the drum," Anton said. "If you're going to wake the dead, please leave them outside my house."

Luka sucked in his cheeks, considering. He turned, seeing a hedgehog cross the stones and disappear into a thicket of ground cover. The house was far from the road, with a treacherous stone staircase that led down to the cliff, and beyond that, water. Anton had locked the gate behind them and secured it with a metal chain as thick as the old man's wrist. Luka did not believe anybody could get to the house easily, but he didn't feel comfortable leaving the drum by the front door. He looked through the house, past Sara, seeing the balcony through the window. He pointed.

"There."

Anton turned. "I said you can't bring it inside."

"I want to leave it on the balcony."

"The balcony?"

"Yes. So I can see it through the window."

Anton considered, not knowing that the boy really wanted to drum with a view of the sea. The blue waters reflected off the white walls and ceiling, bouncing with a kind of rhythm he wanted to match.

Anton sighed. "Hurry up."

Luka looked up, cracking a smile, and ran through the hallway, past Sara and the old woman, flinging open the door to the balcony. He placed the drum on a thick slab of limestone, appropriately beside a planter of lavender.

"Not there," Anton said in Croatian.

"Why not?"

"Because it's not a shelf."

Anton set the drum on the ledge above, brushing off the stone as if the drum had left a residue. He traced the jagged edge with his fingers, Eva's name split where the tombstone had been hit by mortar. He tossed the plastic wreath of roses to Sara, who had walked up behind him, reading the name on the stone.

"Was Eva your wife?"

"Milan's mother. She worked for me as a housekeeper."

Anton stood, blocking Sara's view of the island. He threw his gaze to the cove.

"She was killed down there."

Sara swallowed, picking at the seaweed that had dried on the plastic wreath of flowers. She wondered if the woman had drowned or fallen from the cliff, if somebody had pushed or if she had possibly pushed herself.

"Do you still want to know about *The Sound of Blue*?"

Sara nodded, confused, frightened by the grave tone in the old man's voice.

"You come to right place."

Anton spoke as if his thoughts had already defeated him from keeping the secret from her for long. He threw up his hands, surrendering, then crossed to the door, leaving Sara and Luka alone with the view of the island, hoping they would not see its ghosts the way he did.

~

Luka needed to use the bathroom and walked down the hall, searching for it, unsupervised. Anton's house was big with hallways that turned at sharp angles leading to large rooms whose doors remained locked. Luka had tried them all, unable to open any except for the door with the blue glass knob at the farthest end of the hall. Light came through a circular skylight window and illuminated the knob. It was smooth and dull, and when Luka reached out to touch it, he realized it had been crafted from sea glass.

Luka opened the door slowly, looking back over his shoulder, making sure he was alone. Anton and Sara were setting the table for dinner, and Mirada had stepped into the kitchen to cook. Luka walked into the room, closing the door behind him. It was small but bright, with a child's desk and single bed; sheets were pulled tightly around the mattress as if the bed had been made years ago and had not been used since. He sensed that a boy had lived here from the fishing rod and soccer ball lying inside an empty bookcase. Crowding the walls and the floor were scores and scores of incomplete music, fragments of sound drawn in black pen, the plaster signed like a cast, as if the room itself had the capacity to heal broken things.

Luka turned to the closest wall and traced the music with his finger, slowly, delicately, realizing the walls—like the bed—had not been touched in years. He looked down at his fingertip, which was black with dust, not ink. The handwriting seemed restless, hurried, resulting in an unintelligible checkerboard, leaving no room for silence in the spaces. It made the boy anxious. Even though the room had few pieces of furniture, there was something claustrophobic about it, as if the music there wanted desperately to move beyond the walls or whatever held it back. Luka had never learned to read music and had no idea how to start here. The music had no beginning or end, but seemed to loop around and over itself, a highway of sound, determined to repeat, as if it understood what the boy himself knew—the more a sound was heard, the less its chances were of being forgotten. Like a drum. Or a heart. The sound of life itself. And Luka could understand if the boy who wrote the music believed it was the only sound worth remembering.

Luka turned, hearing the door open.

Anton stood with Sara in the threshold, looking angry and startled. "This is Milan's room."

"Milan the composer?"

Anton stared at him and nodded, impressed. "You've heard his music?"

"No."

"How do you know him?"

"We met the night he left."

Luka looked back into the room, making the connection to the starkness of the composer's studio. It made sense.

"Did he sleep here?"

"Yes."

"Can I sleep here, too?"

"No. You will never sleep here."

Luka shrank from the old man's bark. He was surprised Anton

appeared so ruffled. He had broken nothing and had touched only the walls. It was a boy's room, not a museum.

"Do not open any doors unless you ask me first."

Anton marched over to Luka and lifted his fingers from the wall. He wiped them briskly against his own wrist, sparing the boy not from dirt or dust but from human stain.

~

At night, in the safety of darkness, Sara and Anton would go outside to sandbag the doors and windows. Anton was grateful for Sara's height and hands, knowing he would not have been able to protect the house without her. They had said little, mindful of their voices, wishing not to provoke attention from the Chetniks on the hill and in the harbor. They worked in silence the first week, edgy from the stillness and heat. Even the breeze coming off the sea was warm, diluting the blue, the waters turgid in the haze of June. But working there, filling old burlap sacks from a pile of wet sand, they experienced the general discomfort strangers feel when they are forced to trust each other's fates, to trust that the family they had suddenly and inexplicity created would sustain them until they could move on. They could handle the temporary, the day-to-day moments, eating, cooking meals, cleaning, bathing in the sea. They had tried to resume some kind of routine to deliver themselves from the demise of their misfortune. Anton insisted on finding other ways to pass the time than to sit and wait and worry. Sandbagging the doors and windows seemed like a good idea, but he had no idea the windows would open another part of himself that he had hoped to keep closed.

Sara stood, wiping her face on her shirt, catching the reflection of the island in the window. From where Anton stood, the island seemed to hover over him, round and dark like a cloud.

"You don't like it," Sara said.

"I am too old man to play war."

"You don't like the island."

"It's cursed."

"Cursed?"

Sara smiled. She could not tell whether he was teasing. He had been drinking grappa since dinner. Anton slung a sandbag over his shoulder, eyes darting around the image of the island, as if he were trying to avoid whatever had been stranded there.

"I tell truth," he said. "Richard the Lionheart had shipwreck there. Very long time ago. He pray if he survive, he build monument for God. He live and build monastery."

"How does that make an island cursed?"

Anton caught her reflection hanging in the window from the moon like an ornament for an unknown holiday.

"I tell you. Nobody ever sleep on island. Whoever stay overnight die tomorrow."

Anton leaned toward the door, nudging the heavy sandbag off his shoulder and onto the ground. It landed with a definite thud at the threshold of a narrow root cellar. Sara nudged it into place with her foot. She was too tired and hot to bend over again and wondered where the old man found his energy. He seemed to move with anger, and although she did not want to provoke him, she wanted answers.

"Mirada lived there for years, but she's still alive. I can't believe the curse takes exception to the caretakers of the botanical garden. You don't really believe it."

"I believe island is cursed," Anton said.

"Is that how Milan's mother died? She was cursed?"

"I don't make joke. You make joke?"

"No. I'm sorry, Anton."

Anton wiped the sweat dripping from his nose and neck and walked away from the house, leading Sara through a terraced garden lined with pomegranate and pear trees. The fruit had fallen and rotted, bullet riddled and pecked by crows. A retaining wall bordered the garden, which at first appeared to be made of shiny black rocks until Sara stood next to it and realized the wall was not built from stone but from grenades. Hundreds and hundreds of grenades.

"Don't sit," Anton said, eyes gleaming. "My hobby."

"You have odd hobbies."

"You and that boy wake the dead."

She stared at him, perplexed by a truth she had not yet considered. "I wouldn't consider waking the dead a hobby."

"Okay, but you must know. It is very important to find something to do other than fight in war. Boredom is real battle here."

Sara stepped away from the wall and crouched, taking in the length of it, unable to see where it began and ended, a dark, sinewy line dividing Anton's property from that of his neighbors, a demarcation of humanity or sanity, she could not tell the difference.

"How many are here?"

"About a thousand. Inactivated, of course."

"Of course."

"Where did you find them?"

"Kitchen sink. Bathtub. Many people find them sitting like dirty dish or child. They find three thousand. I find one-third." He beamed.

Sara rolled her eyes. She withdrew her hand from the wall, uncertain anything was inactive here. She imagined the old man clambering up the hillside, defiant, scouring the bushes for mortar and grenades that hadn't detonated, dreaming of the wall he'd build. She could give him credit for his perverted pragmatism. At least Anton was determined to create something useful from the tragedy.

Anton reached up to the pomegranate tree and plucked a fruit from the branches, holding it in one hand, a grenade from the wall in the other.

"Do you know difference?"

Sara nodded. It seemed obvious. "Only one respects life," she said.

He tossed the grenade to Sara with a force that startled her, sending her backwards down the hill a few steps, as she tried to catch it. She was surprised to find the metal still warm from the sun. Her hands trembled.

"It's lighter than I thought."

"Have you ever held a weapon?"

Sara looked up, the whites of her eyes glowing. "My grandfather's hunting rifle."

"Did you ever kill anything?"

Anton walked closer to her and held out his hand for the grenade or her confession, she did not know which. He stared at her, expectant if not intrigued that she nodded.

"What did you kill?"

"A toad."

"Toad? What is toad?"

"It's like a little frog, but brown. I didn't see it crossing the road. It was dark."

"You step on it?"

Sara shook her head as the moment returned. "I was driving too fast. I didn't have a license," Sara said, recalling the single-lane road that connected the fishing cabin to the general store, the road on which Mark had taught her to drive, showing her how to steer with one hand and still avoid the hundreds of toads gathered in packs on the road at night.

When she improved, Mark allowed her to take the Jeep out for a quick errand—a gallon of milk or eggs when the family was too relaxed to notice she was gone. She could see in her mind the fireworks exploding in the rearview mirror as she sped away from the cabin, the whole carnival of the holiday compressed and framed, traveling with her for years after she finished the errand that night. The owner of the general store had offered penny candy for free, sour balls and lollipops, but Sara said she didn't want candy. She browsed the bare shelves, finding only a dust-covered package of disposable diapers, then made her way to the outhouse be-

hind the store to sit until she stopped bleeding. She bought mint
ice cream when she left. Mark did not eat ice cream. Dairy made
him sick.

"Why you drive so fast?"

Sara lifted her chin high enough to let the tear on her cheek
catch the moonlight. Anton stood beside her, and she pressed the
grenade into the palm of his hand. "To get away," she said.

"From what?"

"The toad," she said, and swallowed, pressing the tremble out
of her bottom lip.

"Did you stop?"

Sara turned, feeling a warm breeze graze the nape of her neck.
She realized she had not stopped that night. She had never
stopped running from that night. Even standing here on the edge
of the world in a place she had never been, she was still running
from the memory, running from the pain, avoiding it, ignoring it,
wishing it would go away one day, waiting for that day every day,
every year, wondering if it was possible to recover fully from hurt-
ing not the little toad, but the young girl she abandoned at the
fishing cabin because she was too ashamed to help her.

"Stop?"

"Yes. For little toad."

Sara shook her head. "It was already on the tires."

Anton grimaced. "I guess there are many kind of weapon," he
said. "We chose what work for us. What protect us best."

Sara nodded, hearing Luka and Mirada laughing about something from inside the house. She had not heard the boy giggle before, and it made her smile. He had wanted to help them with the
sandbagging, but Anton said it was no job for a boy and that Luka
could stay inside and play cards with Mirada. They were playing
Go Fish.

Anton shifted, agitated by the boy's laughter, as if it were
inappropriate now and had purposely interrupted his conversation with Sara. He had said little to Luka since he had found

him in Milan's room the first night they were together in the house. Anton had kept the door locked ever since. He made it obvious that he wanted no proximity to the boy and would take his dinners into the study, too nervous to eat, gaze fixed on the drum that remained with its uninvited ghosts on the balcony.

Anton turned to Sara. "Why do you want to help the boy so much?"

"Because I can," she said.

"The boy is not toad. Just because you can help somebody, doesn't mean you should."

Anton turned and climbed back up the hill, fingering the fig and olive trees he had planted years ago at Eva's request. Eva wanted Milan to have many trees to climb, to give him a view and a challenge, but Anton always wondered why, since Milan had been born with both. He paused inside the grove of olives, hearing Sara behind him.

"Do you regret helping him?"

Anton turned. "You the crazy one. You sign for that, not me."

"I meant Milan."

Anton shook his head. "I wanted to help Eva more. She needed most help but never ask it."

"Housekeeping?"

Anton laughed, amused by the simple vulgarity of the question. If it could only have been that easy, his help in the form of a new bucket and mop, the best products from Germany and a clothes washer, too. If it had only been an issue of cleaning, Damir would still be alive. But there was no cleaning of the man's hand who stained Eva for life.

Anton continued to walk deeper into the olive grove, leading Sara with his story, his heels sliding down the dry hillside, puffs of dust like clouds around his ankles.

"The year they moved here from Belgrade, Eva worked for manager at hotel," he said, pointing north to the road they had passed. "But Zarko had bigger plans than making Eva employee or Milan brunt of his joke."

"Why?"

"Milan's seizures embarrassed him. Sometimes they frighten guests. Zarko would not have that and found ways to make up for lost money. Milan play piano for guests, but Zarko collect money and spend on booze and smokes. It was guests who honor Eva and Milan's playing. Hotel always fill with flowers. We met with flowers."

"You gave Eva flowers?"

"Not me. I just deliver for shop. From admirers."

"His mother was popular?"

Anton smiled, the whites of his eyes bright in the shadow of the trees. He liked this part of the story best and wished it ended here. Happily, the right way.

"Eva always had admirers from all over world. She intrigue them with love she had for music. She sang with Milan. Zarko very jealous of Milan. Eva adore Milan. Love him so much even with his fits, you know? Eva never adore Zarko. He knew. He hate so many men who come to meet Eva and listen to voice and music Milan play for her. I can remember Milan had seizure day I bring flowers. I find little boy crying in bushes outside storage room. His face with stripes from shutter marks as if he sleep against them. Very strange boy, I thought. He was so sad. So upset to see me."

"Because you gave his mother flowers?"

Anton circled the tree. "No. He see something in storage room, but he never tell me. He never talk about it. But I find out. Anton always find truth. Next time I deliver flowers, Eva and Milan disappear for nine months."

"Where did they go?"

Anton threw his gaze on the island. He spoke to it, feeling condemned by its superstition. "They hide on Lokrum with Mirada and husband."

"Why were they hiding?"

"For refuge."

"Refuge? But that was the seventies. There was no war."

Anton shook his head, traced the pockmarked bark of the olive tree beside him. "They suffer war that never end. Invisible war."

"What kind of war never ends?"

Anton searched the darkness for Sara's eyes, not knowing the word for *rape* in her language. "Eva pregnant with Zarko's son."

"What?"

"Not her choice. Never her choice."

Sara gasped and slapped the tree. *"The worst choice is the one that is made for you."* The Swedish woman's comment pierced her ears, and a silent rage seized her body. She shuddered uncontrollably, lungs and stomach contracting, jaw stiff, eyes scratched and swollen with the horror of what a six-year-old boy had seen inside the hotel storage room. Sara cried out for the boy she did not know and the man she did, her voice hoarse, unconcerned if the snipers could hear, because she wanted everyone this time, the world itself, to hear her cry.

"He never told you, did he?"

"His mother was raped?"

Anton lifted her chin, gently.

She was shaking, and he had to lean closer to understand, her words garbled. "How could he ever tell me?" she said, wiping her cheeks. Her skin was prickly and stung with salt. "We didn't speak. We couldn't speak each other's language."

"His music," Anton said.

"His music?"

"*The Sound of Blue* tell all of us. Music was Milan's way to say everything he and Eva could not. His war cry."

Sara felt her face grow warm. She stepped back from Anton and studied him, the flow of a tear sliding down his nose, his body suddenly limp with grief, collapsing into itself. Anton did not need grenades, Sara thought, knowing grief had built his walls.

Sara's lip curled, disgusted by the grave conclusion that Eva had taken her life to spare herself and her son the shame of the rape and to salvage their honor. Sara understood for the first time precisely why Milan had played for her at the refugee camp. Had Milan known that she, too, was a refugee and had fought the same war that his mother had lost? She had survived what Eva had not, but her surviving still remained without meaning, and this was the invisible burden she had carried with her when she crossed the border.

"Silence," Anton said, lowering his gaze, locking eyes with Sara, as if to seal a fate she had yet to know. "Silence killed Eva."

Anton stepped into the center of the olive grove and looked up, wishing to climb the trees to his own view, high above the treetops and into the buzz of cicadas, beyond the darkness he knew of Dubrovnik.

～

The sky was heavy with heat and thick with ash from fires when Luka and Sara walked into town for water. The local Red Cross permitted citizens to fill a two-liter bottle every other day, odd days, from trucks parked inside the city walls. The line was long and snaked into alleys where cats napped lazily in the sun, making beds of debris and rubble.

Sara and Luka approached the end of the line outside a small café. The lantern had been fixed and decorated with swags of lavender as if to announce a grand opening and renounce the terrorism of the Chetniks—or better, to reestablish the spirit of the city. Despite recent attacks, Dubrovnik seemed to buzz with expectancy and excitement, counting the quiet days like the seconds between lightning and thunder, certain the storm had passed. It was Friday, June 19, eleven days after the last attack and the longest period between gunfire in two weeks.

The people standing in line turned and smiled at Sara and Luka. The locals seemed shell-shocked and too exhausted to discern Sara's nationality, and for this she was relieved to feel their eyes pass over her without judgment. But she felt like a fraud standing there to wait for water, feeling their sympathetic and welcoming glances, thinking perhaps the boy was her son, that she was one of them. She had not thought to bring identification, preferring anonymity.

Luka stepped out of line and walked ahead of her. He had been eager to leave the confines of Anton's house, confident the nuns would not be out to get him now. It was a much different experience to walk freely through the old city without worrying he would end up in the orphanage. Any day was a good day outside an orphanage, and for the last ten days, he felt as if he had taken some kind of strange vacation at Anton's house. He had kept to himself, trying not to bother the old man. Anton growled like an arthritic dog whenever Luka got too close to him. Rather than sleep inside the house, Luka slept tucked inside a lounge chair on the balcony, cradling the drum as though it were a dog. The old man was a grumpy man, and for all the food he had given Luka and for the roof that still covered him, Luka would have liked to go back to the composer's studio, where no one would bother him and he was free to drum. He didn't like to talk to the old man or the old lady Mirada. She asked too many questions about his mother, none of which Luka could answer with certainty. He refused to reveal anything of his relationship with the war correspondents, fearing the old lady would warn them to stay away from him. He preferred only the privacy of Sara's company, and this was worth all the aggravation they had both caused Anton.

Luka signaled for Sara to follow him, even though the line was moving and they were close to getting water. Sara gestured for Luka to return, but Luka doubled over, faking sick, making a vomiting sound. He ran into the shadow of the next alley and disappeared, leaving Sara no choice but to find him. She had heard the locals say *"Adio"* when they left stores and restaurants, and she nodded her head shyly, pronouncing the word as softly as she could, each letter like a crystal on her tongue. *"Go with God,"* she said to them not knowing she had blessed herself, too.

She found Luka in the alley removing what appeared to be a network of wooden planks nailed over a doorway, but it was an unreliable facade. The planks were held in place with finishing nails on one side only, allowing Luka to lift them like levers, one by one, and crawl through the space with an ease that suggested that he not only had done this once, but also had built the facade himself. Sara laughed, amused that nothing about the boy could surprise her now. She wondered how much of his story had been reliable, to make her believe his mother was still alive. His faith was a clever faith, she thought, and essential to his survival. Even if he did lie.

"What are you staring at?"

Luka ran his fingers nervously over his hair; it was growing back but too short to curl yet. He gestured for Sara to come through the doorway. Her face was backlit, but he was struck by the light spun through her hair, bringing out the flecks of copper and gold.

"Nothing. It's just . . ."

"What?"

"You look like angel," he said, recalling again the stained-glass image in his church before it exploded in the fire, the faceless angel escaping.

"Just like them."

Luka turned, pointing behind him, but it was too dark to see. Sara stepped through the opening, feeling the cool air rush down around her feet as she climbed around the broken lumber. She kept her head down, sensing the ceiling was low. Luka stood by the opening and readjusted the planks, making certain nobody would follow them. He turned in time to catch the look on Sara's face when her eyes adjusted. Needles of light threaded their way through a series of narrow windows, illuminating the faces of the statues crowding the floor, hundreds of half-formed women, limbs missing, torsos emerging from blocks of local marble from the island of Brac.

"They're beautiful."

"I make name for them."

Luka walked up to each one, holding out his hand as he had seen the priests do while administering last rights and wafers. He kept his hand steady and placed it on top of the statues' heads, pronouncing their names with deference and awe as if they were the saints he had always wanted to meet, wishing one of them were named Elana. He liked the idea of resting, if not falling asleep, for a moment, among so many women who looked like his mother. It had never bothered him that they were made of stone. He felt in their gentle expression, in the kindness of their smiles, that they loved him. Where they were missing limbs, their faces were detailed, but it was their mouths he noticed most. Each had the same mouth, lips full, parted slightly, shaped like small hearts. He imagined the stone mason had sculpted them from the image of a woman he knew, a wife or his mother, a sister perhaps, or an angel that had kissed him once. Luka understood that an angel did not need eyes to be an angel, but without a mouth, she could not sing. And it was her voice, he believed, that made her holy.

Sara watched him, impressed by his gentle caress over their cheeks and neck. He touched them not as though they were made of stone, but of flesh, his fingers shaking. It occurred to Sara that the boy did not touch anyone, only the drum. He had walked close to Sara but had never touched her directly, refusing any sort of embrace from her or Mirada. The boy did not have to worry about Anton, who would have liked to touch him as much as he would have wanted to drum. That Luka had permitted Sara to clean and dress his wounds made her curious as to why he trusted her but no one else. Sara wondered if perhaps Luka was protecting himself, saving his touch for the things that could never hurt him.

"You've come here before?"

"Every day."

Luka spoke with authority, as if he had been offended. Visiting the stonemason's studio was part of his routine. He took the bread from the bakery in here, sometimes soup or sausage, and sat eating, feeling less alone with the women watching him, drawing his company from stone. He imagined the conversations the women might have had among themselves when he wasn't there, the jealousy evoked by those who were completed. Luka wondered how the stonemason could have started working on a new statue when the others were left incomplete. Something must have gone right and wrong with each of them, but he would never know why. He had wanted to meet the stonemason, but the man had been killed by gunfire according to the war correspondents. He was a young man. Thirty-five. Not much older than Luka's mother. He had discovered the stonemason's studio the day after Christmas and sat there listening to the bells play "Silent Night" against sporadic gunfire.

The stonemason's studio had comforted Luka in a way the composer's had not. Although he did not have the luxury of a key, there was no piano and nothing else to threaten him. Luka never felt as if he owed the stonemason for squatting there from time to time. The man was already dead. He would never return to claim the space, unlike the composer who had left his studio in a hurry, tossing Luka the key to his flat as if he had no choice but to hope the boy would hand it over when he returned. Luka had doubted that Milan truly wanted to help him, but for months after he left, the composer lurked in Luka's mind. Luka had recurring dreams that they had met crossing over a bridge. They were going in opposite directions, trading places. The composer was coming home, and Luka, it seemed, was going to the place from where the composer had come.

Luka reached his hands out to the torso of the only completed statue—and the smallest by far—then lifted it and nudged with his knee the wooden box sitting beneath. it. He set the statue on the ground and opened the box.

"Come here," he said, and looked up.

Sara stepped behind him and stared over the boy's shoulder. Luka rifled through the box, removing the contents, CDs, books, candlestick holders, a set of pearl earrings and a matching necklace, which he draped around the statue's neck, silver wine goblets, the reliquary of an unfamiliar saint's arm he had taken from the Franciscan monastery, surprised nobody else found it first when they cleaned up after the fire. There were wristwatches and pocket watches, shoes and shoehorns, metal and plastic with the names of fancy hotels, playing cards, tarot cards, Christmas cards sent to people he did not know but presumed had died, a bag of hard candy, a half-eaten chocolate bar, a transistor radio, a Walkman held together with duct tape, headphones whose foam was missing around the earpieces, a headless rag folk doll, socks, shoes, belts, bullet shells—and hidden beneath all of this and removed last, as if it were the boy's holy grail, a simple cigar box that smelled of wine and was engraved with a Serbian cross.

Sara stared, incredulous at the boy's treasures. "You found all of this?"

Luka shrugged. "I find most."

"You stole the rest?"

"No steal. I make *IOU*."

"What?"

"*IOU*."

Sara frowned, unable to understand his pronunciation.

He was frustrated and drew with his finger over the box the letters *I O U,* as if he were hanging a promise on the cross.

"I owe you?" Sara asked.

"Yes."

"You owe me what?"

Luka sighed. She did not understand, and he was speaking perfectly good English. For everything he had taken, he had promised to return it when the rightful owners returned, bargaining with God.

"For you music," he said, digging through the pile of loot for the Walkman and shoddy headphones. He offered the box to Sara. She took it and stepped back, stunned by what the boy did next. Luka took off his shoes, knocking them hard against the stone floor, and from the heel released two double-A batteries, a rare and coveted item in times of war, his currency in case of emergencies. He inserted the batteries into the Walkman.

"Open box."

Sara looked at Luka, suspicious. He was beaming, his grin revealing a missing tooth, an upper right bicuspid that she had not noticed before because the boy rarely smiled or displayed much of any emotion since the day she had found him inside the church confessional.

During the few days they had lived in the basement of the orphanage, neither the boy nor Sara revealed much of anything about how they really felt. They renounced the terror by holding back, permitting their faces a display of emotion no more revealing than the faces of the women carved in stone. But Luka's expression looked entirely different now. He was as animated as any child standing before a Christmas tree. He had gained back weight from Mirada's cooking, and the color had returned to his cheeks, his skin bronzed but lighter without the dirt. Most distinctly, his face was no longer strained by trauma but radiant with the unabashed joy exploding inside him.

"Why do you trust me?" Sara asked.

"Why you believe my mother is alive?"

They stared at each other, eyes locked, knowing exactly why they did not need to answer, knowing why in fact their answers were the same, that faith, not fate, sealed the bond between them.

Sara opened the box slowly, her hands shaking. *My god,* she thought, *it was you.* Sara looked up at Luka with a marked hesitation, knowing the significance of the twelve cassette tapes inside. *The Sound of Blue.* Milan's final recording. It was everything she had come to hear and to understand, knowing now that the voice contained within it was in fact her own, that everything she had wished to feel again and every way she had wanted to be touched remained inside the box. She traced the Serbian cross with her finger, heart pounding, tongue twisted. No sooner could she utter any word than gunfire shook the city. There was one definitive boom followed by another, mortar and grenades raining on the old town. Sara slammed the lid on the box and ran with Luka into the corner of the studio, away from the windows, where the glass had already shattered, emitting the sound of human panic on the streets, the sporadic thud of bodies hitting cobblestone—dead or alive, neither Sara nor Luka could tell from inside the stonemason's studio.

Sara and Luka sat with their backs against the wall, the box between them. They pulled their knees to their chests and covered with their arms and hands as much as they could of their heads and necks. It was Luka who took the risk of uncovering his head to reach down and open the box for Sara. He took out the first tape, knowing the order, and stuck it inside the Walkman. He tossed the headphones to Sara.

He shouted. "Listen," he said.

"How can I hear anything?"

Sara counted the silence between the gunfire as she had learned to do to determine if this were a momentary burst from the soldiers on the hill, a prank to alleviate their boredom, or if perhaps this was the impending attack the Canadian had warned her about—the attack, he said, that would not be worth risking her life. She wondered if this were it. If her journey had come down to this singular moment, the gradual instant of terror or truth she could not discern. What lesson had she really learned in taking sides? Milan's or Luka's or her own, for that matter. Had it been the seed lie, deferring Harvard for Hungary, a chance of a lifetime to make a difference in the world that had brought her here? For what? What had all of it meant? She could not think and stared stoically at the women carved in stone, unable to move. She was surprised she felt nothing, her body and mind numbed by the shock of the attack.

"You must listen!"

Luka pulled Sara's hands off her head. Her limbs moved freely like a doll's, dead weight, he thought, remembering the burden of carrying the Serbian reservist a kilometer through the streets of Vukovar. He refused to have Sara be dead weight. He clapped in front of her face, attempting to startle her into a mild expression, but she seemed to have slipped into another world. He fit the headphones over her ears then pressed play before she could protest. He did not need to listen. He knew the music by heart and trusted his memory to play it again, wondering why anybody in their right mind would have hidden it inside a wine cask. It was the most beautiful music he had ever heard in his life, and he believed it was meant to be shared, not locked away from the people and places that needed to hear it most.

It would take twelve hours to hear the entire piece, but they had time—all the time in the world, it seemed—to sit and wait until the shelling stopped, because it always stopped eventually. At some point the men on the hill would run out of bullets and bombs, he thought, wondering why they would ever waste them on Dubrovnik in the first place. Luka wanted to give Sara the chance to listen to something other than the war, to remind her that there was something more important to hear. He expected her to smile, not cry. She held out her hands, surrendering to the power of the music, tilting her head back for a tear to slide down her throat and flood the voice trapped inside it with love.

∽

On the twelfth hour, the shelling stopped, but the music had ended long before, when the batteries in the Walkman died. Sara and Luka carried the song in their heads, minds hung with the notes as they made their way past firemen and Red Cross volunteers, water trucks surrounded by National Guardsmen. Scattered palm fronds fanned the road to Anton's house, as if the road itself had prepared a ceremony to honor them, the beleaguered war heroes who stumbled home. They found nothing of the same welcome when they pushed back the front door, finding to their surprise Mirada crouched in the corner, murmuring prayers, the wall cast with the snakelike shadow of rosary beads dangling from her fingers. Mortar had gouged the ceiling, and flakes of plaster flittered in the light.

Mirada turned and crossed herself, seeing Luka and Sara. She stood with her back to the window that overlooked the balcony. She was backlit, and they could not see her face, but they were certain from the stillness of the house that she was not smiling. Her shadow stretched long through the hallway, and they were careful not to step on it when they crossed the room to meet her. She said nothing, jaw stiff with the shock of seeing them alive. She held in her eyes a strange, brittle love, as if her sight had been weakened by whatever or whoever currently haunted her. She turned and slowly moved toward the door, crossing herself one last time before she stepped away and let them enter the balcony.

It wasn't the broken pots and lawn furniture, twisted by shrapnel, or the cushions scored by gunfire that caught their attention first but the drum that lay split, half on a pile of roof tiles, the other at their feet, outside the door, cocked, unmoved as if it were merely a prop in the theater of war that had played unrehearsed without them. Everything about the balcony had changed since they had left the house for water. Yesterday. Thirty-two hours ago. A lifetime, it seemed. Anton had been watering the lavender plants. Mirada had hung wash, towels encrusted with salt.

Luka dropped to his knees and sank into the floor of the balcony, too grief-stricken to notice the grout between the tiles had turned black with blood. His cry echoed from the cove below the balcony, scaring into flight the flock of ravens that were perched on Anton's wall of grenades.

Sara followed the seam of blood with her eye to Anton himself. He held the garden hose in his hand but was now only a body
slumped over the broken tombstone as if it always had been
meant for him, not Eva. It struck Sara that he looked comfortable
there, rested, eyes still open, imprinted with the last thing he saw
before he had lunged to save the drum from gunfire.

"He tried to save it," Mirada said, and laughed softly. "Can
you believe old man die trying to save drum?"

Her lips quivered. She bit back the tears, clutching her elbows against her sides believing they would keep her from falling
apart. She appeared to have shrunk overnight, shriveled inside
her pain. She slid her fingers over the rosary beads trusting that
the longer she rubbed them, the more efficacious her prayers
would be. Her eyes darted from the island to the hill, speculating on the duration of the next attack. She did not believe it was
over yet and refused to trust or savor the silence.

Luka stopped crying and stood, leaving the halves of the drum
on the balcony. He seemed uninterested in saving the parts.

Sara picked up the half from the roof tiles. "Don't you want it?"

"Why should I?"

"We can put it back together."

Luka wiped his nose. "It won't sound right."

"How do you know? We can try."

"For what? It has no power now."

Luka flicked his wrist, dismissing the idea. He knew there was
no way to put a skull drum back together again. It was not a toy.
Sara did not know the rituals of waking the dead, and Luka was
not about to tell her or anyone what he understood about keeping people alive with rhythms. He felt as if his own heart had been
the drum itself, seized and split, conscious of the loss it could not
see but felt resonate deep within the walls of its chambers.

⤺

Luka sat cross-legged for days on the balcony, losing himself
in the blue water. He was not prone to temper tantrums but

lashed out against Mirada and Sara regardless, feeling powerless without the drum. He knew it was not their fault but needed somebody to blame for destroying the thing he cherished most and needed more than ever. How could his mother hear him without the drum? She would never find him now. That much was obvious, and he would have to learn how to swallow the razorlike truth of the matter. He damned the old man for keeping the drum outside, although he was not sure if it would have been safe from the debris that still fell through the roof. Luka doubted any of them could ever be safe again without the protection of the drum.

He was angry with himself. He felt foolish. He had made a huge mistake by hiding. The orphanage would have been better than this. If he had agreed to choose the protection of the nuns, he would probably be in Italy, eating lace cookies and gelato, playing with kids his age—not running for cover from grenades. What a stupid game he had invented. Hiding for what? To bring his mother back from the dead? What was he thinking? How could she have possibly survived that day in Vukovar?

Luka considered that the woman he had seen boarding the bus might not have been his mother at all, but somebody else who was already with her children getting their lives together. The Yugoslav Army had killed many people fleeing the hospital that day. Elana could easily have been one of the hundreds of corpses on the streets. Luka was uncertain now if the game he had been playing with the dead had been controlled by God, not by the drum.

Luka did not even get up for Anton's funeral but crawled into a date palm through the hole in the roof to watch the priests bury him, their voices floating up from the cove. They were worried about the boy. Even Sara, for the first time, acknowledged her concern. Luka refused to eat or sleep, more insistent than ever in staying awake should he miss the chance to meet his mother. When he did doze off, even momentarily, he woke himself up, choking on tears. The priests offered to take him to either

monastery, to take him off Sara's hands. They had tried to per-
suade her into leaving Dubrovnik with the United Nations delegates who had come to assess the damage and determine whether
or not Dubrovnik deserved the world's extended sympathies.
Sara declined. She said she had to fix something before she left.
The priests admonished her to fix herself, but she was determined
to fix the boy.

⤳

Sara had felt awkward rummaging through Anton's drawers,
looking for glue. She found only reels and reels of fishing line
and electrical wire, chunks of resin and broken guitar strings.
She needed adhesive but wondered if the boy had been right.
There would be no way to repair the drum. The bone was
chipped. It was impossible to join the two sides. Sara was about
to close the drawer when she found a small iron file. It was old
and rusted, flaking on her fingers, but it worked well enough.
She began to grind away at the fractured skull, trying to smooth
out the sides and perhaps glue the drum later; however, she
pressed too hard, and the file slipped across two small screws,
tearing through a beaded silk brocade that crowned the base of
the drum.

Sara dropped the file on the floor.

It took a moment for the bone dust to settle enough for her to
discern the prize. She was made too rapt by what lay behind the
brocade to notice that her fingers were bleeding. Pasted against
the bone and hidden, it seemed, from the silk crown was a small
black-and-white photograph. She peeled it off the drum and held
it to the light, making out the image of Luka and a woman who
shared the same mouth and the same intelligent, wily eyes. The
woman was tall with a long neck and high cheekbones, hair
pulled into a twist, tucked under a nursing cap. She was hugging
Luka, the drum between them as it had always been, keeping
them together, driving them apart. Sara set the drum down,
catching her breath. She rubbed her eyes, thinking at first she was

seeing things, that all of this had been a mirage. But she was certain that the woman she saw in the photograph was the nurse she had met at the refugee camp, the nurse from Vukovar who had been searching for her son, *the* nurse from Vukovar whose only son believed she was still alive.

～

Sara expected to find the boy seated on the balcony, but he was not there. For a moment she believed it was the old woman who got him to move. Mirada was on her hands and knees, with a bucket and brush, scrubbing blood off the tiles. It was hot, the soap drying as fast as she cleaned.

"Where is Luka?"

"He go to town."

"You let him leave the house?"

Mirada dropped the scrub brush into the bucket, bleeding the water. "He can do what he wants."

"But it's not safe."

Mirada glanced up at the hole in the roof and laughed. "Nothing safe here. You know that."

"But you let him go out there," Sara protested. "He has no supervision. What if something happens again?"

"Something *will* happen. But it no matter."

"It does matter. How can you say that?"

"Because he no son."

"So you don't need to care?"

"No. So you don't," Mirada said.

"I don't have a choice."

"You do. He not your son either."

"He's a child," Sara said, disgusted by the old woman's tone. "That should be enough of a reason to care."

Mirada threw her gaze into the bucket, face flushed with heat. She had stopped wearing her glasses since the attacks had begun, preferring not to see anyone or anything too clearly these days. She and Sara had spoken little since Anton's funeral, but there was less somberness than annoyance that Sara detected from her now.

"Why do you encourage him? It is no good idea. You go on and on. Make him believe his mother is alive."

"You believe she's dead?"

"I no need to believe anything. I know that's why he play drum. He want to bring her back."

"What if I told you she was alive?"

"You are fool girl."

"I know her. We met at the camp."

Mirada slapped her hands on her hips. "*You* know boy's mother?"

"I'd bet my life on it." Sara held her hand out, shielding her eyes from the light. It was harsh and bounced off the wet tiles.

Mirada sighed. She had no energy to argue. "You need to go home."

"I am going home," Sara said, knowing she could now.

"Don't you have family?"

"I do."

"Don't they worry about you?"

"Yes," Sara said, sobered by the truth, knowing her family had always worried about her for the wrong reasons. She could remember calling from the general store before she drove back to the fishing cabin, uncertain she could sleep there that night in July years ago. She told her mother what had happened from the pay phone outside the store. Her mother had listened. Sara knew this because she heard her swallow before the phone went dead. When her father saw her mother's face and asked what was wrong, she told him Sara had run over a toad.

Sure, her parents worried. They worried when Sara talked. They worried when she didn't talk. She had called them only once from Dubrovnik, using the Canadian's mobile phone. She left a message when they didn't answer. She had made it a habit of calling once a month, not only at the camp, but also throughout col-

lege. It was enough, she thought, for them to grow accustomed to
her silence as much as she had grown used to their own. She knew
it was not geography or fiber optics that separated her family, but
the latitude and longitude of their hearts—for the truth about her
they refused to accept and the fiction they did.

"You can't hide from them forever," Mirada said. She pushed
herself off the tiles, groaning when she lifted the bucket of dirty
water. Her eyes narrowed. "Don't make me scrub for you."

꩜

Sara entered the lobby of the Hotel Excelsior. She did not
need to give her name. The National Guardsmen armed with M-
16s recognized her face. They no longer smiled when she passed.
Her novelty had worn out. They looked at her now more in awe
and fear, unable to understand her reason for staying this long,
speculating that she was a spy. She had learned to avoid unsolicited eye contact and look instead at the sidewalk, stepping by
them unnoticed. It was June 30, the twenty-eighth day without
electricity. The only light in the hotel came from the screens of
laptops whose batteries were charged with a generator donated
by a German tech company. A group of British correspondents
waited impatiently for a turn to file the stories crowding their
heads. They presumed Sara was one of them.

"Is it true?"

"What?"

"Your story."

"Yes. Yes, of course."

She stared at them blankly, horrified to think that the stories
they were reporting as news were fiction.

"Is yours?" she asked, recognizing the man who talked to her.
She had seen him in the bar with the Canadian. He fingered the
antenna of the mobile phone sticking out of his left pocket.

"Hard to think any of these stories are true."

She nodded, although she thought it would be harder to believe
they were false or ignore them entirely like most people did when

they skimmed the nutgraphs of world news buried inside their local newspapers. But at least the story would be told, true or false. It would be in print. It would matter to somebody, eventually.

"You ever see that boy again?"

"Once," Sara lied.

"Have you seen him? I'd thought he'd be here."

The man shook his head. "Figured he was killed," he said carefully, emotionless, trained not to take sides, to honor the objective. "None of us saw him again. He never came back."

"Maybe if you listened to him, he would."

Sara looked around at the reporters, fixed in their maniacal poses at the computers, penning the stories they thought would make them heroes. She felt for a moment the tingle that comes with triumph, knowing she had a story that would make them all heroes and put Dubrovnik on the map, guaranteeing the world's sympathies and pledges to rebuild it. But she was uncertain now if Luka's story and Milan's for that matter would make a difference to anybody else beside herself and his mother. She eyed the phone.

"Can I use your mobile? It'll be quick."

The man nodded. He smiled, trying to joke. "As long as it's somebody important."

"It is," Sara said, knowing it would be the most important call of her life.

"I need to call a refugee."

◡

Sara left the hotel, determined to find the boy and tell him the good news. Luka no longer had to wait for his mother. His mother was waiting for him. A bus had been arranged for the boy. He would be in Hungary in two days. He would spend the summer in Lake Balaton, where Elana had found a job at a small clinic for tourists. He would swim and sail and eat sunflower seeds. And Sara? Sara had a wedding to attend. She was the woman of honor.

She crossed the drawbridge, entering the old town through the Ploce Gates, thinking perhaps she would find Luka inside the stonemason's studio. She walked slowly, retarded by the heat and a certain finality, sensing that it would be the last time she would enter the old town before she left. She paused in the middle of the bridge, seeing her shadow cross the boatyard as if it were the part of herself she had intended to leave here forever. She wondered how many bridges she had crossed since she arrived in December, a lifetime ago, countless crossings that took her from there to here. Standing there, she realized that it was the bridges that had whispered to her from the camp, giving her a sense of direction and a chance to teach her what she had been too scared to know about refuge.

It was quiet and still. A hot wind blew across the drawbridge and carried with it the smell of epoxy from a fisherman repairing a boat that had been hit by gunfire. Groups of men wandered lost through the harbor, practicing a sort of triage, identifying the boats that would sail again, marking those that would not with X's. Sara was relieved to see them pass the overturned fishing boat in the yard where she had returned the drum to Luka.

She continued through the Ploce Gates, expecting to find the boy in the stonemason's studio, but the building had been destroyed. A gaping hole the size of herself opened the wall facing the street. None of the statues remained, reduced to rubble and dust. The only thing she recognized was a spool of tape from one of the cassettes and one of Luka's shoes. She felt her stomach sink and followed the unspooled tape through the alley, running down Prijeko Street and along a narrow flight of stone stairs leading to the main street Stradun, where a small crowd had gathered around the monastery walls across from Onofrio's Fountain.

At first Sara thought somebody had been hurt, seeing the Red Cross truck parked outside the monastery. But the workers had come for entertainment, too. Apparently rumors had circulated about the competition, and even the priests had arrived to spectate and deliver Communion to those who waited. The contenders, a group of local boys, stretched in the street. They wore old soccer jerseys, to commemorate the teams that the war had destroyed and rekindle the spirit of good sportsmanship. They divided themselves, forming two lines from the fountain to the wall of the monastery cloister where Sara watched, seeing Luka sitting on the edge of the fountain, crouched between sandbags, hands in his face, studying the advancing teams. Separating them was a strange, grotesque face with bulging, alien eyes carved in stone that jutted out a few inches above the street. Sara remembered passing it once with Anton, who told her the stone was a landmark in Dubrovnik and a tourist attraction for nearly a thousand years. Its mouth hung open, hungry or horrified; Sara had never asked and could not decide from the fixed expression. The point of the gargoyle since medieval times was to test human endurance. Whoever could stand balanced on the gargoyle's forehead the longest won.

The boys took turns running to the wall, stepping up on the forehead, arms outstretched, hands smacking the hot stones for a split second before they lost their balance and slipped off, running back in line to try again. The boys cheered for one another, excited by the prospect of earning a place in the city's history, defying their parents and the guardsmen who ordered them to stay inside until the attacks had officially ended, at least until the deputy commander of the EC monitor mission visited. But after thirty days without electricity, no TV, no radio unless they had batteries, they did what most children would do when they're cooped up. They played. For one hot afternoon in June, they had a chance to be children again.

When it was Luka's turn, the crowd got quiet. Nobody knew his name. But everybody knew his face from the composites posted around town. It was the first time in seven months that the boy had made an appearance, allowing himself to be seen in public. He felt them staring and fixed his eyes on the gargoyle, trying not to lose his focus. He pushed himself off the sandbags and stood in his bare feet, quickly pulling up the jeans that sagged around his waist. The older boys turned, seeing the boy walk up behind them at half their size and weight.

Luka did not run like them but approached the gargoyle slowly, his movements calculated as if he had practiced for this moment again and again in his mind. He paused two meters from the face, eyes sweeping over the polished forehead, trusting the ledge would hold him where the others had fallen. The older boys snickered, but he knew what he was doing. He understood the game, having watched it over the months from time to time, hidden behind the sandbags of Onofrio's Fountain. Even the police played at night when nobody could see them. Once he saw a few nuns try and they reminded him of penguins flapping against the wall. Nobody, not even the priests, had stood for more than six seconds, and he figured the priests had the help of God.

Luka had no help and nobody cheering for him. He took a deep breath and held it until he was ready, waiting a few moments until he launched into a sprint for five and a half paces, stepping up on the face with his right foot first, then left, digging his toes into the stone. He managed to fit both feet on the ledge, arms outstretched, pinning himself against the wall, not only for seconds but minutes. Luka wanted to break the curse of Lokrum once and for all. If he were to die today, he wanted the snipers to see him first. He was the perfect target on the wall. He figured if he made it easy for them, the snipers would be bored and no longer interested in taking his life. Regardless of what they decided to do, Luka knew the curse of Lokrum had more power than the snipers, determined to break it himself.

The longer Luka held his balance, the more the crowd mushroomed. Shutters, closed for months, suddenly flung open from the old apartments overlooking the square. A few policemen and priests emerged from an alley and soon the entire street was packed with locals and dogs even though everyone knew better than to gather in a sniper zone. For a moment they didn't care, they trusted that the boy's timing was right, that all of them were protected under God or Saint Blaise, whoever looked over Dubrovnik now. They had never seen such a stunt from a child. The stuff of legends. The feat of medieval knights. The crowd erupted into applause and the dogs barked, but still, the boy held his balance.

Luka stayed on the wall for at least four minutes before his body began to quiver. His arms shook. His back muscles erupted into spasms. He began to sweat and his hands slipped from the rocks. He curled his fingers, fighting for another handhold, another wound in the wall. He jabbed at the stones, searching for something to keep him steady, reaching higher, too high, hearing suddenly the boom of gunfire. The crowd shrieked, running for cover. Shutters slammed shut, sirens blared, the square was deserted as quickly as it had filled. Nobody realized that the Red Cross truck had backfired when it was backing up to make room for more spectators. The truck was gone now and the square was empty and silent, amplifying the applause of the only remaining spectator.

Luka did not turn to see who was cheering for him, wishing whoever it was would go away. Didn't they know that holding on wasn't the point? Luka wanted simply to stand up to his past and pin himself against all the ways it had broken him. He was not on the wall to win or lose. He did not believe in either. He had wanted to break the curse of Lokrum, and he did so. He had lived. Survival was all he knew now and would ever know without his mother or the drum to bring her back. He felt a hand on the small of his back, pressing him against the wall. It was a man's hand, strong with long fingers and a gentle touch.

"I hope you still have my key."

Luka swallowed, recognizing the voice. He glanced down, seeing the man's shadow and, in his periphery, a white raincoat draped over the composer's arm.

Sara remained motionless behind the pillar of the monastery cloister, watching with a joy that was too real to convince her that any of this was a dream. They had shared too much anguish, unwittingly, unknowingly, not to matter to each other, even now as strangers. She realized what had happened to them was not their fault. They could let go of the shame of their past, and although parts of themselves they had lost would never be recovered, they *would* heal. They shared a common secret and this was their power and the reason they would survive again; refuge was not a place but a condition of the human heart.

Acknowledgments

Sifting through details of war trauma and the psychology of music were made possible only through the help of friends and colleagues who continue to bless my life. Thank you for letting me explore this territory, accepting the journey, and understanding its necessity.

My editor, Laurie Chittenden at Dutton. It is you, not the muses, who keep me writing when I doubt myself the most. Thank you for your patience, wisdom, and humor.

Peter Miller, at PMA Literary & Film Management. You keep the dream real.

Dan Donnovan, for listening late at night and offering poignant story insights.

Jennifer Hyde, for the courage to tell the truth and your steadfast belief in my words. Your brilliant mind delivered again and has left its mark on this manuscript.

Hilary Blake Hamilton, a true creative partner. Thank you for the calls, the care packages, the constant and abundant flow of love and support. You're up next.

Kathleen Caldwell, for your tireless, discerning eyes, good humor, grace, and attention during the darkest days of *Blue*. Your words alone allowed me to finish: KEEP GOING.

Amy Lanigan, the world's most voracious reader and loudest cheerleader. Thank you for all the support and encouragement to "get my write on."

Peter Chandonnet, for your strength and discipline to define and remind me what matters. Thank you for honoring the solitude, the mood swings, and the bliss of creative living.

Donna Laemmlen, a fellow writer and dear neighbor whose patience, support, and exceptional notes helped to make this story better than I could have done it alone.

My parents, Joan and Ellis Payne, for cushioning the second deadline with compassion.

Thank you Anna, Janet, and Bob Lonklin for opening your winter hamlet in Nesokwin to the muses and me.

And in memory of dear Bosco, who gave me a reason to play in the rain.

The circle of refuge: Lysa Selfon Puma; Rosanne and David Selfon; Tara James Gibb; Matt Henry, Kevin Rasmussen; Amy Todd; Melissa Goldberg; Kristan Sargeant; Greta Rose Zagarino; Adrienne, Bob, and Maureen Hall; Rita Payne; Steve Lawlor; Bruce Eckle; Paul McCarthy; David Defries; Dan Christian; Laura Marquez Christian; Scott Stender; Colleen Lenihan; Aggie and Irwin Hoff; Jale, Perry, Clavey, and Jordan Robertson; Julia and Luke Violich; Daniel Mudimbe; Chris Fenster; Greg Scallon; Mark Scallon; Peter Hughes; and J. Cobe (honesty *is* your charm).

My other readers: L.A. screenwriter Jango Sircus and Daniel Davila of Momentum Cinema. Thank you for the generous notes and exceptional suggestions.

I am indebted to Todd Flora for connecting me with Erin, Carol, and Fred Tanenbaum, whose commitment to working with orphan refugees in the Balkans allowed Luka's character to emerge. Thank you for making the time to meet and educate me on how a child begins to heal from such trauma.

Thank you to the following people associated with my travels to Croatia: Ivana and Francesca Vidovic; Georgia Kelly of the Praxis Peace Institute; Anton Masle Gallery; Brigit Masle; Kate Srezovic; Maja Bacic; Denis Ajdukovic; Rudy and Dinka Spajic; Ivana Tomicic; Ante Siklic of the Bonkan House; Hvar; Manuela and Tom of Carpe Diem; Hvar; Francis Violich; Marilyn Cvitanic; Kelly Nimmer; and

Tihana Borovcak and family, whose hospitality will be remembered for many years.

And for Ivana Ivanovic who found refuge in San Francisco and trusted me with her story.

The village of Ketsprony, Hungary, and the University of Richmond graduates who have dedicated their time and talents to teaching English there: Erin Kenny; Matt Washburn; David Lynn; Nate Hulley; Lora Toothman; and Jay Budner, the first teacher who pioneered the way for the rest of us. Also for Christine Lipscomb Duckworth, whose leadership teaching in Bekes, Hungary, also inspired many moments in this story.

Several books were helpful if not critical to my research and my limited understanding of the conflict in the Balkans. I am not an authority on this war. I have only gained a deeper respect for the courage it took to witness it. I will be forever indebted to Peter Maas, author of *Love Thy Neighbor: A Story of War*, whose work provided the cornerstone to my understanding of Balkan refugees.

For those interested in learning more about the details of the Balkan War, the following books proved especially helpful: *Yugoslavia: Death of A Nation* by Laura Silber and Allan Little; *Ethnic Nationalism: The Tragic Death of Yugoslavia* by Bogdan Denitch; *Serbs and Croats: The Struggle in Yugoslavia* by Alex N. Dragnich; *Sarajevo: A War Journal* by Zlatko Dizdarevic; *Balkan Ghosts: A Journey through History,* by Robert D. Kaplan; *The Fall of Yugoslavia: The Third Balkan War* by Misha Glenny; *Croatia: A Nation Forged in War* by Marcus Tanner; *Dubrovnik in War* by Matica Hrvatska; *Black Lamb and Grey Falcon* by Rebecca West; *Trauma and Recovery* by Judith Herman, MD; *Waking the Tiger: Healing Trauma* by Peter A. Levine with Ann Frederick; *The Man Who Tasted Shapes* by Richard E. Cytowic, MD, who helped me to understand the complexity of synesthesia; *Planet Drum* by Mickey Hart; and *The Mysticism of Sound and Music* by Hazrat Inayat Khan.

And finally, thank you reader, for letting these characters live in your heart.

ABOUT THE AUTHOR

Holly Payne has traveled extensively throughout Turkey and Croatia and lived in southern Hungary for a year, where much of *The Sound of Blue* takes place. She holds an MFA from the Master of Professional Writing Program at USC and teaches screenwriting and creative writing at the Academy of Art University in San Francisco, in addition to private fiction workshops throughout the country. She is the founder of Skywriter Ranch, a summer fiction workshop in the Rocky Mountains. She is currently at work on her third novel set in her hometown, Lancaster, Pennsylvania.